MACKINAS
RHAPSODY

S.B. Meier

Arete Books   New York

For Kevin
with love

MACKINAC RHAPSODY

Prelude

The group of four women resorters, resplendent in Worth gowns and old family jewels, laughed out loud and clear. The joke was told by James Reddington Hayes, popular proprietor of the Grand Hotel. "Jimmy" had a bit of the devil in him and the women loved it.

"'Mr. Flirtleigh: May I kiss you?
Miss de Muir: No you may not.
Mr. Flirtleigh: Will you let me kiss you for your sister?
Miss de Muir: I might if you had not been kissing my sister for me!' "

Other fashionable guests, lounging with the admired four on the great column studded veranda, joined in the merriment. Even those swagger gentlemen anxious about the financial panic, put aside talk of stocks and bonds and congress and how much margin to put up before the silver question settled itself, and chuckled with a faint glimmer in their bloodshot eyes. The smartest groups in the Grand Hotel set, they were full of fizz, and fairly glittered in the fugitive pleasure and opulence of that summer scene on Mackinac Island in 1893.

Their laughter floated down the longest porch in the world, all 650 feet of it, touching every guest there who dreamed of falling in love—but would settle for a little delicious foolishness, like romantic flirtation and pointless conversation that evening.

It took four minutes to stroll leisurely from one end of the

1

veranda to the other without stopping. It took a few seconds for the harmonious laughter from the group of four women, surrounded by admirers, to travel the length of the porch and dissolve into the soft discordant strains of the Salisbury Orchestra, tuning up for the nightly outdoor concert to come.

The other resorters, some 500 of them, welcomed the jolly sound of that group's laughter. It added gaiety to the watery sunset scene, which stretched east and west and south as far as they could see.

From their commanding viewpoint, one hundred feet above the Straits of Mackinac, the resorters scanned the vast narrow straits, the commercial bloodstream between the Great Lakes of Michigan and Huron. Their eyes followed the far away wooded shorelines, and rested on the green islands nearby called Round and Bois Blanc—where most of them pictured wild half-breed French Indians and endearing white-tail deer living together in uncivilized harmony. They glanced at sailboats gliding in from the west, at rowboats floating below the hotel, at fishing boats rocking dangerously close to a steam yacht, which appeared to be cutting straight into the path of a huge whaleback freight steamer crawling in from the east.

The sun's setting rays, as orange as fire, melted into the lucid green blue waters of the straits. And the well-traveled guests thought, this everchanging maritime scene is as splendidly showy as any Riviera view on the Mediterranean Sea itself.

Soothing music commenced and floated along the veranda, serenading their senses with "If You Love Me, Darling, Tell Me With Your Eyes." The melody resounded off the facade of the old colonial style hotel and its thirty-four doric columns, wandered down beyond the hotel's velvety front lawn graced with rustic seats and cooling fountains, and landed one half mile below in the old-fashioned village nestled between the hotel and the straits.

A big whistle from an enormous iron steamer drowned the orchestra's music with a rousing salute. The huge "boat without sails," hung with star-like lights from bow to stern, passed the hotel like a floating electrified village.

"A boat without sails is like a man without his thing-amabob," loudmouthed a liquored up lumber baron, former jacktar himself, to a very small group of newly rich bumpkins and flashy clodhoppers. (One bumpkin was a pork butcher who employed 8,000 men and made $66 million in '92.) The men agreed wholehog about the sad demise of commercial sailing vessels.

A group of society old maids sitting nearby did not agree. Their perpendicular faces flushed passionflower red. Avoiding each others eclipsed eyes, they pretended not to have heard that unspeakable, why, unthinkable reference to a man's private parts—thingamabob.

These same unattached women belonged to clubs back home for the suppression of spitting in public places, swearing in public places, and erecting nude statues (with fig leaf covered thingamabobs) in public places. The embarrassed old maids felt duty bound to cover up the lumber baron's crude ejaculation. Something had to be said. With volume.

"I will never step foot in the National Gallery of London, or the Louvre in Paris again. Why, that "Exposure of Luxury" by that Bronzino is lustful, and that ancient "Venus of Milo" statue is indecent, and I must mention that naked "David" by Michel Angelo in Florence, Italy . . . oh . . . that statue is glorified magnified sin if I ever saw it," blurted out a slightly titillated, youngish old maid, who like most society women at the Grand, changed dress for breakfast, lunch and tea, and undressed for dinner by exposing her shoulders and breasts in all the glory she could muster—which wasn't much. These dreaming celebates seemed satisfied that one of their own had rebutted the lumber baron's crudity, by exposing more of it.

As the steamer harbored at Arnold's dock in the village, Salisbury's fifteen piece orchestra crescendoed into the stirring finale of the overture to Rossini's "Semiramide," and without missing a beat plunged into "The Midway Plaisance." Some resorters listened to the cheerful music, named after the exotic international carnival they had just visited at the Chicago World's Fair. But most were only vaguely aware of the lively stringed accompaniment to what they considered the most interesting thing in the world—their own conversation.

That evening as usual the guests enjoyed chatting on and on about what an utter relief it was to be away from the noisy, dusty, hot pestholes of Chicago, Detroit, New York, Philadelphia, Baltimore, Mobile, Galveston, New Orleans, St. Louis . . . . And although they raved on and on about Mackinac Island—legendary island of giant Indian fairies with its fragrant balsam woods, and shady serpentine drives, and copious crops of wildflowers, and bracing lake breezes—it was the city they called home that was the chief theme of their conversations, and which they used to play off each other for social supremacy.

One Chicagoan, who spoke of little else other than the world's fair, secretly missed the unforgettable stench of the tanneries and reading the daily typhus statistics in the newspaper. Of course he owned a tannery, and the newspaper.

One New Yorker, who kept declaring openly what a "joy it was to escape the constant brainfagging tensions" of his city, and how life on the island had been "simplified to the bare essentials," whooped it up at more lively parties, twelve course dinners, moonlit yacht rides, sunny afternoon picnics, serenaded carriage rides, and midnight suppers, than he would have attended out east. In between the feasting and entertainment, the New Yorker could not sit still for more than an hour at a time, and longed for an exhaustive read of the *New York Times*.

On the veranda that lovely mid-summer evening of 1893, if the resorters were not talking about home, they discussed the Chicago World's Fair. While the orchestra played "Voyage of Columbus," great numbers of resorters exchanged excited talk about the 22,000-pound cheese from Canada, the thirty-eight-foot chocolate castle weighing 30,000 pounds from France, the Maitland Bar gold nugget weighing 344.78 ounces, the Ferris Wheel with a capacity for 2,000, and a 120-ton rifled Krupp gun—sixteen-inch caliber and forty-six feet long—said to be able to shoot a one-ton projectile twenty miles.

Many of the 500 strangers felt relaxed and almost "at home" in each other's company as they passed the evening hours outdoors exchanging recharged memories. Reliving the world's fair together, it hardly mattered what part of the country or what social class or what nationality a fellow fair goer hailed from.

"I am afraid to admit it, but everything in my life seems so unimportant, so smallish, after visiting the Chicago World's Fair. Everything except this fabulous veranda," admitted Cynthia Price, a pretty if placid twenty-eight-year-old maid, not part of the old maid group. She announced this to her MaMa, Mrs. Price, to her tomboyish fifteen-year-old sister Priscilla Price, and to a large group of society MaMas.

These society MaMas, members of the "matriarchal group," were all ideal American ladies of the old school who professed not to understand modern ideas, dressed modestly, and showed their wealth behind charming manners. That evening as usual they kept a protective eye on their precious unmarried daughters, strolling on the long veranda with new acquaintances—preferably rich and unmarried gentlemen.

The entire matriarchal group agreed wholeheartedly with Cynthia Price about everything in life seeming so "smallish" after the Chicago World's Fair, which the MaMas from out east persistently called the "Columbian Exposition," by its other name, still stinging that the affair was held in the west.

The western MaMas overlooked this poor sportsmanship from the eastern MaMas, because the westerners adored every well-bred, well-born easterner who was that and little more. The eastern MaMas found the western MaMas refreshingly energetic and only a notch below them on the social scale, which was certainly "most acceptable." It was the southern MaMas who charmingly avoided this large matriarchal group as much as possible, judging the "northern" MaMas too moderate and too protective of their precious daughters.

It was obvious to every resorter promenading and flirting and wishing and conversing as the evening darkness approached, that for once, a summer grand hotel was swarming not only with enough celebrities and a real live countess, but most importantly with enough—"male animals." The supply of men was due to the fair, which brought a flood of the national and international set through Mackinac Island, enroute from New York to Chicago, on the Great Lakes—"God's great highway."

In fact, there were enough eligible men to go around for all the eligible women (and even a few extras for the ineligible women). No one could remember a summer when so many imminent marriage proposals, elopements, love affairs, and scandals seemed likely.

Regarding the subject of eligible men, a related subject most frequently on the minds of eligible women—love—must inevitably pop up. So when a healthy-looking young college girl from New Bedford, Massachusetts, suggested to her group of college girls, as she gazed out at the mundane moon loitering above Round Island that evening, "Lets talk about love," the subject was greeted with lackadaisical sighs by her college sisters.

There were two distinct groups of college sisters. The healthy-looking college girl from New Bedford belonged to a group that mimicked the "New Woman;" they all wanted to be men, and remain women. That way they could retain all the privileges of the female sex, and secure the privileges of the male sex in addition. Extremely athletic "sisters" who were not much good at flirting, they bicycled or rowed together in the mornings, hiked in the afternoon, read Ibsen aloud during tea, and discussed art and politics on the veranda in the evening with college men from Harvard, Yale, and Princeton whom they could outrow.

(It must be said that young women attending college were called "college girls," and young men attending college were called "college men.")

"Let's talk about love if there is something new to add to the subject," piped up a New Woman college sister from Kansas City, altogether suspicious of the subject anyway.

A New Woman college sister from Pittsburgh proclaimed, "I think that love is no longer the subject in the comprehensive sentence of life. I think it has become a frivolous adjective. How, pray tell, can little old love be the pinnacle of life's experience when a thousand other things, like steel and railroads and steam looms and electricity and literature and art and corn and hogs and horse racing and politics and education, share our attentions and, mind you, affections."

The greatly admired group of four women—would not have agreed.

Another New Woman college sister from Detroit added, "The love of ancient times does not exist any more. We have more interesting things to do than sit around writing love sonnets to each other."

The group of four women—would not have entirely agreed.

"I would love to receive a love sonnet," chimed in a hopeful New Woman from Peoria, Illinois. The group, some fifteen of them, stared her down with dubious expressions. One after another New Woman college girl from the east, west, north, and south, proclaimed her opinions about love.

The orchestral music crescendoed into "There's a Sigh in the Heart."

"Our lives today are more influenced by Hymen than Cupid, and that condition is not condusive to composing love sonnets," spoke up a New Woman from Grand Rapids, Michigan.

"Anyhow, what young man do you know who is really a marrying man. A man who would sacrifice anything for love. The young men today have puny passions," sighed a New Woman from Brooklyn, New York.

One woman—in the group of four women—would be able to answer the college girl's question, regarding one "young" man willing to marry and sacrifice for love and whose passion ruled his life.

"Here, here. Who would die for love these days?" a New Woman from Baltimore demanded to know.

The hopeful New Woman from Peoria, pining to receive a love sonnet, answered intensely, "Perhaps someone from a culture not yet modern would die for love these days. A culture founded on human relations, rather than relations to the stock market and price of food and price of clothes."

Little did they know that someone staying at the hotel was to die that summer . . . for love.

The group of New Woman college girls all secretly dreamed of dying for love, as they watched the young women from the second group of college girls, the intellectual flirts, sashaying by to be seen on the arms of "male animals."

That romantic evening, the intellectual flirts and their escorts promenaded on the most convenient veranda for flirting in the world, if not the universe. When their MaMas told them not to leave the porch, the intellectual flirts could be 650 feet away from MaMa, and not be disobeying.

"This is not a veranda. This is flirtation lane."

"So true, Mrs. Muldoon. I call each glorious white column on this grand portico a gossip column. Think how many guests have leaned against those mighty forty-foot pillars, and told the petty news and scandals of the day."

"Yes, Mrs. Muldoon, and how much of it we overheard through the years." The two old Muldoon ladies, who had married the late Muldoon brothers, exchanged angelic, conspiratorial smiles. The white haired ladies enjoyed watching the "young" resorters, that is anyone under seventy, enjoying themselves. They got a particularly big kick out of watching Belinda Gaines, who flirted on the veranda and gossiped near the columns—nonstop.

Miss Gaines, a southern woman from New Orleans, understood the veranda's potency like no college girl her senior. An incomparable coquette, she was younger and shrewder than the college girls. She attached herself to no one except Priscilla

Price, and only when it was convenient. In choosing to spend her non-flirting time with fifteen-year-old Priscilla, Belinda managed to make her own eighteen years look much older and more sophisticated. If Belinda had attached herself to one of the college girls groups, her intellectual and athletic superiors, she would have seemed unknowledgeable and uncoordinated.

There was no doubt that Belinda Gaines knew that her black haired, black eyed, buxom beauty made the men stare. What made the women stare was her "Parisian" wardrobe, bought in New Orleans. Her gowns were so stunning, guests ignored her conniving nature and appreciated the fashion show she provided with four to five changes a day.

The millionairesses at the Grand Hotel did not possess as many white gowns, cream gowns, canary yellow and mauve gowns, rose gowns, green gowns, turquoise blue and soft stone gray gowns as Belinda. But it was her green costumes, the very latest most fashionable color, which drove the female guests green. Costumes of grass green, apple green, bottle, olive and pea green, blue green, yellow green, greens faced with blue-green trimmed with lilac, greens peeping from behind black feathers and ribbons. In the shady island woods she was camouflaged. She displayed more green hues than the ever-changing colors of the Straits of Mackinac—in more respects than her clothes.

That evening, everyone as usual complimented Miss Gaines generously on her gown. Limestone green. But she was slightly despondent despite all of the attention. What kept Belinda eighteen years old, to her chagrin and other's satisfaction, was that she possessed no jewels of the kind that separate the girls from the women. Especially those brilliant diamond rings owned exclusively by official losers of virginity.

The group of four women displayed some of the most beautiful diamonds, sapphires, rubies, emeralds, even coral, amber and turquoise, Belinda had ever seen. Although she prided herself on her youth, a few jewels on her fingers, neck, ears, arms, chest, waist and gowns would have made her feel more of a grande dame; more like the four women she thought terribly old who were in their late thirties. It never occurred to Belinda Gaines that what the four women wore to adorn their bodies only added grandeur to an irresitible charm, which few younger women achieve without having experienced a lot of life.

As twilight turned dusky that evening, the resorters relaxed into the mid-summer night's holiday, soothed by cool balmy breezes, insensible to the outside world. As they half listened to "Actions Speak Louder Than Words," the swell lot of them realized that surprisingly few Grand Hotel guests were caught up in the usual vicious battles for short term, summer social positions, which invariably took place at all colossal watering places in the world. Fought to the finish by seasonal guests, specifically women who scratched and clawed and "bettered" themselves week by week, these social climbing battles so wearied even those resorters who tried to ignore them, that a constant aura of frustration permeated even the restful times of day at these summer sojourns.

Many a status conscious resorter, basking under the full Mackinac moon in utter relief from brainfagging tension and strenuous social climbing back home, noticed a refreshingly foggy social order and rank on the veranda. They secretly attributed this to the democratic spirit of the group of four high society women, who had somehow set a friendly example for all to follow.

Few of them would have described the Grand Hotel as a great universal church to which anyone, who could afford it, could belong. But they would have admitted the gaiety at the

Grand was divine. Especially on the veranda that evening. Especially in the vicinity of the group of four greatly admired, high society women, whose behavior was watched and noted by hundreds of critical eyes. The simplest things they did commanded attention.

The four women were unofficially recognized as arbiters of taste that summer at the Grand Hotel. Had they been men, they would have been officially recognized as arbiters of power.

Jimmy Hayes, a man of great democratic spirit, the Napoleon of summer hotel proprietors, a master in the art of selling leisure to anyone in the world who could afford it, including those races usually unwelcome, looked most disapproving when an old crusty curmudgeon who seldom spoke, rasped to him that evening, "I haven't met one this season . . . thank goodness . . . I hear that eastern resort proprietors keep them out," and then slapped his knee and swallowed a hard laugh prematurely. Usually jovial Jimmy Hayes did not buy that kind of talk and stared a hole through him.

Not only did such talk go against Jimmy's American spirit—it was bad for business. The old curmudgeon felt his disapproval, and in the future spoke to him only when he needed something, like a prettier maid. The old man even went so far as to pick his nose, and take his shoes off on the veranda. All well-adjusted guests usually avoided him. It was not only that they were disgusted with his bad manners. It was because even in the fresh lake air, his feet, in plain words, stank like stinkweed.

That evening marked the third week into the summer season, and by then the old curmudgeon had been dubbed "Old Stinkweed." It was either Mark Twain or Ward McAllister or Teddy Roosevelt or Adlai Stevenson, passing through

Mackinac enroute to or from the Chicago World's Fair, who had conferred the title on the old man. No one remembered. The naughty nickname spread among the guests like wildfire.

As much as Jimmy Hayes did not like it, he needed Old Stinkweed; for he was an armchair voyeur. And every watering place worthy of the title has at least one armchair voyeur— whose wicked observations attract all other crafty crackpots to himself as a spider attracts wasps.

Spying old women with gimlet eyes, hayfever hypodondriacs with dripping noses, artful elderly old maids with lancet tongues, and other crusty curmudgeons, all suspicious of fresh air and unimpressed by the splendor of the scene, hung around Old Stinkweed. Thus, the crafty crackpots attracted to him were not tempted as often to indulge in their favorite pastime—sowing little seeds of discord and dampening the spirits of the well-adjusted and fun-loving guests.

One of the biggest dilemmas Jimmy Hayes faced each summer season was not the unclouded pleasure, which well-adjusted people slipped into at a place as luxuriously pleasurable as the Grand. It was the dilemma caused by well-adjusted guests who—wearied of all the unclouded pleasure.

When guests wearied of the yachting, horseback riding, tennis, bicycling, rowing, fishing, hayrides, steeplechasing and flat races, secret boxing matches, bowling parties, croquet, whist and chess and bridge games, picnics, midnight dinners, teas, carriage drives, sailing parties, trice-weekly hops and dances, balls and cotillions . . . that is when Jimmy especially needed Old Stinkweed.

For when the well-adjusted guests could no longer take the splendiferous surroundings, the utter politeness in intercourse, the absolutely gorgeous gowns and jewels, the talk about romantic island sights, the Chicago World's Fair, and European travel . . . they would unconsciously edge toward Old Stinkweed, get a whiff of his feet, and become thoroughly disenchanted.

The whiff reminded them of the foul air in the cities they called home. The foul air reminded them of the nerve-wracking noise of hammers, horses and carriages. The nerve-wracking noise reminded them of poor people, and of hungry, dirty, overworked city children. Suddenly, like the rush of relief when a cramp subsides, a new rush of admiration for every splendid thing in sight whisked away their weariness with the splendor.

A refreshing sight in an unrefreshing sort of way, Old Stinkweed earned his purpose and position of importance in the atmosphere of the veranda—like everyone else—including the charming group of four high society women, the richest most fashionable groups of married men and women and widows, rich bachelors, college men, college girls and belles and millionairesses and their MaMas and chaperones, the rich bumpkins and flashy clodhoppers, the society old maids, the crafty crackpots, and the transients staying a few days.

Yes, as the dusk turned to the star-shine hours of night, as the Straits of Mackinac vanished into dark inscrutable space, as the orchestra played "Vive la Compagnie," vibrant theatrical exchanges among the various groups and between the sexes swelled upon the veranda, like pulsed waves.

It was the MaMas' daughters, struck with mating fever, who felt most deeply the pulsating energy on the longest porch in the world that beautiful evening. They sensed that the rhapsodic waves, rushing hidden along the veranda like a river inside a mountain, originated with the magnetic group of four women. And they were right.

1

The Big Four

"You must learn to tolerate corsets. Its part of bein' a woman," advised eighteen-year-old Belinda Gaines, in sweet slow sounds. At the same time, she kept a sharp lookout for any eligible-looking rich gentleman promenading the veranda during the evening concert.

"But I hate corsets!" whined fifteen-year-old Priscilla Price. "Why do we wear corsets anyway?"

"So we don't appear to look pregnant," drawled Belinda authoritatively.

"What is wrong with looking pregnant?"

"You scare off gentlemen by lookin' pregnant."

"Why are they scared off with looking pregnant, when you are not pregnant?"

"Dear young thing . . . gentlemen have enough economic burdens, especially with silver worth sixty cents to the dollar these days, without havin' to think of the additional burden of a baby because a woman looks like she's goin' to have one."

"But if you are not going to have a baby, so what?"

Belinda Gaines took a deep breath, wondering what northern MaMas taught their daughters anyhow, and continued, "Priscilla honey, you will never get a man by lookin' like a MaMa. You get a man by lookin' like a mistress and keep a man by actin' like his MaMa; any man worth havin', monetarily, that is. Is that clear?"

Priscilla thought long and hard. "No."

Priscilla's mother, Mrs. Price, overheard this grown-up conversation. She did not approve of Belinda Gaines, who had the instincts of Eve, nor her mother who had bequeathed the capacity.

To the surprise of all the other MaMas in the matriarchal group, Mrs. Price, a generally conservative, careful woman, allowed her Priscilla to associate with Belinda on a regular basis. What the other MaMas did not know was Mrs. Price's rationale: Priscilla might learn some feminine tricks from Belinda Gaines that she herself was too proper or too embarrassed to teach her daughter.

Mrs. Price had witnessed too many "matrimonial engagements which had not materialized" with her oldest daughter, twenty-eight-year-old Cynthia. Having failed to marry off Cynthia, she accused herself of not understanding modern times, modern men, and even rearing her Cynthia to sexlessness. She did not want to have to accuse herself of the same fault with her second daughter, Priscilla.

Mrs. Price had never understood more clearly than on the veranda that evening (due to Belinda's practical talk to her Priscilla), that women had become romanticized vessels of temptation, with swelling breasts lacking milk and corseted abdomens almost defying the conception of life. Feeling herself locked into a cozy cell of introspection and antiquarianism, Mrs. Price shuddered at this understanding. She did not want to dwell on it. Not now. Not while she was trying to relax on the magnificent veranda for the sake of her precious daughters. She needed to relax in order to think of a way to prepare them for such an unnatural role in the life and times of 1893.

Mrs. Price said to herself, any one member in the group of glamorous four women could prepare my Cynthia. They understand what it means to be modern.

"Why is it that the Big Four are so popular?" Belinda Gaines had stopped lecturing Priscilla Price, and as if guessing Mrs. Price's thoughts directed the question to her.

"The Big Four . . . whatever do you mean, Miss Gaines?" asked Mrs. Price with measured coolness.

"I mean the one married and three widowed belles who are dominatin' the social scene this season. I am wonderin' if you have an opinion as to why those four ladies are so popular?"

Indeed, Mrs. Price had very definite opinions about the four women in question. She discerned that their costly manner was the bridge between the "proper customs of the past" and the "improper new behavior." Their politeness and etiquette were akin to the old-fashioned ways. Their lavish dress and sensuous forms, and their quietly confident opinions, were modern. She wondered why the four women were so admired by the gentlemen, and came to the conclusion that they were most admired for what they did not do.

Mrs. Price observed that the four women did not consider it fashionable to copy the blase, spiritless, and emotionless manner that most American women imagined were the characteristics of ancient lineage, lofty birth, and high breeding. They did not act like the New Woman, trying to enter the ranks of men as non-women; instead they appeared to strive to impersonate everything that men and women fabricate as feminine—loveliness, relative innocence, and majesty.

The four women did not act meek and subservient, or try to overpower the powerful, or wear diamond bracelets and brooches to breakfast. They did not take opera glasses to see the breathtaking view from Fort Holmes, the highest point on the island; they took field glasses, bought or borrowed.

The four women did not walk awkwardly on rough ground in high heeled boots, hold their skirts up mincingly, twirl their parasols over their shoulders, or laugh immoderately at funny things male companions said. They walked on rough ground as if born to it. They wore skirts that inched above the ground and freed them from having to hold them. They laughed at a male companion's funny remark in accordance with how funny they thought it was.

After weeks of careful observation, Mrs. Price finally came to the ultimate conclusion that the four women were not the kind to love men—who admired small feet.

Mrs. Price replied to Belinda's question, "I have formed no opinion, Miss Gaines." Her fibbing eyes could not meet Belinda's black orbs.

Noticing that the stuffy Mrs. Price did not want to talk about the four women, Belinda pursued the subject with renewed vigor. She continued, "They're constantly together, yet constantly visiting with everyone . . . simply everyone on the veranda . . . why, I declare . . . even the old maids and the crafty crackpots. They're the life of the entertainments they attend. And they all attend most of them."

Mrs. Price interposed dryly, "I do not like the new fashion of bare arms during the daytime . . . those short puffed sleeves stopping between the shoulder and the elbows . . . the gloves do not meet the sleeves by a hand's breadth. There are few women whose arms are soft and white enough to carry it off. At night cosmetics and powders cover up defects on the arm. But by day, these bare arms are not a lovely sight."

All the MaMas agreed and secretly hoped the conversation would swing back to the Big Four. The matriarchal group had talked about their daughters' clothes most of the day, avoiding any subject bound to disrupt their cowlike harmony. Silently, they goaded Belinda Gaines on.

"My opinion exactly, Mrs. Price. Do you think the Big Four could wear this style well? Or do you think they're too old?" purred Belinda. She detected Mrs. Price's eyes narrow slightly. Most of the MaMas, including Mrs. Price, were not much older than the four women in question.

Controlling her tone, Mrs. Price replied, "My guess is that such ladies who have inherited generations of culture in action and bearing, who have natural intelligence and natural tact, avoid anything brusque or unpleasant. The question, Miss Gaines, is not could they wear this style well, but would they choose to be seen in such an unbecoming style at all."

An outburst of agreement issued forth from the MaMas, drowning the orchestra's first bars of the popular "Mockingbird Song." If they enjoyed talking about the elegant and magnetic four women who inspired thoughts of glamor and intrigue, the matriarchal group, except for Mrs. Price, absolutely adored chatting with the four women personally. The four women made the conservative MaMas, who were at the Grand Hotel without their husbands, feel glamorous in their presence.

The members of the matriarchal group were, on the whole, not envious that the Big Four had taken over the social scene at the Grand, without seeming to have exerted a drop of manipulation. They were far too busy trying to marry off their daughters, and consequently had no time or inclination to pursue competitive roles as short term society leaders. Back home, where they lived to be in battle for life-time roles as generals of society, it was quite the opposite for the matriarchal group members.

Back home, the group of four women would not have taken over without a fight. And if they had snubbed the MaMas, or worse, had not introduced the MaMas' daughters to eligible gentlemen of their acquaintance, the MaMas would have called the three eligible women "grass widows," and the fourth ineligible woman a "married siren," without hesitation and without feeling a smidgen of sisterly guilt. Not only did the

MaMas make personal social sacrifices, they used whomever necessary to lure a husband for their daughters. They were old-fashioned committed mothers. A dying breed.

"Listen to their laughter . . . look who's sittin' and standin' around them . . . all the young men. Those four women must be forty years old at least and still flirtin'," Belinda Gaines addressed the entire group of MaMas and daughters while the orchestra played the hit tune "Our Cat."

Mrs. Price shot back in her most leveling tone, "I doubt that one of the four ladies in question is forty years old."

Belinda's mother, an accomplished though somehow unaffected coquette herself, who would have preferred to sit with the Big Four that evening, but was stuck with the northern MaMas, did not like the tone Mrs. Price used with her Belinda. She decided to take her daughter's side, though young Belinda did not need her mother's support.

"I declare it's true, Mrs. Price, that gentlemen talk about what they . . . as my daughter calls them . . . the Big Four . . . say or laugh about or imply. The gentlemen talk about what dresses they wear, the stories behind the jewels adornin' their ears, necks and fingers, and how they wear their hair. The four women monopolize all the partners on the dance floor, even if it's unintentional and . . ."

Belinda interrupted her mother. She directed her speech at the daughters rocking idly, with an air of expectancy, on rustic chairs near their respective mothers. "The Big Four attract far more than their share of admiration. All you blushin' timid maidens pale before their charm. I tell you all . . . they're enemies to you social buds. Their pleasure is all they think of. If you're forced to be forward with gentlemen, such an unlady-like vice, it's because the married and widowed flirts, especially the Big Four, force you to compete with them."

The northern daughters, many of them college girls who had strolled away from their New Woman or intellectual flirt groups to the matriarchal group and their respective MaMas when suspect nighttime came calling, found Belinda's speech offensive. They did not want to be called "timid maidens" and "social buds" by a southern coquette beauty who attracted every "male animal" who set eyes on her.

"I have never seen the Big Four . . . as you call them . . . flirting with the young men. They are friendly and warm. I do not call that flirting. In fact, the countess has introduced me to many young men of her acquaintance," replied a northern girl. Her MaMa beamed upon her.

"How do you all think that they make the acquaintances of the young men? By ignoring them, I suppose? Why are young men always seeking their sympathy and advice? I tell you," Belinda paused dramatically and fluttered her Watteau fan fast and loose, " . . . the Big Four are traitors to our sex. Take your heads out of your books and watch what goes on on this veranda tonight. You'll see what I'm tellin' you all is true."

Most of the MaMas secretly thought what Belinda Gaines declared was true. The married matrons at the Grand, especially the group of four women, had more attention paid to them than their never-before-married sisters. Some MaMas reasoned that the married ladies were not afraid to speak to a man because they feared he wanted to elope with them. All the MaMas thought that everything was mixed up in 1893. Young men seemed to be attracted to well-formed figures with well-informed minds. Old men seemed to go after unformed girls with uninformed minds.

Just then a pudgy, gnome of a man, fumbling in his vest pocket for a toothpick, dropped a wad of money near the matriarchal group. Trying to avoid his stomach, he stooped down to pick up the wad, and out flew a crisp green bill picked up by a playful breeze and placed down amidst the matriarchal group's protective circle.

"Excuse me ladies . . . excuse me . . ."

The women watched him go after the bill as the soft wind teased the green paper just out of the reach of his ringless, chubby fingers, again and again, while the orchestra played "Good Sweet Ham" as if in accompaniment. The little paper turned somersaults near Belinda. She could not take any more of this interruption to her cant against the Big Four, nor the round man's pitiful movements. When the bill landed near her, she stayed sitting and nimbly placed her small foot directly on it. She noticed one zero. She thought, all this fuss over a measly little ten dollar bill.

"Thank you so very much for your help. I am deeply grateful and most appreciative," effused the blimpish middle-aged man.

Belinda dismissed the round man's self-conscious rattle with a cold quick smile. Then she moved her foot slightly and released the bill as the man carefully squatted to pick it up. Three zeros and a one, she read backwards. Belinda's cold smile defrosted as she cooed, "You're most welcome . . . I've never seen a one thousand dollar bill before!"

"Oh . . . well . . . in that case . . . I would be most gratified to show it to you. Most gratified." The man, having forgotten to get up, handed Belinda the bill, lost his balance, and bounded down onto his roly poly buttocks.

All the women's eyes waltzed with laughter. With the exception of Belinda. She was all business when she broke into a huge smile and offered him her hand.

"Would you kindly help me up? Perhaps I can look at the one thousand dollar bill under the incandescent light. It is too difficult to see here." Belinda transformed the ridiculous looking man into a gentleman, in a swoop of a sentence.

The MaMas grudgingly marveled at such quickness in one so young, and sized up the object of Miss Gaines' attention as he scrambled to get up, in order to help Belinda get up. Almost anyone with money and a kind face was a possible candidate for their oldest daughters.

"Aren't you frightened to carry such a large bill?" Belinda prodded him.

"I would be gratified to explain that. As I came through Chicago I collected a two thousand dollar note. I personally knew nothing of the banks there since the general collapse two months ago in May. The newspapers, why, the very air is so full of rumors, that I thrust the bills into my vest pockets thinking them as safe there as in an average bank at present."

Formal introductions were made, and Belinda, accompanied by her MaMa, walked with the recently transformed gentleman to an electrified glass globe, where they examined the one thousand dollar bill with exaggerated interest.

The matriarchal group members exchanged knowing glances. They were too considerate to gossip about Belinda when she was within hearing distance. But when she strolled some one hundred feet down the veranda, one northern girl, a millionairess, pointed out, "In one breath Belinda Gaines is ranting and raving about young men flirting with married and widowed belles, and in the next breath she is baiting a hook for a man twenty-five years her senior."

"Who but a man of his age and income could afford to dress her?" remarked a college girl.

Cynthia Price, who sat silent most of the evening except for her remark about how "smallish" everything seemed after the world's fair, rekindled the former conversation about the group of four women that Belinda had whipped up and stated, "It is well known that the most courted ladies in the world are widows. It is no wonder that three of the Big Four are courted so enthusiastically, even from afar, by the married men."

Mrs. Price was always discomposed to hear her Cynthia make such mature comments. Mrs. Price had a hard time admitting to herself that Cynthia was pushing thirty. She wished her daughter had not opened the subject again. She knew that a dozen MaMas and daughters would throw in their two cents, because a Price had reopened the subject of the Big Four.

"Yes . . . but the countess is the most popular of the four ladies, and she is married . . ."

"Yes . . . but she is almost a widow. Her husband is quite ill I have heard rumored . . ."

"Yes . . . I am sure that the widows to whom we refer are very well off from their late husbands' wills . . . and from the look of their jewels, their husbands held them in great esteem . . ."

"Yes . . . the countess' jewels are rare and must go back at least twenty generations . . ."

"But we have not answered why the Big Four are so popular?" interjected Cynthia Price.

The uninvited but most welcome male company of Professor Loral Bellamy infiltrated the matriarchal group like a grandfather showing up at a bridal shower. Pleasantries were exchanged and the orchestra cresendoed into "The Old Easy Chair By The Fire."

"May I answer your question, Miss Price?"

"Please do, Professor Bellamy. Would you care to sit down?"

Professor Loral Bellamy had a smile and brain as broad as the northwest. Mrs. Price and all the MaMas showed their teeth they were so happy to smile upon his presence. Not only was the retired Notre Dame professor a manly man, he was learned and athletic and romantic and a widower too old for anything but the sincerest friendship. The entire group relaxed ready for his customary entertainment.

"Dear ladies . . . would I shed some light on this question

if I were to say . . . that quartette of reigning beauty of which you speak . . . that tetrachord of voguish vividness . . . is so admired, because not only are they ideal ladies with perfect manners, behavior, and dress . . . they are ideal gentlemen with generous tendencies, considerate feelings, and magnanimous spirits."

The group turned as green as a pea-green gown belonging to Belinda Gaines, but ate up every word the professor politely hewed. Just to hear the professor speak in that way of his was verbalistic music to the ears of the MaMas. The daughters found him flowery and archaic. But now and then his opinions and stories were original, so they tolerated his excessive expression.

Of course Professor Bellamy was no fool, so he quickly added, "And may I say . . . ladies and gentlemen . . . that I find the same light and spirit here among all of you."

The MaMas giggled, delighted to hear his flattery. They so seldom heard a compliment in a deep voice, that even collective flattery caused each of them to flutter a little inside.

Loral Bellamy, a professor of English literature and classical history, did not articulate the thoughts that struck him as he observed the circle of motherly, procreative women and their daughters. A patch of nearby electric light softened the MaMas' mildly lined facial features, and lit up their pregnant eyes, and rocking, life bestowing bodies. The electric light light dulled their daughters' dreamy faces, and lit up their untapped eyes, and rocking, yearning bodies.

The professor imagined them as a modern version of an ancient interreligious vision; the daughters were like Roman virgins keeping vestal vigils, alongside their MaMas who were like cult worshippers of the Egyptian goddess Isis—honored as the great mother of all, devoted wife, enchantress, speaker of spells, and mistress of magic.

The professor imagined the Big Four, whom the MaMas and daughters secretly esteemed, as a four-in-one Isis godhead adored by the MaMa and daughter cult. He asked himself if the four women had somehow awakened dim primeval memories of female worship among the modern Grand Hotel set. Because all adoring eyes, including his own, were on the group of four women that evening like never before.

Professor Loral Bellamy conversed with the MaMas and daughters until, one by one, they reluctantly began to remark that it was becoming chilly and time to retire for the day. He bade them cheerful goodnights and strolled in the direction of the Big Four. The matriarchal group gradually dispersed, except for Mrs. Price, Cynthia, and Priscilla. They sat in silence, listening to Hawley's "I Love You Dear," the last musical piece of the evening concert.

The softest, most vulnerable moments of the evening blossomed like a delicate moonflower yielding inflorescence. No one on the veranda wanted to let go of the music and conversation and enjoyment and developing love affairs and friendships, and be reminded it was time to go to bed. For many went to bed . . . alone.

And it was no wonder that at that time of the waning evening, lonely Cynthia Price interrupted her family's listening in a voice so sad, that even her inattentive fifteen-year-old sister Priscilla looked startled, and actually listened to her sister's discourse. Cynthia had clearly been affected by the dramatic attentions bestowed upon the Big Four.

Staring into the black space of night, Cynthia said in a voice barely above a whisper, "I wish to be admired and loved openly . . . only by one man . . . .I wish to hear emotions put into words . . . .I wish my life to be expressed beyond ordinary routine. Those women whose lives stretch beyond ordinariness, are unusually beautiful or talented. And the rest of us who are not so exceptional . . . suffer longfully . . . for one to admire us for our little lovelinesses."

Cynthia breathed in the cool air of night hoping to calm the heat of her emotions; she spoke deliberately, as if fighting the resignation of impatience and its consequent dullness.

"I am not brashly beautiful . . . I cannot recite dramatic poetry with flair . . . my charms could never match up to any one in the group of four women. But am I any less of a woman . . . any less sensitive to the vanity of experiencing expression . . . reaction . . . from a man. . . . Could I not be admired and loved openly for . . . one little loveliness I may possess?"

Mrs. Price's heart flew to her lonely daughter who longed for something uncommon to happen, but she replied firmly, "Sit up straight . . . and quit dribbling such nonsense. Very few women have that kind of excessive admiration and love bestowed upon them from a man. Be thankful for the attentions of a devoted mother and her friends. It is enough. Never . . . never . . . and this is meant for you too, Priscilla . . . never . . . make up romantic expectations from a man . . . it is not the way of life."

"I do not believe you! I see all sorts of romance here. A woman has to make herself into the kind of woman a man wants to love in a romantic way." Cynthia suffocated her urge to cry out, even lash out at the mother whom she loved dearly.

"Tell me dear, what kind of woman is it that a man wants to love in a romantic way?" Mrs. Price predicted the answer.

"A woman like the countess or any one of her three friends."

"If I hear any more about that group of four women, the so-called 'Big Four,' I am going to forbid you to talk with them. Their appetite for attention is excessive."

"They are fun loving and full of life . . ."

"Not everyone comes here to be pumped up, my dear. Some of us simply want to rest in comfort . . . breathe in the fresh air . . . be left alone." Mrs. Price did not add, and marry off our daughters.

"I cannot wait till PaPa comes to be with us here. I only wish he could stay for more than a fortnight, when we are here for the entire summer." Mrs. Price and Cynthia agreed whole-heartedly with Priscilla.

The Prices stared out into the darkness, down to the electric and gas lights in the village below. Mrs. Price and Priscilla thought of Mr. Price, while Cynthia wondered what romantic entanglements were weaving themselves in the smaller hotels in the village, such as the Astor House, Island House, and The New Murray.

Mrs. Price became increasingly perplexed over Cynthia's sad outburst. She began to wonder if she should have brought her Cynthia to a summer resort again for the sole purpose of finding a husband. She was thankful Mr. Price had not heard his daughter. He had warned Mrs. Price that a summer setting so full of momentary enjoyments was a questionable place for establishing, for Cynthia, a lifelong marital relationship—a relationship which in no way would resemble the enchantment of summer, momentary enjoyments.

Mrs. Price wished Mr. Price were on the veranda with her that evening. She felt a longing to discuss this sad outburst from their oldest daughter. And she knew how her husband would respond. He would say in that practical way of his, we must explain to Cynthia that people who enjoy summer so-journs are quite different in the spring, autumn and winter. Remind her, that during the rest of the year, these same active women resorters bound out of their homes to attend lectures, and devote themselves to charity or civic work. Remind her, these same men resorters go to work and after attend their clubs, card parties, and banquets. The women seek all the excitement and intellectual stimulation they can find. The men seek all the relaxation and simple companionship they can find. Tell her, in the summer the sexes come to frolic together, but the rest of the year, they go their separate ways. He would say, Cynthia is old enough to understand these differences.

Yet, Mrs. Price did not have the heart to directly confront Cynthia with this practical approach to weaning her from ideas of romance. She thought, if only my Cynthia would not take the romance this splendid setting inspires so seriously. If only she would concentrate on making matrimonial alliances rather than imagining romantic escapades.

Mrs. Price thought, if only that group of four women, with all the traditional manners of our class and the magnetism of women of the night, did not influence my Cynthia. She does not see their clever manipulation of language and gesture, how they build invisible walls around their vulnerability, how they escape unwanted passion in their union of four.

Just then Mrs. Price overheard the four women's liberal laughter float down the longest porch in the world, again, and she felt pangs of disenchantment with their new charms and old manners. She almost wished their laughter was forced and immoderate. She almost wished the four women's infectious sense of fun was exhaustible. She wished her Cynthia had not been influenced by their obvious magnetism. She wished her Cynthia to be happy, so she could be happy.

Mrs. Price did not know that the admired Big Four, sitting some three hundred feet down the veranda, had responded gaily to an impromptu poem recited by Jimmy Hayes' best friend, Eugene "Sully" Sullivan:

" 'It's when the sun sinks in the west

The summer lady's at her best,
For when the nighttime charms her soul
Tis then she loves to take a stroll,
And by these presents be it known
She hates to take that stroll alone.' "

Whereupon, the group of four magnetic women rose gracefully, their silk and lace gowns rustling rousement. The surrounding eligible, swagger gentlemen, except Jimmy and Sully, moved in. Much to the eager gentlemen's obvious surprise and disappointment, the four women took each other's arms, bid good night pleasantries, and began strolling two by two along the veranda to the orchestra's encore piece, "Though Your Sins Be As Scarlet."

If the admiring gentlemen appreciated the four women's ironic response to Sully's poem, they did not talk about it. They stood about grinning to themselves and gazing after the four lovely forms until they vanished into the dark distance. Then they lit up their pipes and cigars, and resumed discussing stocks and bonds and congress and the silver question, and more importantly, what time they would go fishing the next day, and whose boat (meaning yacht) they would take to catch the finny devils.

And as the Big Four strolled the longest porch in the world that evening, past hundreds of admiring critical eyes, their fine minds teemed with thoughts. Secret thoughts—not one of the resorters would have guessed at in their wildest midsummer nights' dreams.

2

Meetings

"Yes, Mrs. Muldoon, I was in London and Paris for their respective seasons this spring. London was dull. Speaking of dullness, I received a letter yesterday from my brother. He wrote that it is the dullest season in Newport in years. He is yawning mentally . . . worn out with the weariness of inactivity for over a week. He wrote Bar Harbor is gayer than ever. I also received a letter from an acquaintance. Can you imagine . . . the envelope was sticked before sealed? Unpardonable."

"You must tell us about the season in Paris, Mr. Haverhill," spurred on the second Mrs. Muldoon.

"Paris? So so. Piety has suddenly become chic . . . bad form to be an atheist. When religion becomes fashionable in Paris, piety can no longer be considered bourgeois."

The two jolly chatterers, the Mesdames Muldoon, basking in the morning sun on the veranda, stuffed from a breakfast of fresh strawberries in cream, fresh orange segments, eggs croquette, piping hot buns, newly made butter, marmalade, and hot chocolate, barely followed the talk of Mr. Rutherford Earle Haverhill V. His talk was resolute, abbreviated, and had inflections similar to an English public school accent. They thoroughly enjoyed listening to his accent. And they thoroughly wondered why Rutherford Haverhill kept looking over at the entrance doors leading to and from the veranda.

The western born Muldoon ladies did not seem to mind that Mr. Rutherford Haverhill was an elegant, scornful American

31

anglophile, born into the highest level of eastern society. He copied English manners, bearing and fashion, with cooly patronizing, arrogant airs, seen in aristocratic circles in England. He was the type who opened an umbrella under sunny skies in the states because he thought it might be raining in London.

Rutherford Haverhill was too perfectly shaven, pronounced words by dropping a letter, and laughed in a mirthless, jerky sort of way. The western men called him a dandy. The southern men called him a Yankee dude. The women called him fussy. Although he was handsome, only a fortune hunter would put up with his fussiness; all the eligible women, including the Muldoons, admitted reluctantly. He discussed small matters in detail with a persistence few important matters merited. As a result of his fussiness, he had never found lasting love, and concerned himself soley with the improvement of his character—and other people's character.

"How do you account for the religious revival in Paris, Mr. Haverhill?"

"Quite simple, Mrs. Muldoon. The French churches today look like the salon of a duchess. Flowers everywhere. The floors, once bare, are thick with carpets. The music, the singing, compete with concert hall performances. Walls drip with paintings and tapestries. Priests drape themselves in gold embroidered vestments. Dear ladies . . . it is like participating in a grand performance at the Paris Opéra."

The Muldoon ladies, both society matrons who had made the grand tour of Europe but once, were most entertained by Mr. Rutherford Haverhill. They met with him every morning after breakfast and often challenged him to a nip and tuck game of croquet. Although they knew his family hobnobbed with the Astors of New York and Newport, and he had hosted his acquaintance, that "strange man" Ward McAllister, at the

Grand just one week ago—these credentials, hot fodder to any social climber, did not impress the Muldoon ladies. They simply liked to listen to him.

In return, Rutherford liked to have an audience. The old Muldoon ladies reminded him, remotely, of his beloved mother. He felt comfortable with them.

While the Muldoon ladies listened to yet another of Mr. Haverhill's opinions—about a lady who strolled past wearing a skirt with fifteen ruffles, "She looks like a ruffled chicken . . ."—they looked the fashionable gentleman over. His black flannel lounge coat, perfectly pressed, was as black as his white duck trousers, starched and creased in front and back, were white. The four solid gold disk buttons on his lilac shirt sleeves bore noble crests from both sides of his family. The ladies did not know that gold crests kept a man like Mr. Rutherford Haverhill moored to his family's social caste, no matter how far away from home he strayed. What they did know was that Mr. Haverhill proved to be the best dressed gentleman at the Grand.

The ladies also found Rutherford Haverhill a handsome man. What man would not be handsome in his late thirties who never worked a day in his life, they often pointed out to each other. To keep busy, Rutherford told them, he traveled Europe, shot quail and caught trout on Long Island, shot crocodiles in the Nile and jackals in the Nairobi desert and mountain lions in the Rockies.

He did not tell them, that as a rich man of leisure, his greatest emotional concern was keeping his valet happy. This was because his valet took care of his morning, afternoon and evening clothes which included: for the morning—six pairs white duck trousers, three pairs white flannel trousers one striped and two plain, a black flannel lounge coat, a blue flannel lounge suit, six ordinary morning suits of tweeds and other mixtures, and tan shoes either low or laced; for the afternoon—one Prince Albert coat of vicuna, one cut-away or morning coat of vicuna which could be worn with white duck double-breasted waistcoats, a number of fancy cashmere trousers, and *de rigueur* patent leather shoes; for the evening—two Cowes suits, three suits of usual evening style, gloves, and patent leather low pumps or shoes, broadbrimmed straw hat, top hat for coaching; and for formal wear—swallow tail coat, low cut waistcoat, vicuna trousers, white lawn tie, black silk stockings, patent leather pumps, top hat; miscellaneous items—silk ties of gray and light blue and pink, derby or Hamburg rain hat, Wellington tan or patent leather riding boots, riding clothes, yachting clothes, shirts of pinks and lilacs with two buttons and white collars high with ends slightly bent, not to mention underclothes, pajamas . . . .

Rutherford Earle Haverhill V had more costume change possibilities than Belinda Gaines and the Big Four high society women put together. And it must be said that he wore his costumes with as much elegance as they wore theirs.

Yes, Rutherford's valet was almost the most important person in his master's life. He brushed his master's clothes, cleaned his top boots and shooting boots and dress boots. He put out his master's clothes for dressing. He assisted in packing and unpacking his master's clothes. Although the valet complained that he would rather work in a factory, he never left Rutherford's employ. In fact, the valet was Rutherford Haverhill's unacknowledged, closest friend. Rutherford did not have many close friends. The reason was simple. He was not well liked.

Rutherford Haverhill was unkind, if sincere, in his opinion of others. The men at the Grand called him a know-it-all. He was notorious among the guests for his remarks such as:

"Smart men do not wear monocles."

"His crease is always in the wrong place."

"He is too short to wear knickerbockers."

"Only ruddy-faced men should wear that peculiar shade of green."

"I do not think colored handkerchiefs chic."

"Tailors, like family doctors, should always be retained."

"Good blood so seldom means good looks."

In spite of Rutherford's crisp remarks, guests decided that his character consisted of gentlemanly breeding that outshone even the notorious Ward McAllister himself, a former companion to Rutherford's dear mother's dear friend, Mrs. Astor. It may even be true that Ward McAllister used Rutherford Earle Haverhill V as a living example for his own, so-called, gentlemanly behavior.

Old maids and couples with children and college girls and their MaMas and crafty crackpots and bachelors began promenading the veranda for their after breakfast, morning constitutional, dressed in their 9:00 a.m. to 12:00 noon costumes. Rutherford kept one eye on the Grand Hotel's entrance doors leading directly onto the veranda, and kept the other eye on the attentive Mesdames Muldoon. The ladies wondered whom he was looking for. They were soon to find out.

"Were the salmon and trout as fresh in Paris as the Mackinac salmon and trout are here, Mr. Haverhill?"

"We did not touch salmon in Paris. It is considered much too bourgeois. And trout is considered too restaurant. No one eats sole there nowadays either. Shad is all the rage."

"How does the food here at the Grand compare with the food in Paris, Mr. Haverhill?"

"Oh, my dear hearts . . . it would take days to describe the differences. I shall say this. The Grand's specialty is its table. J. R. Hayes knows how to feed his patrons. I know a hotel's worth by its butter, bread, coffee, cream, as I know a resorter's worth by his linen, neckware, fingernails, teeth. But the patrons eating the food here are quite beyond my comprehension." Rutherford inhaled a sniff and continued. "Last night I noticed a diner cutting a salad leaf with a . . . knife. Certainly a fork is sharp enough for so delicate a plant. Then I saw him drink coffee with his . . . soup. I could not bear to watch after that."

The western Muldoon ladies smiled, so amused with the eastern Haverhill man. Rutherford did not understand what it was he said that provoked such smiles. Again, he looked at the hotel's entrance expectantly. Ah, there she was. And she was alone. He sneaked a look at his tan morning shoes. Really, no need to look. But, yes, they were perfect. She would notice his shoes. All women, even American nobility, look at men's shoes first. His speech quickened and his artificial English colored voice rose in volume, as she approached his group on her morning constitutional.

Rutherford continued, "Speaking of food . . . years ago I went to a party at Delmonicos in New York . . . oh . . . good morning Countess Gianotti." Rutherford arose from his wooden chair. Good morning pleasantries were exchanged by all.

"Would you care to sit a spell, Countess?" asked one of the ladies. Countess Gianotti accepted because cheerful Mrs. Muldoon asked. If Mr. Haverhill had asked, the countess would have declined, most graciously.

"Thank you, Mrs. Muldoon, I should like to relax before my morning drive," the countess replied in a full and mellow voice. Countess Elizabeth Anne Gianotti sat down, her legs begging to get up for a brisk morning walk instead. She stole a brief look at the water-filled straits stretched out like a shimmering wet ribbon, the early morning sun casting silver reflections upon it in the east. She longed for a moment alone, to breathe in the morning dampness heavy with fresh scents.

"I was just telling the Mesdames Muldoon about a party I

attended at Delmonicos. A bachelor friend of mine gave a dinner party for forty guests. For a centerpiece someone designed a miniature lake that ran down the center of the table. It was large enough for two living swans to paddle up and down the water. One swan died from the heat and fumes of the dinner, wine, and gas."

The Muldoon ladies looked wide-eyed and bewildered.

Rutherford continued, "It was the talk of the town."

"Well then," the countess quipped charmingly, "the host must have been delighted."

"He was tickled to be on the tongues of every New York society name worth mentioning," Rutherford replied, trying to hide his excitement in the presence of the grand countess, one of the most admired ladies at the Grand—if not the most admired lady because of her noble title.

One of the Muldoons blurted, "I live to hear such stories. I understand that royalty entertains even more voluptuously. Is that true, Countess?"

The youthful grande dame decided to oblige the sweet old Muldoons with a description, if not an ending, to top Rutherford's black braggadocio. She told her story in a voice so perfectly natural, so free from affectation, so downright friendly the effect charmed the Muldoons, and even Rutherford whose put-on accent was an unwitting burlesque on pompous English aristocracy.

"You have reminded me of a ball given by Baroness Jules Koenigswarter, which I attended in the spring. I shall always cherish the memory. The baroness had large cherry trees in full bloom brought in. The blossomy boughs were laden with a hundred small gold cages, alive with tiny song birds with brilliant feathers. We could hear their chirping above the strains of the music while we danced. It was as if the birds were singing along."

The countess paused. Noticing the Muldoons enraptured by

the description, and Rutherford Haverhill seemingly envious that he could not have been a part of it, she continued, "The supper room was just as enchanting. Its frescoed walls were covered with gold encrusted trelliswork on which thousands of red and yellow and pink roses, and green vine leaves, and luscious bunches of hot house grapes, and forced peaches, appeared to grow. In the center of the supper table was a huge roast peacock, with a gilded beak and eyes bejeweled with emeralds, its iridescent feathers spread out like a giant fan. At either end of this table were great cages spun from sugar. They were decorated with candy, and inhabited by bullfinches and hummingbirds and canaries. The room was well ventilated and the birds seemed to enjoy the scene as much as I did. And Mr. Haverhill," the countess added engagingly, "not one of the birds died."

Rutherford Haverhill smiled insincerely.

The Muldoon ladies were transfixed. They sighed at the leftover images stimulated by such description, and wondered how such dreams were realized. But not for long.

Soon one of the Muldoon ladies began wracking her brain to come up with an equally entertaining food related story. "The most unusual dinner I have ever attended was the funeral dinner of a friend's husband. My friend had the table decorated in black, purple and white. The napkins were white with black monograms and embroidered with dark purple pansies. The silver vases at each corner of the table were filled with dark colored flowers. I cannot remember what kind . . . can you dear?" she asked the other Mrs. Muldoon.

"No dear, I cannot remember."

"Too bad . . . one forgets so easily. But I do remember the ices. They were colored violet and white. Of course we were requested to wear black. And . . . what I shall never forget . . . never . . . was the male guest who presided at the foot of the table wearing a broad band of crape around his left arm." The two ladies exchanged loaded glances. "That same male guest ended up—marrying the newly widowed hostess!"

The countess obliged them with a scandalized look. The ladies were simply delighted. They noticed the corners of Rutherford's mouth looked compressed, and that his eyes were on the countess.

To Rutherford, the countess' whole being seemed aglow with morning energy. He felt like tapping into her energy, then and there, in front of every resorter on the veranda.

"Countess, where will you be buried, in Italy or America?"

"I must confess, Mrs. Muldoon, I have not thought seriously about it."

"But it is never too early to consider such things. I must say I have one of the most beautiful spots in the city of the dead. Bushels of roses grow on it. I go out to my plot and pick the most sumptuous pink roses for my table decorations. Of course, I never tell my guests the roses are from the cemetary. Most people do not care to be reminded of the city of the dead at dinnertime. In fact, the flower arrangements for my funeral will come from my own graveplot. But I must be sure to die when the roses are in season," she grinned at her own eccentricity. "Indeed, I have never found a more restful spot on earth."

The countess added, "With the exception· of Mackinac Island perhaps? Would you spend the season here if you did not find it restful?"

"On the contrary. I find this spot invigorating. So many people coming and going. And so many delightful spots to visit on the island. Have you been to the graveyards on the island yet?"

"Yes," the countess replied wistfully, "many years ago."

"And you, Mr. Haverhill, have you visited the graveyards yet?" one of the Muldoons demanded to know.

"No . . . I have not . . . Mrs. Muldoon," Rutherford answered dropping more letters in his words than usual. "In fact, I do not intend to visit—any graveyard."

"Ah . . . but some day you must . . . ," sighed a Mrs. Muldoon gravely.

Rutherford was thoroughly dismayed that a chat involving the enchanting countess, on a perfectly beautiful morning, should be ruined by such talk. Talk about death in his circle out east was generally taboo. He was also embarrassed, for the sake of the aristocratic countess and himself, to be in the company of ladies who dwelled on such a subject.

"My sister's smile was as cold as ice, but she looked so natural."

"Yes . . . that she did, Mrs. Muldoon," agreed her counterpart.

"Even the young ladies today do not look natural anymore. I have noticed they brighten their hair," Rutherford added, glad to get off the taboo subject. He wanted to ask the exquisite countess, sitting so very near, to promenade; but did not want her to think him rude to the Muldoon ladies, by taking leave just then.

"The term is dye, I believe."

" . . . Die?" Rutherford asked absentmindedly.

"The young ladies dye their hair."

"Oh yes . . . of course."

"Getting back to my sister . . . she was the most natural looking I have ever seen," remarked a Muldoon.

"You are prejudiced because she was your sister," suggested the other Muldoon, her sister-in-law.

"I tell you only what I have witnessed in my lifetime."

"Still, she was your sister."

"My sister looked exceptionally natural."

"Everyone thinks their family members look more natural than their neighbors."

"Heavens and earth. I tell you, she looked more natural dead—than alive!"

Rutherford Haverhill, usually delighted with the Muldoons, could take no more of it. He noticed the countess' eyes bright and lively, her full lips holding back a smile. He was relieved to look upon such a lovely, cultivated creature who embraced life as if she would never let go. He excused himself to the old matrons, and turned to the countess.

"Countess Gianotti, would you care to accompany me on my morning constitutional?" To himself, he quipped that he might well have said, mourning constitutional. He noticed the countess hesitate slightly, as if she would rather not walk with him. But she turned to him with such an easy smile, he knew she would not refuse.

"Mr. Haverhill, a brisk stroll would be most welcome before my ride. Good morning, Mrs. Muldoon . . . Mrs. Muldoon."

By now guests streamed onto the longest porch in the world with satisfied faces and bellies big from breakfast. Rutherford, his heart pounding, led the countess to the eastern end of the porch. They heard the bugle for guard mount at Fort Mackinac, located one half mile away on a bluff directly to the east, beyond the nearby village pasture.

The distant sounding bugle seemed to alert the tranquil looking cows in the pasture. Their cowbells clanged or clunked, depending on the quality, in quicker succession when the fort bugle was played or the drums rolled for drill, than at other times of the day. Many of the Grand Hotel's more sensitive guests could not take hearing the "cursed cowbells" percussing the resultant metallic sound. The countess loved the sound of cowbells and the pastoral scene before her.

"Countess, what do you think of the extraordinary collection of people here at the Grand?" Rutherford twitted the word, extraordinary, and stole a stimulated, penetrating glance at her intelligent eyes.

The countess ignored his high toned implication. "I have met friendly people of every description, Mr. Haverhill."

"I noticed in a listing of the social register that of 5000 prominent families of New York, Chicago, Philadelphia, Boston, and Baltimore, whose summer addresses are published, 367 families are in Europe, 2,400 are at inland resorts, 2,200 are at the seashore, and a handful are here at the Grand."

"Surely more than a handful are at this hotel, Mr. Haverhill."

"Lets just say the swellest families, Countess Gianotti." Rutherford noticed a cow defecating, quickly turned his face west, and continued, "With the refinements of your court life as a lady-in-waiting to Queen Marguerite of Italy, the most elegant monarch in Europe, you must feel like a fish out of water on rustic Mackinac Island."

"There are no marble palaces, mosaics, or artistic masterpieces on the island, Mr. Haverhill. There is nothing on the island which makes pretense of competing with the grand monuments of Europe. And that is exactly why I enjoy it here. Where else in the world do you find a quaint New England style village on a remote northwoods island in a clear freshwater sea? My dear husband, had he been well enough to accompany me here, would have recuperated on this island."

With not-so-honorable intentions, Rutherford purposely ignored the mention of her husband and pointed out, "How generous, your poetic appraisal of this island."

"It is not an appraisal, Mr. Haverhill. It is a feeling I have about the island and its people."

The countess' words, "it is a feeling" echoed in his mind while Rutherford answered, "If you mean you find the peasants on this island picturesque, I do not. The smirking hotel servants and others here all have aspirations to be something other than what they are . . . preferably president of the United States. Only the Negro waiters are professional, agreeable, and know their place. I especially enjoy Europe because the picturesque peasants know where they fit in life."

"Yes, Mr. Haverhill, the European peasants have no chance to better themselves." The countess realized Rutherford had no idea how she felt about the island and its people.

Rutherford persisted, "But how friendly, polite, hospitable the European peasants are."

"Yes, the European peasants are subservient, unlike their American counterparts."

Again the countess' words, "it is a feeling," echoed in Rutherford's mind. He could not remember a high society lady in his set at home use the word "feeling"; he considered it an old world word. It sounded old-fashioned in the modern new world. He fixed his eyes on the countess, a feminine blend of old world charm and new world vitality. She was the most exotic American he had ever met. He thought her enchantingly fresh, free of conventional pretense, worldly in a refined way. The embodiment of health and strength, she stood erect and straight. No curve was exaggerated—but they were all there. If she was a bit statuesque, he figured it was because of her lady-in-waiting position at the court of the king and queen of Italy.

Rutherford knew of the American countess' reputation in Europe. He knew she was one of the few Americans married into European aristocracy who was welcome in the most exclusive circles even outside of Italy. He heard it was because she did not pretend to be an American aristocrat. The European aristocracy laughed at the idea of an American aristocrat, so opposite to all American principles.

Rutherford Earle Haverhill V knew this firsthand because

they had laughed at him. It was one of the few times in his life he had been put down by his own kind, and the other two times it had been by his own father. The put-down had happened in France the past June, before the Paris season was over. It caused him to return to America for the summer and distract himself at the Chicago World's Fair. All this led him to the Grand Hotel on Mackinac Island.

He was still smarting from the put-down, and downright jealous of the countess' European success. The only criticism he had ever heard of the countess among his aristocratic European friends was that, perhaps, she was too much of a lady. In other words, the European heads of state had not added her to their list of seductions.

"I read there has been a forty-five percent falling off of departures to Europe this summer," Rutherford stated in a spiteful tone of voice.

"Perhaps it has to do with the world's fair . . . even the financial panic," added the countess in patient, even tones.

"Perhaps . . . ." Rutherford could never tell the countess why that percentage, causing leaner times for many arrogant Europeans, satisfied him. He hoped that the percentage somehow affected the arrogant aristocratic Frenchman who had poked fun at Rutherford's affected English mannerisms. And somehow affected Rutherford's longtime aristocratic English friend, who had laughed along with the Frenchman whom he confidentially declared to hate. It was all too humiliating to tell the countess, though Rutherford was aching to tell someone who understood the British and the Europeans.

He wondered if the countess seemed gentle and humble because she had absorbed the style of popular Queen Margeurite, or because she too had been put in her place many years ago when she had entered the royal Italian court, by her marriage to Count Gianotti, the king's chamberlain. Rutherford, still smarting, preferred to think she had been put in her place as he had been.

Rutherford questioned why the countess, a lady reputedly well liked by the Prince of Wales, Emperor Franz Joseph and Prince Rudolf of Austria, King Alfonso of Spain, King Christian IX of Denmark, Prince Napoleon, would choose to spend two months at a northwoods watering place made up of a mishmash of society people.

Since it was the first time Rutherford had managed to spend that much time alone with the exceedingly admired countess, he did not want to put her off by too many direct questions. In fact, had he been honest with himself, he might have admitted that the resorters might learn to like him more if he promenaded with the popular countess. But Rutherford was too proud to admit, even to himself, that he longed to be well-liked. It was no wonder. Rutherford Earle Haverhill V often pooh-poohed popularity as "common."

It took the countess and Rutherford ten minutes to promenade from the east wing of the longest porch in the world to the west wing. The countess preferred to walk faster. Rutherford wanted to be seen with the countess and deliberately slowed their pace.

"Countess, in our conversation with the Mesdames Muldoon, you mentioned visiting the graveyard on this island many years ago . . . ."

"I visited as a child . . . .I summered on Mackinac Island for eighteen years, Mr. Haverhill. And this summer is the first time I have been here . . . in twenty years."

"You have not been back here for decades . . . why the Grand is but six years old . . . .Where on earth did you stay thirty years ago?"

"Almost forty years ago, Mr. Haverhill," the Countess Gianotti smiled, "I came before I was born. The first ten summers my family stayed at Mission House, and the next ten were spent at Island House. I remember when the Indians camped on the beaches near the village, and when the villagers used to fish rather than take Kodak armed tourists on carriage rides around the island."

Rutherford, clearly taken with the countess and clearly entertaining hopes to take her into his arms (if not into his bed) before summer's end, strained to sound sincere in his disguised verbal pass, and even inflected a bit of the American accent he was born with. "Countess Gianotti, your memories make you sound ancient. Yet I see before me a woman whose beauty presupposes she is much younger than she admits. I should like to possess such a fountain of youth myself."

Realizing that Mr. Haverhill would like to "possess" herself, the countess responded carefully, "Thank you, Mr. Haverhill. Your compliment reminds me of similar sentiments my dear husband . . . Count Gianotti . . . conferred upon me before our difficult parting two months ago." Countess Elizabeth Anne ("Anna") Gianotti smiled knowingly, and by mentioning her husband, forever dashed the hopes of arrogant Rutherford Earle Haverhill V to court her, in a clandestine fashion, for the summer.

Rutherford had been dreaming of complimenting the countess for days and days. He was obviously let down that she did not even bother to flirt in her rejection of him. But he was still thrilled simply to be standing next to her, especially in front of the entire veranda crowd.

By now Rutherford had gathered enough information about the countess to understand more clearly why she possessed the presence of a youthful grande dame. He calculated that she was about thirty-eight years old, as old as her Queen Marguerite; she had the advantage of years to accumulate all that was best of Europe, and the wisdom of age to retain all that was best of America.

Rutherford was dying to ask her how she could leave her sickly count in Italy to spend an entire season at an American resort. It was the unanswered question on every resorter's mind. But he was too proud. He was afraid she would not confide this to him. He could not take another rebuttal after she had refused his romantic advance. Rutherford decided he would find out some other way. Perhaps the Muldoon ladies could squeeze it out of her, he thought. Rutherford led the countess back to the Muldoon matrons. He knew she liked the old characters.

Anna Gianotti did not wonder or care why Mr. Rutherford Haverhill chose summer hotel life in the middle of the Great Lakes over cottage life at Newport, Rhode Island, where his family occupied one of the grandest summer houses in the nation. She heard him claim again and again that he was merely stopping off at "rustic" Mackinac Island enroute from the Chicago World's Fair to New York, and then on to Newport. That was three weeks ago.

Anna found Rutherford too arrogant for an American. In Europe his arrogance might have been acceptable had it been seasoned with royal blood. Anna jested to herself that Rutherford Haverhill's uncovered personality on rustic Mackinac Island was as obtrusive as the idea of hanging Renoir's "Nude in the Sunlight" painting in Mission Church in the village.

"Countess, would you consider writing a book?" asked Rutherford in a voice plainly flattened from her poised rejection of his disguised romantic pass.

"On what subject, Mr. Haverhill?"

"Instruction to the masses about things they should know. An etiquette book for Americans."

"What things should they know?" Anna tried to ease the seriousness of his voice by answering in a lighthearted tone.

"Observations about life in general would be of good use to the masses. Our existence must have some beneficial and refining influence. We need to explain our methods of living and enjoying life."

"Our methods, Mr. Haverhill?"

"Whenever we make an appearance in public, we are doing good in the world. I know that our method of behavior, without attracting undue attention, gives the masses a lesson in good manners and dress."

Countess Gianotti lowered her voice. "I hardly believe that the underprivileged Americans and their children who mine the coal for our stoves and weave the lace for our windows, ever see our behavior as a refining influence for their behavior."

Rutherford was amused to see Anna's eyes narrow ever so slightly. "I see that you have misunderstood me, Countess. I refer to the provincial, snobbish bourgeoisie who pretend to our class but fall dreadfully short."

"Excuse me . . . I misunderstood you. In the past I heard you refer to the masses as 'those evil smelling, rude crowds of roughs and their children.' I could only think you were referring to them when you spoke of the 'masses.' "

"Since that class of people cannot read . . . I could not refer to them as readers of an etiquette book."

Countess Gianotti never lost control. Rutherford Haverhill grew excited hoping she would. He noted her eyelashes, those elegant lashes, move up and down once too often. By now mixed emotions of jealousy, admiration, rejection, longing, were so strong that he desired to ruffle her feathers. Break the Dresden mold. With his bare hands if he could. They stopped walking in front of the Muldoons.

"Thank you, Countess Gianotti, for your brilliant company. I did not sleep well last night. Your presence awakened me more than my morning coffee," Rutherford said in a smarmy tone.

Before the countess could take leave politely, Mrs. Muldoon detained her by asking Rutherford, "Isn't your mattress comfortable, Mr. Haverhill?"

"I always carry an India rubber sheet to cover the mattress in addition to my own sheets, counterpane, and blankets. Hotel mattresses cause me nightmares. Think . . . of all the people who have slept on the very mattress you are sleeping on. Think . . . of the disease and dirt creeping about in the stuffing of the mattress . . . ."

The countess interrupted Rutherford, " My mattress was entirely clean, Mr. Haverhill."

"Do you suppose the mattresses really are clean, Countess?" Mrs. Muldoon asked suspiciously.

Countess Gianotti, realizing that Rutherford was trying to upset everyone, as he had tried to upset her before, happened to see Jimmy Hayes, caught his attention, and beckoned him over to their group.

"Good morning, Countess . . . good morning Mrs. Muldoon, Mrs. Muldoon . . . Haverhill," Jimmy Hayes exclaimed with his customary gusto, as if these were the last "good mornings" he would ever utter. "What can I do for you this morning?" he asked the countess.

"We are discussing the condition of the mattresses here, Mr. Hayes."

"The mattresses? Have you not been sleeping well?"

Mrs. Muldoon answered for the countess, "I never slept so soundly since I was here last summer."

"Well then . . ."

"Jimmy," broke in Rutherford, "we were discussing the condition of the mattresses."

"They are all quite new, Haverhill."

"The cleanliness in particular . . ."

"Yours was certainly clean, Haverhill . . ."

"Since I cannot see inside the mattress anywhere I travel, I carry an India rubber sheet for that purpose."

"A clever man you are," grinned Jimmy Hayes and slapped Rutherford a bit too hard on the back. "But I can assure those guests without rubber sheets that their mattresses were combed and cleaned before the season." Jimmy, a state champion amateur pugilist, felt like wading into Rutherford Haverhill in a businesslike way—with a corker on the ear. He had to shut Haverhill up before a rumor was started about the mattresses that would be harder to control than the plague. A rumor like that could ruin a season.

"Well, that is of credit to your establishment, Jimmy." To himself Rutherford added, if it is true.

Jimmy Hayes figured Rutherford Haverhill got the message to keep his mouth shut about the subject. After all, they were both sportsmen.

Having heard their discussion, a Mrs. Muldoon declared enthusiastically, "This is truly a first class hotel."

"Did you know that the queen of England carries not only her bedding, as I do, wherever she goes . . . she also carries her bed and other bedroom furniture," Rutherford tried to get in the last word.

"Must be heavy for her," Jimmy countered.

The women giggled lightly.

"The queen insists that wherever she travels, the rooms she stays in must be recarpeted, repapered, recalcimined, before she places one royal foot in them. Other royalty simply carry their mattresses with them . . ."

"Simply?" asked Jimmy, provoking another round of light giggles.

"Countess, may I inquire, did you bring your mattress with you from Italy?" asked a Mrs. Muldoon in all seriousness.

"I did not even bring an India rubber sheet," replied the countess with a straight face.

"Neither did I," replied a Mrs. Muldoon.

"Neither did I," replied the other Muldoon.

"What's an india rubber sheet anyhow?" Belinda Gaines appeared and begged to know in her dragging southern accent.

Before anyone answered Belinda, the countess excused herself. All eyes watched the lovely countess leave, including those of a rather young man new to the hotel scene standing a respectable distance away. The countess noticed him as well. She figured that he was in his early thirties, and that he was eligible. She thought the young women would swoon over him. She glanced at him again and felt somewhat disquieted by his expressive, intelligent looking face.

Jimmy Hayes watched the countess leave as well. Then he reminded everyone about the lecture that afternoon on the bloody massacre at Fort Michilimackinac.

Belinda exchanged polite greetings with everyone, and Rutherford Haverhill felt dutifully obliged to educate her on the advantages and history of the rubber sheet, in response to her question. She did not listen to a word he said. But she managed to maneuver Rutherford away from the Muldoons, who began exchanging news (that the mattresses were cleaned and combed before every season) with some youngish old maids.

Belinda Gaines lived to be seen with Rutherford Haverhill. Such a perfectly dressed, coifed, shaved, manicured, handsome, eligible specimen of a rich old family of New York and Newport, she thought, and little ol' me from New Orleans; all the cities begin with the word new   it must mean somethin'.

It must be told that Belinda Gaines went so far as to bribe her maid to wiggle her substantial hips in front of Rutherford's valet, in order to extract information on his master.

The only tidbits the maid learned from the loyal valet was that Rutherford did not use scented soap, and could not bear standing next to a man whose hair dressing smelled like a perfume factory. The valet also confessed that Rutherford used a violet wash on his hair. One of the valet's many intimate duties, in addition to hand washing Rutherford's silk underwear, was to fan his master's head vigorously for an entire half hour every "goddamned morning" to quench the smell of the sweet perfume. The valet hated fanning his master's hair, which is why he revealed the secret. And he hated the mornings for the rest of his life.

After Rutherford explained rubber sheets to Belinda, she used her bribed knowledge on him and cooed, "I like a gentleman to smell like a man. I am opposed to men usin' scents. I notice you do not use scents, Mr. Haverhill," proclaimed Belinda.

Rutherford thought, girls these days are in a terrible hurry about their future.

Belinda thought, so what if Mr. Haverhill is unpopular, he's grudgingly respected; just be to seen on his arm would establish me as a young lady of taste and sophistication and refinement. She especially wanted the Big Four to see her with a mature catch.

Belinda Gaines was out to catch a millionaire that summer. She knew they usually did not come in twenty-year-old packages. She figured Rutherford was not much older than thirty-five. Certainly not over forty. He abandoned his family in Newport to come here. She reasoned that Mackinac Island must be the "Newport of the west" for such a fine figure to grace it with his presence.

"Would it be too forward of me to suggest a stroll along this marvellous . . . simply marvellous . . . portico, Mr. Haverhill?"

Rutherford was too much of a gentlemen to say no.

"Yes," he responded carefully, "it would be a pleasure to stroll upon this magnificent porch." He did not add, with you.

Rutherford was just about to offer his arm when it occurred to him to look at his pocket watch. "Will you accept my apologies, Miss Gaines. I have quite forgotten the time. I must place a call to Newport."

"Newport . . ."

"Yes, a dear friend of my mother's, a Mrs. Astor, is expecting me to call her. You will excuse me?"

"Mrs. Astor, of course! Then you must know the Astors' fortune practically began on this humble island in fur trading back in the 1830s."

"Yes . . . but Mrs. Astor informed me, upon learning of my visit here, that her father-in-law, John Jacob, never set foot on this island."

"That's because there was no Grand Hotel then," gushed Belinda.

"Undoubtedly. Excuse me, Miss Gaines."

"See you later, Mr. Haverhill . . . ." Belinda turned around and just avoided walking into Professor Loral Bellamy. "Oh . . . my goodness . . . almost a collision . . . good morning, Professor . . . good morning, Mrs. Venn, how are your children today?" Everyone exchanged greetings. Belinda stole a few once-over glances at Mrs. Beatrice Venn and questioned why everyone thought her so stunning.

Belinda thought that Mrs. Venn, a high society lady from New York, was much too tall, her waist too long and slender for a MaMa, her feet too small for her size. She was far too straight featured, her carriage and impervious glance too proud. By any of Belinda's standards, Mrs. Venn did not look like a strictly beautiful woman. She decided that everyone exaggerated Mrs. Venn's good features.

But then Belinda ignored Mrs. Venn's luxuriant golden red hair, her flawless complexion, lovely sloping shoulders, well-modulated, friendly voice, and instead concentrated on what she perceived as the New York woman's flaws. That Beatrice Venn's personality was as spirited and lively as the countess' proved too much for Belinda to bear. Even more difficult for young Belinda to bear was that Beatrice Venn—belonged to the Big Four.

Mrs. Venn's little four-year-old boy Frederick touched Belinda's hand and announced, "We're going with the 'fessor to the village and the fort today."

"His name is not 'fessor. His name is Professor," corrected his ten-year-old sister, Monica in her most adult voice.

"How fun for you," Belinda bubbled sweetly.

The children liked Belinda very much because young Miss Gaines was one of the few "big people" who had the energy, and the mentality, to match their own.

Mrs. Beatrice Venn did not like Belinda because she noticed the children were always unruly even after a short visit with flighty Miss Gaines. What Beatrice Venn did not know was that the children were unruly because Belinda sneaked rock candy or peppermint patties or chocolate bon bons to the children, whenever their MaMa or German born nanny, "Nanna," were not looking. The children knew they were disobeying by eating the candy and devised all sorts of sneaky maneuvers in order to eat it, without their mother or Nanna catching them at it. There was no end to their mischief whenever Belinda Gaines was around.

"Your delightsome children most certainly enjoy the island, Mrs. Venn," uttered Belinda with unforced effervescence.

"Nowhere have I seen such a paradise for children, Miss Gaines. I am never afraid for my children's safety here."

"This idyllic island must be a genuine relief from your dirty, ugly city, where cold stone meets you at every corner. Why, I declare, there are no tree-lined streets to speak of, and there are no parks for the children exceptin' Central Park. I hear the poor are afraid to go there. You must be relieved to be away from the awful . . . awful noise. My former cousin who married a . . . northerner . . . now lives in New York. I heard, via the grapevine, that she swears she lives off her nerves caused by the noise and . . ."

"Miss Gaines," interposed Mrs. Venn politely, "I am sure you will be relieved to learn that your former cousin will have less stress to her nerves because the roads are gradually being paved with asphalt. It lowers the noise and one can now actually converse in cabs and carriages and rooms facing the streets."

"Oh really . . . my former cousin declared, via the grapevine, that all New Yorkers' lives are being worn out by the noise, but they don't realize it."

"You must tell your former cousin, via the grapevine, to move to a more secluded quarter uptown where the noise is less." Beatrice Venn was just about worn out with the noise of the conversation.

"Oh look . . . look . . . Mr. Sydney Froilan is settin' up his easel. Why, he's walkin' towards us," Belinda exclaimed. Everyone looked at the artist and Belinda slipped the children two maple cream filled bon bons she had wrapped in a hotel tea napkin marked with the letters PGH.

"Professor Bellamy asked, "Is that the world famous Sydney Chase Froilan?"

"It certainly is," replied Belinda importantly, "he told me he recently completed a portrait for Mrs. Potter Palmer . . . the Mrs. Palmer of Chicago!" Belinda emphasized Bertha Palmer's name almost as much as she had Mrs. Astor's name. Is was no wonder. Mrs. Palmer ruled Chicago and Mackinac Island even as Mrs. Astor ruled New York and Newport. That Mrs. Palmer was not to grace Mackinac Island with her presence, until late in the 1893 season, was due to the Chicago World's Fair. She was chairman of the Women's Building, a consuming and enslaving position.

"When did Mr. Sydney Froilan arrive?" inquired Professor Bellamy.

"Last night," Belinda answered excitedly.

"And you have already met," said Mrs. Venn, amazed at such quickness in one so young.

"Oh yes," Belinda drawled proudly. "I was examinin' a $1,000 bill when Mr. Sydney Froilan came up to my little group and explained he overheard and asked if he could see the portrait of the president of these United States on the bill because he was a portrait artist. The gentleman who owned the $1,000 bill asked his name and introductions were made all around. He's world famous . . . of that there is no doubt." She did not add what was doubtful in her mind. If Sydney Froilan were eligible. He certainly acted as if he were eligible.

Sydney Froilan finally arrived at the group.

"Good morning, Mr. Froilan," Belinda practically purred.

"Good morning . . . young lady. How lovely you look this beautiful morning."

If Belinda Gaines was not insulted that Sydney Chase Froilan forgot her name, she was crushed that he called her "young" lady. Yet she was determined to prove herself a gracious young lady by making introductions. Just as she was about to commence with introductions, middle-aged, American expatriate Sydney Froilan spoke in a voice which summoned up all the youthful spirits he could rouse so early in the day.

"Good morning . . . Mrs. Venn."

"Good morning . . . Mr. Froilan."

Belinda Gaines flew into an inner rage. One of the Big Four moved in already and Mr. Froilan arrived only last night.

While Mrs. Venn introduced Professor Bellamy, young Belinda felt relegated to a mere bystander.

"Miss Gaines tells us you met last night over a $1,000 bill," prompted Mrs. Venn, purposefully easing Belinda's wounded young pride.

"Ah . . . yes . . . Miss Gaines," Sydney Froilan immediately caught Beatrice Venn's intention, " . . . do you know . . . Miss Gaines . . . that you are more lovely by day than night?"

Belinda just about burst with pride at this compliment coming from a world famous artist who painted the queen of England and members of the royal family. Who painted Mayfair and Belgravia in London. Who painted most of Fifth Avenue in New York. Who earned the praises of the English and French public, and the Royal Academy and the Salon. While Belinda indulged herself in the compliment, she failed to notice Sydney Froilan gazing deeply into Beatrice Venn's eyes.

Professor Bellamy did not fail to notice, and interrupted the steamy eye contact. "Is it safe to assume you are stopping at this fairy isle enroute to New York from the Chicago World's Fair?"

"Yes it is, Professor. This is the final leg of my journey back to Paris. I have been traveling for four years."

"Four years . . . it must have been difficult to be away from your wife and family that long," uttered the professor with emphasis, shooting a glance at Mrs. Venn.

Sydney Froilan produced a man-of-the-world smile and answered, "I have found that the best marriages are with people who ignore they are married."

Professor Bellamy, shocked, purposely did not respond.

Sydney Froilan continued, "My French family has been most supportive concerning my work and where it takes me

. . . and well supported by my work. They have no needs
. . . their cousins have no needs . . . their cousins' cousins
have no needs . . . and of course their wants are met in
addition. They are quite spoiled," he admitted with a world-
worn air.

"I thought your paintins' utterly divine in the Art Palace at
the Chicago's World's Fair, Mr. Froilan," chirped Belinda.

"Thank you, Miss Gaines," Sydney Froilan smiled, "so
did I." He rested his attention on Mrs. Venn.

The group fell into an uncomfortable silence. By this time
Belinda Gaines gleaned that Sydney Chase Froilan was a man
with a history—which made him irresistible; and a man with a
wife elsewhere—which made him ineligible. Practical Belinda decided then and there not to waste any more precious time
on a married man.

"Well, I am obliged to write letters of a thoroughly confi-
dential nature to my dearest, truest friends immediately,"
Belinda excused herself.

"How many do you need to write, Miss Gaines?" asked
Sydney Froilan, who wondered if he could count one true
friend to his name.

"At least twenty-one," Belinda replied seriously. She wondered why they all looked so amused. As she was about to take
leave she spied Rutherford Haverhill approaching. She chided
herself for announcing her intention to write boring letters.

"Mr. Haverhill . . . your call went through?"

"Perfectly, Miss Gaines."

"Mr. Haverhill, I'd like to have you meet Mr. Sydney
Froilan . . ."

"I know Mr. Froilan. Thank you." Rutherford's voice was
colder than the frozen waters of the Straits of Mackinac in the
dead of winter.

Belinda exchanged departing pleasantries and left. The
professor announced his intentions to leave for the village.

"Be good children . . . and thank you, Professor," said Beatrice Venn, smiling warmly.

"My pleasure, Mrs. Venn . . . we will be back in time for lunch." The professor and children headed down to the village.

Sydney Froilan peered at Rutherford Haverhill. "It has been four years, Rutherford, since our last meeting in Paris . . ."

"Has it really?" Rutherford did not peer at Sydney in return; he looked down his nose at him.

Beatrice noticed the animosity between the men. Rutherford managed a smile and gentlemanly greeting in her direction. Beatrice did not understand why Rutherford, who appeared to be the most hostile, approached the artist.

"I just spoke with Mrs. Astor. She had asked me to look you up, Froilan, when I was in Paris this past June. You had not answered her letters. You were not in Paris. When I saw you last night . . ."

"Come, come, Rutherford, let us not speak business in front of Mrs. Venn."

"I have little to say, other than that Mrs. Astor wishes to know why you have not finished the portrait of her son."

"Then I must let Mrs. Astor know that I have traveled from Paris to the Cape of Good Hope to sketch Zulus, from Africa to New Zealand to sketch Maori, from New Zealand to South Pacific islands to sketch Polynesians, from Tahiti to Japan to sketch the little dods there, from Japan to Alaska to sketch the Esquimaux, and across the plains of our great United States to sketch what is left of the Indian children of the forest . . . since . . . I began her son's portrait which, by the way, is an uncommissioned sketch for her personal boudoir. A favor."

"You could have saved the unnecessary trip, Froilan, and sketched these people, if you can call them that, at the Chicago World's Fair. The Midway Plaisance was full of them." Rutherford smothered his admiration for Sydney Froilan's adventurous travels and continued, "Considering all of the commissions you received through the fine lady, it is a wonder you have not completed her son's sketch."

Beatrice Venn, beginning to feel as relegated to the sidelines as Belinda before her, intervened. "Mr. Froilan, so many of my friends in New York have been painted by you."

"Did you recognize them in their portraits, Mrs. Venn?"

"I recognized their more ideal features," Beatrice answered, her eyes sparkling honesty.

"Ah ha," Sydney laughed with charged abandon. "I wonder if you would consider sitting for me on this magnificent porch. In all my travels I never saw such a grand piazza, nor a lady who could grace it the way you do. But understand, in your case, I will use my most realistic technique. And I fear, the portrait will appear enchantingly ideal."

"You flatter me, Mr. Froilan."

"But do you succumb to flattery, Mrs. Venn?" Sydney's twinkling, trained eyes followed the outline of Beatrice Venn's ruddy, ready lips.

Rutherford, not only felt relegated to a bystander, he was embarrassed by Sydney Froilan's and Mrs. Venn's obvious flirting, and was attacked by yet another twinge of jealousy. For weeks he tried to interest eligible Mrs. Venn in a simple carriage ride, alone together. Instead of accepting his proposal, she always answered with a gracious invitation to join her in a group activity. Rutherford was a sideline witness to Sydney's quick seduction. In a matter of minutes, the artist had maneuvered Mrs. Venn into the possibility of sitting for him, for God knows, how many hours on end. Alone together, to boot.

Before Beatrice Venn could answer the artist's veiled pass, Rutherford intervened, "Froilan . . . I wonder that your wife has not divorced you."

Sydney shot a glance at Beatrice. She looked him straight in the eye, but softened the directness with a charming smile. He answered, "I have been away from . . . society . . . for so long, I had not realized society spoke of divorce during morning small talk, in mixed company."

"Divorce . . . why Froilan . . . the very best families are using it." Rutherford glanced at Mrs. Venn. "I was told about a recent case of most interest. One individual, a gentleman from Baltimore, and the second individual, a lady from Philadelphia, were married, had two children, were divorced. The gentleman . . . if you can call him that . . . from Baltimore, married the sister of his former wife. The lady . . . if you can call her that . . . from Philadelphia, married the brother of her former husband. All together they had four children," Rutherford paused to let the matrimonial maze sink in.

He continued sardonically, "Dwell on the cozy domestic scenes at Thanksgiving, Christmas, funerals. Think of the menagerie of in-laws—brothers, sisters, grandmothers, grandfathers, children. But can you imagine when these new couples have additional children?"

"It should be a game of live chess, I would imagine," Mrs. Venn replied rather uneasily.

"Yes, especially when it comes to inheritance rights. Both families are quite well off." Rutherford was satisfied that he effectively marred Sydney's romantic advances to Beatrice by bringing up divorce.

Sydney Froilan was not going to let Rutherford Haverhill V get away with it unscathed. "Rutherford, you should have been an artist or a musician or a writer or a . . . anything . . . for that matter. You have such a keen sense for observation and memory of the minutest detail." Sydney's voice was laced with spitting sarcasm. He would regret his statement.

In return, Rutherford Haverhill despised Sydney Froilan for a reason other than the artist's hurled insult—implying Rutherford's seeming lack of talent or usefulness. That moment, Rutherford thought to strike Sydney's seductive base balls right off the veranda. Instead he sliced Sydney's painterly macho into mincemeat.

"In the Haverhill family, Froilan, we are brought up surrounded by the paintings of Rembrandt, Titian, Raphael, Velasquez, Gainsborough, Rubens, Ingres . . . masterpieces . . . to name a few. We invite Paderewski and Metropolitan Opera divas to perform in our home. We sit down to read in front of our marble fireplaces with illuminated manuscripts from the Middle Ages, and the oldest editions of literary masterpieces . . . ."

Rutherford looked narrowly at Sydney Froilan who spent his youth milking cows on a farm in Vermont and dreaming of becoming a famous artist. Rutherford continued, "Look with me beyond the conceit of having. Imagine . . . one brought up in the jeweled arms of splendor . . . inducted with the greatest art, music, literature known to mankind . . . imagine.

"I never had the desire, Froilan, to duplicate what was around me, because I was surrounded with all that was the summit of desirability. It held no mystery, awe, or fascination for me. It was there to decorate my life and entertain my soul. It was not there, to inspire me to aspire to enter the ranks of its originators as an artist, musician, writer."

Rutherford lowered his voice and continued bombasting Sydney barely above a whisper. "Furthermore, Froilan, I understand what you imply, my uselessness as a man. I know you do not like me. Please do not hide it with pleasant denials."

"I have no intention of doing so." Sydney said crisply.

"I make my life my art. And by doing so, Froilan, I quench any creative artistic endeavor which I might have pursued." Rutherford finally went in for the kill and dropped, "You see Sydney, I do not care to be second rate."

To himself Rutherford added, Sydney Froilan may be popular, but he will never go down in history as a master. Rutherford evened the score. Rutherford Earle Haverhill V would rather be useless than a second rater like Sydney Froilan. But as usual, he explained too much. And he made the mistake of bashing the artist in front of Mrs. Venn.

Sydney, wounded, breathed in agitated excitement but continued speaking in his devil-may-care attitude for the sake of Mrs. Venn and his pride, "I understand what you have not said. You may think portrait painters today are second-rate artists. I have been accused of excessive taste for portraiture among my fellow artists in France. I tell them that my taste for portraiture is purely American. That in America the personal worth and individual independence of a human being are part of our national character. They find this very conceited. At the same time, they are terribly jealous of our personal liberty, and of the great amount of money I make painting portraits. Mrs. Venn, where are our manners . . . ."

Beatrice Venn was not sure how to respond to the drama. She had no idea whose side to take. Though she was not fond of Rutherford, they were acquainted in New York circles. Yet it would hardly do to show favoritism to Mr. Froilan, whom she had met a mere fifteen minutes ago.

If Beatrice had known that Sydney Froilan indirectly caused the put-down of Rutherford Haverhill by his aristocratic friends, she could have decided with more ease. But she did not know that Sydney met Rutherford four years ago at the Paris Exposition of 1889. In that same year Sydney sketched a cartoon depicting Rutherford for a major magazine. The cartoon showed Rutherford looking up at the brand new Eiffel tower, dressed entirely as an upper class English gentleman except for high-heeled cowboy boots. The text read:

Frenchman: Averill, why do you have your umbrella up when it is not raining?

American Anglophile: Because . . . dear heart . . . I heard it is raining in London!

Beatrice also did not know that one of Rutherford's aristocratic French friends came across the four-year-old magazine, and showed it to Rutherford in June. Rutherford recognized his own face immediately, and might have laughed at himself, if his aristocratic English friend had not eyewinked the French aristocrat and laughed first. When Rutherford saw the name Froilan on the bottom of the cartoon, he vowed to get even with the artist.

"It is apparent that Rutherford and I have an old score to settle, Mrs. Venn. Please excuse our heated words."

"Mr. Froilan, I witness the most proper morning manners daily. It is a relief for me to hear human emotion awake at this time of the day. And I should be delighted to sit for you." Mrs. Venn stole a look at Rutherford, who turned his eyes away realizing Beatrice favored Sydney.

Rutherford realized too late that his verbal swordplay inflicted wounds on Sydney big enough for Beatrice to want to bandage.

"Are you free this morning?" Sydney asked Mrs. Venn.

"I am going on a carriage ride to Robinson's Folly with the three ladies you met last night."

Before they could make arrangements for Mrs. Venn's sitting, another admirer of the world famous Sydney Froilan engaged him in discussion. Beatrice noticed, as Sydney graciously talked with the newcomer, that he was not pretentiously arty like so many of the artists she had met. He looked like a man capable of great physical strength.

Rutherford interrupted her thoughts and said, "Portrait artists are as necessary as undertakers. They preserve our memories. But they are mistaken when they think to enter our circles as equals." Rutherford turned the knife, knowing full well he had not fatally slain Sydney Froilan in Mrs. Venn's mind.

Though Beatrice was a blue blooded high society New York woman, finished at Miss Porter's School in Connecticut, somehow, she was not a snob. She replied, "Mr. Froilan is known world wide. He is accepted in the best circles in any of the world's capitals, except possibly New York. But then it is no wonder. I met an ultra-elite personage here but a week ago who told me that he met no artists, historians, poets, explorers, scholars, generals, or naval heroes in New York, because not one of them is in society."

Beatrice smiled and greeted some college girls and their MaMas passing by. She continued, "Since Mr. Froilan is everything a New York society personage is not . . . it is no wonder that a society man like yourself, Rutherford, would not consider him an equal."

Rutherford thought that Beatrice should have stood behind a podium, her words flowed so freely. She chastised him in a tone so agreeable her words lost their sting, and gained too much meaning. In other words, Rutherford could not be distracted, by a bitchy style, from the truth of her words. He was incensed that a fellow New Yorker had taken the side of an outsider.

"I do not pretend to speak for all New York society, Beatrice."

"But you do, Rutherford, you do." Beatrice allowed a few moments for her words to sink in and then asked, "You will dance at least one waltz with me at the ball tonight?" She took Rutherford's arm in a conciliatory fashion.

He was taken by surprise and felt a rush of relaxation after his morning of one confrontation after another. "I would be honored, Beatrice."

"Ah, I think see Owen Corrigan's carriage coming up from

the village. As I mentioned to Mr. Froilan, my friends and I are going to Robinson's Folly this morning. Would you care to meet us there?"

"Thank you . . . perhaps I will." Rutherford had no intention of visiting Robinson's Folly and invading the four women's little female party. But he brightened up considerably. Rutherford was growing so accustomed to Mrs. Venn's group invitations that if she stopped offering them now, because of Sydney Froilan, he would begin to despise her almost as much as he vengefully despised the world famous portrait artist—whom she obviously liked.

Beatrice Venn walked in the direction of the grand stairway leading to the porte-cochere. She noticed a presence following her and suddenly felt a warm hand grip her wrist. She saw a hand which looked like that of a field worker. Confused and startled, she tried to pull her arm away not thinking to look at its owner. The grip was so strong she could not. She looked up, recognized the face, tried to conceal her surprise at such boldness, and was relieved she had not been able to pull her hand back dramatically, causing any onlookers to gossip.

"Why, Mr. Froilan," she caught her breath and finessed it, "I believe you are feeling my pulse . . ."

"I am feeling your spiritual pulse, Mrs. Venn," he said quietly and slowly.

"My spiritual pulse is buried deep inside my heart, Mr. Froilan."

"Well then . . . I am feeling both your physical and spiritual pulse." He said this in a tone so deep she just managed to understand. It was as if she had to translate his words from an exotic language borne in the depth of his voice. She felt a rush of youthfulness.

Beatrice Venn could not decide whether Sydney Froilan had

seduced her or shown real feeling. He slowly let go of her wrist, as a group of old maids approached pining to meet the world famous artist. But the old maids passed by with knowing looks and kind hearts. They did not stop to chat with their friend, Mrs. Venn, who looked unusually flushed and would have introduced them. After all, Mrs. Venn was eligible. They did not know that Mr. Froilan—was not.

"From your accent, Mrs. Venn, I know you were born in the east, but I am not sure which city?" Sydney stepped back a respectable distance.

Beatrice recovered and replied, "Let me provide you with a clue. I was born and raised in a city where the illustrious dead men are more alive than the living, and where you will find one of the greatest mutual admiration societies in the civilized world."

"Tell me . . . were Daniel Webster and Benjamin Franklin born in your city?"

"Ah, you have guessed." She smiled, tongue in cheek.

"You are much too cosmopolitan, having been born and bred a solemn Bostonian, Mrs. Venn . . ."

"I left Boston for Europe before I married a New Yorker and settled on Fifth Avenue. Of course, I am partial to dear old Boston despite my family's and friends' constant worship of the noble, heroic dead . . . .Where is there a river more sparkling than the Charles River? Where are the sunrises comparable to the sunsets as on the Charles?"

"Last night, everyone on this veranda claimed that the sunrises and sunsets on Mackinac Island are the greatest in the world."

"Yes, I must admit, they are breathtaking. But the Charles River still holds my heart."

Beatrice Venn coaxed herself to end the chitchat and board

Owen Corrigan's carriage. She did not move an inch. Sydney suspected he might compromise Mrs. Venn by showing her too much attention. He doused his suspicions.

"May I ask, Mrs. Venn, what brings you out west for the summer? Certainly the finest summer resorts such as Bar Harbor, Beverly Farms, Newport, Saratoga Springs, Cape May, to name more than a few, are right in your back yard."

"I came to this western island to get away from the east, Mr. Froilan. My husband departed this life from me two years ago and—" Beatrice paused, trying to decide if she should tell the artist a partial truth she shared with no one but her group of four.

Sydney Froilan's rugged face and searching eyes looked so free from pretense, Beatrice decided to tell him. "I do not wish to go to the places where I would meet my in-laws and my departed husband's friends. They are all too polite, too pedantic, and speak in monologues. The people out west have not found such intercourse . . . proper . . . yet. I hope they never do. As for my family, they are in England making the acquaintance of new found relatives. I declined their invitation to accompany them. Imagine, the overbearing politeness demanded in such meetings."

Sydney wondered how it was possible for a lady with Mrs. Venn's prudent eastern background to behave so openly. Perhaps it was the western setting which inspired her spontaneity. She was full of humor and irony and animal spirits, and Sydney wanted nothing more than to slip his arms around her lithesome form.

He said, "There is a ball tonight . . ."

"Yes . . ."

"I am an excellent dancer, I have been told . . ."

"I believe you have been told many times . . ."

"I would rather have you believe that I am an excellent dancer . . ."

"Then you must prove that to me tonight. . . ."

Beatrice Venn had no idea that Sydney Chase Froilan wanted nothing more in his life, that minute, than to prove himself to her.

"Ah, Mr. Froilan, I see old Owen Corrigan is driving our carriage into the porte-cochere."

3

Go Lang, Charley

"Whoa, Charley."

Owen Corrigan, a wee cockalorum of a man, and the oldest hackman on the island with the oldest hack, pulled up in front of the glorious Grand Hotel in the most inglorious carriage on the island. Most Grand Hotel resorters would not step foot in it.

"Good morning, Owney," called out Jimmy Hayes, who happened to be in the porte-cochere quietly reading the riot act to an irresponsible coachman. Jimmy walked over to his seventy-four-year-old buddy.

"Wish ye good mornin' Jimmy Hayes. Are the four fine prancin' leddies ready for their mornin' drive?"

"Well, Owney, I see Countess Gianotti coming out and I see Mrs. Venn walking this way."

"What about the other two fine leddies?"

"I haven't seen them since breakfast."

"Well, I wish the leddies was on time . . . for me Charley, he's an impatient beast today . . . and he might not put up with the waitin'."

"Why is that Owney?" Jimmy glanced at Charley. The old horse was so calm, he might have been dead and stuffed. Jimmy patted shabby old Charley on his neck, expecting a good yarn from Owen Corrigan.

"Ye see, Jimmy Hayes . . . last night I was a wee bit late gettin' out of the beer shop . . . and when I stumbled out of the door . . . thare me Charley was a chompin' his bit . . .

smack-dab in front of the beer shop door." Owen sighed, "Ah, Jimmy, ye should 'av graced yer fine presence thare last night. Biff, bang and everything but bite 'em went. I could 'av pulled a tooth last night and mostly of a young girl. Ach ya.

"Anyhow, so I says to me faithful steed standin' at the beer shop door . . . lookin' like he was ready to bite off me nose . . . I says, so I beg yer pardon, Charley. But he stamped his foot and snorted . . . not a listenin' to a word of me apology . . . why me gracious words slid off himself like water off a duck's back. Then I tried to explain to Charley, I did, that I'm a honest man with a special weakness. I canna pass by a beer shop without takin' just a little. But he bristled at me with that piercin' stare of his. And then ye knows what me Charley did? He dumped a mound of horse apples. He couldn't 'av said it better."

Jimmy had a good laugh.

Owen grinned and his fine features, as delicate and small as a woman's, wrinkled. His left eye twinkled. His right eyelid folded over his eyeball, hiding it. Most resorters thought he was blind in his right eye. Jimmy knew that Owen's eyesight was as sharp as his tongue. Crowning his small Irish face was an immense Scottish Tam o' Shanter given to him by a resorter some year in the past. Yes, Owen Corrigan cut quite an amusing character on Mackinac Island.

"By the ways, Jimmy, ye knows I've been married three times, and ye knows I've survived all me wives, in spite of . . . may the blessed saints preserve me . . . in spite of wishin' them dumb—but never deaf—at times."

"I know, Owney."

"Ye also knows . . . I've taken a heap of ribbin' about those three wives . . . most of it from ye, Jimmy Hayes, who's nearin' thirty-eight and never taken the holy vows yerself. Well, just yesterday, a young lady who's married to a millionaire older than meself and is stayin' at yer grand palace, meant to make a joke of me. She asked me dainty like, 'When are you going to get married again?' I asked, 'Married . . . again?' I thought a moment and said, 'Well . . . I'm a waitin' for the auld man to die first.' She asks, 'Which old man, Owen?' I says, 'Your auld man, of course!' The young thing turned redder betwixt the ears than a woman bent over pickin' spuds. I put the like of her voice to rest, I did."

"You certainly did, Owney," added Countess Gianotti brightly. She had arrived at the carriage along with Mrs. Venn. The coachman helped the elegant ladies into the dilapidated vehicle.

"Wish ye good mornin', Countess Anna and Mrs. Venn. Where are the other two fine leddies this cheerful mornin'? I'm a wee anxious because me Charley is an impatient one today."

"Why is that, Owen?" asked Beatrice Venn.

"Last night I was a wee bit late in gettin' out of the—" he winked at Jimmy, "out of a special meetin' I was obliged to attend. And like a nervous cow chewin' her cud, me steed was a chompin' his bit right thare in front of the door."

"Who was a chompin' his bit at the door?" inquired a voice as good natured and cultivated as voices come.

Owen turned around to see Mrs. Clare Gilbertson, a refreshing sight for sore eyes. "Me Charley, Mrs. Gilbertson, he is an impatient beast today."

"Why is that?" asked Clare Gilbertson with her customary friendliness.

"Last night, after attendin' . . . a most important meetin' . . . I found Charley at the door a chompin' his bit, neighing notes so short and sharp I felt as if me own dear mother had given me a tongue lashin'. Begorra . . . before I knew what was happenin'—he tried to bite off me nose."

"Who tried to bite off your nose, Owen?" asked a lovely lilting voice with a touch of southern rhythm.

"Ah, Mrs. MacAdam, ye who knows horseflesh like few others . . . can ye imagine . . . 'twas my faithful steed Charley who tried to bite off me own nose. It's no wonderin' why he did it. He has a wild past he has. As a young bucko he was the worst horse demon I ever laid me eyes upon . . . a young Lucifer he was, I swear. Why the beast wouldn't let himself be shod until I threw him down upon mother earth herself, with me own bare hands. Look leddies . . . Charley doesn't blink an eye or move a muscle . . . but his ears are peaked like a pyramid . . . he's a listen' he is."

The four women smiled broadly, picturing, little Owen Corrigan, barely five feet tall and as thin as a spruce sapling, throwing down a sixteen-hand-high horse weighing over a thousand pounds.

Jimmy Hayes had another good laugh and exchanged morning pleasantries with the Big Four, who had gathered for their thrice-weekly morning sightseeing ride with Owen as their comical guide.

"Go lang, Charley."

The veranda crowd, watching the four elegant women in the rickety carriage, was befuddled as to why high society ladies would set foot in Owen Corrigan's dingy old hack. They collectively concluded that the four ladies commissioned Owen out of charity and would not be seen in the hack at any other time of day than morning. They noted that the four women were seen only in a high hung barouche or a victoria or a C-spring carriage in the afternoon.

What the veranda crowd did not know was that Owen Corrigan was the funniest guide on the island and took his time showing the sights. He spun legendary stories about Arch Rock, Devil's Kitchen, Skull Cave, Crack-in-the-Island, Lover's Leap, Sugar Loaf . . . which no one else on the island seemed to know. Owney had more than a bit of the devil in him, and the four women loved it.

It was an utter relief, those morning sightseeing rides with Owen. It was a relief for them just to sit and watch the scenery pass by. Owen Corrigan sensed that the four women were fagged out from all the fine doings and fancy chatter at the grand palace. As much as Owen enjoyed gabbing, he could not have kept up with what he called the "neverendin' lingo bingo contests of them swells" up on the Grand Hotel bluff.

Owen turned Charley around and headed down the road toward the village. To the left they passed the public pasture full of cows and calves grazing, mooing, clanging their bells, and drinking water from the pond. The countess requested Owen to stop nearby a certain pregnant cow she recognized standing near the road, whose name was Glendora.

Owen thought the Countess Anna unusually fond of cows. Her three companions, who felt no particular affinity for the bovines one way or the other, were good sports, and alighted from the carriage when the countess did. Owen had scrambled down to help them out, all the time wondering why the Countess Anna chose Glendora out of all the other cows to dote upon.

He called out, "Why . . . that cow with an udder like I've never seen the likes of in all my livin' days . . . seems to know ye, Countess Anna."

"That is because I know her, Owney. The last summer I spent on the island, twenty years ago, Glendora was born in this field. I will never forget that day. See the star on her forehead? That is how I recognized her. Do you remember, Owney?"

Owen took off his Tam o' Shanter and scratched his head. Dandruff fell lightly on his shoulders. A dim memory materialized in Owen's mind of Countess Anna. Yes, young spirited Anna, the whole town called her "Anna." But she was not alone in his recollection. She was with a man. Who? Ach ya, he said to himself, Anna was almost engaged that summer.

In bits and pieces, picture flashes of young Anna, and who was it, who was the young man, a widower with a boy, recalled buried romance in Owen's head. Ah, they were so in love's embrace those two, he thought. Owen remembered driving Anna and the faceless young widower and his son about.

Owen dimly remembered driving them to a pasture . . . the birth of a calf . . . a young woman with tears in her bright eyes, it must have been Anna, ya, happy tears they were . . . a faceless young gallant widower about to touch her hair . . . a small son pulling Anna's hand . . . the son and Anna running hand in hand toward the newborn calf . . . the father too proud to run to a beast . . . too concerned he might smoosh into cow plats scattered like soft brown stepping stones in the pasture . . . too careful not to step in the muck . . . the son pulling Anna . . . the son and Anna frolicking like gazelles, her golden honey-hair flying and splendid in the hot sun of midday . . . running hand in hand and jumping the plats, trying to avoid other plats nearby . . . missing one by two by three by chance . . . laughing with abandon . . . ach ya . . . it was more fun jumping cow plats hand in hand—than solo.

Owen sighed at the heart felt reminiscence he strung together like Indian popcorn on a string. He waxed nostalgic. His steed Charley was practically a baby then. Owen's old eyes moistened. Everyone was young but himself. Even twenty years ago the Countess Anna was young, Charley was young, but he was already old. He could not remember what if felt like to be young. He lied to himself.

Owen Corrigan watched the four fancy youthful women talking to the cows, especially Glendora. He knew that Glendora must have been Glendora's daughter, and had inherited the star from her mother. But he was not about to ruin Countess Anna's belief that it was the cow she had seen born twenty years ago. It's queer enjoyments they like, he said to himself, and doubted if a milkmaid herself would show such concern for a pregnant cow.

Owen began to think that the four women were his favorite passengers. They were always interested in the historical and legendary sights, and treated him with kindly talk. Most of the other daily tourists he took around the island were either too rude, too quiet, too uppity, or put on airs.

But what a vain sort this group of four fancy women are, he thought. Owen could always tell a vain woman. Hadn't he known a few fancy saloon women in his early days? He grinned, fancy women are always vain. That Owen made no distinction between fancy society women and fancy saloon women might have dimmed his popularity, considerably, with the four ladies. Even his buddy Jimmy Hayes, a hale fellow, would not acknowledge such a comparison. Some things Owen kept to himself. He instinctively knew his role as island jester could only go so far.

Owen helped the Big Four climb back into the carriage. Each one had her own suspicion when Glendora was due. Owen knew the cow would calve any hour. The ladies were off by days but he did not correct them. Owen only told stories. He did not converse with the swells much. He knew his place; and that is why he was so well-liked in spite of his dilapidated carriage.

The driving party continued down the hill and turned left onto Market Street. They drove past the old Edward Biddle house, of the Philadelphia Biddle family, which was one of the island's oldest houses. They drove past the blacksmith shop, and city hall, and noticed that all eyes were on them from the

Astor House hotel porch (certainly less than one hundred feet long).

The eighty-year-old Astor House hotel building had been John Jacob Astor's American Fur Company trading post. Owen informed them that what used to be the great trading room, overrun with Indians and French voyageurs bearing bundles of skins to be sorted and valued by company clerks, was now a ballroom. Thirty- five million dollars worth of pelts destined for fur coats went through the—ballroom—back in the 1830s.

As they turned right onto Astor Street they faced the water and sighted the ferry steamer *Manitou* approaching the dock. The upper decks were packed with pleasure seekers sporting yellow and green and pink and blue dresses, and white trousers and blue suits set off by the black background of the steamer. The tourists stood with their lunch baskets and kodaks and parasols, attempting to show they could retain their equilibrium on the gently rocking ferry.

On the wharf stood a motley reception committee, a swarm of porters and hack drivers, all ages, anxious for the passengers to disembark. The reception committee waited to capture new arrivals and whisk them off to their hotels, or talk a daily tourist into a hack for a trip around the island for one dollar.

The ferry landed. Trunks were taken ashore. The bell sounded and tourists streamed off carrying small grip sacks and parcels. Owen turned left onto Main Street.

The four women overheard a hackman nearby squabbling with a tourist, "If you spect me to race my animal to land you and your load of trumpery for 'alf a dollar, you've figured it wrong. I'll do it for $3."

They could not help hearing, from a block away, the subcellar voice of a black man, a member of the reception committee, who was on the dock to send new arrivals to the hotel that employed him.

The black man bellowed like a fog horn in the straits, "Astor House! Astor House! I well do remember the old familiar homestead. That's where the people all go. I don't do anythin' to stop 'em. John Jacob Astor House up the street, to the right and a little to the left. You can't miss it, I declare."

Owen, noticing that the four women noticed the tall black man in the tall black hat bellowing near Doud's mercantile company, stopped Charley and volunteered, "That nigger man's name is Isaac. The darky has the habit of addressin' tourists with titles dependin' on the amount o' tips they give him. Let me give ye an instance. Whosoever tips him ten cents, he calls Captain. Whosoever hands him a quarter, he calls Colonel. A great many swaggers 'ave given him a dollar and those he addresses as General or Mrs. General dependin' on the sex.

"I heard he got a five dollar bill from a swell leddy just a week ago. 'Thank yeh,' he drawled to the swell leddy and then wondered what title to give her for a tip twould buy twenty-five frothy beers. So the darky said, 'Thank yeh . . . Mrs. Queen,' and added, 'for a Queen you is.' "

Owen's comical brogue rendition of the black man's accent was as thick and unauthentic as Irish stew with black-eyed peas.

The four women laughed and kept to themselves what they really thought about Mrs. Queen's tasteless display of wealth. Most porters were tipped twenty-five cents.

Owen and the four women drove past Foley's Art Gallery, which had windowed walls for the taking of photographic portraits; past Views of Mackinac, which sold novelties and specialized in superior Petoskey agates; past Highstone's gift shop, which had an advertisement in the window describing its goods.

The advertisement in Highstone's read: "Scalps! Scalps! Call and see the Indian Dudes and Dudines—lineal descendents of Hiawatha and Minnehaha—Call and hear the blood curdling Chippewa war-whoop—the defiant Ottawa battle-cry—the victory-shout of the Iroquois—the heart-rending Huron deathsong—get tickets for the Dakota scalp-dance." It was no surprise that Highstone's sold scalps, scalping knives, Indian pipes, wampum, tomahawks, war-clubs, boomerangs, and bows and arrows.

They drove past McAdams next door, which sold Indian curiosities as well as "fancy" goods and books and magazines, fine stationery and nuts and fruits in season; and past the Mackinac House hostelry and The New Murray hotel.

They drove past Dr. J. R. Baily and Son's National Park Drug Store. Dr. Bailey (the island's doctor) advertised that he was a dealer in "carefully compounded" drugs in medicine all the way back to 1845, and that he sold all "goods usually found in a first class drug store" in addition to guide books, charts, maps, and pure wines and liquors—for medicinal purposes, of course.

Next to Dr. Bailey's was the impressive Fenton's Indian Bazaar, the tallest and fanciest building on the main street, with the Opera House occupying its second floor.

"Leddies, would you care to stop and take a wee look at the fine gew gaws at Fenton's? Charley looks as if he could do with a breather," Owen coaxed them—with one eye, his hidden right eye—fixed on a tavern nearby.

Although the four women were not in the mood to climb out of the hack and go into Fenton's, they decided instantly to get out and go shopping, as they had many times before. The four women cooperated because they suspected that Owen was treated to a beer by every shop owner in town whom he recommended to his passengers. The Big Four joked among the guests back at the Grand that they did not want to be held responsible for denying Owen Corrigan his free, liquid treat. In return, Owen always showed the four women something no other "still wet behind his ears guide" could show a tourist.

Owen helped them out of the carriage and said, "Fine leddies, how 'bout fifteen minutes . . . that'll do fer a rest fer ol' Charley." Charley had barely walked a mile. But the group of four all sportingly agreed and headed for Fenton's.

Sending four such elegant women into an Indian Bazaar was like setting four flawless diamonds into a wooden nickel. They entered the shop and Mr. Fenton, the proprietor and leading citizen of the village, dropped what he was doing and with forced calm rushed over to the ladies.

"Good morning, ladies. If I may be of any assistance, please do not hesitate to ask . . . look to your heart's content . . . I will be nearby if you should need me."

The four women walked to a dazzling display of semi-precious gems, and rock crystals, and rare seashells, and polished stones. They gazed at the—glimmering amethysts and garnets and opals—the crystalline masses of rose quartz, and blue celestine and yellow sulpher—the pearlescent tapestry turban shells and hump-back cowries and cuban tree snails—the glossy Lake Superior agates and Petoskey agates and Canadian pudding stone—all shining and brightly in the morning sunlight.

The four women glanced at the Indian moccasins, Florida ornaments and Japanese goods. They examined the Indian hand works of porcupine quill, moose hair, and sweet grass basketwork, as well as scented table-mats, portfolios, canoes, satchels and reticules. They bypassed the miniature mococks of maple sugar, and the imported and domestic cigars.

Beatrice Venn chose a handkerchief box because it was her turn to purchase something, and she really had a use for it.

Although they were not "gew gaw" addicts, the four elegant women never left Fenton's without a purchase, which was usually Whitman's famous chocolates. They always felt obliged to buy something at the Indian Bazaar, because they liked Mr. Fenton and they regularly came in contact with him at the hops and special events up at the Grand.

Mr. Fenton pretended to appreciate the ladies' little purchases. But he was really grateful to Owen Corrigan. Simply having four such elegant ladies seen walking into his store, brought in greater revenue from tourists who practically followed them in, than from their little purchases. Mr. Fenton noted that the four high society ladies were like magic. Already the daily tourists began to stream in. Mr. Fenton's eyes lit up as he added projected numbers in his head. For the majority of the tourists who entered the Indian Bazaar would leave with a satchel chock full of genuine souvenirs. And Mr. Fenton would end his day with a brass cash register chock full of green bills.

While the Countess Gianotti, Mrs. Beatrice Venn, and Mrs. Philippa MacAdam chatted with Mr. Fenton, Mrs. Clare Gilbertson spyed a well-blackened meerschaum pipe in a case at the other end of the store and walked over to give it a second look. Childhood memories played upon her senses. Was it so long ago, so far away, that her beloved father smoked a pipe just like it? As she waxed nostalgic she smelled tobacco, the memory was so strong. She smiled, remembering a happy and gentle time in her life.

"I have a meerschaum similar to that one. It is my favorite pipe."

Mrs. Clare Gilbertson was startled by the presence, so near to her, within the close confines of a dark corner of the shop. The tobacco aroma she imagined was not a flash in the memory. She observed that the hefty gentleman near her was puffing away on a St. Claude pipe with an ebonite mouthpiece. Nothing surprising about that.

What startled Clare was that the gentleman smoked the same semi-sweet tobacco her late father doted upon. The aroma triggered recall. And for a few moments, Clare fell vacant as to where she was or why she was in the remote dark corner of the shop. She oscillated between past and present realities like a flower in a breeze bending into the light and back into the shade. Her sense of time and place popped back as fast as it had vanished.

Clare's smile turned from the sweetness of youthful remembrance to mature friendliness. The gentleman noticed the difference. She looked up at him and spoke in a direct manner, "I always imagined that my late father's meerschaum possessed a mysterious if friendly spirit. I felt that spirit soothed my father more than I knew how to. I was always a bit envious of my late father's pipe." Clare's renewed smile was warmly distant. She felt her heart pounding, and was upset with herself for feeling as excited as a schoolgirl meeting a towering strange man in a dark corner of a shop, alone. Exactly what she was doing.

"Your father was blessed twice. Once with a spirit-filled pipe . . . and twice with a spirit-filled daughter."

Clare wondered if anyone in the Indian bazaar overheard the stranger. It was not that he was loud speaking, but he had not exactly whispered this rather intimate appraisal. She scolded herself in no uncertain terms to wish the gentleman good day, and take leave of him. Her friends were waiting.

Actually, the countess, Mrs. Venn, and Mrs. MacAdam were wondering who was that gentleman with the muscular neck and why was he keeping Clare. They had run out of small talk with Mr. Fenton. And he in turn was anxious to get over to the well-dressed gentleman talking to Mrs. Gilbertson, but felt he could not until she rejoined her lady friends.

Clare sensed all this but stood near the meerschaum as if her boots were nailed to the floor. She really stood near—Mr. Philmore Calhoun—magnetic mining baron, who had just dropped anchor at Mackinac Island for a couple of days. Philmore Calhoun visited the island every year to pick up supplies and a bit of local color. This time, Clare Gilbertson was the local color.

Philmore Calhoun managed a good look at striking Clare Gilbertson. He noticed that the lower portion of her face was a little long, but her brow was beyond competition. He liked a woman with a well-formed brow. Her expression was bright, her smile amiable. Her dark hair set off her light eyes. In the dark corner, it was puzzling for him to decide the exact color of her eyes. Though he could see that Clare's eyes had a faraway, almost wounded look.

Clare glanced at the meerschaum for a moment, and Philmore quickly checked out what appeared to be a shapely classical bosom. Considering she was not "fashioned up" in her afternoon costume, lovely Clare Gilbertson, wearing a dainty jacket and simple natty skirt, made quite an impression on Philmore Calhoun in her morning clothes.

Philmore trusted the sight of Clare more with every moment. He never liked a woman too dressed up all the time, because he never knew whether he was attracted to the color and texture of the woman's clothes, or the color and texture of the woman herself. Many a fetishistic friend of Philmore Calhoun could not keep his hands off women dressed in mink and silk by day, and satin and laces by night. He suspected himself prone to this same tactile fetish, and never trusted his true feelings about a woman all "fashioned up," as he put it. Or as other men put it, "dressed for conquest."

Mr. Fenton could wait no longer. He interrupted the *tête-à-tête* with a polite, "Good morning, Sir. Ah, it is you, Mr. Calhoun. Welcome back. I did not notice you until a few minutes ago, and then with my failing eyesight, I could not distinguish your face in this dark corner."

"Good morning, Mr. Fenton. You look as fine and well fed as ever. How are you charming daughters and son? How is business?"

"My children are fine and business is not. Not what it was last year at this time."

" That is what you say every year I anchor here and pay you a visit."

Mr. Fenton regarded Clare and said, "Mrs. Gilbertson, I am so surprised to recognize Mr. Calhoun, I failed to ask if I can help you?"

Philmore answered for Clare, "We have been looking at your meerschaum and discussing pipes, Mr. Fenton. But we have not yet introduced ourselves."

Mr. Fenton made formal introductions and grumbled to himself, what am I running here a merchandise store or a mating parlor, noting the obvious interest Mr. Calhoun showed in Mrs. Gilbertson.

"I would like the meerschaum, Mr. Fenton," added Philmore Calhoun as if paying off Mr. Fenton for the introduction and his time. Mr. Fenton congratulated himself on a sale well done. The meerschaum was quite expensive.

Clare pulled herself away reluctantly. "Good day, Mr. Fenton . . . and Mr. Calhoun, it was a pleasure to meet you. I hope you will enjoy the pipe."

"I do not intend to smoke it. I will add it to my pipe collection on my boat."

Boat! Mr. Fenton thought. Philmore Calhoun had one of the largest yachts and crew in the Great Lakes.

Philmore followed Clare, as she walked toward her three friends who were dying to meet the impressive yachting clothed gentleman in the Norfolk jacket, blue shirt, white collar, tweed trousers, and white shoes. Philmore Calhoun managed to maneuver introductions with the ladies as well as he steered his "boat." He thought the three ladies imposing types who aroused favor's comment. He was not impressed that an American countess numbered among them, though he was impressed with the countess. After the four women left the store, Philmore asked Mr. Fenton if he knew where the ladies were staying.

Mr. Fenton replied, "Philmore, all I know about the ladies is that they are staying the summer at the Grand Hotel . . . they are the reigning society queens up there . . . and all three, except for the countess, are eligible."

"I have always known you to get to the point. Come Sunday night to the boat for a drink if you can. Bring your son, the West Point cadet, and bring the meerschaum."

Mr. Fenton relaxed for a moment and said, "I will be there with pleasure, Philmore." He looked forward to an evening on Philmore Calhoun's yacht. There would be storytelling, banjo playing, singing, and general good fellowship.

The four women, who were ten minutes late getting back to Owen's carriage, found Charley looking the same as when they left him. It was Owen who looked rested. A short visit to the beer shop, for Owen, was as rejuvinating as a long visit to Baden-Baden for the rich, and much less expensive.

Owen helped the ladies into his carriage, took his place, and called out to them, "On to Robinson's Folly," above the surrounding sounds of horses clopping and harnesses jingling and tourists talking and children laughing and seagulls crying and ships whistling and dockworkers yelling and liverymen shouting. The life avowing noise was an improvised symphony of unmusical energy. Everyone on the island shared this energy when they were on the main drag, whether they liked it or not.

Owen drove past Mike, a full-blooded Indian driving an ice wagon, and bid him the time of day. He drove past LaChance Riding Stable, and a shooting gallery and peanut stands, all within a block, and then left the area of the merchandise mongers' shops. Bicyclists whizzed past Owen's carriage and ten other horse-drawn vehicles crowding nearby.

The four women looked to their right and sighted a southeast scene of sparkling, crescent shaped harbor waters. The harbor was filled with canoes and rowboats and Mackinac boats and steam yachts and sailing yachts. They recognized John Cudahy's new sailing yacht the *Gerald C*, and Michael Cudahy's steam yacht *Catherine*, and General F. H. Winston's sailing yacht *Flying Mist*, and D.A. Blodgett's steam yacht *Adele*.

They noticed that Commodore George W. Gardiner's trim double-master, the *Wasp*, with a cabin fit for Neptune himself, slowly left its mooring and headed into the straits toward the morning sun. Merrill B. Mill's bird, the steam yacht *Grace*, carried a unique electric flag with eighty-five lights, which someone had forgotten to turn off. The four women recognized these vessels, because they had been invited on every one of them. And, invited back.

"Whoa, Charley," yelled Owen.

Livery wagon drivers and bikers and other carriage hacks halted abruptly for the big fellow lounging in the middle of the road.

"Does the lumbering scoundrel think he himself owns the public road . . . doggone it anyhow. Get out of me way ye mug faced hippopotamus."

The fellow, looking unimpressed, ignored Owen and the other drivers hurling threats and cuss words, and turned his face in the direction of the picturesque harbor.

"Move yer fatty muscles afore I move them for ye . . ."

Having stretched his legs and laid down his bulky weight in the middle of the busy road, the massive St. Bernard dog, who usually sat around the wharf, was not about to accommodate the drivers. The burly creature refused to move, especially after Owen hurled a few choice four-letter words at him.

A man of little patience, little Owen Corrigan jumped down cantankerously from his carriage and began trying to pull the dog, which weighed almost twice as much he did, by the scruff of his neck. To Owen's utter surprise the dog got up . . . got up on Owen's shoulders. The St. Bernard was not only as tall as Owen, he was stronger and had better breath. And whether Owen could not bear the weight of the St. Bernard on his shoulders, or the dog could not bear Owen's beer breath, no one will ever know. Because for some reason, the little man and big dog called it a draw and retreated from each other simultaneously. Except for one hitch. Before Owen could drive his carriage away, the St. Bernard lifted his heavy hind leg and watered Owen's front wheel. Generously.

"Do you see the eighty-foot steam yacht next to the schooner rigged yacht?"

The four women, barely able to contain their laughter over the St. Bernard's trick on Owen, turned in the opposite direction from the waterworks scene and recognized the bronze-faced, pewter-haired, healthy-looking Philmore Calhoun smiling up at them.

In turn, Philmore Calhoun noted their jolly, radiant faces. The morning sun highlighted every lovely feature the gracious ladies possessed. What a beautiful sight the four women were to him.

The four women, slightly surprised to meet with Mr. Calhoun again, looked at the steam yacht he pointed out. They murmured what a handsome steam yacht it was, assuming it was his.

Philmore continued, "I think it is the most rakish looking high speed steamer I have seen. It has a ten foot beam . . . a three-foot-six-inch draft . . . its keel and frame is of white oak . . . it's double planked with clear yellow pine . . . its deck is white pine . . . its machinery . . . Seabury triple expansion engine . . . Seabury patent safety water tube boiler of bent tube type allowing a working steam pressure of 275 pounds."

He watched the ladies faces as he spoke. They looked thoroughly interested in what he was saying, with the exception of Clare.

Clare's expression was not the look of a society lady listening intently. It was the look of a woman wondering why a man she had just met, exchanged an intimacy with, and left, was again standing next to her and talking shop. It was a spontaneous, questioning look.

Philmore Calhoun liked it.

"What is her speed?" Philippa MacAdam asked gamely in her soft Virginian accent.

"Her speed is nineteen miles per hour, but will be increased."

The ladies oohed and aahed over such velocity.

The countess asked, "You must be looking forward to finding out how fast she will go."

Philmore looked at Clare and thought, very much looking forward to finding out how fast she will go. He was amused that the ladies referred to the craft in the feminine form. He could not remember a lady referring to a boat as anything but an "it." He answered, "No, Countess, I have no care how fast she goes. It is the 144-foot schooner-yacht next to her I care about. She's mine. And very fast."

The four women felt slightly misused having wasted their efforts eyeing up the steam yacht they thought was his. Even

Owen thought it a waste of eyeballin' himself. That is until Philmore Calhoun invited the four women for a moonlit sail around the island, on the next night there was a good breeze and a good size moon.

"I am sure you will be quite comfortable on her." He did not add that the deck was adorned with an oriental rug and white wicker furniture. He did not add that inside he had a ladies' cabin with step lockers and sofa, a library, two staterooms, a middle cabin embellished in silver and gold with two sofas, a smoking room, a mess of pantries and ice boxes, a pastry room, bread room, coal bin, carpenter store, quarters for a crew of sixteen, and his own room complete with a water closet, water basin, bookcase and sofa over a bathtub. He did not add that he had a wine list, which stretched from stem to stern and rivaled the wine cellars of France. He did not add that he had a phonograph, and a collection of records including Sousa selections performed by the U.S. Marine Band and operas such as *Aida, Carmen,* and *Tristan and Isolde.*

"By the way, her name is *Calla*, in case you cannot tell her apart from another craft." Philmore proved himself a master at understatement. There was no other pleasure craft like *Calla* in the entire Great Lakes and possibly only one or two like it out east. The four women thanked him for his kind invitation and wondered whom *Calla* was named after. They smiled brightly at Philmore Calhoun, but no more, no less, than the degree they had smiled before the invitation. Philmore noticed this as well. He bid them morning pleasantries and took his leave.

"Go lang, Charley."

As Philmore walked over to his launch to be taken back to his schooner, he was not quite sure what to make of the group of four ideal ladies. He had even forgotten what the hell Clare Gilbertson looked like. He wanted to remember.

Old Charley barely walked ten steps, when one half of the

New Woman college girls group whirred past Owen's carriage on rented bicycles, calling out friendly "hellos" to the four ladies. The bicycling college girls also hailed their other half, rowing in the harbor in the direction of Round Island, with a sororal "ahoy there" and vigorous waving.

The oarswomen in the five rowboats did not see or hear their sisters' greetings because they were singing at the top of their lungs, "Nothing Can Stop Us Now," while plunging their oars into the cool waters, as fast as the local Indians who rowed tourists around the island. And almost as fast as the French voyageurs had for two centuries.

Way back, the French voyageurs had sung lively chanteys and mournful ballads. Today's college girls sang bright songs of promise. While songs had lightened the labor and hours of toil for a voyageur who paddled eighteen to twenty hours a shift—songs enlivened the college girls' unneccessary exercise. Songs were magical incantations to the slaving French voyageurs, and a good singer got extra pay. Songs were not magical to the New Woman college girls, rowing to Round Island for the fun of it.

One can only wonder what a French voyageur from the 1700s would have said, had he seen young (educated!) women rowing a boat for no other purpose than to keep fit. He probably would have said—nothing. He probably would not have believed his eyes.

Charley took a number of steps and the four ladies asked Owen to stop near the earliest merchandisers of Mackinac Island, the Indian squaws, sitting in front of a teepee made of woven mats set up on the harbor's edge. Their intricate basketware, including mammoth hampers big enough to conceal a man, were spread out for sale nearby.

The countess observed that the Indian wares had changed much in forty years. She remembered boxes and baskets and fancy articles made of birch bark and decorated gaily with colored porcupine quills and beads. Those wares had possessed a crude aboriginal beauty. She remembered that some of the last souvenirs, she had taken home from Mackinac Island, back in the 1870s, had sweet grass woven into the baskets. In the dead of winter, she would smell the baskets and their fragrance brought back her happy Mackinac summers.

The countess did not recognize the new baskets made of black ash. Some were white, some colored in yellow, red and green. In fact, the countess did not recognize a lot on Mackinac Island. When she had visited the island from the '50s through the '70s, it was a fishing village with a few hotels, not a resort village with a few fisherman.

She looked in the opposite direction from the squaws' teepee, beyond the fort garden, and up to Fort Mackinac sprawled securely upon a high limestone bluff. The fort's white buildings, set against a deep blue sky, gleamed in the morning sunlight. The fort's flag fluttered livelily in the cool morning breezes.

Fort Mackinac overlooked an immense shipping zone where at one time tens of thousands of Indians, French voyageurs and traders in birch bark canoes paddled through the straits of Mackinac—a shipping zone where up to 1880, sailing cargo schooners had passed through.

Yes, Fort Mackinac was still recognizable to the countess. The legendary sights and natural curiosities such as Arch Rock, Devil's Kitchen, Lover's Leap, Sugar Loaf . . . were still recognizable. The countess even remembered certain old inhabitants and trees.

But the log cabins, stockade fences, antiquated houses and other century-old relics were almost gone. The venerable old buildings had been torn down for boarding houses and hotels and modern summer cottages painted blue and red and yellow, rather than with the whitewash she recalled. The stores, once picturesque and homely, were now filled with fancy goods and trinkets. Where coopers' shops for the building of shipping barrels once stood, where warehouses for icing and salting fish once stood, there were now saloons and restaurants and shooting galleries and gift shops.

Owen interrupted her thoughts with his guide's talk about the fort. Apparently it slipped his mind that he had told it to the four women on other tours. The ladies were either too considerate to interrupt him, or they had other things on their minds.

"Fort Mackinac is a reg'lar Gibraltar. It was considered an important fortress in its early days by white men. Yeh fine leddies, may know its a reg'lar fort of these United States, havin' thare year round a reg'lar garrison.

"In 1715, the fort yeh see up thare on the 150-foot bluff—wasn't up thare. But thare was a fort 'cross the straits at Fort Michilimackinac, built by the Frenchies as a trading post for furs.

"Then in 1760, the imperialist British hoodlums took over Canada, and a year later took Fort Michilimackinac 'long with the whole damned country. By 1781, the thievin' British moved their fort 'cross the straits here to Mackinac Island 'cause of the deep harbor and big bluff, and named it Fort Mackinac . . . whoa, Charley, where do ye think yer goin' . . . I ain't a finished yet . . . .

"Leddies, the flags of two nations 'ave floated oe'r its white bastions here on the island. The bloody British lion growled up thare 'til George Washington whipped the roarin' beast into its iron cage in the Revolutionary War, and we Americans finally took the fort in 1796.

"Once more unto the breach, in 1812, the fort was surrendered to the royalist British, who surprised the brave lot o' American soldiers one night, by landin' at British Landin' and attackin' the Americans from behind.

"But Fort Mackinac came back into our democratic hands, it did, in 1815." Owen suddenly stood up in the carriage for the finale, and addressed the ladies directly. His voice grew louder and louder as he rhapsodized, "Fine Leddies . . . from that momentous time 'till this very moment we breathe . . . the star spangled banner has waved its reds, whites, and blues at us above the snowy white battlements of Fort Mackinac . . . and may God . . . himself . . . grant that our flag may never be taken down agin in our lifetime. Ach ya."

Owen Corrigan should have been an orator.

To Owen's satisfaction, the genial ladies looked as if they were listening intently to his rapturous speech. Nothing could be further from the truth. Their minds were far away.

Clare Gilbertson was fighting temptation to turn her head in the opposite direction from Fort Mackinac, to the harbor, and snatch another look at *Calla*.

Philippa MacAdam, a fine horsewoman and painter of horses, was restless and thinking ahead to her afternoon ride on Dude, the nobbiest gelding in the Grand Hotel's stable.

Beatrice Venn, thinking of Sydney Froilan's strong grip on her wrist, caught sight of Professor Bellamy and her children waving wildly from the long ramp leading up to the fort; she began waving back energetically, as did all her friends in the carriage.

The countess continued wading through old memories of the island with increased abandon.

"Go lang, Charley."

Countess Anna took another quick look at the harbor. She recalled a sacred scene enacted during the lilac festival in a June too long ago. A large cross, covered with sweet smelling lavender lilacs, was blessed by the priest of St. Anne's and propped up in a flat bottomed, thirty-foot Mackinac boat. When the Great Lakes' wind filled its three graceful sails, the boat carried the lilac cross, gently rocking to and fro, out into the glimmering straits. The islanders believed the sacred cross would bring good luck to the jack-tars, as the sailors were called. And so did young Anna.

Twenty, thirty, forty years ago, the harbor and wharf and straits were a forest of sailing masts interspersed with rigging and halyards. The countess pictured the husky jack-tars working the ropes and halyards. She remembered the sounds of the sailors chanting.

As if reading her thoughts, Owen said, "Leddies, I can remember when the sparklin' straits were fully full of cargo schooners. Sometimes I'd be wakened in the dead o' night, with the jack-tars' chantin' the rhythm of the capstan weighin' the anchor, ach ya, and the haul on the halyards while they mastheaded the yards to the rhythm of . . ."

"'A-hay! A high! A-ho-ya!'" chanted the countess gleefully.

If the other ladies looked surprised, Owen looked dumbfounded. He shrugged and thought, first the cows and now jack-tar talk from Countess Anna. Even if she was a born American, he just plain did not expect such behavior and talk from genuine royalty.

The countess continued, "They set sail to a solo chant, 'haul on the bowlin', the fore and mainstop bowlin' . . .'"

"'Haul on the bowlin', the bowlin' haul!'" interchanted Owen, alive to bygone rhythms, forgetting his surprise with Countess Anna. "One giant sail a spread to port, the other sail a spread to starboard . . . with a lubber's wind dead aft toward Lake Huron."

Owen and Countess Anna felt a camaraderie the other ladies could not have shared. An awkward, mutual bridge of memories connected their polar social classes. It made both of them feel somewhat uncomfortable. The countess had unwittingly brought Owen into her past memory with Glendora, which she regretted, and now again with nostalgic exchanges about the former wildness of Mackinac.

Having sandbagged a sentimental flood of recollection for three weeks, Anna and her emotions suddenly erupted and sizzled inside soothing images from eighteen happy summers in a fishing village she could never bring back to life. What she could bring back were double-edged visions of a wild lost island teeming with aborigines, fisherman, sailors, soldiers, their wives and children. And engaged to those images, like sea lampreys to fishes, were wildly tender, forgotten, resurging memories of first love.

Owen drove past Island House, one of the first hotels on the island, where Anna had stayed her latter ten summers. He pointed straight ahead and said, "Looky yonder, leddies, you'll recognize St. Anne's church with her mighty newish belltower. What a white sight laid against a blue sky. Looky at the gleemin' white church, leddies, if yer eyes can take the firey sun upon her. I believe, begorra, that the blessed Holy Ghost, himself, mixed the white paint and cast his own blessed light into the whitewash of St. Anne's."

As they passed St. Anne's, a bold-looking clapboard church dominating the street, the four women craned their necks to look at the tall new belltower shooting up from the middle of the facade. St. Anne's was not a passive-looking church just sitting around waiting for people to visit it. The church looked as if it were cheerfully bidding all to enter its flung open doors.

Another old building replaced, thought Anna. She remembered the auction of the old, much smaller St. Anne's, in the summer of 1873, when they tore the church apart before her eyes and sold it off piece by piece. When she came back in 1874, her last summer on the island, the congregation celebrated Mass at Mission Church up the street. St. Anne's . . . Mission Church . . . Mission House . . . the countess drove past these buildings as she had all the other places, filled with memories her three friends in the carriage could not relate to.

She did not attempt to explain. She sat in the carriage culling through the the first ten summers of her life, spent at Mission House hotel. She recalled the eleventh summer her mother insisted on staying at Island House hotel, because it was newer and more fashionable. She suspected that her mother never did care to write to her new set of rich friends that she was staying at the Mission House hotel, whose name reflected its former function. Although Anna and her newly successful father pushed to remain at Mission House, her father gave in to her mother in the end, as usual. Anna eventually grew fond of Island House, but it was always back to Mission House her mind would wander.

No wonder. It was at a dance at Mission House, one of those outdoor dances they held on the night of a full moon, twenty years past, that Anna had fallen in love with the young widower, her first love. And it was one full moon later, while summer revelers danced on the Mission House lawn by the light of the silvery moon over Round Island, that the young widower embraced Anna near Mission Church, and asked her to marry him with a passion Anna still cherished. The day after the proposal, Glendora the cow was born.

Anna never came back to Mackinac Island after the summer proposal of '74, until the present. Her mother saw to that. And Countess Elizabeth Anne Gianotti had never seen or heard from her first love again.

"Whoa, Charley. Here we are, leddies . . . Robinson's Folly finally."

The women, except for Anna, looked around but saw no dramatic rock formation as they expected.

"Leddies, its been told, that a thievin' if gallant-like English officer from Fort Mackinac, Robinson was his name, was a helpless admirer of yer fair sex . . . and had a mind filled with a vision . . . a she-vision more ideal than real.

"At every day's ending . . . when the orange orb of daylight crawled into its cradle of rest . . . when the twilight gloamed in the evenin' sky . . . when the whip-poor-will's soft music floated through the bosky dales and green dingles of this fairy isle . . . the she-vision lay a waitin' in her lover's bower for the officer. The she-vision's angel smiles and devilish charms beckoned Robinson's soul from tameness to love's wild landscape.

"One chilled night, her lustful eyes lured him toward the high cliff up yonder," Owen pointed to the legendary rocky precipice, " . . . and the she-vision jumped off the cliff. He like a lover crazed, jumped after her . . . plungin' himself into this very cedar tree to my left . . . where he broke his bloody English neck." Owen sighed dramatically and sneaked a look to see how his version of history had affected the Big Four.

They had that look in their eyes they got now and then. Owen thought the look meant lets get back to the Grand Hotel. Little did Owen know that the look in their eyes meant the Big Four were not entertained by Adam and Eve stories.

"Tank ye, leddies, fer yer fine attentions. Now its back to the Grand palace we'll be a goin'." Owen knew he had to push old Charley to get the four fancy women back before lunch.

"Go lang, Charley."

As they drove back to the Grand, the same young man whom the countess noticed on the veranda rode past her on a chestnut mare whose coat gleamed like a bolt of shot silk in the sunlight. Their eyes met. He grasped his reins and whip in his left hand and raised his hat with his right. The countess recognized his dignified gesture with a smile and slight nod of her head. She wracked her brain, wondering where they might have met. She thought it was possible they had met in Italy, at the court of Queen Marguerite. Yes, that was it. She was . . . almost sure.

4
Fishing With Ladies

"Fishing with ladies is dangerous sport. Too many years ago, I went out bait fishing in a little rowboat with a young lady. Swarms of perch played about our hooks. The young lady said she had a big fish on the line and would I assist her. I had to drop my fishing pole and help her land the big catch. The lady exaggerated the prize. The fish did not weigh more than half a pound. I landed the fish for the lady but she landed the big prize for herself. For I was the catch on her line."

All the gentlemen laughed.

"We were married a year later. That is what comes from bait fishing. Since then I only go fly fishing. And I must add, that I never had the urge to go bait fishing again," admitted Professor Loral Bellamy, smiling broadly.

Jimmy Hayes, Eugene Sullivan, Rutherford Haverhill, Sydney Froilan, John and Edward Cudahy—meatpacking millionaires with cottages on the island, and their friend Richard Anders—the son of a fellow cottager, a world traveler, former rowing champion, and professional race horse gambler, all chuckled at the ending to Professor Bellamy's fish story. It was the kind of after-lunch talk they liked to hear. That they believed his fish story was to the professor's honor. For it was likely to them that the old-fashioned professor had a good marriage, and never really needed to do a little bait fishing on the side.

Rutherford Haverhill quenched the afterglow of the professor's humor and said smugly, "Anyone who uses a worm for the hideous catfish, and uses a worm for the beautiful lake trout, cannot pretend to be a sportsman. Bait fishing is entirely inferior to fly fishing."

"I know a sportsman when I see one," Jimmy Hayes spoke up supportively, "and Loral Bellamy is one of the greatest fly fishermen and finest sportsmen I have seen. Loral's an early riser, he's temperate, he's patient of disappointment, and courageous, and intent upon his business, and cool and confident. He's always ready, kind to a dog, civil to the girls, and polite to a brother sportsmen." Jimmy landed a playful pat on the professor's broad shoulders.

"I did not mean to imply, Loral, that you are not a sportsman. I was only emphasizing my delight when a frail tackle, such as an artificial fly, overwhelms a furious and stubborn prey, such as a fish," Rutherford Haverhill defended himself without cause.

John Cudahy, a well-liked cottager always welcomed at the Grand by Jimmy Hayes, knew the area near Mackinac Island well and replied, "There's unequaled bait fishing at Sault Ste. Marie and at times excellent fly fishing. You see, Haverhill, bait fishing is preferred there because it will kill the largest trout . . . because of the depth and strength of the water there. Did you fellows know that a few miles below the Sault, at Garden River, there's good sport and fair sized trout? It's a difficult stream to ascend."

The group of sportsmen discussed the possibility of fishing at the Sault, until swagger Richard Anders, the youngest adventurer among them, brought up another daring sport available at the Sault.

"Have any of you run the Sault rapids?" None of the men had. "Years ago I rode the rapids in a canoe manned by half-breed Indians. Damned exciting. Imagine busting a bronco, rushing like a locomotive, in a rocky downhill river. If you go for that idea, you'll have the courage to take the rapids midstream, at their most dangerous. However, I don't have the courage. I'll take them again. But I'll take them near the shore."

The group of sportsmen liked Richard Anders. He was not a show-off in spite of having rowed in an open boat across the North Sea, from the German coast to Goteborg, Sweden, some five years before. They liked him in spite of his being a race horse gambler who had won a million dollars without doing an honest day's labor to deserve it. They liked him in spite of his rather manly good looks. And they even liked him in spite of his relative youth—which is the most difficult detail of all to believe.

Whether the group of sportsmen was uncommonly generous or Richard Anders was uncommonly likeable, is questionable. Knowing that the overly successful sportsmen's group could afford to be generous and Richard Anders could afford to be likeable, it was probably a bit of both.

"What say all of you to a trip to the Sault, a run on the rapids, a day of fishing, and an overnight at Sault Ste. Marie sometime soon?" asked Richard. He did not add that his thirtieth birthday was coming up and he would like to celebrate it at the Sault. He did not want to call attention to himself.

Rutherford Haverhill noted that western men who knew one another for only a few hours—men like Richard Anders—invited each other on the most intimate journeys without thinking twice. It was simply the way of western men with common tastes and interests. Money and position were not the primary uniting forces with men in the west, unlike most of their counterparts in the east.

The group of sportsmen went into a lengthly discussion about going fishing and shooting the rapids at the Sault. They decided to make the trip on one condition and one condition only. No ladies allowed. The one condition was to change that very evening. After midnight. After the grand ball.

"Ah . . . the seduction of fish," cooed sporty heartcracker Eugene "Sully" Sullivan. "Let's get out our rods and reels and lines and flies and fishing suits and tackle boxes and head up to the Sault." The sportsmen beamed at the thought of it all.

Sully was always the first man to answer in any event proposed. He was usually the life of the party and therefore always included in the invitations for just about everything. Not only was he the first man to buy another man a drink, he was the first man to dance with a rich and youngish old maid. Sully was a heart breaker by avocation and a "Mayor of the Detroit River" by appointment. With a long and lively career in swell society, he acted to the manner born though he never owned a *manor*. He looked fifteen years younger than he was and Grand Hotel dances were his paradise. The summer of 1893 was his third season at the Grand and he knew all the ropes.

Sully continued, to the sportsmen's great satisfaction, with more talk about fish tackle. "Only the creative power of genius, of great men like ourselves, can make an artificial fly come alive . . . move . . . and have being.

"I remember throwing a fly such a distance, with such utter delicacy and suspension, that when it dropped down upon the lucid waters for a single moment in the breezeless air . . . as if defying the law of gravity . . . right before my trusty eyes could verify it . . . the fly took wings and life and might have flown away . . . .But just then an old finny five pounder, who had eyeballed the fly's imminent ascent, darted up and jumped at the fly a full foot out of the water."

Sully's rendition started a flood of fish-related stories. Among the believable stories, the Cudahy brothers told about the time they went fishing in the straits, not far from the island and about two miles from Mackinaw City. They caught a whopping number of twenty lake and salmon trout, weighing in at 160 pounds, in less than six hours. The biggest one weighed eighteen pounds and took one-half hour to land. "Nine of the fish were red fins . . . and splendid fellows they were . . . game to the very end."

Rutherford Haverhill told of having fished in Scotland, in the Caribbean, and off of Long Island. Then he explained, at length, where he hunted all winter—for the latest fishing outfit for spring.

Sydney Froilan countered that he fished in Vermont, and stripped to his underclothes in a trout stream, rather than lug a fishing outfit he inherited from his grandfather.

The sportsmen got a good laugh out of that contrast. Even Rutherford, on the warpath with Sydney before lunch, gave in after lunch, with a half smile.

A net brimming full of fish stories was brought up from a pool of memories. These fishy stories gushed forth from the sportsmen like Old Faithful—when young and unreliable.

But there was one fish story told by reliable Professor Bellamy that was truly verifiable. "A friend and I caught a monster muskellunge in the north channel . . . St. Clair Flats . . . that was a twenty-five pounder . . . almost four feet in length. It fought an hour before we landed him. He ran our line out 300 feet and it towed the two of us 150 feet." The sportsmen, eyes agog, lived to hear such finny feats.

Jimmy Hayes added, "Fellow anglers, what my good friend Loral says is one hundred percent true. For the monster muskellunge, given to me by Loral and his friend now passed away, God rest his soul, hangs preserved and mounted on a wall in my office. You must come to my office and see the twenty-five pounder some time."

Some of the sportsmen had already drooled at the sublime sight of the monster muskellunge on the wall behind Jimmy Hayes' desk. The mounted monster fish somehow blended into Jimmy's huge office, with its finely finished dark hardwood walls, Brussels carpets, chairs and sofas of heavy green upholstered leather, curtains of lace and heavy chenille, and other personally hunted trophies such as a stuffed grizzly bear and a mountain lion.

Jimmy shot the mountain lion in the Shasta Mountains of California when he was there checking out his mining claims. He had boasted that he was out to break Teddy Roosevelt's record in killing mountain lions, and managed to shoot, one. When Teddy Roosevelt had stayed at the Grand Hotel and saw the mountain lion in Jimmy's office, he had claimed that he had never seen a bigger one. It would be hard to say whose affability and nineteenth century sportsmanship was greater— Teddy Roosevelt's or Jimmy Hayes'.

One of the great disappointments of Jimmy Hayes' life was that he never killed a buffalo. Since he was not the kind of man to buy another hunter's trophy, he never had a buffalo head "to grace his office," as he put it. That Jimmy Hayes felt less of a sportsman because of it there was no doubt. He was downright angry, when he learned from Teddy Roosevelt, that there were no more than 1,000 buffalo left on the North American continent, and 500 were protected in Yellowstone. With those low numbers, Jimmy knew he would never even get a chance to shoot down one of the beasts.

Not one deer trophy ornamented Jimmy's handsome wooden office walls either. But this had nothing to do with extinction. When asked why there were no deer trophies Jimmy replied with his usual candor, "Deer? No offense to you deer hunters, why, I wouldn't go across the street to shoot a deer. You have to stand in one place for four or five hours waiting for the deer to come, and then you shoot them down same as you would a cow. Give me the grizzly or the mountain lion, where it is nip and tuck. Why, great scott . . . I would just as soon go on a chipmunk hunt."

Not all the men agreed. But they all liked Jimmy Hayes, a hale fellow, a tasty dresser, and a popular gentleman with the ladies. They knew he was as active as a cat and strong as an ox. He jumped ten feet four inches in the standing broad jump and had won twenty gold medals in amateur boxing matches in his day. He was not a snob, and most importantly was not married. Having escaped the snare of matrimonial obligations, he was admired for it by the men; he was also admired for it by the women. Especially the MaMas, who considered Jimmy Hayes an excellent catch.

Jimmy noticed the hotel's riding master, John Fuller of England and New York, walking up rapidly to the sportsmen's group with Donny, a three-year-old English setter belonging to Jimmy. When Donny saw his master, he bounded to Jimmy like a hungry young pup to its mother, his tail wagging like a metronome set at allegro, his mouth gripping a carrot. The handsome dog threw the wet carrot onto Jimmy's lap, leaped up, and splashed a few licks on Jimmy's shiny ears made shinier by Donny's polishing. Donny did not calm down until Jimmy gave him a belly rub.

"What's this, the dog eats carrots," commented Edward Cudahy.

"Donny, you son of a bitch, what are you doing with a carrot in your mouth again?" Jimmy asked playfully, but not loudly enough for any ladies nearby to hear.

John Fuller answered for Donny in an English public school accent, (Rutherford Haverhill wondered where the riding master had picked up the upper class accent, so like his own), "Donald has been into the kitchen's vegetables again. Your chef is fed up, Mr. Hayes."

"Oh, is he now," replied Jimmy, trying to figure why his

riding master, John Fuller, was coming to him with both the chef's complaint and Donny.

"He has threatened to quit if he catches Donald rummaging through the vegetables again. He says it is unsanitary and that Donald ruins the best vegetables."

"Never saw a dog go after vegetables. How does he get in where the vegetables are anyway?"

"I have no idea. But I found out today why Donald's after the vegetables . . ."

All the sportsmen looked at John Fuller's poker face expectantly.

John Fuller revealed, "Donald is stealing the carrots to give to my best gelding, Dude. Ever see a dog and a horse friends before?" All the sportsmen declared they had never seen it, but heard it told.

"That explains it. They are good friends," exclaimed Jimmy, who not only understood friendship, but elevated friendship to a creed. Jimmy also understood that John Fuller did not like Donny hanging about the stables during the day.

"Ah, Donny, my boy. In spite of your eccentricities, you are quite a dog." Thinking to coax John Fuller into letting lonesome Donny hang around the stables during the day, as Jimmy had little time for the dog himself, he invited John Fuller to sit with the group of sportsmen.

"Thanks Jimmy, but I have to get back to the stable." John Fuller volunteered, in a voice verging on the proud, "Mrs. Philippa MacAdam is riding Dude this afternoon, and I promised to accompany her. I am giving her hurdle jumping lessons."

Most of the sportsmen knew that Philippa MacAdam was not only a fine horse painter, she was a fine horsewoman. She took four-foot hurdles sidesaddle as if she were born to it. They also suspected the divorced riding master had his eyes on the eligible and youngish widow.

John added, "Also, I am expecting Colonel Marshe Williamson's bay mares to be up from the dock any hour soon."

"Marshe Williamson, is he back this summer?" asked Jimmy Hayes, knowing the answer. "I didn't expect the colonel. Gentlemen, for those of you who do not know the colonel, let me tell you, he is a true southern gentleman, a fine horseman, polo and billiard player, and the finest judge of horseflesh in the country. He also happens to own of one of the largest stud farms in Kentucky."

"What should I do with Donald?" asked John Fuller rather crisply, slightly envious over Jimmy's effusive compliment about Marshe Williamson's skills as a horseman.

Jimmy noticed John Fuller's bad sportsmanship and quickly mentioned, "But of course, if Marshe Williamson is the best southern expert on horses, then our John Fuller here is the best northern expert. Certainly you can rest your legs a few minutes, John."

John Fuller calmed down and sat down after the compliment. Donny, as if mimicking Jimmy's complimentary and pragmatic mood, grabbed the carrot off Jimmy's lap, threw it over on John Fuller's lap, and lay down at John's feet.

All the sportsmen concealed their amusement—that Don the dog, instinctively knew he had to butter up John Fuller the riding master, in order to be with his friend Dude the horse. They also could tell that the riding master did not like dogs, and became suspicious about John Fuller's unsportsman-like behavior and, consequently, his character.

"Regarding Donny," Jimmy continued, "take him back to the stables. If the dog enjoys it there, let him stick around your horse, Dude, if he is not in your way."

John Fuller tried to cover up his anger.

Jimmy tried to humor his riding master and began, "You know boys, there is no better bird dog than Donny in America. Last autumn I took him to a field trial of hunting dogs at

Bicknell, Indiana. And this story you will get a kick out of, John Fuller, because it has more to do with horses than with dogs," Jimmy Hayes smiled brightly and began his story. The sportsmen were expecting a good one from Jimmy Hayes. They never knew him to tell a bad one.

"Gentlemen . . . my talents lie with driving horses . . . not riding them. Well, at the field trial, eighty of us dog owners, on horseback, had to follow the setters and pointers that were being put through their paces. A few of us dog lovers, including myself, were not expecting our minds and behinds to be concentrating on the horses instead.

"You see . . . for the first time in twenty years I mounted a horse, and as a result I was the stiffest man in Michigan for a week after. The only steed I was able to secure was a big, lumbering gray horse sixteen hands high, whose only gait was a clumsy trot.

"Cross country riding under such circumstances is not the hilarious and exhilarating sport that one might suppose. I can't help laughing when I think what a sorry figure I must have cut, perched up on the ridge pole of that old gray horse, trotting across a plowed field in the wake of some eighty well-mounted men.

"In order to relieve the monotony of the exciting chase, I occasionally dismounted and walked a mile or two. By that method I found I could make better time than when on the back of my prancing charger."

The sportsmen grinned, undoubtedly thinking of a similar experience on a borrowed horse. John Fuller masked his impatience and smiled insincerely.

"Finally, for a consideration, I induced another member of the party to exchange horses with me, and I climbed on top of his hunter, which could lope very nicely. Unluckily, the stirrups were too long for me, and when my loper, in reponse to a cut from my whip, broke into a run, I flew gracefully through the air in fully a dozen different attitudes. As soon as I was able to check the mad rush of the new horse, I dismounted, led him back to where my big gray was and made another trade.

"I finished the day on my trotter's back, but did not urge him to any bursts of speed you may rest assured. Now that it is all over, I will tell you in confidence, that I am convinced a man may be able to 'keep tavern' all right, and at the same time, not prove a conspicuous success as an all-around equestrian, as John Fuller is here."

Jimmy Hayes not only lampooned his ability on the saddle, the story served to humor proud John Fuller, who felt intimidated into taking on the added task of looking after Donny. John Fuller tried to hide the resentment he felt working for the Napoleon of summer hotel proprietors, Jimmy Hayes. Out east, John Fuller had worked for himself.

The group of sportsmen caught on to Jimmy's purpose in relating the story; but the hard nosed businessmen among them never would have catered that way to an employee, even if that employee, like John Fuller, was successful in his own right and had brought his own thoroughbreds to the hotel. The businessmen would have simply told John Fuller to take on the added responsibility of looking after the dog. If Fuller did not like it—so what. The businessmen thought Jimmy Hayes a bit soft. But then the businessmen knew nothing about running a summer hotel, nor about dealing with temporary summer help.

They were to get another taste of Jimmy's style and the joys of running a mighty successful summer hotel, or 'keeping tavern' as he called it, when a new problem came up to Jimmy, borne in the form of the hotel's maître d', Bludsoe.

"Ex 'use me, Mr. Hayes, suh," interrupted the courteous, but nervous black man dressed up in his fancy maître d' costume, including the swallow tail coat and patent leather pumps any white man of means wore to a grand ball.

Jimmy Hayes looked Bludsoe over and joked for the benefit of the sportsmen. "Which are you, Bludsoe, a maître d' . . . or . . . a gentleman?"

"Suh . . . I endeavor to be both," replied Bludsoe with a toothsome smile, looking directly at Rutherford Haverhill. All the sportsmen guffawed, except for Rutherford who looked dubious and wondered if the Negroes really knew their place on the island, as he had favored that impression to Countess Gianotti that morning.

Bludsoe continued, "There's a unusual problem, Mr. Hayes . . ."

"What is it, Bludsoe?"

"Well, suh . . . it's like this, suh . . . a dishwasher just fell into the cistern . . . suh."

Jimmy put a hand through the hairs on his head—which were numbered—and rubbed the shiny expanse where their brothers had once been. He replied, "This is a new one . . . well, gentlemen, excuse me, and remember I am counting on you to take part in the cigar and umbrella race this afternoon after the lecture." Jimmy Hayes hurried into the kitchen.

John Fuller suddenly realized that he was running late for Philippa MacAdam's ride and hurdle jumping lesson.

All the sportsmen, including John Fuller, were so attentive to Jimmy Hayes' attention-getting narratives, they had not noticed Mrs. Philippa MacAdam leave the hotel and walk in the direction of the Grand's stables some time ago.

Everyone else on the veranda noticed her leave and noted that Mrs. Philippa MacAdam wore the plainest dark-blue riding habit most had ever seen. When the college girls asked her why she did not wear a veil over her face to avoid flying pests, she answered that it veiled her vision, which could cause an injury to her horse. To the observant college girls, she seemed more concerned for the horse than for herself. If

Philippa MacAdam were not such a feminine-looking horse-woman, or so smart and spirited and cultivated, or a member of the admired Big Four, the female guests would have called her "horsey"—gladly.

When Philippa MacAdam entered the Grand's stable, which smelled of varnish and fresh straw, she found Dude and another thoroughbred named Mackinac Belle saddled and tied up near a window. The afternoon sun, filtering through layers of cobwebs clinging to the window, landed on Dude's glossy chestnut colored coat. Philippa admired the nobby looking horse, his lustrous coat deliberately brushed to reflect the light. Deliberately brushed, because Mrs. MacAdam would be riding him that afternoon.

She approached Dude gently and firmly, wondering why neither John Fuller nor his groomsman was in the stable. Dude placed his ears forward and tried to scent her, his sensitive upper lip wrinkling, driving away a pesty fly. Recognizing Philippa, the horse rubbed his nose against her sleeve and accepted her caresses docilely.

Philippa MacAdam, in a daring if somewhat impatient mood that afternoon, decided to mount Dude alone. No easy feat. She seldom was mounted on a horse properly the first time, with a man's help, anyhow. That she decided to mount from the floor was a gutsy move. That she decided to mount alone was a resigned move. For no one mounted her as well as her late husband used to. No one.

Philippa managed to mount, but displaced her sidesaddle and twisted her thick skirt underneath as she sat down. Frustrated and more determined than ever, she had no choice but to dismount and try again, unaware that a man in a dark corner of the large stable was gazing curiously at her every move.

With expectant eyes, the stranger watched Philippa take her foot out of the stirrup. He watched Philippa remove her right leg and skirt from the sidesaddle crutch, and move her right gloved hand to the upper crutch. His racy eyes followed her curvaceous athletic body slip down from the horse, and alight near Dude's foreleg.

Never had the stranger seen a more comely woman dismount a horse so suggestively. In fact, Philippa MacAdam had never dismounted so suggestively in her entire life. Nor would she have ever consciously tried to dismount a horse in a suggestive fashion. Not alone in a stable, at any rate. No, like almost everyone else, attractive Philippa MacAdam usually came down off a horse as if she had thirty-pound weights stuck to her behind.

"I see there are no groomsmen to be of assistance. May I assist you?" offered the stranger in a basso profundo voice, with a slight southern accent.

Philippa, startled to the core, saw a man walking toward her. Gripping her whip tightly, she moved closer to Dude and tried to make out the stranger as he approached. She did not recognize the black-haired, black-bearded man with the military bearing. She wondered if he was an officer from Fort Mackinac, out of uniform for some reason she was too shaken to make up at the time.

When he stopped a respectable distance from her, she could see that he dressed like a gentleman. This did not convince Philippa that he was a gentleman. Nor did his gentlemanly accent convince Philippa that he was what he appeared to be. By this time, Philippa figured the stranger had been in the stable since she arrived. Had he seen her mount? And why had he not shown himself, immediately, to be of assistance.

With forced calm, Philippa answered, "I have never been much good at mounting a horse alone."

"You're mighty fine at dismounting," the stranger said in voice too appreciative to Philippa's ears.

The groomsman, Karl, hurried inside the stable to Philippa's utter relief.

"Young man, come steady the horse, this fine lady wants to enjoy a ride this afternoon."

"Ya, sir, Colonel Williamson. Why, Mrs. MacAdam, I didn't know you vas here at all. You should have called out to me."

"I am a bit early, Karl. Thank you for having Dude saddled up so well." Philippa relaxed. The stranger was known to the groomsman.

"I didn't saddle 'im up. Mr. Fuller did before he vent to the hotel. How long vill you and Mr. Fuller be out, Mrs. MacAdam?"

"Not more than two hours, Karl."

"Colonel Williamson, are your altogether fine bay mares settling in?"

"Very well, Karl, thanks to your attentions. They're not fond of the ferry crossing, you know."

"Well, I'll be stymied . . . excuse me . . . Mrs. Mac-Adam, Colonel . . . but I see a lady outside and I think she's riding our Kentucky Jean . . . she ain't a horse for a sidesaddle . . . vhat the hell, excuse me, Mrs. MacAdam, but I'm goin' to find out what's goin' on here." Karl ran out of the stable.

"May I assist you to mount?" asked Colonel Marshe Williamson, with a gallantry Philippa had not expected from a man she thought a common sneak but a minute ago. She told herself to wait for Karl or John Fuller, but her instincts told her to accept the attractive colonel's offer.

"Yes, thank you."

Philippa watched Marshe Williamson while he checked to see if Dude's bridle and saddle were secure. A most thoughtful gesture, she noted.

Marshe also checked Philippa's left hand, to see if any ring bulged beneath her glove. No ring.

From outside the stable came the voice of Karl shouting,

"But, Ma'm, you can't ride Kentucky Jean. And vhere the hell did you come from anyvays, riding our horse vithout permission?"

Inside, Philippa took the whip and reins in her right hand. She wondered why Karl was making such a fuss.

A woman's voice outside, her accent born in a cornfield and her r's punched like a steer on the arse, answered Karl urgently. "I've saddled up this horse here. It was the only one left in the stable. No one was here, and I've got to go for a ride. I waited till you got back before I left, didn't I?"

Philippa raised her left foot and Marshe Williamson bent down.

They overheard Karl reply, "Ma'm that ain't a horse for a sidesaddle . . . vithers too thin . . . please let me help you dismount."

Dude suddenly became restless and twisted around slightly, as if in response to Kentucky Jean's undoubtable pain from the sidesaddle. The colonel caught Dude's mane.

They overheard the woman shout back, "I'm meeting someone at a place where a carriage can't get through. I'm an experienced rider. Besides," she lied, "I met John Fuller at the hotel and he said it was all right."

Whatever happened next outside the stable, Philippa and Marshe Williamson would never know. For when—the colonel was bending down again, and placing the palm of his broad hand under the waist of Philippa's left foot . . . and Philippa was feeling the warmth of the colonel's hand through her fine thin soles . . . and he was feeling her left hand on his right shoulder . . . and she was straightening her leg and standing on his ever so warm hand and grasping the upper crutch of the saddle . . . and he was imagining her comely soft legs maintaining their balance under her heavy skirt . . . and she was feeling his manly strength lift her . . . and he was watching her lovely body turn to the left and sit sideways in the saddle—they both forgot about the argument outside, and could not help but think of two distinct possibilites during such a perfectly harmonious act. Mounting the horse, and mounting each other.

Colonel Marshe Williamson had raised Mrs. Philippa Mac-Adam with utmost ease to a sitting position on the sidesaddle. That they both breathed a little heavier than usual, and both tried to cover it up, had nothing to do with over-exertion in their perfect little act of harmony.

The colonel was downright surprised he managed to put a lady up on her horse the first time. Ladies were usually saddle shy.

Philippa's mind raced with memories of clumsy attempts and the surprise of this first-time-up success. Usually the man helping her, whether a gentleman or a groom, trying to show off the strength he did not have, used only one hand and brought her foot too far forward, dashing any hope to mount. Or worst of all, the man tried to raise her before she straightened her knee and rested her weight on his hand. She had even suffered clumsiness at the hands of John Fuller, who sometimes raised her too soon out of nervousness. Yes, Philippa thought, men and mounting, men and mounting. So few knew how to . . . really knew how.

Marshe Williamson was obviously strong enough to do it one handed. Philippa could not help but look over the gentleman, who knew, by feeling her weight in his hands, when she was in the proper position to be lifted up. The full-bearded stalwart gentleman with the military air, so close to her, showed a free and easy readiness. She assessed his age at forty, plus or minus a couple of years.

Marshe gently pulled the right side of her heavy skirt straight. Standing back, he watched Philippa put her right leg over the sidesaddle's horn. His eyes stirring, Marshe fancied himself as the sidesaddle, and imagined pretty Philippa putting her leg over his horn.

Philippa felt the gentleman placing her foot in the stirrup, and felt his warm hand lingering a stolen moment.

Finally, Marshe pulled down her skirt—and dashed his desire to pull it up instead.

Philippa took both reins and Marshe led her out of the dark stable.

"Thank you . . . very much," Philippa said warmly and smiled brightly when they were out in the open air and sunshine.

"May I introduce myself, Madam?"

"Please do . . . ." Philippa tried to contain her amusement with the thought that two strangers of the opposite sex had just performed a most trusting and intimate act in a dark stable, but waited to be out in the open before making formal introductions.

"I am Marshe Williamson, from Kentucky."

"I am Philippa MacAdam, from Virginia."

"A pleasure to meet you . . . Miss or Mrs. MacAdam?" He was surprised she omitted her title.

"Mrs. . . . Mr. Williamson . . . or is it colonel?"

"An honorary title, Mrs. MacAdam." Eligible Marshe Williamson was clearly let down with Philippa's title. Since he had not seen a wedding ring bulge beneath her fine white chevrette glove, he had assumed she was not married. Caught up in the excitement of the moment, even an accomplished horseman like the colonel forgot that no experienced rider wore rings when riding. It was too dangerous.

Caught up in the excitement of the moment, Philippa neglected to drop to Marshe Williamson, that she was a widow, having spied his ringless left hand. Nor did she notice his less predatory, if still interested, dark eyes.

"Enjoy your ride, Mrs. MacAdam."

"It should be especially enjoyable with such an excellent start. Thank you again, Colonel Williamson." Philippa answered Marshe Williamson in such a fresh and simple way, it was bound to make an impression on him.

Never had Marshe met a southern lady, of Philippa's obvious stature, who had swept him off his feet without clever flirtatious remarks and a little horsing around. He watched Philippa, this time in a friendly open manner, ride Dude in a circle near the stable. He wanted to see if she knew how to handle a strange horse as well as she handled a strange gentleman.

What a horsewoman, he thought. This fine lady knows how to sit a horse. In one long look he saw that Philippa sat forward in the saddle, with her elbows in, and her pretty head raised. Her perfectly formed shoulders held up a body free from rigidity, and fitted in one of the plainest riding habits he had ever seen. A tall, black silk hat sat on her black hair done up in the old-fashioned way, gathered at the nape of the neck with plenty of hairpins.

He liked that as well. He saw too many ladies go out riding with "manes" as long and loose as Lady Godiva. When the "Godiva ladies" as he called them, galloped, their hair flew wildly in all directions and clouded their eyes. He thought the Godiva ladies handled their freedom from hairpins stupidly, causing danger to the horse, to people around them, and lastly, to themselves.

Although Marshe Williamson reveranced ladies like any good old southern boy, he drew the line when it came to ladies on horseback. He was merely tolerant of ladies who rode without grace. But the ladies who rode without care or feeling for the horse, he called "horseback whores."

Yes, the lovely sight of Philippa MacAdam, with her friendly manner and elegant bearing in the plainest of riding costumes, was a vision almost too tempting for Marshe Williamson. Especially, when he considered the lady was married.

That Marshe Williamson was a connoisseur of horseflesh and had not given proud Dude a thorough once-over proved only one point. He had finally found a woman whose personality, form, and bearing was like in quality to his beloved stallion Armande, who stood sixteen hands high, had earned $150,000 to date, and bore perfect shoulders. He imagined handsome Philippa riding handsome Armande. He jested to himself that if a woman who sat a horse like Philippa Mac-Adam, wore a price, he would pay top dollar for her, and enjoy watching one perfect-shouldered thoroughbred riding another.

While Philippa rode Dude in a circle, waiting for John Fuller, who had been detained by Jimmy Hayes, she glanced every now and then at Marshe, smiled, and felt a rush of lightheadedness. Over and over again her mind replayed the mounting in the stable—the warmth of his hand on her foot, the strength of his shoulder under her hand, the sensation of his eyes on her body. She thought of a scratched phonograph she had heard repeating, "heart to heart and lip to lip . . . each the other's breath we sip . . . heart to heart and lip to lip . . . each the other's breath we sip," from *Tristan and Isolde* and Wagner.

Philippa MacAdam's buried libido resurfaced and ambushed her emotions. Into her husband's grave, three summers ago, she had buried her genitalic life made duller than virtue after his tragic death. She continued riding Dude in a circle, thinking back over the years gone by, made dreary without the excitement of sexual emotion.

After her husband's accidental death, Philippa had thrown herself into creating her paintings. Even a year of study among the Italians in Rome, where she observed that instinctual sexual urges were still up-and-coming in the human race, did not awaken her emotions. It was as if her instinctual self had died. She felt nothing for men. It was all she could do to concentrate on the techniques of painting horses, which she learned from the famous painter Rosa Bonheur—made infamous by dressing in turkish pants.

At thirty-five years of age, having lost a husband, having put her three sons with astonished in-laws, she headed to Rome and lived like a university student changing her clothes only twice a day. When she got up in the morning she took off her nightgown and put on her turkish pants, and when she went to bed at night she performed the reverse. Solo.

From a Virginian southern belle, who was educated at finishing school, changed clothes four to five times a day, and produced a family with a stud farm owner—to a widow studying art in Rome in turkish pants—Philippa MacAdam had made gigantic leaps in a few short years. It is a wonder she was so surprised and lightheaded when her emotions suddenly leaped alive due to Marshe Williamson from Kentucky.

John Fuller finally appeared, perceptibily flustered, having noticed the all too obvious energy slipping back and forth between Philippa MacAdam and Marshe Williamson.

Donny threw down his carrot and blurted out barking at Dude, just as John Fuller tried to speak in a normal pitch.

John said to himself, I will go to hell before I will compete with a dog. He cursed cocky Jimmy Hayes for his effrontery in telling him to look after his goddamn dog.

Not only did John Fuller's prize horse Dude appear to be listening to the dog, but Dude ignored John, and looked to see if his canine friend brought him a carrot. Indeed, Donny had not forgotten Dude when he raided the hotel's root cellar. The dog picked up the carrot and bounded over to the horse. Philippa and Marshe were amused to see Dude take the carrot right out of Donny's mouth. John was not amused.

"Oh, Mrs. MacAdam, you have mounted Dude," John

Fuller blurted the obvious and continued, "please excuse my lateness. I was obliged to speak with Jimmy Hayes. Karl should have Mackinac Belle saddled up for me. I will be with you in a moment." Turning to Marshe he asked, "Colonel Williamson, has Karl been of assistance to you?"

"Yes, Karl has been of fine assistance. Thank you, Mr. Fuller."

Karl brought out Mackinac Belle and John Fuller mounted her with ease. Philippa and John Fuller bid parting pleasantries to Colonel Williamson, who looked ever so disappointed that he was not invited to join them. As they trotted Dude and Mackinac Belle along shady and scented Tranquil Trail, Philippa wished she had invited the colonel.

Donny followed uninvited at Dude's side, and refused to go back to the stable even after John insisted repeatedly to the dog to turn back. Philippa thought the dog and horse friendship humorous, even rather touching, but did not say so. She doubted that John Fuller had a sense of humor.

From Annex Road, Philippa and John turned left onto Gratiot Trail which led to British Landing Road, and headed to the downs of the Early Farm near the middle of Mackinac Island, where John had set up hurdles in a pasture. As they neared the farm, a woman galloping at break neck speed passed behind them from a left fork in the road. They stopped their horses to see if she was out of control or riding the horse recklessly.

"She must have seen the giant demon himself at Crack-in-the-Island," quipped Philippa, "and stepped on his fingers."

John Fuller was about to chuckle, when his face tightened as taught as deerhide stretched on a tom-tom, and he uttered, "My God, I believe that's Kentucky Jean she's riding to her death." He turned his horse around quickly. "Who in hell's blazes allowed her to ride that horse sidesaddle!"

Philippa quickly went to Karl's defense as she turned her horse around, explaining what she and Colonel Williamson had overheard.

"That's no excuse. The animal is in pain. Who the bloody hell is riding her? Excuse me, Mrs. MacAdam." John Fuller tore off on Mackinac Belle at breakneck speed.

Philippa wondered if John were really concerned for the animal's pain or concerned that he might have one less riding horse in his stable. Maybe it was both. It was hard to tell with John. She decided, at that moment, not to think about attractive-looking, but humorless, John Fuller. Marshe Williamson's warm hand on her foot and that whole scene replayed itself in her mind again, until she heard grave hoarse neighing and a piercing scream.

In the distance, she saw Kentucky Jean trying desperately to rear. But the horse could not get up and began spinning around and around until it became giddy and fell. She made out a red colored skirt flying about in all directions and landing on the ground. Urging Dude to a gallop, Philippa raced him to the accident, Donny barking and bounding next to them.

The reckless horsewoman, her startling get-up covered with dust, looked stunned. She yelled at John, "I jumped off the stupid animal's back or I would 'ave been killed."

John Fuller did not bother to answer the reckless horsewoman or go to her assistance. Desperately trying to disconnect Kentucky Jean's tush from a ring on the martingale, John spoke gentle words to the powerful animal, and the horse made grave sounds after each belabored breath.

Philippa dismounted Dude and hurried over to the woman to help her and asked, "Are you quite sure you should get up?"

"I can get up, thanks to my own wits. What kind of horses does the Grand Hotel let out? I'll report this to the police, or worse, the newspapers."

Helping the reckless horsewoman get up, Philippa quickly replied, "I am quite sure this was an unusual accident. I know John Fuller's horses at the Grand are some of the best riding horses in the country." Philippa even brushed the dust off the woman's skirt with her white chevrette gloves. "Are you sure you are all right?" She did not recognize the woman's face as anyone she had met on the Grand's veranda.

"I can't say . . . for sure. By the way . . . thank you," the woman said awkwardly, with a noted change in her accent; it jumped from raffish to semi-finishing school in one sentence. She looked Philippa over.

Out of breath, John Fuller finally released the horse from its pain. He barked at the woman, "The animal was annoyed by flies . . . she turned her head . . . to drive them away from her shoulder . . . she caught the tush of her lower jaw in this ring. John glared at the woman seeing she wore a loud checkered vest, and her Bordeaux colored hair free flowing. She was older than she looked and she wore lip rouge artistically applied. By looking at her get-up, he guessed she must be a parvenue. He knew that she was a fearless, ruthless, reckless horsewoman.

"I shall have to ask you to mount my horse, and I will walk Kentucky Jean back to the stables," John informed the reckless horsewoman and continued in a gentler voice, "Mrs. MacAdam, I am very sorry, but I shall have to cancel your jumping lesson today."

"I understand, Mr. Fuller. Of course." Philippa's heart went out to poor Kentucky Jean when John removed the side-saddle. The horse's coat, over her thin withers, was stained with blood.

"You ladies may ride on ahead. Together if you please. Of course, a lady never rides alone."

The reckless horsewoman ignored John Fuller's remark and

ignored Kentucky Jean's groans, which sounded like a series of suffocated coughs. But she did agree to ride back with Philippa, if for no other reason than she was more shaken than she let on.

No introductions were made between the two women. But Philippa managed to get the reckless horsewoman to agree not to go the police or to the newspapers, before they rode away from John.

John Fuller should have been grateful to Philippa for intervening. He was not. He was disgusted with Philippa for lowering herself to talk with the lowly "bitch." He would have rather dealt with the police and newspapers than dirty his hands with the parvenue.

For a moment, John seemed to forget that Jimmy Hayes would rather have John Fuller not deal with the police and newspapers. Jimmy would rather have Johnny dirty his hands. It was possible that John Fuller did not care that the bad publicity alone might taint an entire season at the hotel. He was not unaware that Jimmy tried to humor him back on the hotel veranda, in front of some of the richest men in the world. He put up with the patronizing because he had not wanted the sportsmen to think him a bad sport. But he did not like it. He thought, Jimmy Hayes' humorous hazing was nothing more than conceited horseplay; Hayes can play with his Negro maître d'—but not with me.

On the way back to the hotel stable, the reckless horsewoman attempted conversation but once with Philippa, declaring in her raw-toned voice, "I refuse to ride a gray horse. The white hairs come off like rabbit fur and the hairs stick to a riding habit like flies to a web."

With careful cordiality, Philippa answered her and repeated what she had said about John Fuller's horses. The rest of the way back to the hotel, they rode in silence.

As she rode, Philippa groaned a bit to herself. She would be back in time for the lecture on the "Massacre at Fort Michilimackinac" given by, of all people, a boring, unintentionally comical, little Muslim from Egypt who called himself Ibrahim G. Kheiralla. He had lectured on "Hindu Breathing," "A Turkish Bath in Every Home," and "Seven Ages of a Mohammedan in Egypt" in the past three weeks.

One of the few details Philippa and the most of the Grand Hotel guests remembered from his lectures was the Egyptian's matter-of-fact depictions of Egyptian babies. He said the babies enjoy life in Egypt, because they never get washed; when the dirt gets thick it is scraped off. Philippa smiled to herself, as she ducked a tree branch, and pictured the astounded looks on the MaMas' faces in the audience.

She smiled again when she remembered the audience's reaction to Ibrahim's request during his Hindu Breathing lecture. He had asked them to lie on the floor so he could inject oil in their noses, after which he would bid the audience to relax and think beautiful thoughts. His audience grew nervous at such a compromising proposition and thought the man had lost his senses. Nevertheless, the audience was three times larger for his next lecture. Everyone was curious to know what crazy thing the little Muslim would come up with next.

Yes, Philippa had promised the countess and Beatrice and Clare that she would join them for Ibrahim's undoubtedly unconventional lecture, if she got back from her hurdle jumping lesson in time. Once again Philippa smiled, this time at the foreign idea of an Egyptian Muslim as a resident lecturer on a remote American island. And Philippa never would have dreamed that the little Egyptian would serve her dear friends— and the reckless horsewoman riding next to her.

Through an extraordinary perversion of fate, Philippa's

amusement with the little man was to change before the end of the summer.

From a distance, Philippa heard welcome singing and laughter resounding through the scented woods. A merry chariot party of intellectual flirts and their beaus and chaperones, packed together in five carriages and hurrying to get back to the hotel in time for the lecture, passed by Philippa and the reckless horsewoman. She knew they had picnicked on the beach at historic British Landing, located some three to four miles from the Grand Hotel.

Singing "Won't You Be My Sweetheart" with animated spirits, the young men and women sounded drunk on food and love and sunshine and youth and freedom from worry. As they sang, the young beaus secretly hoped to kiss their flirting loves, and the young flirting loves secretly hoped they would be proposed to, whether they wanted to marry their beaus or not, after the grand ball that evening.

The lively youth greeted Philippa, who felt almost as high-spirited, in a friendly if not too sincere fashion. If the young intellectual flirts had not been with their beaus, they would have exchanged gossip about Philippa and the mysterious lady with the rouge tinted lips riding next to her.

As Philippa rode on she resisted the impulse to break away from the reckless horsewoman, gallop down Indian Road, cross over to Cupid's Pathway, and take a longer route back to the hotel, thereby ensuring her lateness for the lecture. But she felt John Fuller had entrusted his horse, Mackinac Belle, to her without saying so. And she did not trust the woman riding next to her to treat Mackinac Belle any differently than she had poor Kentucky Jean.

Passing by the fork in the direction of Cupid's Pathway, Philippa, under the influence of rascal Cupid anyway, was struck with the idea that Colonel Marshe Williamson might be at the lecture and might attend the cigar and umbrella race after it. If Philippa could have wished a four-in-hand into existence that very moment, she would have driven the four horses speedily back to the hotel, in order to be early for the lecture.

She smiled to herself and became anxious to get back to the hotel and change into her afternoon clothes. Only yesterday she had cursed having to "dress up like a corsetted peacock" all day. She preferred turkish trousers and a white shirt, her painting costume. She sighed. What delicious freedom from corsets. And in the next sigh tried to decide what corset she would wear with what costume when she got back.

A bit of the belle in Philippa MacAdam bubbled to the surface for the first time in three years. She wanted to look especially dashing that afternoon . . . and that evening for the grand ball. But first things first. She had to figure out what special afternoon costume to rush into when she got back to the hotel.

Ah yes, Philippa envisioned, the black and white silk with the hairline stripes and ruche of black lace trim around the bottom of the skirt would do nicely. She knew how dramatic the throat ruffle of black lace with a narrow line of white lace on its edges looked next to her fair complexion. But what hat? Why, my white and black straw sailor hat trimmed with a black velvet band and black loops and scarlet berries. Of course. And she smiled to herself, realizing that three years ago a decision like this—would have been one of her major decisions in a day. She completed her picture with tan gloves, patent leather slippers, and black stockings.

Philippa knew her maid would be cross with her, for she decided to wear an entirely different costume from the one she had asked her maid to have ready. She smiled to herself, thinking of the excited commotion and gentle scolding the quick change in costume would ignite. She smiled because she knew that Tessie, the old black maid who had mothered her for thirty-eight years, would be secretly happy for such commotion—and something to complain about.

The reckless horsewoman, who was beginning to feel less shaken, and less grateful, stared over at Philippa and began noticing the lovely smiles popping up every few minutes on Philippa's face. She interpreted Philippa's smiles as those of a smug, good for nothing society lady who had never seen any hardship in life. She wanted to slap the smiles right off Philippa's cultivated face. The smiles reminded her of someone. Someone she hated. Someone staying at the Grand Hotel.

5

Rising to the Bait

Philippa MacAdam, having dressed hastily to the accompaniment of Tessie's good-natured scolding, asked her maid if she knew where the lecture was being held. Her hotel room was on the third floor and it always took extra time to get anywhere.

"Usual place, I suspect."

"But they change the location every week . . ."

"Well, honey, if it ain't in the writing room, it might be in the reception room . . . if it ain't thare it might be in the ordinary or in the parlor. It won't be in the rotunda seein' that that room is the entrance and chekin' in and checkin' out meetin' place. I can tells yeh where it won't be . . . in the writing room, nor the private rooms, nor the billiard hall, nor the bowling hall, nor the monstrous dining room, nor the casino dance hall, since that's readied for the grand ball tonight, nor the . . ."

"Thanks Tessie . . . .I will gamble on the parlor."

"And right you'll probably be. Should I move your paints out of the harsh sunlight, sugar?"

"Oh my, I do not remember putting them there."

"Yeh did when yeh come in . . . but with the mad rush and all, I plum forgot yeh did it myself." Tessie saw how excited her mistress was and wanted to ask her why. She never dreamed it was on account of a gentleman. Tessie reckoned that no man would ever fill the shoes of the late Mr. MacAdam.

Why, hadn't Tessie herself prayed Philippa MacAdam out of jumping right into that dark cold grave with her beloved husband?

The old black maid imagined her mistress for thirty-eight years now, how fast time passes, hurrying to the parlor as she sauntered over to a window. Tessie looked out at an overwhelming expanse of blue sky and green shorelines and shimmering waters of the Straits of Mackinac, filled with pleasure sailboats she called "sea butterflys" and other commercial "boats without sails." Overcome with ecstasy she gazed and gazed at the magnificent ten mile view, and finally focused in on the whitewashed church spires in the village below. The old woman whispered a prayer. From up on the third floor of a grand building, high up on a cliff, the enrapturing view before her seemed to swell to the very borders of heaven and pulsate to the rhythms of the heavenly host; and Tessie felt nearer to her God than she had ever felt before in her life.

Philippa entered the Grand Hotel's parlor and scanned the audience. They sat in a most agreeable and comfortable room decorated with hearty African curly palms and Australian elkhorn ferns, lively-looking oriental rugs and red damask draperies, white wicker rockers and overstuffed green sofas, American presidential portraits in gold-leaf frames and huge mahogany book cabinets, an eighteenth-century English secretary and a new player piano. And a couple of brass spittoons. Plain wooden chairs, occupied by resorters, were set in the middle of the large room. The little Egyptian had just begun lecturing.

Within a few seconds, Philippa recognized Professor Bellamy, Eugene Sullivan, Rutherford Haverhill, the Muldoons, the Prices, Belinda Gaines, the MaMas and daughters, the intellectual flirts and their beaus, the New Woman college girls, college men, the old maids, Old Stinkweed and crafty crackpots—but no Colonel Marshe Williamson. Let down, ever so slightly, Philippa glided over to one of the empty chairs next to the countess, Clare and Beatrice.

The little Egyptian lecturer gushed flowery borrowed words, which the audience recognized from a local newspaper, in an accent thick and musical. The Muldoons were the only two resorters who enjoyed his accent immensely.

"Among the jewels of the inland seas, the island of Mackinac rests fairest and foremost like a living emerald of rarest green amid a setting of exquisite pearls.

"This jewel throbs with life, and is radiant in its picturesque beauty. Nature was in ecstasy when the Creator touched this spot with the magic wand of beauty—the Earth smiled, the heavens sang, the heavens kissed the earth, and the kiss was Mackinac Island . . . ." The little Egyptian breathed heavily. From his sleeve, he dramatically drew a red handkerchief and waved it through the air in a broad arch.

"Truly fair and beautiful is this island, a queen among the resorts where man makes merry, where woman woos worldy wonders, where the tired body needs rest, where the fatigued brain requires recreation, where the soul seeks new inspiration for its winter's work. There are no bad eyes here. It is here that man can best prepare for the stern realities of life when the hallowed sounds of summer are transcribed into an ethereal anthem of action, joy, and praise . . . ."

The audience, as fond of Mackinac Island as the little Egyptian, began to wonder what his rhapsodizing had to do with the "Massacre at Fort Michilimackinac," which happened five miles from the island.

"It is here that the trials of the year are forgotten, the

troubles dispelled, and the tribulations wafted into nothingness, for nature is a lavish hero with her comforts and blessings for the weary. The perfectly pure air of the lake steals gladly through the pines and cedars and gladdens all with a new life. It brings rest and a new creation of the senses. Physical pain is touched by the balm of the atmosphere and is driven away . . ."

By now the audience members were shifting their well-padded weights upon the hard wooden chairs. The restless hypocondriac members of the crafty crackpots began hallucinating the odor of sneezeweeds, and started making little explosive noises while blowing their noses. The well-adjusted guests simply yawned.

The little Egyptian noticed he was losing the attention of his audience and, as if inspired, threw up both short arms, ripped a loud hole in his jacket under his left armpit, and shouted like a born-again preacher.

"The sun shines brightly here, with a new warmth that kisses the face and gives it a ruddy, healthy hue; the system is invigorated, a new energy is born. Man lives in the open air, is on friendly terms with the waters and the woods; he cherishes a new love for his fellow man, and grows more fond of his neighbor, especially if it be a pretty girl or a handsome woman, or a . . ."

Eugene "Sully" Sullivan clapped. The audience got his message and joined him. "What about the massacre at Fort Michilimackinac?" spoke up Sully in a friendly voice trying to get the lecturer on the subject.

The little Egyptian finally got the hint and replied, "Yes Mr. Sully, I will get to that without delay . . . without delay." He wondered why Mr. Sully was in such a hurry to hear about a massacre which went back one hundred years ago. Uh, he thought, all Americans are always in such a big hurry. Even in a big hurry to go backwards. Where do they think they are going anyways?

He finally began, "Genteel ladies and men. Across the straits from this enchanted island, this home to the giant Indian fairies, was Fort Michilimackinac. I'm sure all of you know your history," he added with masked sarcasm. The statement served him well, for the audience appeared more attentive.

"You will remember that the French and Indians were big buddies over there since the fort was built in 1715. You will also remember the fort was taken away from the French, in 1761, by the English. The Indians did not like the stuffy English controlling the fort and developed a bad eye for them.

"One day, the brave Indian chief Pontiac, who was fed up with the English at the fort, united all the tribes of the region for a sneaky attack on the English.

"The Indians banded together outside Fort Michilimackinac to honor the king of England's birthday in the summer of 1763, and began playing an exciting Indian game of baggatiway, pretending to celebrate the king's birthday. This game was played for great purpose. I will read to you of the exciting massacre that resulted from this game."

If the little Egyptian did not know that he made a big mistake in choosing to read, rather than creating a more favorable impression by extemporaneous speech, he did know what happened to his audience—when the world famous artist Sydney Chase Froilan entered the parlor. All eyes, bad or good, turned away from him and onto Sydney. The little Egyptian, feeling insulted and upstaged, quickly threw up his fat short arms, ripped a loud hole under his right armpit to match his left, and raised his voice to regain the audience.

Beatrice Venn's eyes observed that Sydney Froilan strolled

in wearing his worldly air, and looking cockier than when she met him in the morning. She wondered why Mr. Froilan, who had painted little Islamics riding big camels near the pyramids of Giza, chose to come to a lecture on obscure American history given by a little Egyptian muslim. Certainly Sydney had enough to do with them over there. And certainly after traveling around the world for four years, he could not hope to be entertained in the telling of a local massacre.

Sydney was quite amused when he saw the little Egyptian throwing his arms about. So amused that he forgot himself, and made a beeline for the chair next to Beatrice Venn. His conspicuous attention to Mrs. Venn was noticed by all.

Beatrice's cheeks brightened. She barely recognized Sydney. She knew the whole core of the full season guests would be wagging their tongues about Sydney's mistaken action after the lecture.

If Mrs. Beatrice Venn were not a well liked member of the admired group of four women, and if Sydney Chase Froilan were not a world famous artist, Sydney's tactless display would have compromised Mrs. Venn, and stamped Sydney as less than well bred.

Sydney Froilan, sitting uneasily next to stunning Mrs. Venn, realized his faux pas and the irony of it. He thought, half the world's men and women were running after each other cooing, "ready or not hear I come," whether bonded by the vows of matrimony, or not. Meanwhile, the second half of the world's men and women were pretending the game of illicit hide and go seek did not happen, but were secretly trying to catch the players hiding. He reasoned that was how the second half got in on the first half's play—and did not feel left out of the game.

On top of it all, Sydney's realization turned to embarrassment when the little Egyptian, indignant and more animated by the moment because of the upstaging, kept staring exclusively at Sydney and Beatrice as he lectured. The sneaky little foreigner happened to catch Beatrice hiding her eyes from Sydney, and saw Sydney go seek the eyes of Beatrice.

By this time, Sydney gathered that the tricky little muslim caught on to his faux pas and was gloating at innocent Mrs. Venn and himself, on purpose. Sydney determined to do something fast, as the little Egyptian, his head bobbing up and down, continued reading about the Indian game of baggatiway.

"At the beginning of the game the main body of the players assembles half-way between two posts. Every eye, bad or good, sparkles and every cheek is already aglow with excitement. The ball is tossed high in the air, and a general struggle ensues to secure it as it descends. He who succeeds starts for the goal of the adversary holding it high above his head . . . ."

The little Egyptian held a ball over his head, his armpit hole agape. In his other hand, he held a long handled stick with a triangular head and a loose mesh pouch for catching and carrying the ball.

"The opposite party, with merry yells, is swift to pursue it . . ."

"Whoopee!" shouted Sydney Froilan with abandon.

The audience was taken by surprise.

The little Egyptian, flustered, finally averted his eyes from Beatrice and Sydney and blurted, "His course is interrupted, and rather than see the ball taken from him, he throws it, as the boy throws a stone from a sling, as far toward the goal of his adversary as he can and—"

By this time Sydney Froilan had run up to the little Egyptian, grabbed the ball away and interrupted him calling out, "Eugene Sullivan . . . whoopee!" and threw the ball to Sully, who stood up and caught it right smack in the sock-er-roo.

"Now what do I do with it?" Sully called out, grinning boyishly.

The astonished audience laughed.

The little Egyptian did not know if the men were making fun, or making fun of him. So he continued unsurely, "An adversary catches it, and sends it whirling back in the opposite direction and—"

Sully threw the ball back to Sydney who jumped in front of the little Egyptian to catch it.

". . . hither and thither it goes; now far to the right . . ."

Sydney ran right up to Rutherford Haverhill, curtsied like a belle, and tried to hand him the ball.

Rutherford smiled, bowed comtemptuously, and waved Sydney away. It was well done. And it was hard to say if Sydney had made a fool of Rutherford and the foreigner in one stroke . . . or Rutherford had made a fool of Sydney making a fool of the foreigner.

". . . now to the far left; now near the one goal . . ."

Without uttering a discourteous sound, Sydney turned and threw the ball to a college man standing away from the audience, who threw it to a fraternity brother, who threw it to Sully. The little Egyptian kept on talking, trying to regain an audience thoroughly delighted with the show.

" . . . now as near to the other goal; the whole band crowding continually after it in the wildest confusion, until, finally some agile figure, more fleet of foot than others, succeeds in bearing it to the goal of the opposite party and then . . ."

Sydney began running around the room passing the ball at close range to one college man after another game enough to enter the charade.

" . . . as many as six or seven hundred Indians sometimes engage in a single game, while it may be played by fifty. In the heat of the contest, when all are running at their greatest speed, if one stumbles and falls, fifty or a hundred who are in close pursuit and unable to stop, pile over him and . . ."

Sully started running after Sydney followed by a pack of college men. Sydney made one flying leap landing on the oriental rug under the oriental lecturer's feet. Sully fell on top of Sydney shouting "whoopee!" and the college men piling one by one on top of both of them, chanted apologetically, "Whoops!—oops!—Whoops!"

". . . and formed a mound of human bodies . . ."

The audience roared. The women especially loved the show.

The flustered little Egyptian did not know what to do so he plowed on, " . . . and frequently players are so bruised as to be unable to proceed in the game." He hoped Sydney or Sully were bruised enough to discontinue the distracting rough housing.

Quietly, the pile of athletic-looking men struggled up, red-faced after the splurge of energy, making toothy smiles, and rambled back to their respective seats. Except for Sydney. This time around, Sydney sat next to Sully.

Beatrice Venn appreciated this action, and Mr. Froilan's considerate comical distraction from his former inconsideration. For with all the excitement, guests would be gossiping later more about the wild ruckus at the massacre lecture, than the faux pas committed by Mr. Froilan in sitting next to Beatrice Venn.

The little Egyptian, maroon-faced and oily from all the excitement, continued reading short of breath, "This game, with its attendant noise and violence, was well calculated to divert the attention of English officers and men, and thus permit the Indians to take possession of the fort.

"To make their success more certain, they prevailed upon as many English as they could to come out of the fort, while at the same time their squaws, wrapped in blankets beneath which they concealed the murderous weapons, were placed inside the enclosure.

"The plot was so ingeniously laid that no one suspected danger. The discipline of the garrison was relaxed, and the English soldiers were permitted to stroll about and view the sport without weapons of defense," read the little Egyptian, who began to calm down and perk up for all eyes were upon him once again.

With renewed vigor he continued reading, his head bent over, his voice growing bolder and louder with every word. "And even when the ball, as if by chance, was lifted high in the air, to descend inside the wooden pickets of the fort, and was followed by four hundred Indian savages, all eager, all struggling, all shouting, in the unrestrained pursuit of a rude, athletic exercise, no alarm was felt until the shrill war-whoop told the startled garrison that the slaughter, the massacre at Fort Michilimackinac, had actually begun."

The little Egyptian's eyes practically popped out of his head when he looked up, for Eugene Sullivan was standing next to him with a shiny scalping knife. Sully suddenly grabbed him and held the sharp knife above his dark wavy hair. The audience giggled expectantly. The little Egyptian tittered not knowing any more what was real and unreal among these crazy Americans. He decided to close the lecture before things got out of hand.

Perspiring and dry mouthed, he licked his chubby lips and managed to sputter, "Nearly the entire garrison was indiscriminately massacred by the Indians. Years later the fort was removed to this island for greater protection. Thank you genteel ladies and men."

Eugene released the little Egyptian, who ran like a frightened fattened calf out of the parlor and plowed right into Jimmy Hayes.

"I lecture no more for you. No more."

"What's the problem?" Jimmy asked.

Eugene Sullivan appeared and winked at Jimmy.

The little Egyptian ranted, "I lecture no more. I lecture no more."

Jimmy and his friend Sully pulled the little man further down the immense hallway, away from the parlor door and guests' ears.

Jimmy asked, "But the Shah of Harremajarra, when is he coming? You promised me you had made arrangements for his coming here enroute to the world's fair. In turn, I gave you room and board, and in turn you lecture only when you feel like it. For three weeks now I have been waiting for confirmation of the shah's arrival, and feeding you well and providing you with a comfortable room. Where is the confirmation, Ibrahim?" For Jimmy, the Shah of Harremajarra would have been a real publicity getter.

"The shah is on his way . . . on his way. He is traveling incognito."

"But do you have this in writing?"

"In writing . . . in writing . . . you Americans always have to have everything in writing. A man's word is not enough for you."

"Well, Ibrahim, maybe it is for the best that you leave. I have given you free room and board for three weeks, and you have given me nothing."

"The shah will come . . . but I will leave!"

Sully could not resist poking fun at what he considered a comical liar and dropped, "Does this mean he will miss the cigar and umbrella race, Jimmy?"

Before Jimmy Hayes could answer the little Egyptian clamored, "Cigar and umbrella race. Cigar and umbrella race. That's all you Americans think of. Your pleasure. In the rest of the world poor people have no food. No such enjoyments. Even in your own fertile country the poor suffer. I spit on your cigar and umbrella race."

Jimmy Hayes gripped Ibrahim's arm tightly and uttered strongly, "And I spit on your goddamn lies. I will make arrangements for you to leave at once. And I suggest you do so quietly if you know what is good for you . . . ."

The audience cleared out of the parlor and strolled to the veranda for the cigar and umbrella race to come. Sydney Froilan walked out surrounded by a flock of fawning ladies, who gradually left his larger than life presence. The group of four women were the last to leave, and Sydney fell back from the crowd and approached Mrs. Venn in the hallway, away from prying eyes. The countess, Clare and Philippa stood a protective distance from Beatrice and Mr. Froilan.

Beatrice spoke before Sydney had a chance. In low if friendly tones, she admonished him, "Mr. Froilan, when I agreed to—sit for you—this morning, I did not mean—sit with you—this afternoon at a public lecture, after only one brief introductory meeting."

"I was obvious. I apologize, Mrs. Venn. But I shall grow more obvious, I warn you."

"Then I must warn you, Mr. Froilan, that I am not attracted to obviousness."

"Then, Mrs. Venn, you should view the paintings I usually do not show. My genre scenes. They are full of masked symbolism. You would enjoy the subterfuge . . . ."

"Perhaps . . ."

"Would it be improper to ask if it would be proper to sit with you for the cigar and umbrella race?"

"I am sitting with my children, four-year-old Frederick, and ten-year-old Monica, and their nanny, and Professor Bellamy, and Countess Gianotti, and Mrs. Philippa Mac-Adam, and Mrs. Clare Gilbertson."

"I see . . . then I must join the race and you will . . . perhaps . . . secretly . . . cheer me on?"

"Perhaps . . ."

Sydney flashed a charming smile at Beatrice. He noticed her face brighten up like tarnished sterling—polished. But her lips remained closed as she smothered the pleasure she felt in his presence. As much as she tried to deny it to herself, Beatrice always fell for cock of the walk types. With one refinement. The cock had to walk an uncharacteristic straight and narrow path without bends or turn-offs. A straight path toward Beatrice Venn.

The spectators gathered on the western end of the 650 foot veranda for the cigar and umbrella race to come. Directly below them, standing on the road that led past the Grand Hotel to large lavish cottages on the west bluff, were all the swell men who generally agreed to participate in the race— only after Jimmy Hayes promised them a Pilsener beer on the house after their efforts.

Jimmy did not have to bribe the college men with beer. They claimed they would join in just for the fun of it, but would, most certainly and most graciously, accept a beer for their efforts. The truth was that the race gave the college "men" an opportunity to show off before the college "girls."

"All right, good fellows," Jimmy called out, "listen up and we'll be ready to start. Each one of you will be given a cigar, matches, and an umbrella. At the word go, you are to light your cigar, raise your umbrella, and run like an Injun. The first gentleman under the wire near the porte-cochere, with a lighted cigar mind you, wins the race and a box of genuine, premium, Havanna cigars. So pull up your britches . . . ready your cigars and umbrellas . . . get set . . . go!"

Some thirty men lit their cigars, raised their umbrellas and took off full steam ahead. One of the Harvard men got it wrong and raised his umbrella before lighting his cigar.

Spectators on the veranda cheered for their favorite man on

the road below, as he fought the gusts of wind playing havoc with his umbrella. Jimmy Hayes ran alongside boosting the racers boisterously. Some racers stopped to relight their cigars. One lost his umbrella to the wind.

Eugene Sullivan was in the lead with the young Cudahy boys close behind, followed by other swagger resorters such as Marshall Fields Jr., Robert T. Fort, Honorable Hempstead Washburn, James Gallagher, J.M. Hughs, Darby Hull, Chug Byram, Alexander P. Hannah, Sydney Froilan and others.

Philippa MacAdam, growing disappointed, searched the crowd for Colonel Marshe Williamson over and over again.

Clare Gilbertson had one eye on the straits, where six yachts, including Philmore Calhoun's *Calla* in a class by itself, were racing around the five-mile buoy and back; Philmore Calhoun was not exaggerating when he said that *Calla* was fast.

Beatrice Venn, watching the cigar and umbrella race, saw that Sydney Froilan could not, for the the life of him, get his umbrella under control because of the air currents. She laughed. Though she was still undecided whether to secretly cheer Sydney on or not.

"Countess Gianotti, what do you think of this cigar and umbrella race?" Even if the countess had not recognized the voice, she could have guessed who would ask such a dampening question in the middle of the excitement. She also knew that by Rutherford Haverhill's tone of voice, he thought it corny.

"What do I think, Mr. Haverhill? I think I should have a hard time keeping my cigar lit," the countess countered with a smile. She gently placed her hand on little Frederick Venn's shoulder; he was rooting for the Cudahys, and jumping up and down for the pure excitement of it all.

All too soon the cigar and umbrella race was over. Eugene Sullivan claimed victory and passed out the premium Havana cigars he won to the men who had competed with him. The racers' jovial camaraderie affected the onlookers, who broke out into exuberant applause. Jimmy Hayes invited all the racers for a drink while most of them relit their racing cigars.

"I heard that the Empress of Austria smokes several strong cigars by night and smokes fifty Turkish cigarettes by day," said Rutherford Haverhill, who loved to be seen conversing with the countess, and tried again that day to strike up a conversation on a friendly basis—without disguised passes. He thought that talk about royalty would be much more to the countess' taste than discussing the silly, childish, fun and games they had just witnessed.

"Although doctors warn us against the smoking habit, it is surprising how lovely the empress' teeth are in spite of her excessive smoking," replied the countess politely.

Rutherford thrived on this kind of privy information about royalty, coming from the lovely mouth of one who knew kings and queens personally.

A gentleman's voice not familiar to the countess intervened before Rutherford could continue, "I saw a woman arrested in Paris a few months ago, because she puffed away on a cigarette in the street."

Anna turned and recognized the familiar stranger she had bowed to in the village that morning. Rutherford recognized his new acquaintance from the sportsmen's group, Richard Anders.

"Anders . . . so you were in Paris for its season as well . . . why did we not run into each other? I think smoking is a dirty habit for men, but for women, it is sinful." Rutherford noticed younger Richard Anders smiling openly at the countess. "Countess Gianotti, allow me to introduce Richard Anders . . . recently arrived . . . who is a son of a cottager."

Of all the weighty accomplishments which Rutherford knew about Richard Anders, like millionaire race horse gambler and champion rower, he called Richard "a son of a cottager." He might as well have called him a son of a bitch; it would have been a helluva lot more colorful description in the eyes of a woman, if not a lady.

Rutherford intentionally, ungenerously, avoided an interesting description of Richard Anders. But then Richard Anders' manner was strong enough to prove himself interesting without listing his many accomplishments. Much to Rutherford's disappointment. And much more to Richard Anders' esteem in the opinion of the countess.

"I am glad to meet you, Mr. Anders. At last . . . ." Anna smiled warmly, and bowed slightly with slow and measured dignity. Richard Anders returned the bow, but far more deeply.

"I thought you had not met," intoned Rutherford.

"Not formally," pronounced Richard, openly smiling at the countess' eyes and thinking them similar in color to a blue jay's wings.

Rutherford felt caught in a crossfire. Never had the countess released such enveloping warmth in his presence before. Proud Rutherford Haverhill suspected that he himself had probably not aroused it in her.

It would have been no surprise to find Rutherford envious of Richard Anders' instant appeal. But he was not. He became envious of the countess' ability—to release such feeling. Rutherford Earle Haverhill V, one of the richest men from one of the oldest families in America, who could recognize beauty and feeling in life and art—could not express deep feelings himself.

The countess tried to feel out Richard Anders and said in a friendly manner, "I assume you are not staying at the Grand."

"That is right. My father has a cottage in the Annex. Though I would much prefer to stay here."

"Where is the Annex, Anders?"

"It is beyond the west bluff cottages, Haverhill."

"Where do you call home, Mr. Anders?" the countess asked in a mildly interested fashion.

"Wherever there is a racetrack." Richard Ander's look sparkled with the frivolity of a gambler and the spontaneous warmth of a man of the world. In a mere five words he told more about himself then most people tell after three paragraphs. It was not only what he said, but the way he said it, and the way he looked when he said it.

Whether or not he really was the worldly-wise warm young gentleman he appeared to be, the countess had yet to determine. She knew his type was as rare as truffles in America. Though there were thousands who acted the role with great aplomb in the new world.

Yes, Richard Anders, turning thirty years of age, not only displayed the dash, verve and similar experience of Rutherford Haverhill some ten years older, he showed a freshness and sense of humor which Rutherford, who took life as humorlessly as a Norwegian metaphysician, probably never possessed.

The countess thought that there would be a hundred young feminine traps set for Richard, and a hundred old feminine traps set to avoid such a match. Every girl pined for such a swashbuckling type of man. But no MaMa wanted her daughter married to one. And definitly not a swashbuckler with the modern vocation of a race horse gambler.

Why, a MaMa who would even consider such a thing, might as well sacrifice her precious girl to a Russian roulette player. The MaMas perceived little difference between the two bravado actions. No, a race horse gambler, who never did a day's work, was no matrimonial match. Although he may be rich today, tomorrow he might be as poor as a debtor's prison mouse. Even the most aggressive MaMas did not want their daughters to suffer such sanctioned uncertainty.

"When I am not at a racetrack I am in London or Paris or New York," Richard added in a matter-of-fact, unaffected tone, "and I arrived on the island a few days ago from Chicago. Have you both seen the world's fair?"

After the countess and Rutherford replied in the affirmative, Richard Anders eagerly asked, "What did you think of it, Countess?"

"I found it strangely picturesque, Mr. Anders. To see boats and gondolas sailing in temporary lagoons, surrounded by temporary buildings of magestic proportion . . . to see this in a prairie city in the middle of the west which did not exist one hundred years ago . . . was as disconcerting to me as seeing the Grand Hotel and the new cottages for the first time on this primitive, remote island. Yet, the lagoons at the fair mirrored the floating godolas in way which rivaled Venice. I have spent a lot of time in Venice, Mr. Anders, and never thought I would be comparing Chicago to that fascinating city."

Richard Anders and Rutherford chuckled. Richard encouraged the countess with more questions about the fair, while Rutherford kept quiet, observing that the countess never spoke quite so enthusiastically and openly in his presence before. Proud Rutherford suspected her lively expression might have something to do with younger Richard Anders. Though Rutherford could not understand what the countess found appealing in a race horse gambler.

The countess explained, "I was sent to Chicago by Queen Marguerite to oversee the safe arrival of her priceless collection of laces. Some of the laces, from Egyptian and Etruscan tombs, date one thousand years before the birth of Christ. Did you both see the collection of her laces?"

Richard Anders owned up to not having set foot in the Women's Building.

Rutherford, who covered every inch of it claimed, "Yes, I

saw the outstanding Italian laces . . . and . . . a mouse scampering about them." Rutherford managed, as usual, to throw a dampening spirit into the circumstances of what he perceived as a budding older woman—younger man friendship, so common at the Grand Hotel and all hotels like it throughout the world.

Richard saw the countess' face cloud in concern for the laces, which she was ultimately responsible for.

The countess decided to send Mrs. Potter Palmer a telegraph about the mouse that very afternoon. In the meantime, she was not about to let Rutherford Haverhill think he disturbed her. She even wondered if Rutherford made up the fishy mouse story in order to trouble her, because of her rejecting his romantic advances that morning.

Countess Gianotti smiled and said, "I enjoyed the fair for an entire week and saw just about everything, including the city of Chicago and its people. Mrs. Potter Palmer saw to it that I had invitations at least twice a day. I do not know where she found the time to make arrangements for such gracious introductions, considering her position of leadership at the Women's Building. I attended all the invitations she arranged for me, and I found the hospitality in Chicago quite Russian."

Rutherford asked in his most anglophiliac voice, "Do you mean Russian hospitality . . . in the sense of . . . barbarism?"

"Only if Russian hospitality is a . . . relic of barbarism, Mr. Haverhill. True . . . heartfelt hospitality . . . as I enjoyed in that prairie city . . . is seldom experienced anywhere in society these days," the countess counterblowed with the sweetness of a madonna.

The countess and Richard Anders, both western born, understood the eastern man's slur against Chicagoans. Although Richard Anders was originally from Michigan, he could not have cared less what the eastern society man thought of western society. But he rallied behind the countess out of respect for her adroit answer, and decided to take on Rutherford Earle Haverhill V for the fun of it. And to show off his verbal skills in front of the most captivating woman he had ever met.

Rutherford continued talking about Chicago, hoping to ruffle the countess' composure. "When I was in the black city, I saw nothing I enjoyed but the white city, in other words, the fair. I stayed away from the black city, smothered by black smoke, as much as possible. Those boisterous buildings in the black city, how can they call them architecture? No width, all height, so unlike European buildings. A mixed up composite of Byzantine, Roman, Gothic, somehow become painfully modern. But the domestic architecture . . . well . . . the word—odd—comes most readily to mind."

"Haverhill, I beg to differ."

"Anders, please do."

"Chicago architecture is a medley of styles. An ingenious confusion. A harmonious discord. As for the domestic architecture, if you had been invited to their castles complete with turreted gables and inviting porches, I wager you would find them highly imaginative. Their interiors are filled with antique furniture and tapestries and paintings, just like out east. Art and literature are discussed within their walls. Why, I have heard child labor and women's rights discussed and debated among Chicago society women. They even open their castle drawbridges to those less fortunate. Is that a fair description, Countess? Does it meet with your observations?"

"I could not have said it more eloquently, Mr. Anders," the countess replied with an ironic smile, delighted to learn that Richard Anders was an entertaining conversationalist.

Amused, Rutherford had not expected a race horse gambler and rower to speak as well. But then Rutherford did not know that Richard Anders graduated from Harvard with a double degree in law and literature, followed by a year of study in Heidelberg. The subject: philosophy.

The closest Rutherford ever got to the university at Heidelberg—was Baden-Baden for the baths. Although he had a mere twelve credits to complete, Rutherford had not bothered to graduate from Yale in liberal studies. With all the monetary numbers and generations behind the Haverhill name, he did not feel the need for letters like BFA or Ph.D. behind his name as well. To Rutherford, academics, or "professional students" as he called them, were as "necessary as clergy."

Rutherford continued, "I have never seen such dirty streets as those in the black city."

Richard answered, "I have never seen such a diverse confrontation of people, sights, and sounds. Splendid parks lie adjacent to acres of wasteland. Grand architecture loaded down with onyx walls and mosaic floors stands next to breweries, oyster palaces, winerooms, beer saloons and public houses."

"Forgive my candor, but I could not stomach the stench of the slaughter houses," Rutherford stated without a repentant note in his voice.

"Forgive my candor," lampooned Richard," but the blood of the pigs flows like a red flood in the stockyards. And Chicago's butchers . . . such philanthropic butchers. Are you aware, Haverhill, that some of those multimillionaire butchers have cottages on this island . . . such as the Cudahys, the Armours . . ."

Rutherford was not interested in hearing of any more ultra rich society upstarts. He could not remember one tenth of the new names as it was. "Are you aware, Anders, there are only 300,000 native Americans in a city of one million one hundred thousand?"

"Surely, Haverhill, there are not that many Indians in Chicago," Richard said wryly. "I know of Poles, Swedes, Germans, and Irish, Negroes, Bohemians, and Israelites—a human multinational flood without our langauge and ignorant of our law. And I know Chicago's women try to help these exiles in a new world relieve their poverty in this age of unrelenting competition. Countess Gianotti, you will excuse us for our exclusive discussion."

"Mr. Anders, please do not hesitate to continue your discussion on my account. All this brings to mind an interview in the papers with Ward McAllister, which I read. His appraisal of Chicago society left many from that most interesting city— livid. It caused somewhat of a national stir among those who are affected by such comments. Are you aware of it, Mr. Anders?"

"Countess, I have heard it mentioned but did not read that fop's comments myself."

"Wait a minute, my good man," interjected Rutherford insincerely, "I must inform you that Ward McAllister is a close acquaintance of mine. Though right now most of New York society looks the other way when he passes by. Ever since he wrote that scintillating book."

"I understand, Haverhill, and will curb my contempt for the man in your presence. However, I missed his stinging words about Chicago society, and like most people, society or otherwise, I am curious to read the articles under the most malicious headlines."

"Well then, Anders, I just happen to have a copy of the article in my coat pocket. Would you care to read it? And before you do, please rest assured that I did not condone these statements made by Ward McAllister. He went too far with the truth. Too much truth destroys, not enlightens."

The countess and Richard wondered what Rutherford could

have meant when he said that he did not "condone these statements."

Rutherford took the newspaper article out of his coat pocket. It looked as starched and clean and pressed as a fresh handkerchief. Instead of handing it to Richard passively, he seized the moment to dominate the threesome, and to read snappy snippets from Ward McAllister's hot and spicy comments aloud.

"The contrast of New York and Chicago society during the World's Fair cannot help but open the eyes of our Western natives to our superiority . . . .I do not need wish to belittle Chicago in using the word 'superiority' . . . .The society of Chicago is behind that of New York, but there is no reason why it should not eventually catch up . . . .

"I could name many men and women who have been forced to spend a large part of their early lives in the West, but who have nevertheless established themselves in good positions in Eastern society. . . . I may say that it is not quantity but quality that society people here want. Hospitality which includes the whole human race is not desirable . . . .We, in New York, are familiar with the sharp character of the Chicago magnates."

Rutherford knew he had opened a Pandora's box, and now he was curious as to what Richard would say to impress the countess. He knew that Richard Anders was not the type of man to take society seriously, and really did not care what old has-been Ward McAllister had to say. He also knew that Richard Anders cared very much what the countess thought of him, and would choose his words carefully to win her charming approval.

Richard looked Rutherford straight in the eye and responded, "Haverhill, would you agree that Ward McAllister's remarks are hardly worthy . . . for as to sharp characters, New York society is based on the Astor fur thieves who had a base here on Mackinac Island, and Jay Gould's and Fisk's outright swindling and stealing from orphans and widows, and Commodore Vanderbilt's well-known lecheries and disreputable commercial maneuverings, and J. P. Morgan's stock-kiting, clubbing of small companies, and womanizing, and John D. Rockefeller's illegally breaking strikers and competitors with the hiring of Pinkerton for murder in Colorado, not to mention burning out rivals' oil fields.

"I could name some sharp characters among the Chicago magnates . . . but not one to rival the whoring cast of New York society whose vast fortunes were founded on the corrupt abuse of integrity and honesty."

Rutherford laughed and stated, "Well said, Anders, I quite agree. But do not rant too loudly about the Pinkerton name. Mrs. Pinkerton of Colorado is sitting but twenty feet away." Rutherford cleverly managed to quell the impact of Richard's enlightened speech by warning him of potential embarrassment. If Rutherford had not warned him, the countess would have.

Rutherford continued, "Not all of New York society is based upon your exaggerated claims. There are a few of us left who were established long before these new arrivals, and some of us have a spirit democratic enough to accept the newly arrived. Let me add, I would not be at the Grand Hotel on Mackinac Island in the north woods, even though it is a most beautiful setting, if I were not democratic about society.

"Getting back to Ward McAllister . . . not only is he newly arrived in New York society . . . and already dismissed . . . he makes himself obvious when he asks in the newspapers," Rutherford read from the article, " 'Really, an exposition to honor who? Christopher Columbus? In a social way Columbus was an ordinary man.' His remark about Columbus' ordinariness . . . well . . . even I do not agree with that. Granted, McAllister is absolutely correct about New York and Chicago society, but I did not agree to his talking, through his hat, about the acute differences of New York and Chicago society to the pencil pushing press."

Rutherford was to change his tune about New York and Chicago society when he met Mrs. Potter Palmer, queen of Chicago and the world's fair Women's Building, at the Grand later that season.

Richard commented, "McAllister is some sort of actor. Decadent remarks are his opium . . ."

"Oh no . . .no no no . . . the man is terriby bourgeois. He actually believes what he says. In fact," Rutherford drew long looks out of the countess and Richard, "in fact, McAllister usually quotes me."

The countess and Richard were both taken by surprise and could not help but show it. But it was the countess who knew from her morning conversation with Rutherford that his greatest wish was to improve the masses, and to instruct the bourgeosie who pretended to his class. Never in her wildest imagination would she have dreamed that Rutherford Earle Haverhill V hid behind Ward McAllister's mouthpiece for that purpose, without anyone, including McAllister himself, realizing Rutherford's masterful manipulation.

The countess changed the subject and directed her attention to Richard. "Have you been to Italy, Mr. Anders?"

"Next to Switzerland, Italy is my favorite country, Countess Gianotti."

"Have you by any chance been introduced at the court of Queen Marguerite?"

"No, I have been introduced only in England. I have turned down the few other court introductions offered to me."

Rutherford, who jumped at court introductions, could not believe his ears.

Richard continued, "Please understand, Countess, I am not indifferent to European royalty and aristocracy, unlike many

Americans, but it seems they always want something of me. Tips about horses, racing, that sort of thing. In fact, I have noticed they always want something from the Americans, but never want the Americans themselves." He glanced at Rutherford.

"I see, Mr. Anders. I must explain my questions. I feel as if I have met you somewhere in Europe."

"I know I have never met you, Countess Gianotti. I would remember," Richard's eyes sparkled, "and you may ask as many questions of me as you wish. Perhaps . . . at the grand ball this evening . . . you will honor me with some more questions set to *L' Invitation à la valse*. I overheard Mr. Salisbury say he will be conducting it this evening."

"You have struck upon my favorite waltz, Mr. Anders. I would be delighted and will write your name upon my dance card next to it.

Rutherford observed the countess a shade shaken.

Richard did not. For he took out his pocket watch and stated, "Please excuse me Countess Gianotti, Haverhill, but I must hurry to be late for tea with my father. He will be peeved I am not on time. He is an extraordinarily punctual man who believes a great life is composed of little charges faithfully kept, and little burdens cheerfully borne." Richard smiled without reverence for his father's disposition. "It was an honor to have met and spoken with you, Countess."

"Thank you, Mr. Anders. I look forward to *L' Invitation à la valse* this evening.

"Richard asked, "See you this evening, Haverhill?"

"Of course." Rutherford waited until Richard was just beyond hearing range, gazed down at the countess' glowing eyes following Richard's exit, and admitted, "The man has wit and understanding . . . for one so young . . . ."

"Not so young, Mr. Haverhill . . . Mr. Anders is not much younger than yourself."

Rutherford smarted from Anna's unusual interest in Richard Anders. He replied, "It is the times. Superior education, world travel, money, personal achievement . . . all these advantages ripen youth very fast. I often wonder what will become in the end of such old youth. I suspect a deep cynicism or worse complete intolerance for the dull and mundane."

"Perhaps . . . .Yet you, Mr. Haverhill, had all these same advantages . . ."

"Yes . . . ." For the first time in three weeks, Rutherford let down for one moment. That one "yes" betrayed a biting truth. Having achieved all there was to achieve in life, he was like Richard Anders, in desperate pursuit of personal happiness and someone to share it with. That someone would have to reflect himself. It was like searching for a treasure without a map. Everything had come so easily to Rutherford. Everything but personal happiness. Everything but the ability to feel deeply.

The countess and Rutherford watched Richard walk away swinging his heavy walking stick like all the young men in Paris, who were trying to build up their arm muscles. When Richard was out of sight, the countess gazed out silently at the shimmering straits, and the racing yachts, their sails swelling in the Great Lakes' breezes.

Rutherford thought to himself, look at the woman Anders chooses . . . a countess . . . a youngish grand dame . . . married . . . older. But of what interest could the young budding beauties of limited experience be to Anders? He wants to live life now. Not wait for a college girl . . . as bright as they are . . . to grow up and be able to converse beyond fifteen minutes. They cannot even sit still that long . . . they have to be off riding their bicycles, or rowing against the waves of the straits, or riding in the woods . . . proving . . . always proving their artful physical abilities. But conversation? They have none. Anders . . . so young . . . sees all this clearly. I did not at his age. How will the countess handle this ardent young admirer? I think I will stay another week to see how this infatuation develops.

"I think I will be staying on another week, Countess Gianotti."

"I can understand why."

"Can you?" inquired Rutherford.

"Yes. The island is too beautiful to leave."

"Yes . . . ."

If Rutherford Earle Haverhill V's dispassionate curiosity about Richard Anders and the countess had not gotten the better of him, he would have travelled back to Newport. Back to the same well-worn, worn out cast of rich cut-out characters.

Rutherford saw that Richard Anders was looking for some-one to share his life. He also perceived that Richard, some ten years younger than himself, was capable of deep feeling and of arousing the countess' interest. Rutherford envied Richard's capability, for he did not possess it himself. Rutherford needed someone . . . to teach him to feel deeply. How he suddenly longed for more than the parasitical life of a fancy animal, as he called it. At that moment, with the lovely countess standing next to him, instead of conversing with her, Rutherford's mind, as if a loom interlacing yarns of truth, finally contrived to realize after forty years of living, that life without passion of deep feeling was merely a series of self-indulgent survival tactics.

Yes, Rutherford's quick decision to stay on at the Grand Hotel was to have far-reaching effects. For if Rutherford had left the island, he would have missed what became the most passionate time of his entire life.

In the long run, the rest of Rutherford's life would have been easier without having suffered the passion of deep feeling, which was to introduce itself to him a number of days later. But

Rutherford's life, without the peculiar passion to come, would have remained as empty as it was that very moment he made the decision to stay a little while longer on Mackinac Island. For someone outside of the group of four women, someone outside of society, was to change his life.

"Mr. Haverhill," the countess interrupted his thoughts, "this evening, if you are free, would you attend the grand ball as my escort?"

Rutherford's mouth dropped open, gaping like a mountain peasant seeing a stranger cross his remote path. He was so surprised that he hesitated before his answer. When he finally answered, he spoke in an accent which sounded almost American.

"Countess Gianotti, you honor me with such a request. I am free to escort you and hope you will consent to dance one waltz with me." Rutherford's voice almost sounded pathetic he was so tickled with her request.

"Mr. Haverhill, thank you for honoring my request. I should very much like to dance a waltz with you, if not two." The countess noticed Rutherford beaming and began to soften her heart just a bit toward him. She began to see that Rutherford could barely help who he was. And in what he was—he was sincere. Obnoxiously sincere.

Also, she needed another neutral gentleman, besides Professor Bellamy, to accompany herself and her three friends to the grand ball that evening. Little did Rutherford know that if another neutral Professor Bellamy type were known to the four women, they would have chosen that type to escort them instead.

And little did Rutherford know that he was to escort two ladies that evening. The countess reasoned against all the rules of fair play, if not etiquette itself, that there was no point in bothering Rutherford with that little detail, until he came for her that evening. Why ruin his anticipation. That was half the fun of a grand ball. The countess knew that Rutherford would have felt used rather than honored. So a careful explanation later would honor Rutherford even more. After all, how many eligible gentleman at the Grand Hotel would even dream of accompanying—two—members from the universally admired Big Four.

Rutherford, obviously excited, excused himself for tea. But he really rushed to personally pick out the most beautiful orchids for the countess to carry to the ball. He trusted no one, not even the florist, to really know how to choose the most beautiful orchids extant on Mackinac Island.

The countess heard Frederick and Monica Venn giggle, and rejoined her group. Jimmy Hayes, after a drink with the cigar and umbrella racers, had stopped to chat a few moments with the children and Professor Bellamy.

"Have you any rinktumditty for tea?" asked the professor with a wink at Jimmy.

"Not only don't we have it, Professor, why, great scissors, I do not know what rinktumditty is made of." Jimmy pronounced the funny sounding word comically, causing the children to giggle, and causing the four ladies to enjoy the little ones' merriment.

Professor Bellamy explained, "It is cheese, seasoned tomato sauce and egg served on toast."

"We would like rinktumditty! Please, Mr. Hayes?" enjoined the happy-looking children.

Jimmy bent down to the children's level and said, "We do not have rinktumditty so . . . how about . . . some . . . pigfish?"

"Pigfish?" the children guffawed, anticipating something funny.

"Ever heard-a saltwater grunt?" asked Jimmy, his eyes as mischievous as Owen Corrigan's after a visit to the beer shop.

"Noooo . . . does it sound like this?" Four-year-old

Frederick misunderstood and grunted, "Oink, oink!" Then inhaling loudly through his nose, he let out a rip roaring—snort. Nanna shushed little Frederick just as he was about to let another snort go.

"Very similar indeed . . . well . . . if you would rather not have pigfish for tea, how about hasenpfeffer and hasty pudding?"

"Nooooo . . . thank you . . . we would like tea and cakes!"

"Tea and cakes? At four o'clock in the afternoon?" Jimmy asked disbelievingly. "All right. Sounds good to me. Tea and cakes it is then. Come follow me, children."

Professor Bellamy, holding the children's hands, and Beatrice, Clare, Philippa and the countess, all followed Jimmy into the hotel for tea. The four women had so much to confide in each other. The "so much" meaning disguised talk about Sydney Chase Froilan, Philmore Calhoun, Colonel Marshe Williamson, and allusions to Richard Anders.

Every guest the group strolled past noticed that the Big Four looked more radiant than ever. They thought Beatrice Venn a wonderful mother and her three companions delightful adopted aunts.

Especially the old maids and MaMas and daughters and college girls examined the glowing women and happy children passing by. These onlookers assumed, instinctively, that the four women's radiance had something to do with gentlemen.

Yes, the four women's radiance fell like raining fire upon the feminine onlookers, to illuminate their faces and heat up their anticipation for the grand ball that evening. Without it being stated, mating fever was in the air and spreading like wildfire.

6

Expectation Waltz

"Oh, how lovely!"

"Well done . . ."

Hundreds of lips buzzed excited exclamations, while exhilarating melodies from the overture to *Die Fledermaus* tickled hundreds of ears. Guests glided into the casino ballroom and the festive spirit of the first gala ball of the Grand Hotel's 1893 season.

Hundreds of expectant eyes gazed about the casino ballroom. They looked up and to their amazement saw billowy snow white bunting, two thousand yards of it, flowing across the ballroom ceiling in rolling masses of fabric, like frozen waves of ice. Row upon row of festooned laurel branches, aglow with electric lights, decorated the fabric furrows of the white ceiling waves so cooling to summer eyes.

Cozy corners enclosed by ornamental evergreens, and African palms, and boxes defined by carved wooden railings, surrounded a dance floor as shiny as glass. Voluptuous bouquets of hothouse roses and orchids and lilies of the valley and stephanotis scented the soft air, alive with contagious temptation. Temptation—to seize a brief moment of bliss

The balcony above the dance floor, hung with national emblems energized by incandescent lamps, was crowded with resorters like the Muldoons, Old Stinkweed and the crafty crackpots, the oldest old maids, old couples, and old transients. These spectators in the gallery, except for Old Stink-

159

weed, enjoyed looking down upon the romantic fantasy picture.

Five calcium lights shot pastel blue, yellow, and red beams of illumination upon women's gleaming white necks and arms and shoulders, as they were whirled about the dance floor in colorful costumes of rustling satins, silks, and laces, their long trains held gracefully, their jewels flashing. The couples danced in an elaborate maze of motion to "On the Beautiful Blue Danube," the first waltz of the grand ball.

MaMas and chaperones lined the walls, and a rosebud garden of young women in flowing gauzy gowns sat in front of them. Between the ensuing promenades and waltzes and polkas and quadrilles and pas de quatres and marches and galops, young women returned to their seats, and eligible gentlemen, dressed in black swallow tail coats and low cut waistcoats and vicuna trousers and white lawn ties and pearl studded shirts and patent pumps, crowded around the MaMas and chaperones making dancing engagements with the young women of their choice by writing their names on ballcards in pencil. Sounds of voices repeating the same formulas could be heard floating up to the gallery.

"Will you honor me with your hand for the quadrille?"

"May I have the honor of dancing the next set with you?"

"Thank you, I shall be very glad."

"This is our dance, I believe."

Elsewhere, groups of lively people congregated or promenaded around the ballroom floor. Ladies without male escorts did not wander about the ballroom but sat together in boxes. Ladies accompanied by their husbands did wander about and were complimented by other husbands and bachelors as to their beauty; many husbands could not believe it was their wives being praised—so each took a good look at his wife wondering if the compliments bestowed upon her were true.

"The Big Four have not yet arrived. I suppose they think it

fashionable to arrive as late as possible," declared Belinda Gaines, outfitted in a peppermint green gown with twenty rows of ruffles, and out of breath from her last dance with a Fort Mackinac officer. She boasted to Cynthia Price, "My ballcard would be entirely filled if I had not left a few spaces open for possible surprises. What about yours, Cynthia?"

"I doubt if the four ladies you refer to are so self-conscious as to purposefully arrive as late as possible. I noticed that they were never very late at the other dances and hops here at the Grand." Cynthia Price would not have answered Belinda Gaines' rude, boastful question about her filled up ballcard—even if Cynthia's ballcard had been filled with gentlemen's names as well. In fact, the only name on Cynthia's ballcard was Professor Bellamy's. At dinner time she had promised him a promenade.

Belinda looked away from Cynthia, and saw the Fort Mackinac officer she had danced with approaching Cynthia. Belinda responded in double quick time. "Oh Cynthia, don't go after him. Why every good quality he has you have to invent." No sooner had Belinda said this, she was off dancing "At the Hunt Polka" with her new invention. Belinda somehow captured the officer's eye before he approached Cynthia. She happened to have saved her next dance for any "surprises," and ended up spoiling Cynthia's chance to enjoy a dance with one of the best male dancers on the ballroom floor.

Mrs. Price observed the guileful scene and was secretly relieved that Miss Gaines stole the Fort Mackinac officer away. She spoke in a comforting tone to her Cynthia, "My dear, his social standing is somewhat ambiguous. I think it is best to remain indifferent when he accompanies Miss Gaines back to her mother. Remember, you are looking to socialize with your peers." She noticed her Cynthia's pretty, if placid face harden perceptibly.

Cynthia reponded in low tones, "The only kind of man

attracted to Belinda Gaines is a man who ends up marrying a flirtatious woman sought after by many men. That kind of man bids and bids until he has won his prize . . . like a bidder at an art auction who does not know the value of a painting."

Mrs. Price was about to answer her daughter with an even more profound opinion, when she noticed the rest of the MaMas' attentions riveted to the ballroom entrance.

A rush of pure admiration from the gallery, from the boxes, from the dance floor, greeted the gorgeous and esteemed Big Four. The calcium lights seemed to scan their glittering gowns, ecstasies of creativity, outlining their Gibson girl, hour-glass figures—in cream and white satin, spangled thickly with silver paillettes—in pink and silver, adorned with large shoulder diamond bats—in white and gold, cinched with a silver diamond studded serpent belt—in pale rose, spangled with ruby sequins. The four women's heads, ears, throats, chests, waists, wrists and fingers were adorned with sparkling diamonds, sapphires, rubies, emeralds and pearls set in rings, bracelets, brooches, rivières, earrings, tiaras and fans.

The quartette of beauty—triumphed like a full orchestra.

At first no one could distinguish who wore what; the sight of the four women's vainglorious extravagance, fabulous wealth, and reckless gratification was so visually overwhelming.

The guests noted that the four ladies were accompanied by only two escorts, elegant-looking Rutherford Haverhill, and distinguished-looking Professor Loral Bellamy. It somehow looked correct in spite of two men short. If the crowd was let down that the Big Four had not arrived with gentlemen admirers to gossip about, they were pumped up again at the sight of the four women's sumptuous costumes and radiant smiles.

The magic of the Big Four's combined charm was that in spite of their bejeweled wealth, few guests at the ball felt commonplace in their presence, including the well-off who were not rich. Everyone who wanted to felt more glamorous because of the four women's presence. If the four had been royal queens, the guests would have bowed gladly to them on bended knee. In fact, the guests wished the four women were queens, but settled for a genuine countess among them.

As the two gentlemen escorted the four women to their box, the next rush began. The rush to engage a dance with at least one of the Big Four.

Mrs. Price observed, without trying to be obvious, that the group of four women timed their arrival perfectly. At the moment they sat down, the next dance began. The group of gentlemen surrounding them appeared less obvious when the dance floor was full. Mrs. Price had watched the four women at other dances manipulate the gentlemen with charming delicacy. She wondered that the reigning women could keep every dance straight, for two of the four were somehow keeping each other company in the box at the same time. Such consideration, Mrs. Price thought. Such self-possession was truly to be admired. And Mrs. Price began to quench her former disenchantment with the Big Four.

Mrs. Price also observed that the four women ended up dancing relatively little, considering all the gentlemen milling about them, and sent the gentlemen back over to specific eligible women at her end of the ballroom. Mrs. Price found this gracious gesture more than generous and fitting for matrons nearing their forties, because the four women did not keep all the choice gentlemen to themselves. And especially because they never overlooked her Cynthia.

While Mrs. Price finally relaxed and wondered what respectable gentleman one of the four ladies would send to Cynthia that evening, she turned to see tall, blond Eugene Sullivan at Cynthia's side. He asked her to dance the "Wine,

Women and Song" waltz. Cynthia accepted without asking her MaMa.

Mrs. Price was no longer relaxed and wished the group of four had arrived sooner for the sake of her daughter. She felt what she called, "an instinctive maternal distrust" for Eugene "Sully" Sullivan. She saw that he was too popular with the females, too genial, too handsome, too entertaining—which meant that he was a heartbreaker by avocation; and he was from too questionable a social standing, in spite of being accepted by the highest society. But the most suspicious detail of all about Sully was, unlike most men, he danced like an archangel.

Cynthia Price danced with archangel Sully, as so many other young and not-so-young eligible women did. Stiffly. As if her MaMa was watching her. She was. Those eligible women, especially the intellectual flirts and Belinda Gaines, who danced as if their MaMas were not watching, were the most popular belles of the ball.

Eugene Sullivan tried to loosen Cynthia up a bit by telling her a joke as they danced to "Wine, Women and Song." It helped. She relaxed substantially in his arms. After the dance, Cynthia did not rejoin her MaMa as was her custom. She accompanied Eugene to the refreshment area where he served her strawberry acid punch and brought her into conversation with a fun-loving, pleasant group.

Observing her daughter's actions, Mrs. Price suddenly felt a disordered stomach coming on. She asked the adolescent boy, doting upon her Priscilla, to kindly find her a glass of water. Mrs. Price intended to dilute the Horsford's Acid Phosphate which she carried in her evening purse, into the water for a soothing acidulated drink.

"This is our dance, I believe . . . *L' Invitation à la valse*." Dignified-looking Richard Anders appeared at the elegant Countess Gianotti's side as if from nowhere.

The countess smiled warmly and accompanied Richard to the dance floor as the waltz music burst forth. It was the first time she had seen him that evening. His formal suit added years to his age, she convinced herself. Like Rutherford, Richard did not wear a boutonniere. The countess knew that gentlemen had stopped wearing flowers in Paris, and Rutherford and Richard, men of the world, had followed suit.

"I have been waiting for this moment for many hours, Countess . . . ." Richard smiled and spoke in a level, slightly intense tone as he whirled Countess Elizabeth Anne Gianotti around the dance floor in perfect time, if imperfect ease.

Anna's body swayed gracefully, in the gorgeous gold and white gown with diamond belt, responsive to Richard's every move. In a voice melodious and expressive, Anna replied, "I have been looking forward to this dance, Mr. Anders, and I am pleased to find such a pleasurable partner."

Richard felt Anna respond in his arms; her whole being aglow with energy, alive to his aliveness. Anna noticed Richard's ears grow red; this was not caused by the red calcium spotlight.

"You do not wear a boutonniere, Mr. Anders . . ."

"Having been in Paris, where they are not wearing them, I forgot we are still wearing them here."

"I see."

The waltz music lasted minute upon minute. Fleeting notes formed floating melodies. Enticing carefree sounds tempted Richard to sieze a brief moment of bliss alone in the rhythmic crowd with Anna. Alive to Richard's intention, Anna let go from within and held back from without.

Sensitive to the inner woman in his arms, Richard barely spoke above a whisper to Anna, "I should like to preserve the very motion and heat of these moments with you . . . ." He anticipated her outward reaction as he skillfully guided her into a simple box step.

Anna smiled but did not say a word in response to Richard's risqué comment. Richard thought, how like the countess not to answer me; it is what she does not do, what she does not say, which sets her apart from all other women. Richard began to hold her tightly and step into a giddy twirling step, circling around and around and around as the piece drew to its climax. That is when Anna answered Richard Anders. Loud and clear. Without saying a word.

Anna's answer was that she did not drop her left hand from Richard's shoulder to bring it down between their bodies, as she had done so many times in the past with the Prince of Wales and Prince Napoleon when they held her too tightly. She left her hand just where it was and she danced, with the younger gambler who was holding her too tightly, as if no one was watching.

Richard spun Anna around and around and oh, how she loved it and did not care if she showed herself meeting his prime with red cheeked youthfulness and giddy lightness. Within in each other's arms, their energies, like dumb clouds colliding, quivered and fused and banged silently. Anna fancied their bodies spinning as one, like a top, whirligigging till heady, splitting apart, falling to the floor and lying there catching breath upon breath. Richard fancied spinning Anna to the floor—and landing on top of her.

Yes, Anna and Richard danced as if no one was watching. And yes, Mrs. Price, the MaMas, and entire gallery watched every graceful, highly charged move. They figured that the countess could not control Richard Anders' youthful exuberance, because the rather young man did not realize his strength. After all, he was at least five to ten years younger than the countess.

Any gossip among the MaMas was immediately extinguished by Mrs. Price because after *L' Invitation à la valse*, a waltz few were to forget for a couple of days anyhow, the countess sent Richard over to Cynthia Price for a dance. Richard conceded with gentlemanly unwillingness to dance with Cynthia Price, on one condition: if Anna would allow him to escort her back to the hotel that evening. Anna said she would think about it. Richard showed consideration and did not press the matter.

Richard Anders danced the rather impotent "Pizzicato Polka" with Cynthia Price. Mrs. Price observed that Richard did not dance in the same overheated style with her Cynthia as he did with the countess, thank goodness. Yet, she would not have minded if he had, and she wondered why he did not, growing a smidgen suspicious of the countess' probable enjoyment dancing *L' Invitation à la valse* with Richard Anders.

If the truth were known, all the suspicious MaMas would have given their eye teeth to have danced the way the (married) countess had with younger Richard Anders. Mrs. Price finally consoled herself with the thought that her Cynthia, after all, was dancing the "Pizzicato Polka" with Richard. She asked herself, what could be expected to grow from such music. Certainly not cucumbers. Mrs. Price smiled to herself and wished her husband were there. She could have shared this naughty little joke with him after the ball, when they were snuggly settled into bed for a good night's sleep.

After the last sprightly note of the "Pizzicato Polka" was played, Richard accompanied Cynthia back to her MaMa. He spoke a few polite sentences to Mrs. Price, took leave of them, walked in the direction of the Big Four, and never thought twice about Cynthia again.

Cynthia Price, however, had fallen in love with Richard Anders, in spite of the innocent nature of the music or perhaps because of it. Richard Anders had not overwhelmed her with his manliness, as had Eugene Sullivan. Richard Anders had not scared her. Cynthia found Richard considerate and intelligent and a perfect young gentleman. She could barely wait to tell her MaMa, who was smiling to herself about something, about Richard's education. Although Cynthia had failed to ask him what he did for a living, she figured a gentleman like Richard was independently well off.

Belinda Gaines, "pooped" from the "Pizzicato Polka," graced herself next to Cynthia. She took one long look at Cynthia and declared to herself, sleeping beauty is finally awake. Belinda caught on that Cynthia was head over heels over Richard Anders.

"I declare, you waste yourself dancin' with that Anders fella. Why, he's just a transient. Why, he's not even stayin' here at the marvelous Grand Hotel. Really, what other hotel is there?" Belinda continued, changing the subject, "I wish I could ask the gentlemen I really want to dance with to dance. How I envy the freedom of the servant girls. I have been told they ask the men for dances if it pleases them. What freedom. If my pap spoon had been lead instead of sterlin', I would not have to be chaperoned every minute of my life."

Belinda saw that Cynthia was watching Richard walk back to the Big Four's box. To Belinda, Cynthia looked almost radiant for the first time that summer. She asked Cynthia, "Does the Anders fella flirt?"

"No," Cynthia answered absentmindedly and with a sudden surge of energy, ripped into an astonished Belinda, "and you have no right to talk that way about servant girls. What freedom do they have? They work everyday of the week except Sunday afternoon and then they spend it with some young man who probably has no future but the factory. The girls receive thirty-five dollars a week. Why I imagine you pay twenty dollars a day here at the Grand and . . ."

"I declare, Cynthia Price, you are awake suddenly. But please do not ruin a perfectly marvellous ball with servant talk." Another gentleman admirer collected Belinda Gaines for a quadrille.

Cynthia watched Belinda Gaines dance with a beauty and sensuality beyond her eighteen years, her gown's twenty flouces fluttering flirtatiously. Passing next to Belinda, she saw the countess, in gold and white, dancing with Rutherford Haverhill, while Beatrice Venn, in pink and silver, adorned with diamond bats on her shoulders, danced with Sydney Froilan. Cynthia observed Philippa MacAdam, in pale rose with ruby sequins, speaking with Richard Anders in the box, and Clare Gilbertson, in cream and white satin with silver paillettes, sitting next to a mystery gentlemen in the box. Cynthia wished she could be one of the Big Four. She wished to be as sensuous and entertaining and experienced and confident as the Countess Gianotti, Mrs. Venn, Mrs. Mac-Adam and Mrs. Gilbertson put together. To herself she said, no gentleman could resist me then.

Word got around the ballroom that the mystery gentleman with eligible Clare Gilbertson owned *Calla*, and apparently eligible himself, did not dance. Guests figured that a strong, big fellow type like Calhoun felt self-conscious pulling his weight around the ballroom floor. They reckoned that Calhoun declined to ask Mrs. Gilbertson or any lady to dance, out of consideration for their size six feet. They figured he wore size twelve.

Philippa MacAdam only half heard what Richard Anders said to her. She kept one eye on the ballroom entrance . . . waiting . . . wondering . . . if her afternoon introduction to Colonel Marshe Williamson was simply one of those passing meetings, which take place every five minutes at the grand and little hotels all over the world. One of those chance, short meetings of kindred spirits with equal energies and interests, charged with an emotion embarrassing to admit even to oneself. Meetings never to be pursued. Meetings never to be satisfied.

Jimmy Hayes and Eugene Sullivan danced with one after another middle aged old maid, so enthusiastically, it was as if they danced the last "Explosions Polka" or last "In the Little Jelly Doughnut Woods Polka" or last "Banditen Galop" or last "Radetsky March," the world would ever hear or dance to. The old maids loved it. Jimmy and Sully had hearts of gold for all wallflowers. They saw to it that every guest who wished to dance—danced that unforgettable evening. Jimmy and Sully lost five pounds by sunrise.

Every guest at the ball seized a brief moment of bliss. And those who were not free to plunge headlong into love wanted to do it all the more in a sensuous setting which ignited such illusions.

As the vibrant affair passed midnight, the boxes and gallery were humming with gossip about newly formed alliances, possible engagements by summer's end, chatter about little draughts detected, and effusive compliments about each other's gowns.

The entire crowd watched thirty younger couples dance a german, otherwise known as a cotillion, and exchange favors or a souvenir in between the succession of waltzes, two steps, marches, pas de quatres, and picturesque figures easily followed as the leader called them out.

The countess had talked a reluctant Richard Anders into dancing with Cynthia Price. For Cynthia, that german with Richard was one she would never forget. For Richard, that german was one he immediately forgot.

After the german and a light buffet supper, the gallery crowd gradually bid each other fond good nights, raved on and on about the success of the ball, and retired for the evening wearing satisfied if tired faces. The MaMas and chaperones, stiff from sitting all evening, reminded their flushed daughters and charges of the late hour and gradually left the ballroom.

Cynthia Price asked her MaMa if she could stay on, explaining that one lady in the group of four women might consent to chaperone her. Perhaps the countess. After all, she had sent Richard Anders over and Richard was with her group most of the evening.

Mrs. Price had not heard Cynthia so happy since her last engagement. But she suspected that her Cynthia had enough exhilarating rhythms for the evening and replied, "Cynthia, my dear, let's find out a little more about Richard Anders, shall we? Are we to trust him simply because Countess Gianotti sent him over? For all we know, he may be a transient."

"But Mother, he graduated from Harvard and studied in Heidelberg and . . ."

"That would not make him less of a transient, my dear. For all we know, a man of his age, I believe him to be about thirty, could have a wife elsewhere. Remember dear, I am watching out for your best interests."

Cynthia Price, twenty-eight, left the casino ballroom with her MaMa, while married women, five years younger, remained partying at the ball with their husbands.

For many, including the group of four women, the grand ball began when the gallery spectators and MaMas and daughters and chaperones and charges retired for the evening.

Philmore Calhoun, noting the spectators had left, finally danced with Clare Gilbertson. He managed his Falstaffian figure with surprising ease as they danced the "Aquarellen Waltz." He did not step on her feet.

"Mrs. Gilbertson, you do not dance . . . you float like a leaf upon the rapids.

"Thank you, Mr. Calhoun. If I float it is because of your expert maneuvers."

Tickled pink on the neck, he knew Clare meant what she said, and he knew he was keeping to the beat far better than he had anticipated earlier in the day. He had not danced much since his wife's death. In fact, his first mate back on the "boat" had to dance Philmore through a few steps, after the yacht race that afternoon, in preparation for the ball. In preparation for Clare Gilbertson.

The waltz over, Philmore accompanied Clare back to her box and said, "Speaking of floating and rapids . . . I was talking with some of the sportsmen here . . . Professor Bellamy, Sydney Froilan, Richard Anders, the Cudahy brothers. I offered my boat for a trip they are planning to Sault Ste. Marie, not far from the island. Perhaps . . . you and your friends would care to accompany us. We intend to run the rapids and get in a little fishing. Should be quite enjoyable if you would care to join us."

Clare looked hesitant.

Realizing that she might be questioning the intention of such a proposition, Philmore quickly added, "Well, you see, you would overnight at the Chippewa Hotel at the Sault. And the Cudahy wives might join us as well."

"I have never run rapids or fished seriously in my life, Mr. Calhoun. Are you sure you would like a greenhorn along?"

Philmore chuckled, "You do not look like a greenhorn, Mrs. Gilbertson. Women are doing adventurous things today."

"Yes," replied Clare, "like Kate Marsden and May French Sheldon. I heard Mrs. Sheldon speak at the Women's Building at the world's fair. At forty-three she traveled a thousand miles in the African wilderness without, as she put it, male assistance, though she had 150 Negro porters in her caravan. She put down a mutiny, was almost killed by a python, and on her way back a bridge collapsed beneath her. A very exciting story. Is that what you mean by women doing adventurous things today?" Clare asked with an ironic smile.

"Ah . . . sure . . . yes." Philmore realized he should not have assumed that running a few rapids and a little fishing would be considered adventurous to Clare. For all he knew Clare might have been a mountain climber. Women were certainly changing. "Yes, if a woman can keep up with the men, not carrying heavy equipment, mind you, just keep up, it should be a jolly time for all."

"Thank you for the invitation, Mr. Calhoun. Can I let you know tomorrow?" Clare was thrilled to be included in what was usually a strictly male adventure.

Philmore Calhoun, realizing he had misread Clare's ironic reaction about women adventurers, received great pleasure seeing Clare enthusiastic about a simple fishing trip and a boat ride to the Sault.

"Do you mean you will let me know today? It is Sunday."

"Yes . . . today . . . Mr. Calhoun. I will answer you later today."

Clare and Philmore danced two more dances with each other that evening. Any more than three dances together would have roused talk even among the remaining lively set, who lived life so fully they seldom had time for serious gossiping, and who were the usual fodder for the gossipers. Clare was thoroughly relieved that Philmore Calhoun did not press her for more dances, though he proved himself human when he overstepped his bounds later that evening.

The midsummer night revels were by no means over. By two o'clock, the countess was having a time of it trying to avoid "younger" Richard Anders' adoring eyes. The more Anna tried to avoid him, the more he tried ways to achieve eye contact. The countess had danced three dances with Richard:

the respectable, slightly stretched quota for a married lady with any one gentleman in an evening.

And as the clock ticked away into the early hours of the morning, Richard became more bold and whispered to Anna, "Countess . . . I want you to know . . . I have danced every dance with you this evening . . . ."

Such continental talk from an American surprised Anna. She did not know then that Richard Anders was not a typical American. And she never thought that Richard meant what he had whispered.

Anna had seen too much of life to take an amorous gentleman at a ball seriously.

The countess and Clare were not the only two of the four women who had their hands full. Eligible Beatrice Venn, who somehow lost count, danced with ineligible Sydney Froilan four times. When Professor Loral Bellamy, with total delicacy, gently reminded her of the four dances, Beatrice responded warmly.

"Thank you, Loral . . . you are a new friend and I believe a true friend. If Mr. Froilan danced as well as you, I would consent to dance a fifth dance with him. But if he asks me again, I shall decline."

Sydney did not ask again. He begged. Beatrice laughed with her whole spirit, as she had so many times that evening with Sydney.

Professor Bellamy, observing Beatrice, thought over her response to his gentle warning of the excessive number of dances. Such a clever and complicated answer she had handed him. In the professor's day, a lady would have replied how slow of mind she was not to have noticed she danced too often with the same gentleman, and thanked him profusely for setting her on the right path. Not today's lady. Always a clever and complicated answer.

Beatrice made it clear to Professor Bellamy that Sydney Froilan had stolen her heart. The old professor did not like it. Although he respected Sydney Froilan's position as a world famous artist, he did not approve of Sydney's position as free lance husband. The professor wondered why Beatrice was attracted to Sydney. He did not wonder why Sydney was attracted to well-formed Beatrice. Professor Bellamy feared the steamy attraction had nothing to do with Beatrice's fine mind, cute children, or even wealth.

Yes, the old professor thought how complicated life was for this society woman, Mrs. Venn, who had such expensive freedom, but no freedom to relax in the splendor she paid for so handsomely. There was no doubt about it. Beatrice Venn was a modern woman. The sort of well-off woman with freedoms that did not exist in Professor Bellamy's day. The sort of woman used and misused, with or without knowing it, setting herself up for more. Her freedom of expression with Sydney was almost shocking to the old professor, who doted upon her.

The professor overheard her say: "I have married friends who would take their husbands as lovers—if they were not married to them." After a round of laughter, the professor heard Sydney reply: "The best marriages are by those people who ignore they are married, and realize they are lovers living together." After a round of discussion, the professor heard Sydney remark flippantly: "When an English woman marries she loses her liberty. When a French woman marries she gains her liberty. When an American woman marries she retains her liberty." To which Beatrice promptly added, "Speaking of marriage . . . the very latest fashion this year is . . . postponed marriages." And Sydney howled.

The old professor, who held marriage sacred probably because his marriage was unusually happy, astonished himself at their flippancy. He decided then and there that Beatrice Venn needed protection from herself. Professor Bellamy turned chivalrous protector of Beatrice Venn; and she was more fortunate in his friendship than she had ever been in her life. For in the world of 1893, there were few real chivalrous protectors left. Few men knew how to protect anything but what they personally owned, such as things. Such things as businesses and wives.

With watchful old eyes and straining old ears, the old professor heard Sydney talking clever, animated, mirthful talk with Beatrice. The orchestral music, the perfumed flowers, the low lights, the *joie de vivre* in the ballroom accompanying Sydney's exotic stories, tended to glorify the stories even more. Few women could resist such entertainment, especially because Sydney always invited Beatrice into his conversation.

Professor Bellamy began to realize why Sydney attracted Beatrice. Sydney actually listened intently to Beatrice's conversation and opinions and jokes. The professor wished that Sydney Froilan spoke in monologues with Beatrice, like most of the men who could not converse or entertain. Instead, he saw Sydney listening intently to Beatrice, smiling encouragement, adding tidbits of spice to her stories and opinions.

Loral Bellamy knew no good could come from self-glorifying, world famous, Sydney Chase Froilan. He observed that Sydney was too polished under his purposefully rugged, bohemian exterior. And before the summer was over, Professor Loral Bellamy was to learn to despise Sydney Froilan. Because of Sydney, Beatrice Venn would shock the old professor into the reality of modern times. A reality Professor Bellamy had stubbornly refused to accept.

"Professor Bellamy," Sydney interrupted Loral's thoughts, trying to bring the old gentleman into the conversation out of politeness, "Mrs. Venn tells me you came to the island in a most unusual way."

In spite of the professor's dour feelings for Sydney, he answered him courteously. "Most would call my means of transportation old-fashioned, if not eccentric. Not too very long ago, before the trains, before the big and fancy tourist steamers, if my wife and I did not come up to Mackinac Island by way of a sailing vessel or rustic steamer, we came up by a horsedrawn coach to Mackinaw City, and took a vessel like a Mackinac boat across the straits.

"I dislike trains. They are stuffy and noisy and dusty. And the new steamers are stuffy and noisy and God forbid the wind blows the black soot from the smokestack in your direction. Not only that. The new steamers are so luxurious and so fast you hardly feel as if you have traveled at all to get to your destination. It is all too damn easy.

"Well . . . Mr. Froilan . . . and forgive me, Mrs. Venn, for repeating it . . . this summer of 1893 . . . believe it or not . . . I came up in a coach with four horses I hired, and took a canoe across the straits to the island. It took me two and one-half weeks to get here from South Bend, Indiana, instead of two days. I met ever so nice people along the way in Kalamazoo and Grand Rapids and Traverse City and Charlevoix and Petoskey and . . . well . . . I would be here all night if I named all the towns . . . and I must add that I have been invited to visit them on my way back. As a matter of fact, many people rode with me from town to town to visit relatives and friends, they had not seen for years. I also have invitations from their relatives and friends to visit on my way back. Ah . . . please excuse me . . . my dance with Mrs. MacAdam has come up."

Philippa Mac Adam gladly danced with Professor Bellamy. The old professor moved about the dance floor divinely, and made Philippa look beautiful as he glided her into steps she had never known in the arms of men much younger. Philippa truly enjoyed whirling about the room on the old gentleman's arm, and for a few minutes relaxed, and stopped looking at the entrance door to the ballroom. Beginning to feel utterly foolish, hopeful Philippa still anticipated the arrival of Colonel Marshe Williamson at the late hour of half past two.

The countess, Clare, and Beatrice followed Philippa's elegant form moving around the dance floor with the gracefulness and sensuality of a ballerina. The ruby sequins on her gown caught the glow of the calcium spotlights, which seemed to search her out. Philippa and the professor might have been skating on ice until her three friends saw her stumble slightly.

"Is everything quite all right, Mrs. MacAdam?" asked her partner.

"Quite . . . Professor Bellamy . . . would you kindly take me back to our box."

"Of course, Mrs. MacAdam." Professor Bellamy offered her his arm, and guided her back to the box as if nothing had happened.

"I want to say, Loral, I enjoyed our dance more than you shall ever know . . . ." Philippa's voice shook slightly.

"You honor me, Philippa," replied the old professor kindly.

Philippa asked Clare to accompany her to the ladies dressing room. At the time, Philippa MacAdam had no idea that by asking Clare Gilbertson to the dressing room at that very moment, she had—saved the evening for Clare.

In return, Clare had no idea what suddenly troubled Philippa. Because of Clare's concern for Philippa's stumbling, Clare had not noticed a stunning woman enter the ballroom at the scandalous hour of half past two, dressed in a pomegranate red gown and white diamonds, her bright hair ornamented with a solid gold dagger ornament encrusted with flawless diamonds.

Philippa recognized the woman in red, who was obviously no lady, immediately. But it was not the woman's entrance alone which caused her to stumble on the dance floor. What caused her to stumble was the man who followed the crude woman in—Colonel Marshe Williamson—looking uneasy but remarkably attractive, as he gazed about the ballroom with an air of debonaire interest in the group at large, seeming to look for no one in particular.

If Philippa was visibly disturbed by Marshe Williamson's late arrival and red-gowned partner, she would have been shocked to know that she had saved Clare from a ruthless confrontation with the woman in red that evening. For the woman in red was the reckless horsewoman whom Philippa had dealt with that afternoon. And the "someone at the Grand" whom the reckless horsewoman hated was—Clare Gilbertson.

Philippa could not believe that a seemingly fine southern gentleman like Marshe Williamson would have anything to do with such a crude woman—in public at any rate. She sat down at the dressing table with Clare, and stared at the brushes and combs and pomade and face powder and cologne and needles and thread and hairpins. She grabbed the soap, dipped it into some water and washed her face. Clare remained silent until she noticed Philippa's eyes watering.

"Philippa . . . dearest . . ."

"I am behaving like a schoolgirl going on forty . . ."

"You are behaving like person deeply hurt . . . certainly not Professor Bellamy?"

"Dear Clare . . . of course not. I believe I am reacting to the excitement of the evening . . . .In spite of everything, it was glorious . . . was it not? And now I am selfishly keeping you from Mr. Calhoun, and feel that is worse than the cause of my loss of control. Clare, though I know the professor or Rutherford would escort me back to the hotel, I do not wish to break up the party. Perhaps you would ask another gentleman I know who is leaving . . . or a couple who is leaving . . . to accompany me back to my room."

"Philippa, I shall ask Mr. Calhoun to accompany both of us."

"Do you think it is too soon to leave?"

"It is almost three o'clock in the morning . . ."

"Yes . . . ." Do you mind if I wait here until you come back for me?"

"We shall come for you as soon as I bid good night to our friends."

"Please bid them all good night from me . . . please tell them I am slightly dizzy," Philippa added quietly, with a distant look on her face, " . . . dizzy from freedom. No . . . please do not say that . . . it is no fun dancing with Kierke-gaard . . . ."

"No . . . ." Clare smiled carefully, "I will be back for you soon. You will be all right alone?"

"I am much better already, thank you, dear Clare."

When Clare left the dressing room she was surprised to find Philmore Calhoun standing nearby.

"Is everything quite all right?" he asked with what amounted to concern in his voice.

"Would you escort Mrs. MacAdam and myself back to our rooms, Mr. Calhoun?"

"Of course, Mrs. Gilbertson."

Philmore Calhoun escorted Clare and Philippa from the casino through the covered passageway, and back into the Grand Hotel. Waiting for the lift, too tired to walk three flights, they noticed the big round clock above the lift marked three o'clock. After they rode up to the third floor and walked to Philippa's room, the trio bid each other pleasant good nights.

While Philippa closed her door, Philmore and Clare heard her old black maid Tessie call out: "Well, Philippa honey, I's waited up long enough, passin' the time with my Lord who's a fine listener but not much of a talker . . . and now I want to hear yeh talks to me, cause the suspense of it all will done do me in if yeh doesn't spill the beans. Dids yeh falls into love with the gentleman or what?"

Philmore escorted Clare in silence to her room down the hall. Both had lingered at Philippa's door, listening to Tessie's long loud question, and felt a bit embarrassed. They were trying to figure out what had upset Philippa, until they stopped in front of Clare's door. There Philippa's problem vanished like dust in a sunbeam when a cloud conceals the sun.

"I enjoyed the evening so very much, Mr. Calhoun," Clare extended her hand for some moments, but Philmore Calhoun did not grasp it. Clare wondered if she too had committed some terrible error about a man that evening. She was sure Philippa MacAdam was suffering about an error in judgment—and most likely it was about a man. She dropped her hand slowly to her side.

"Clare Gilbertson . . . you extend your hand to me . . . you tell me you enjoyed the evening so very much, Mr. Calhoun, in a voice so unlike the voice I heard when I met you . . . unlike the voice I heard this entire evening . . ."

Clare did not know quite what to say to this at three o'clock in the morning. Philmore noticed this and liked it. He liked that Clare did not articulate another rehearsed, polite remark.

"Mr. Calhoun," Clare began in a firm but friendly voice.

"Philmore . . ."

"Mr. Calhoun . . . it is three o'clock in the morning . . . no doubt people are sleeping . . ."

"Only the old ones . . ." Philmore almost winked, but thought it was better not to under the circumstances.

"No doubt our voices disturb them . . ."

"Let's whisper . . . but I will have to come closer . . ."

Clare's every heartbeat, like a Clydesdale's hooves on asphalt, pounded loud and hard.

Philmore's face eased into a kind of boy scout grin; the kind of boy scout who dreams of adult fantasies to come, and the kind of grin which has made fantasies come true in the past.

Philmore thought, as he gazed at Clare's mature but soft looking face, this is ridiculous. Here we stand, two middle-aged people who have held each other as we hopped about as merry as larks on a dance floor, and sat together most of four hours laughing and discussing the world, and now, to be so close to a simple, dignified romp in the sack, and instead be handed a hand and a formal good night. It suddenly struck Philmore as very humorous.

Humorous, until he looked above Clare's lips. Her eyes were no vacant orbs which had seen this kind of scene too often. Her lovely, sleepy eyes looked hurt.

Clare blamed herself for his behavior. Philmore blamed Mother Nature. It was a long time since he really wanted a woman. Recognizing Clare's eyes, he realized the mistake he had made.

"Perhaps . . . Mrs. Gilbertson . . . you will understand that Mother Nature plays tricks on me . . . especially since I turned forty . . . some years ago. She keeps telling me I am getting older and life is short. I keep proving it true to her . . . ." Philmore grasped Clare's right hand between both of his hands.

"Good night, Mrs. Gilbertson . . . thank you for more pleasure than I have had since . . . quite some time in the past . . . .If Mother Nature allows me, I will be here for tea today . . . will you honor me with your presence at tea?"

Clare understood and accepted Philmore's veiled apology. She replied in a low mellow voice, "I shall have my answer for you . . . regarding the Sault trip . . . today . . . at tea . . . ."

Clare smiled and opened her door. A waft of warm air and rose scent and soft light greeted Philmore's relaxed senses. It lingered a few moments and faded like a pleasurable dream over too soon. As Clare slowly closed the door to her inviting bedroom, Philmore stepped backward—fighting all instinct to step inside.

Clare locked the door quietly, with a lingering smile on her face and a question in her mind. She questioned how long it had been since Philmore's last pleasure. As for herself, as for her own pleasure . . . .Clare, like her three friends the countess and Beatrice and Philippa, considered moral codes and sin. But she had transcended that early stage in her life when she thought of little else. She was more than ready to reenter the asthetics of human passion. But on her terms. With sanctioned elegance. Not with a one night romp in the sack.

As for herself, as for her own pleasure . . . for Clare, there had been no pleasure since the death of her husband. No pleasure, in fact, even before his murder. She tried to put the nightmare out of her mind, to think of the beautiful ball instead. She said to herself, after all, that is what balls are for, to think upon their brilliance, to help us block our dark memories. Thank God, some of us creatures have evenings like this to enliven the lighter moments of our lives.

Clare did not awaken her maid to help her undress. She began to undress slowly, wishing his hands were taking off her jewels, her gown, her underclothes . . . .

The first gala ball of the season ended at five o'clock in the morning with the sweet strains of "Tales From the Vienna Woods." All eleven minutes of it.

Beatrice danced with Professor Bellamy and thanked him for escorting her that evening. The old gentleman replied that he was honored and delighted and could not remember enjoying a grand ball more since the death of his dear wife.

Countess Gianotti danced with Rutherford and thanked him for escorting her that evening. He answered her with polite remarks. But Rutherford really thought that he had never enjoyed a grand ball more in his life. He asked himself, how is it possible on a remote island made up of a mish mash of society people? And as he danced with the enchanting Countess Gianotti, a woman obviously capable of deep feeling and grand passion, he wished to possess the woman and her ability to feel. But even the old Haverhill money and heritage could not vicariously buy back Rutherford's—lost instinct.

Sydney and Richard watched Beatrice and Countess Gianotti, almost enviously, dance among some one hundred resplendent couples, relaxed and exhausted with the pleasure of it all, gliding through the last glorious waltz of the Grand Hotel's ball—called a "brilliant success" by all.

"Countess . . . may I have the honor of escorting you back to your room?" asked Richard when the countess approached the box one last time. He was hoping for a few moments with her alone.

"Of course, Mr. Anders . . . we shall enjoy it if you accompany us back."

We? Us? Richard questioned if he would ever find a chance to be alone with Anna. He explained, "It is just that . . . I want to invite you . . . to ask you and some of your friends, to accompany a number of us sportsmen to Sault Ste. Marie for a little fishing and shooting the rapids. Philmore Calhoun has offered his schooner . . ."

"Mr. Anders . . ."

"Yes . . ."

"Would you care to join me for tea today? We could discuss it then."

"I look forward to teatime with pleasure . . ."

"Your father will not be unduly upset that you are not having tea with him?"

"Not unduly . . . ." Richard thought, alone at last at teatime.

Sydney Froilan stepped up to Richard and patted him on the back and said, "Is it possible, that a mere twelve hours ago, a group of us sportsmen decided to take a trip to the Sault . . . on one condition?"

Richard smiled knowingly and asked, "What . . . one condition . . . was that, Froilan?

"Hmm . . . I seem to have forgotten what the . . . one condition . . . was." Sydney turned to Beatrice. "Mrs. Venn . . . a few of us are sailing up to the Sault to shoot the rapids and get in a little fishing . . . ."

Beatrice inquired with a smile, "Fly fishing or bait fishing, Mr. Froilan?"

"A little of both, Mrs. Venn. Both bring great pleasure to a true sportsman . . . ."

7

Troublemaking on Sunday

Sunday at the Grand Hotel was the most difficult day of the week. No one said it, but everyone knew that the Grand was a bit too theatrical on Sundays. Many resorters felt guilty about their luxurious surroundings on the Lord's Day, and made a point of trying not to enjoy themselves on the seventh day of rest. They felt it their moral duty to discuss the poor, or at least read about them, because the rest of the week they allowed themselves not to think about the unfortunate.

Indeed, resorters even tried to avoid gossiping on the Lord's Day by reading magazines, preferably of a religious nature. Hospitable weather encouraged them to read on the veranda at least until teatime at four o'clock, when the sobriety of Sunday somehow seemed unofficially over, or had worn off.

Generally, the Presbyterians read the *Evangelist* or *North American Review,* the Episcopalians read *Churchman* or *Harper's Magazine,* the Methodist Episcopalians read *Christian Advocate* or *Illustrated American,* the Unitarians read *Unitarian* or *Altruistic Review,* the Lutherans read *Lutheran Evangelist* or *Home Magazine,* the Catholics read *Pilot* or *Babyhood,* anti-catholics read *Forum* tucked between anti-anti-catholic *Iconoclast,* the Congregationalists read *Independent* or *The Nation,* the Hebrews read *Menorah* or *Commodore Rollingpin's Illustrated Humourous Almanac,* the theosophists read *The Path,* the agnostics read *Open Court,* the Christian

Scientists read *Scientific American,* and the atheists read *Truth*.

But in spite of reading religious or respectable magazines, no matter how sincerely the resorters tried to be good, it was more tempting to be bad on Sunday than any other day of the week. Yes, it was always on the Lord's Day that all hell broke loose at the hotel.

And the Sunday after the Grand Ball was no exception. The damning hell waters of sinful Sunday gossip flooded the veranda just before church services and after breakfast, as guests took their morning constitutionals. They heard whispered gossip that a photographic picture of college men and girls taken in a gymnasium at Drexel University in Philadelphia—showing them together in "an application of Greek art to modern science"—had popped up in the parlor.

In other words, the college men and girls were photographed stark naked, exhibiting their almost perfect Greek forms developed through the modern science of dumbbells, the trapeze, and the latest Swedish apparatus.

Few guests knew the purpose of the university's photograph, to compare students' physical progress from year to year, except for the college men who had hidden the scandalous photograph in between the sheets of a hymnbook on the parlor piano. The dirty discovery had been made before breakfast. In excited response, most guests at the Grand dutifully resurrected their Puritan spirits, being that it was Sunday, and called the photograph "shocking, immoral gymnastics," though they had not, "thank God," actually seen the sexually explicit picture.

One lancet-tongued old maid from the crafty crackpot group, who never allowed her back to touch the back of a chair on Sunday, demanded to know of Old Stinkweed after he told her the gossip, "Do these students fly through the air on a trapeze like naked apes?"

Old Stinkweed answered, "No . . . with the greatest of ease." And he snickered to himself, imagining stark naked girls flying through the air on trapezes. Old Stinkweed wished that someone had planted the dirty picture in between the sheets of his favorite Sunday magazine, *American Checker Review.*

Those guests who were convinced that college was dangerous to the health of women, because it might cause sterility, were doubly convinced after hearing the scandalous gossip. Only the old Muldoon ladies took the news in good stride, and marveled at young people's commitment to physical fitness.

The photograph incident whipped up forbidden Sunday gossip all because members of the "You'll be damned if you play cards on Sunday" group, suddenly inspired by religious fervor right before breakfast, had rushed to the piano in the parlor to play and sing Moody and Sankey hymns. When the piano player had opened the hymnbook, the stark naked Drexel University men and girls exposed themselves to her, and twenty other ladies gathered around the piano straining to catch a glimpse of the photograph.

Those ladies in the group who had never seen naked male bodies before were overcome with palpitations, and had to be helped to chairs by those sister singers who either had husbands or brothers. The piano player, overcome, would not further contaminate the religious songbook by closing its holy pages on the sinful picture, nor would she or anyone else touch it to turn it around or dispose of it. The ladies might just as well have found the magazine *Lucifer,* which avocated free sex, free thought, and individual anarchism. It was all the same to them.

So when Jimmy Hayes had overheard the commotion and rushed into the parlor, almost overcome with the odour of violet sec perfume, and witnessed ladies of all descriptions with mouths drooping downwards and teeth gnawing at their lips, he wondered what the hell was going on.

No one could bring herself to tell him. Not one of the ladies had the nerve to explain that when they opened their Moody and Sanky hymnbook they witnessed young men and women exposing themselves. As a matter of fact, not one lady could look at Jimmy Hayes, naked under his clothes, straight in the eye.

Jimmy Hayes, utterly perplexed, lucked out when Philippa MacAdam, with liquid-looking sleepy eyes, had walked into the parlor. The Sunday hymn singers rushed toward her in a chorus of rustling silk and laces, and explained about the shocking photograph on the piano in hushed voices.

Philippa, who had used nude models in painting class in Rome, remained in control of herself. She turned to Jimmy, who looked small and sheepish in a corner of the parlor, and said in her soberest Sunday voice, "Mr. Hayes, these ladies have had a terrible shock . . . and I think you ought to send a maid into the parlor."

Befuddled, Jimmy had practically tiptoed out of the parlor and immediately sent in a maid. After instructions from Mrs. MacAdam, the maid had wrapped the sinful photograph in her apron and whisked it out of the parlor. The ladies, still stunned, could barely be coaxed to eat breakfast. But worldly wise Mrs. MacAdam, one of the Big Four, no less, enlightened them that good Christians can fight evil better on a full stomach than an empty one.

At breakfast the rumor about the shocking Sodom and Gomorrah photograph began to travel. Carried to the veranda, the juicy story spread quicker than the floozies at the Everleigh Club in Chicago.

When Jimmy Hayes finally found out later he exclaimed, "Great Constantinople . . . but that's rich!" and chuckled, almost sympathetically, remembering the shocked look on the ladies' faces. At bottom, this college men's prank was not good for business. Though it was one helluva rich story to tell the boys, especially after a couple of Pilseners.

Why, this scandalous story even quashed an early morning rumor about to be spread by a member of the crafty crackpots who wore disfiguring eyeglasses. The rumor would have been about Philippa MacAdam, whom the crackpot had seen strolling upon the veranda, at an early hour—alone. But of even more significance—Mrs. MacAdam had been seen picking up a woman's lacy underpants, red in color, that a man with black hair and beard threw to her in clandestine fashion, from one of the many little balconies overlooking the 650-foot veranda.

The rumor about Philippa that never spread was true. Almost. Unable to sleep peacefully, she tossed and turned all morning, plagued by dreams of coal black horses ridden by black-haired men and Bordeaux-haired women jumping over flaming orange hurdles. Fed up with the repetitive visions, Philippa roused herself from slumber, dressed quietly and tiptoed out of her room in order not to awaken her maid. Old Tessie would have insisted on accompanying her mistress. Alone on the veranda, Philippa imagined herself as free as she had felt in Rome. Her release was short-lived.

Hearing voices, she looked up and spied a man leaning over the balcony to a bedroom, about to throw something off of it. A woman's voice protested and begged him not to throw it over. The woman, half dressed, suddenly lunged at the man on the balcony. He pushed her back into the room, disappeared, jumped back onto the balcony, buried his face in the object he was about to throw off the balcony, and threw what turned out to be a pair of red lace panties onto the veranda. A duet of soft laughter and naughty inference, from the woman and man, landed on the veranda as well.

Philippa recognized the voice and hair of the reckless horsewoman, who had worn pomegranate red (and red lace panties) to the ball and had entered in front of—Colonel Marshe Williamson. But Philippa had not recognized the voice of the teasing man, though he was black-haired and black-bearded and resembled the colonel, who had helped her mount Dude so skillfully. So like her late husband. He resembled the colonel, who only yesterday afternoon had awakened in Philippa a deep yearning to meet him again.

Even after Marshe Williamson's shameless display and late entrance at the ball, Philippa convinced herself that the younger-looking black-haired man on the balcony was not the colonel. She convinced herself that the colonel was not a man to be so obvious. Not knowing what to do, Philippa picked up the red lace panties that had fallen in her path, stuffed them in the pocket of her bluish green dragon-fly cape from Worth, promenaded another few minutes, headed back into the hotel, strayed into the parlor, and was rushed at by twenty ladies of the "You'll be damned if you play cards on Sunday" group—all before nine o'clock on the Sunday morning after the grand ball.

It was an hour later when Philippa, standing on the veranda with her back to the glorious view of the straits, was relieved to see the countess, Beatrice and her children and Nanna, and Clare emerging from the Grand Hotel dressed in immaculate white church-going clothes. To Philippa, the women and children were a testimony that the world contained well-adjusted females, as well as women who wore red lacy underpants and parlor ladies who were shocked at life's realities.

No one pretended to be in the mood for chitchat, but the four women exchanged warm knowing smiles and broke up into two carriages waiting for them, among thirty others on the road leading past the Grand. Sunday morning Grand Hotel church goers not attending the sacred services in the unsanctified casino, given by visiting clergyman and singers at eleven o'clock, headed to St. Anne's or Trinity Church in the village.

The countess and Clare climbed into Owen Corrigan's carriage bound for St. Anne's. Beatrice, Philippa, little Frederick, Monica, and Nanna entered the next carriage, bound for Trinity Church. The Edward Cudahy family waved to all of them as they passed by, enroute to St. Anne's, in a showy open carriage big enough for their servants to accompany them. A short whistle from the greenish blue waters below the hotel told the Grand Hotel guests that Edward Cudahy's brother, Michael, had loaded his family into his steam yacht, *Catherine,* below his cottage in the Annex, and was off by sea to St. Anne's church as well.

To the Big Four, the homespun hoopla surrounding Sunday morning church going was a genuine relief from the sophisticated doings at the hotel. Yes, old-fashioned church going was a relief from the world rather than a time of rejuvination to go back out into the world with the good news. The world of 1893 was a confusing place, and not one of the four women could remember a time when religion and the world seemed more separate.

It was the college girls who came out and honestly said what they thought about church going. They agreed that attending church was like putting on old comfortable shoes, which still fit, but you really did not need to wear them. You had ten other shoes far more beautiful and just as comfortable. Yet every once in while, for no apparent reason, you put on the old shoes anyway. It was that simple-minded. Unless you were a Catholic. Then you put on the old shoes every week whether you felt like it or not.

After all, the college girls claimed, who but the holy rollers had time for religion when steel and corn and hogs and art and literature and European travel and issues such as workers' rights, child labor, spitting in the streets . . . dominated the minds of all classes. There was so much to be done in the world that sitting around in church, doing nothing, made some people nervous. They concluded, to many church goers sitting around in church was simply a habitual "time-out" from other more important matters.

But to most working class natives of the island—the families of innkeepers, store owners, tavern keepers, restaurateurs, hack drivers, delivery men, farmers, street sweepers, cooks, waiters, chambermaids, laundresses, (many of them former fisherman and lumbermen), even half-breed Indians—Sunday church going was the focus of their lives. The fundamental life avowing time of the week. It was the time when they were assured that good behavior and hard work during the week was going to be rewarded, if not presently, after death. It was also the time when many were assured that bad behavior would put them in hell.

Hell was a very comforting thought to many of the island natives. For the reality of hell made the reality of their hard work and good behavior meaningful. Not one of them wanted to burn in eternal fires stoked by the devil himself. Why, to most natives, life without the threat of hell would be like life without the threat of death. Boring.

Sunday for the Mackinac Island natives was the time they gathered together to assure each other that life had meaning. No ego-culture had replaced religion in their lives. And they did not come to church in fancy carriages and clothes and steam yachts.

Owen Corrigan and his faithful steed Charley dropped off Anna and Clare at St. Anne's twenty minutes before the service. T-carts and buggies lined the street near the church for blocks. If it were not the Lord's Day, Owen would have cursed the lack of parking space near the church due to the summer influx of tourists and consequent overcrowding. And if it were not Sunday, Owen would not have the Sunday morning shakes from his weekly Saturday night fling at his favorite beer shop.

Due to the fact of his weekly illness, Owen never made it to Catholic church on Sunday. He knew he was commiting mortal sin. But he had a plan to confess the sins and ask forgiveness of a forgiving God during his last sacraments, right before he died. He figured this plan would at least put him safely in purgatory. And his three dear dead wives up in heaven, hearing the news, would eventually pray him up to heaven to spend eternity with them. He did not look forward to eternal harping from his three wives in heaven, but it was better than the boredom of purgatory. So while the fancy society women attended church services, Owen kept Charley company and tried to control his illness, and his guilt, by sleeping it off.

Anna and Clare walked up the steps to St. Anne's porch leading into the church. The porch looked like half a bandstand created for Sousa himself; it added gaiety to the otherwise conservative New England style architectural features of the church. St. Anne's porch, the physical prelude to the main proper of the church, invited the congregation and summer visitors to assemble in a semi-formal, semi-sacred area outside of the church. No one could say damn or hell on the porch's premises, but you could think these words without fear of commiting a venial sin. In its own small way, St. Anne's thirty-foot, bellied out porch was as inviting as the Grand Hotel's 650 foot veranda.

Although Anna and Clare recognized many fellow church goers, they did not join the groups of early bird resorters from various hotels on the island, as they stood laughing on the left side of St. Anne's porch. Nor did they join a group of island natives standing on the right side, quietly exchanging arguments about whether the old church bell sounded better than the new church bell.

The new bell in the new bell tower tolled a call to Mass. The ringing sounds seemed to be a cue, for island natives standing near Anna approached her, without introducing themselves. They figured Anna remembered them. And she did, though their faces had weathered, some beyond immediate recognition. One of them had been a childhood playmate of Anna's when she had vacationed on the island decades ago. Back then the island children and the summer children played with each other; this was not so in 1893, when the two groups kept to themselves.

The island natives did not ask Anna how she was or what she had been doing in the twenty years since they had seen her. It was as if twenty years had not passed. That Anna was now a countess they thought a lot of hogwash. They asked her, point blank, to help them settle an argument.

"What do you think, Miss Anna. Is the new bell better than the old bell? Or what?"

This was a loaded question and Anna knew no matter which side her answer fell, a few faces might turn the other way from her for a couple of Sundays till they got over it. Anna looked up beyond the rose window in the church tower, but could not see the glassless Palladian window in the belfry. Not remembering how the old bell, cast in 1832, had sounded, she listened intently to the new bell.

Anna wanted to answer her old Catholic acquaintances honestly, like an islander, not like the lady-in-waiting pseudo aristocrat she had become who dipped her every really honest phrase into honey before serving it. But she could not tell the whole truth. For Anna honestly thought the bell sounded a bit restrained—really, a bit protestant. She thought, if it is not a protestant bell per se, it certainly is not a Catholic bell. Anna concluded, it is a convert bell, and smiled inside herself.

After a fair amount of deliberation Anna answered the partial truth, "The sound of St. Anne's new bell is not brilliant. But it is pleasant to the ears. It is not boisterous. It is not sweet sounding. It sounds as if means business—come to church or else. Is it not very similar in these respects to the old bell?"

Anna watched the islanders' faces. One by one they broke into half-smiles. Some thought, that like themselves, Anna liked the new bell better. Others thought, that like themselves, Anna liked the old bell better. All of them thought her answer too clever. And everyone was satisfied. (Everyone looked at her again the next Sunday.)

Of all the careful comments the countess was to make that summer, the comment accepted by the islanders about the new bell was the most hard won, and the most meaningful to Anna. She realized the bell was important to the rather poor natives, and she knew that her answer would be remembered for some time to come.

Island natives did not engage in chitchat that went in one ear and out the other. They did not say much. But what was said was remembered for a while—if not for an entire lifetime. And the islanders did not talk with just anybody. They totally ignored an amused, if kindly-looking, Clare Gilbertson standing next to Anna. They might not have ignored Clare if she had not looked so amused. To the natives, Clare's look of amusement smacked of superiority. To Clare, the natives' snub smacked of snobbishness.

Finally the countess and Clare and the natives and other resorters filed inside St. Anne's for High Mass. Generally, the resorters sat on the right side of the center aisle and the islanders on the left. Anna and Clare ended up in the choir loft because there was no room left in the pews.

Up in the loft, Anna felt little sentimental comfort in the structure of the not-too-large and not-too-small St. Anne's; she had no old associations with the relatively new building. Her mind drifting away from the service, she gazed at the brown barrel vaulted ceiling sprawled over the body of the church. From Anna's viewpoint, the cream colored square columns in the nave seemed to hang down from the broad gently arched ceiling; rather than shoot up to support the wooden canopy of the oblong building.

The three modest altars in cream with gold trim, stationed in what amounted to the transcept, were decorated with bunches of blue and white and lavender and yellow wild-flowers. Anna guessed from a distance the bouquets contained harebell and yarrow and smooth aster and common St. John's-wort. Hundreds of white blessed candles, aglow with tiny leaping flames, burned brightly in front of the side altars, which served as pedestals for brightly painted plaster of paris statues of the Virgin and Child on one side, St. Joseph on the other. Behind the main altar, a primitive painting in blues and browns of St. Anne with heavy eyelids and an aquiline nose, her slender hands grasping a vellum scroll, hung on the cream colored undecorated wall.

The remote island church of St. Anne's vaguely reminded the countess of the mountain village churches in the Italian Alps which she loved so dearly. Of course St. Anne's had no frescoes or mosaics or marble floors, nor was it made of stone; but despite the fancy tourists, the atmosphere inside and outside suggested a haven of peaceful coexistence within itself and its surroundings, similar to the remote mountain churches.

"The subject of my sermon today is the renunciation of offspring," proclaimed a young substitute priest who had seen much of life, but experienced very little of it.

Anna, brought back into the service with a jolt, thought of her sickly Italian husband. Clare thought of her murdered husband. The two women heard the rustling of silk and laces rise to the choir loft from the right side of the pews below. The majority of rustling no doubt came from the young college girls, who caught on very quickly that the sermon of the erudite young priest was directed at the generally educated, high society female resorters in the congregation. For all the native islanders who could, bred abundantly.

The young priest practically accused women without children of what he saw as the retrogression of culture, for coarsening the ideals of life. He stated that women who achieve independence—remain single; or in marriage—remain childless. Suddenly the peacefulness of the remote island church vanished for Anna, and the chaos of the outside world rushed in. Both she and Clare knew all too well that their nagging feminine natures never let them forget for one day that they were childless. They did not need to be reminded of this in church and lost all solace in the sanctified surroundings.

In Anna's and Clare's cases, they were not childless by choice. And both women realized the young priest was not wise enough to temper his sermon with mention of the very real services childless women provided to society as doting nannies, governesses, aunts, nuns, and even dedicated old maids. Next week they hoped the old parish priest would be back at St. Anne's again. The wise old priest sermonized on the beauty of Mackinac Island's nature and made announcements about church bazaars and picnics and needed funds for the improvement of the church building.

As the young priest continued sermonizing about degeneration, Anna's mind wandered to a conversation she had been brought into, but had not contributed to, after breakfast by two lancet-tongued old maids from the crafty crackpots. They had not only informed her of the shocking photograph of stark naked Drexel men and girls; they were convinced that college men had planted the dirty picture in the Moody and Sankey hymnbook.

"Those college men are evil from the day they are born."

"They lie as soon as they learn to talk."

"They are self-willed."

"Their mothers call them smart."

"I call them impudent."

"Their mothers say they know how to take care of themselves."

"I call their mothers selfish."

"What their mothers call high spirits, I call insubordination."

"What their mothers call sharpness, I call dishonesty."

"What do you expect from mothers who are as self-seeking and selfish as their children?"

"Children who are as self-seeking and selfish as their mothers."

"Pleasure seeking women feel child rearing is a waste of their lives."

"It's no wonder that maternity is going out of fashion."

"Babies of humble women are better off."

"I knew a young fashionable woman whose baby died at childbirth. When the dead baby was brought to the mother's bed in its coffin, the mother was deeply interested only in what the lining of the coffin was made of."

Anna shuddered to think that many of the childless people in the world, like the young priest who was finally ending his sermon, either railed at others for not having babies, or like the lancet-tongued old maids, criticized those who did.

Like Philippa MacAdam earlier in the morning, Anna had experienced enough bitter awakenings to Sunday, and longed to run from the stuffy choirloft out into the cool morning air, up to the east bluff, and find her way along some old Indian trail into the wild wooded recesses, miles into the interior of the island, away from civilization.

Anna longed to escape into a patch of giant, white flowered, seven-foot-high cow parsnips far off the beaten track, along Swamp Trail, where she had hiked as a child with her father. She figured the huge plants with clusters of white flowers as large as a fan, stalks thicker than a silver dollar, and leaves as broad as a big hatbox, were by that time of summer nearly full grown, heavy with blossoms. Anna longed to run away and walk alone among the towering, concealing cow parsnips; ever more so, because she knew she could not.

Communion began, and the countess felt renewed tinges of sentiment when she recognized the faces, as they got up and turned from the communion rail, of the Bogans and Borisaws and Chambers and Douds and Dufinas and Earlys and Fentons and Gallaghers and Hobans and La Chances and La Pines and Murrays and Peraults and Pelotts and Ponds and a dozen others walking to their pews with folded hands.

How many of those faces she had seen in church for eighteen summers. And they sat pretty much in the same places they had sat for decades. Those who paid the most dues, or were the most religious, sat from the middle to the front. All others sat from the middle to three-quarters back. Only the half-breed Indians, a few wearing lightweight blankets, sat in the very last pew. Anna cheered up considerably when she found she could even guess which families the altar boys belonged to, the resemblances were so strong.

The last hymn of the High Mass sung, the countess and Clare filed out of St. Anne's. From the church porch, Clare spotted Philmore Calhoun walking briskly in the direction of the harbor. Clare assumed he had attended church services, though she had not noticed him take communion. The effects of the dispiriting sermon vanished, as Clare grew excited thinking about the answer she would give Philmore about the Sault trip at teatime. She had not decided what to answer him, though she had decided to wear her most youthful looking promenading outfit at four o'clock.

The countess and Clare, greeted by many passersby, waited for Owen Corrigan to pull up in front of St. Anne's. When Owen did not show up, they walked in the direction of the closed Mission Church and found the sleeping Catholic curled up in the carriage seat, snoring to beat the band.

Anna called out, "Hello, Charley . . . ."

Owen jumped like a hungover leprechaun scared out of a bog, and helped the "fine leddies" into his carriage. He had no jokes to tell, being that it was Sunday, and somehow jokes were not "fittin' " on the Lord's Day, or on a weak stomach. But he had the courtesy to stop Charley when a very old, poorly dressed woman approached the carriage and asked Owen to "delay himself for a short spell."

The poor old woman walked up to Anna, sitting high and regally in the dilapidated carriage, handed her a holy card, smiled slightly, and without saying a word, took her leave. Anna and Clare watched the poor woman hobble away and disappear around a corner. Anna recognized that the beautiful holy card, with its delicate cut-out tracery of white paper lace, was from Paris. But she did not recognize the poor old woman's face or the name, when Owen told her.

Why had the poor old woman given me what was probably her most precious holy card? wondered the countess, who had lived in a splendid palace the past twenty years, overindulged with gifts of old jewels and extravagant gowns, and was struck by the genuine generosity of the paper gift.

Indeed, the old woman who remembered friendly young Anna had no ulterior purpose. She simply gave the holy card for the act of giving, for the joy of it. Something very hard to accept in 1893, when many a gift or favor was suspiciously regarded.

Anna, her mind so full of other thoughts, did not realize at the time that the precious holy card from the old islander was one of the few real gifts she had received in her lifetime—because nothing was expected from her in return. But Anna did realize that she had been given yet another warming memory of the island and its people to cherish. Many times, old happy memories of summer island days in her youth had been enough to sustain her, when other avenues in her life could not.

The poor old woman presenting her a Parisian holy card was a gesture Anna knew Rutherford Haverhill could never understand. A gesture she wondered if Richard Anders, the younger, amorous gentleman who had so obviously fallen in love with her at the ball and asked her to accompany him to the Sault, would relate to—at teatime.

8

Tea, Horses, and Cows

Four o'clock finally arrived. Every resorter on the veranda breathed a sigh of relief, for Sunday was unofficially over. They could put away their religious or respectable magazines, and sober faces and voices, and talk of the poor, and sinful nude photograph, and begin chatting about the glorious grand ball still alive but some twelve hours ago. The resorters' words about the music, the flowers, the decorations, the gowns, the jewels, and the romantic alliances that afternoon at teatime, flourished like the notes of the waltzes, the polkas, the quadrilles, the pas de quatres, the marches, and the galops at the ball the night before.

Many guests went inside the hotel for tea, but Philmore Calhoun, Sydney Froilan and Richard Anders had arranged with the maître d', Bludsoe, to have tea outside on the veranda. They waited expectantly for Clare and Beatrice and the countess in comradely silence, and gazed out at the sunny skies filled with a parade of fat white clouds brightening and darkening the sparkling waters of the straits, like puffy cumulus curtains being opened and closed repeatedly. Sailing yachts, steam yachts, sloops, Mackinac sailing boats, ferries and rowboats glided in and out of the maritime view.

Philmore, his sailorly bones aching to be out in the tempting Great Lakes' breezes, especially enjoyed watching his schooner yacht *Calla*, out for a run in the wind. He wanted Clare to see the pleasure craft from the veranda full masted, mastering the strong clear currents, and had made arrangements with his crew to take her out before teatime.

Sydney, his painterly bones aching to catch the light of the landscape, translate the sunshiny scene into shiny oils, and sketch a lovely Beatrice in the forefront of the canvas, especially enjoyed watching the view ease in and out of cloud caused shadows. Sydney enjoyed watching the free motion of the herring gulls riding the winds in the airspace facing the veranda. His painterly mind imagined freezing the herring gull's flight as seen by Beatrice within the maritime backdrop. But not with a camera. That was too easy.

Richard, his gambling bones aching to know if the countess would say "yes" to the Sault trip, forgot his father who was miffed that Richard could not join him for tea. Richard felt a surge of carefree energy as he looked at the village, the waters, the islands beyond, the resorters playing croquet and lawn tennis below the hotel, the passersby on the road parallel to the veranda riding nobby horses, or driving handsome phaetons, tilburys, and victorias pulled by matching teams with high held heads, high-stepping hooves, and shiny jingling harnesses flashing in the sunlight.

The three men swallowed the tonic of peace and could not remember feeling so exuberant, just sitting around observing life, rather than participating in it actively. Their exuberance turned outward as they stood up at the approach of Clare, Beatrice and the countess, all smiling, all looking lovely and relaxed and rested, dressed in elegantly simple, pastel colored, nipped in at the waist gowns, and elegantly complicated hats of fantastic shapes ornamented with feathers or berries or flowers or ribbons in artful combinations. The gentlemen and ladies exchanged enthusiastic, if formal, late afternoon pleasantries, and each of the three ladies was helped into her chair next to the adoring gentleman who had invited her.

Bludsoe, who had seen that the round tea table was dressed in white Irish linen, silver service, lustrous china, and decorated with fine cut glass bowls filled with water and floating deep pink roses, lost no time in bringing on the goodies for tea that Philmore, Sydney, and Richard had specially ordered.

A mini army of black waiters in white coats placed on the table one silver platter after another filled with attractively arranged ham fingers and deviled eggs, with square cut lobster salad sandwiches and star-cut lettuce sandwiches, with jellied veal and spiced beef tongue and pressed chicken. On three-tiered serving plates, white, pink, and yellow petit fours and chocolate eclairs and cream puffs filled with custard, and Chocolat Menier dipped strawberries were presented upon white crocheted doilies, causing the ladies to "ooh and ahh" much to the gentlemen's great pleasure.

The gentlemen grew even more exuberant, having realized the ladies' delightful feminine appreciation of such a little thing as luscious-looking sweets. And each gentleman took a turn in explaining to his respective female partner that, although it was late in the season, the strawberries were exceedingly fresh. The plump sweet berries were brought to the island directly from the little village of Freedom across the straits.

Yes, Philmore, Sydney and Richard were out to show Clare, Beatrice and the countess that they knew how to entertain with cultivated gusto. In addition to iced orange pekoe tea, they had ordered hot Earl Grey tea, as well as Johannis sparkling water and freshly squeezed iced lemonade. Not to mention the cooled Chablis and Pouilly-Fuissé white wine, which the ladies drank mixed with a few drops of potash water, and the gentlemen drank with utter appreciation.

As a group they conversed about bohemians, post prandial ablutions in the orient, dullness of theatre in Paris, Oscar

Wilde's new play "A Woman of No Importance." Sydney sang the popular new tune "Daddy Won't Buy Me a Bow-wow Comrades." Philmore hummed a melody from *Faust* and complained that *La Gioconda* was above people's heads. Richard admitted he could not hold a tune and recited, "That man that hath a tongue, I say, is not man, If with his tongue he cannot win a woman," from the *Two Gentlemen of Verona*.

Time passed more swiftly than anyone cared to admit. And indeed, not needing to reveal anything about their backgrounds, the men won the women over. Hands down. For the gentlemen's actions, their attention to detail and generosity, spoke louder to the women than any background stories they so easily could have related, whether true or made-up. Besides, there was a whole half a summer ahead to relate their colorful pasts to the charming woman sitting so delightfully close to each of them.

Beatrice, Clare and the countess thoroughly enjoyed the gentlemen's company and enthusiastically agreed to accompany Sydney, Philmore and Richard, as well as Professor Bellamy, the Cudahys and their wives, Rutherford Haverhill, and Eugene Sullivan to the Sault to shoot the rapids and get in a little fishing.

The gentlemen considered the ladies' "yes" regarding the Sault trip as one of the harder won negotiations of their summer. They also felt the effort was well rewarded. And right after the women agreed, as if by plan, all the new friends who were going to the Sault gathered together on the veranda to make last minute arrangements to leave in a couple of days.

New friendships of kindred spirits, mixed with physical allure and shared worldliness, ah, what a sensation it caused in each of them. Each wanted to hold on to those moments of unentangled freshness and excitement in the discovery of each other. And each of them, except Richard, was at an age when he or she knew the elevated emotions were temporary, so they opened themselves to make the most of the sensation.

It had been a long time for most of them, since they had felt exhilarated in the presence of another human being. Usually their excitement came from sailing fast yachts, traveling around the world, betting at the race track or on the stock market, attending extravagant balls and a hundred other modern excitements. Feeling excited in the presence of another human being was—almost—a new feeling.

During this time, Philippa MacAdam was not enjoying the attentions of entertaining gentlemen. She was jumping hurdles with humorless John Fuller out at the Early farm, fully aware that a man with black hair and a black beard sitting a bay mare, watched her from a distance. Philippa had no idea whether the man was Colonel Williamson or the black-haired, black-bearded man on the balcony before breakfast—or both.

Philippa tried to put the colonel out of her mind in order to concentrate on improving her already masterly jumping. Having promised John Fuller that she would participate in the hurdle jumping contest at the annual Grand Hotel sponsored Field Day sporting competitions, Philippa wanted to practice as much as possible with Dude.

Colonel Marshe Williamson watched Philippa MacAdam taking a jump. She sailed over the four-foot hurdle with ease and on landing held a loose rein, straightened her arms and leaned back. He thought, such style, and figured that Mrs. MacAdam cared more for Dude than herself. The colonel could always tell what a person was made of by the way he or she jumped a horse. Most people who jumped a horse leaned their bodies too far forward on the landing, jarring the horse's forelegs. But Mrs. Philippa MacAdam was not most people, and Colonel Marshe Williamson put aside thoughts of horses and began concentrating on the woman riding Dude.

Yes, there was no doubt about it. Eligible Marshe William-son grew unusually interested in eligible Philippa MacAdam the more he saw of her. And having made a few inquiries of John Fuller and Jimmy Hayes about her, found out to his great satisfaction that she was not bound to any husband. He was sorry to have missed her at the ball the night before. Jimmy Hayes told him that Mrs. MacAdam suddenly fell ill and had left just about the time he had arrived. The colonel thought Philippa looked perfectly well jumping Dude, and damned his bad timing in not making it to the ball earlier. As exhausted as the colonel had been last night, he would have found the spirit to dance more than one waltz with Mrs. MacAdam.

"Mr. Fuller, is that Colonel Williamson watching us in the distance?"

John Fuller's face brightened as fast as an incandescent lamp switched on as he answered, "I believe it is the colonel." With a barely audible, "excuse me," he promptly rode away from Philippa to Marshe.

The last person Philippa wanted to see was Colonel Marshe Williamson. Having spent so much of the day before anticipat-ing his presence at the massacre lecture, at the cigar and um-brella race, at tea, at dinner, before the ball, and during the ball—the sight of him now caused more vexation and frustra-tion than Philippa would have imagined herself capable of in reaction to man, a mere twenty-four hours ago. Hormones, she thought, go away.

She decided to ignore the men and jumped Dude over a few more short hurdles with ease. Sensing that the horse needed a drink she rode him to a water trough nearby. Hearing the approach of a horse, she turned and saw John Fuller waiting on the roadside while Marshe Williamson trotted up to her side.

Dismounting, the colonel checked to see that the water in the trough was not stagnant, coaxed his unthirsty $20,000 bay mare to drink, and addressed Philippa in gentlemanly, if extremely friendly, tones.

"Good afternoon, Mrs. MacAdam."

Philippa could not help but notice that the colonel was genuinely happy to greet her. But she regretted that her usually generous nature could not ignore judgment of the colonel's obvious bad taste in women, and she could not reciprocate his enthusiasm. She could not help feeling a bit insulted that the colonel should favor the reckless horsewoman and herself without distinction.

"Good afternoon, Colonel Williamson."

Marshe felt her closed coolness. He figured she was not feeling well. Certainly the no-nonsense friendly woman from their warm afternoon acquaintance in the stable less than twenty-four hours ago could not have changed that drastically. But then he thought, people are so unpredictable these days, as he remounted his horse with noticeable effort, if excellent form.

Marshe inquired with a courtesy seemingly born of old money, "Mrs. MacAdam . . . Mr. Fuller has asked me to convey the message that if you are willing, he will allow me to accompany both of you back to the stables, as soon as you are ready."

"Whatever is agreeable to Mr. Fuller is agreeable to me, Colonel Williamson," Philippa replied politely. Avoiding his slightly offended eyes, she added a quick smile. There was no doubt in Philippa's mind that the black-haired, black-bearded, middle-aged colonel, dressed in a pink shirt and white collar with a simple club tie, a morning coat of black, blue trousers strapped tightly over his boots, and a tall black silk hat, cut a rather decent-looking figure sitting tall on his handsome bay mare.

Most females would have called the colonel downright

dashing. But Philippa, turned upright because of her recharged suspicions about his sneaky spying in the stable, and seeing him with the reckless horsewoman, possibly twice, wished he had the face of a frog and ears like jug handles. She could not feel at ease with the liberating man who had only yesterday reclaimed her hormones from limbo and rearoused her interest in hateful corsets. She laughed to herself thinking she had commited some asinine schoolgirl indulgences. After all, she claimed to herself rashly, no one could fill the shoes of the late Mr. MacAdam—not even Colonel Marshe Williamson, who could have been his brother.

"I'm honored you allow me to accompany you, Mrs. MacAdam."

Philippa thought, aren't you spreading your marmalade a bit thick on the burned toast, Colonel Williamson? But she responded, "Perhaps we can make it back to the hotel during teatime. I have quite an appetite after my hurdle jumping lesson."

"Perhaps you would do me another honor, and join me for tea, Mrs. MacAdam?"

Philippa could not resist replying in her most courteous voice. "But perhaps three is a crowd . . ."

"I beg your pardon . . ."

"Excuse me if I am forward, Colonel, but your other friend, with whom I am acquainted, having traveled these same carriage roads together only yesterday, after the accident on Kentucky Jean, might not take kindly to . . ."

"My other friend . . . of whom do you speak? For I have many friends on this island. And although I am aware of the accident with Kentucky Jean and your involvement, I do not make the connection."

"I am not unaware that you accompanied the . . . friend . . . of our mutual connection to the ball last night . . . and it is of that . . . friend . . . of which I speak."

"I was not aware that you were at the ball when I arrived last night, Mrs. MacAdam."

"And I was not aware that you were acquainted with the . . . friend . . . to whom I refer." Philippa felt a rush of energy and redness creep into her face. Her words were laced with disguised sarcasm and she regretted that she felt the need to show the slightest interest in the colonel's comings and goings.

Marshe looked over at her, noticing a red blush penetrating her soft-looking skin; he liked the color red. He had not figured that Mrs. MacAdam's charming coolness had something to do with him.

Marshe Williamson became quite excited thinking he had aroused that much reaction in Philippa. A woman who could potentially sit his Armande like no other woman he knew. A woman who could grace his library and his dining table like many other women he knew. But there was no woman he knew who could do it all, or he would have married her by now. So he told himself. And he knew plenty of women—though not all of them by any means in the biblical sense.

Anyone with an eye for choice male specimens, even older ones such as Marshe, might construe that he would be popular with the women. But Philippa was disgusted with herself for allowing her emotions to have been so carried away in the seclusion of the stable by such an obvious lady's man. And when Marshe did not answer her as they approached John Fuller, Philippa flippantly figured that Marshe would not even do her the courtesy of making up lies as to why he sought the company of two women at once.

Philippa tried not to convince herself that his silence admitted the clandestine relationship with the crude reckless horsewoman, who could change her accent from raw to ripe as fast as she could open her mouth. And Philippa hated to admit that the black-haired, black-bearded man on the balcony must have been the colonel, looking younger. Because what male, worthy of the name man, would not look younger burying his roguish face in a woman's lacy red underpants before throwing them off a balcony, on the Lord's Day (when such things should not happen, therefore making "such things" all the more forbidden and exciting and youthful).

Although it was one of those glorious Mackinac days—when the sun warmed the scent from a nearby meadow full of pink fireweed and yellow Aaron's rod and white ox-eye daisies, blended into sweetness by fresh lake breezes—the soothing breeze did not blow away the stinkweed of suspicion about Marshe, which Philippa really wanted to deny.

She thought the colonel had quite a nerve asking her to tea on top of everything else. He needed to be answered immediately regarding the seedy proposal and put in his proper place. She knew the Italians regarded such two-timing behavior as an insignificant little peccadillo to be forgiven and forgotten within the greater significance of life. Philippa told herself she was not that continental in her outlook regarding two-timing men. She should have told herself, she was not that stupid.

"Regarding your invitation for tea, Colonel Williamson, thank you . . . I . . ."

"Excuse me, Mrs. MacAdam." The colonel, beginning to grasp Philippa's innuendos, turned to John Fuller and interposed wryly, "John, do you take tea at the hotel?"

"Never, Colonel, I have a stable to run and seldom have time for anything except three square meals a day. Besides, already I feel I have been too long from Kentucky Jean."

"You see, Mrs. MacAdam, there would not be a crowd at tea today." Marshe's eyes twinkled.

"But Colonel. . . ." Philippa realized the colonel purposefully and mischievously connected her former use of the word "friend" to John Fuller, rather than to the reckless horsewoman.

Without appearing to realize Philippa's unspoken accusations toward Marshe, John Fuller interjected, "I am in deep debt to the colonel . . . he assisted me in saving Kentucky Jean's life last night. When her fever broke at one o'clock in the morning, Karl took over watch of her, and the colonel and I decided to celebrate, so we freshened up and attended the ball. We looked for you, Mrs. MacAdam, but were informed you were not feeling well and had left."

"I did not see you, Mr. Fuller," Philippa's voice trailed off as she pictured the colonel and horsewoman.

John continued, his voice verging on the malicious, "And Mrs. MacAdam, you would never believe whom we followed into the ballroom . . ."

"I wouldn't?" Philippa's indignation turned to embarrassment, having subtly accused Marshe of cavorting with the reckless horsewoman, or perhaps, "horseback whore."

"We followed that hussy of our mutual acquaintance who rode Kentucky Jean near to her death yesterday . . . ."

"Oh, Mr. Fuller . . . what a curious twist of events . . . ." Philippa, feeling sheepish, could not look over at Marshe Williamson. She knew Marshe had put two and two together.

Strangely, John Fuller could not keep his mouth shut about the reckless horsewoman and gushed on in a rather affected tone, "But this is too much, I said to myself. Imagine . . . that woman had the nerve to ask the colonel . . . who had just sat up half the night with the horse she nearly killed . . . to escort her into the ballroom because she claimed her husband was already inside . . . or some such nonsense . . . and before I could tell the colonel that it was because of her that Kentucky Jean was suffering, and our evening had been ruined, the colonel graciously agreed to follow her in. Later we

learned from Eugene Sullivan . . . that the woman draped in
. . . I must admit . . . a stunning red gown . . . had in fact
not entered the ballroom before that evening. Of course I
reported all of this to Jimmy Hayes," he added, insincerely.

"Life is full of ironies, Mr. Fuller." And in spite of the
explanation, Philippa had a hard time believing all the little
coincidences between the reckless horsewoman and the colonel. She sighed and said to herself, it is so hard to know whom
to trust, and it does not matter if the trust involves men or
women.

Philippa knew all too well that in the world of 1893, no one
appeared to be what they had been born to be. Industrialists
had been factory workers. Millionaires' wives had been chambermaids. Lumber barons had been lumberjacks. Big city
merchants had been small town shop owners. United States
presidents had been farmers. Whores had been ministers'
daughters.

She realized that transmutants disguised their pasts. They
wore personalities and manners to match their gowns and
suits—changing them to fit their new role and the new fashion.
Their children, doomed to reflect their parents' uncertain
behavior, were fast becoming schizophrenic reflections of both
what their parents were born into and what they tried to
become. Mind boggling changes in technology, coupled with
personal transformations, were just about driving everyone
away from disturbing realities into fantasy world escapes. And
driving them to fairy isles like Mackinac.

Philippa, a kind of reversed transmutant herself from spoiled southern belle to ascetic serious artist, could not even trust
her own weakened instincts to know—whom to trust.

"Colonel Williamson . . . I accept your gracious invitation for tea," she said trying to hide her hesitation.

Marshe took out his solid gold pocket watch and announced, "If we hurry the horses a bit, we should be there before teatime is over."

And Philippa smiled at his lips, because she could not yet look directly in his eyes.

Bagpipe players blew blasts of air through their reed melody and drone pipes as they promenaded the longest porch in the world, as if in parade. And guests streamed back onto the veranda after tea. They noticed the countess, Mrs. Beatrice Venn, and Mrs. Clare Gilbertson enjoying the company of a group of gentlemen they had been seen with at the ball. Bludsoe oversaw his band of waiters clearing the round table, fairly groaning with the extravagant leftovers. It was noted by all the veranda observers that the group was most merry, and each observer would have given up something to be a part of their fun.

Then and there each of the observers resolved to have tea on the veranda, rather than inside the hotel, next Sunday as well. The special tea arranged by Sydney, Philmore and Richard was to cause considerable headaches for Jimmy Hayes. For within one hour's time, having tea in the refreshing outdoors, on the great column studded veranda, suddenly became the *de rigueur* fashion for some five hundred guests at the Grand Hotel on Sunday afternoons for the rest of the season.

It was also noted that Mrs. Philippa MacAdam was not present among the Big Four. Tongues wagged about her absence until she showed up in a cream white grenadine gown with terra cotta satin stripes and a sailor hat of white straw with a white tulle veil. Then tongues wagged about her gorgeous costume—until she was met by a swell southern gentleman some knew to be Colonel Marshe Williamson. And then tongues ceased wagging and started articulating some serious speculation about the two eligible southerners.

Relieved to see that her friends were still on the veranda, Philippa suggested to the colonel to join them. Desiring to be alone with Mrs. MacAdam, the colonel graciously replied that he would very much like to meet her friends. To the accompaniment of a bagpipe schottische, Philippa introduced Marshe Williamson to the countess and Clare and Beatrice, looking so radiant sitting next to Richard and Philmore and Sydney looking so exuberant. It was obvious that tea had been a great success. And the radiance and exuberance was—catching.

More is the pity that lovestruck Cynthia Price, stuck with chaperoning her sister Priscilla and "pesty" Belinda Gaines, promenaded nearby the jolly group and accidentally caught the glow in Richard's eyes when he looked at the countess.

Cynthia, displaying typical Price rationality, told herself that Richard Anders was rather young and naturally enthusiastic, all the time trying to control the urge to cry at the sight of their happiness together. Why she herself had seen that same look in his eyes at the ball as well, when they had danced the cotillion together. But certainly the married countess would not encourage the younger man's attentions, she reasoned, her uncontrollable pulse pounding blood beats, like the wild Dahomeys at the Chicago World's Fair pounded drum beats.

Worst of all, quick Belinda noted the look between Richard and the countess as well and jumped into action practically dragging a thoroughly embarrassed, lovestruck Cynthia over to the group, and infiltrating it with her customary flighty intrusion.

Belinda exchanged afternoon greetings with everyone and then wasted no time in exposing her observations that Mrs. Venn's children looked as if they were having so much fun playing croquet with Professor Bellamy, the "old" Muldoon ladies, Rutherford Haverhill, and some New Woman college girls on the hotel lawn below. They all watched the game and overheard one of the eighty-year-old Muldoons exclaim, after she missed hitting the professor's ball out of bounds, "Oh, to be sixty again!"

The countess, who had observed Belinda's bitchy maneuver, wisely brought an uncomfortable Cynthia into conversation with Richard. And then she tried to bring young Belinda, wearing a tarnished copper green neo-Empire gown, into conversation to keep her from spoiling Cynthia's chance to converse with Richard, a gentleman her own age.

The countess observed politely, "Miss Gaines . . . your dress looks like a perfect copy of an 1830s first Empire gown."

"Countess Gianotti, you must remember how they looked back then . . . ." Belinda shot back an unfounded insult that wished the countess some sixty years old.

"Miss Gaines," intervened Beatrice Venn, glancing at the countess who was holding back a smile, "Your dress is a perfectly delightful copy. Recently, I saw the original gown yours was copied after, in Paris."

Belinda burst with anger inside. She prided herself on her original Parisian gowns bought in New Orleans, and not even one of the Big Four, who deliberately kept all the choice gentlemen to themselves, was going to accuse her of wearing a copy.

"Mrs. Venn, I was assured that this dress is an original."

"You look so lovely in it, it hardly matters whether it is an original or a copy."

"Mrs. Venn, it appears that you and your friends spend so much time in Paris, I mean, so many of your stories relate to that city . . . why one could call you all reg'lar Parisites," quipped Belinda, thinking her green response very grown up, and that it was about time someone finally put the man-grabbing Big Four in their places.

Cynthia Price, having paused in her conversation with Richard, heard Belinda's uncalled-for rude behavior. She wanted to slap the beauty off Belinda's sassy face. Instead, she spoke up with such dignity and poise, even Richard Anders noticed her grace.

"Belinda, coming from New Orleans, I am surprised to hear you mispronounce a word from the language of your family's origins. You are drastically mistaken. Please excuse us."

After quick parting pleasantries, this time, Cynthia dragged a red-faced Belinda away from the group. Yes, somehow the short conversation with Richard had reawakened Cynthia's spirit to the point that she actually cared again what people said to each other. And Cynthia was not going to put up with an adolescent Belinda, not much older than her sister Priscilla, embarrassing the group of four women, especially when she was serving as the adolescent's chaperone.

Filled with an energy similar to the rush she felt at the ball with Richard Anders, Cynthia released and translated this energy into a tongue-lashing at Belinda until young Miss Gaines fell into tears, and Cynthia fell into a state of utter satisfaction. From then on, Cynthia could not get Richard Anders off her mind.

And from then on, Belinda Gaines watched what she said around "frustrated old maid" Cynthia Price, her "best friend's" sister. But Belinda did not watch what she said when the Price sisters were not around; for after Cynthia's tongue-lashing, Belinda Gaines was bound and determined to get back at Cynthia before the season's end.

By this time unattached Rutherford Haverhill had been invited to join the Big Four and their admirers. He would never admit it, but he was delighted to be asked to accompany the group to the Sault and was cheered up by their laughter and their discussion about the trip. For he was still hung over, not from alcoholic spirits at the grand ball, but from the acute emptiness he had suddenly begun—to feel—in the presence of the countess.

Rutherford checked to see whether or not Richard Anders was keeping the married countess interested. He was. Perhaps too obviously so. He also checked out Sydney and Beatrice. And it did not take long before Rutherford purposely engaged Sydney in an argument about what outfits to wear at the Sault, in order to keep the world famous painter from his so obvious enjoyment of Beatrice Venn.

Sydney tried to make a fool of Rutherford by replying, "The superior masculine mind does not bother two hoots with the considerations of what he wears to shoot the Sault rapids. Attention to dress and superior intellect have nothing to do with each other, Haverhill."

Rutherford ignored the implied insult and responded in his most anglophiliac tone, "Froilan, your theory has no foundation. The greatest swell of classic times was Caesar himself. As a matter of fact, we have an ancient bust of Caesar at our cottage in Newport. If you would see it, Froilan, being the . . . portrait painter . . . you are," Rutherford inhaled a sniff through his seemingly chiseled nostrils, "you would have to admit to the intelligence rendered in Caesar's eyes."

At the same time, Philippa and the countess were brought into a conversation with Marshe and Richard, who began discussing their favorite subject. Horses. The two men were distantly acquainted with each other, having met a few times at various race tracks around the country. To the two women, the men's conversation had nothing to do with horses. It had to do with the men. To the men, the conversation had nothing to do with horses. It had to do with indirectly telling the women they meant to woo—this is my life. And the men sportingly assisted each other in the telling.

Richard said, "Ladies, did you know that Marshe Williamson owns 275 acres of the most beautiful bluegrass land outside of Lexington, Kentucky . . . and on it stands the famous stud farm 'Colonel's Thoroughbreds' . . . and on that farm lives one of the best judges of horseflesh in the country."

Philippa recognized the name of Marshe Williamson's farm immediately.

"Anders, you compliment me generously and I thank you for it. Though other long-haired turfmen, I must admit, call me a dude and a faddist. They don't like the high prices I pay for horseflesh. Years ago owners of race horses bought their animals at random and raced them purely for pleasure. But I purchase the best horses at any cost and race them for profit . . . and I must add . . . great pleasure. The long-haired gentlemen turfmen don't like the idea, much less the practice, of racing horses for profit. They despise me for making a business out of it. But I use sound business methods in my horse dealings."

Richard added, "Colonel, everyone of those turfmen who calls you a faddist yearns to copy your success. I know that certain men, like my father, hold onto their old ideas as if they are the sacred cows of India. And many of them stubbornly cling to those old ideas, oftener than not, because they cannot afford financially to compete with the new.

"After all, Colonel, your Armande, that stallion of yours standing 16 hands high, with perfect shoulders and not a blemish on the legs, with the Triple English racing crown, the Derby, the Two Thousand Guineas, and the St. Ledger winnings to his name . . . well, Colonel . . . it was widely publicized that Armande has some $150,000 in earnings to his name . . . and the long-haired turfmen, then dead and buried, turned over in their graves."

Everyone chuckled and Richard added, "I am looking forward to seeing the get of Armande."

The colonel smiled, and stole a glance at Philippa to see her response. She looked neither impressed by nor unappreciative of such a record. She looked extremely interested. Then Marshe noticed she wore a cut crystal horse head scarf pin with a portrait of Sir Hugo, winner of the Derby of 1892. And he knew immediately that Mrs. MacAdam had more connections with horses than she let on.

"Regarding the subject of criticism," Marshe replied, "recently I bought a colt for $30,000. You should have witnessed the dour attitudes which befell me from the so-called gentlemen horse racers. Of course as a result of the exhorbitant sum paid, I have now removed a dangerous rival to my champion, Armande."

Richard, Philippa and the countess smiled in response to the colonel's cleverness. But again Philippa's suspicions about the colonel crept back because he had flaunted money talk in mixed company. No real southern gentleman discussed money among ladies.

"Ladies, you will forgive me for discussing the monetary particulars of the horse racing world." The colonel noticed Philippa's cheeks redden slightly and wondered if she suffered from acid stomach.

He had no idea that Philippa MacAdam was fighting every feminine impulse the colonel had awakened in her. And that she was looking for any excuse, through his social mistakes, to refute the youthful feelings he caused her in the stable.

"But the truth is . . . if I may state it," the colonel paused waiting approval.

"Please do," the countess encouraged him.

"This is the age of money. You may have a street named after you, or a library, but it doesn't matter. Better to sell your ancestral possessions and turn your aristocracy into cash."

The countess added, "Many aristocrats are selling their

family heirlooms in order to keep their palaces and castles. In Italy, I heard of this occurrence daily."

Richard observed the countess turn her regal head and stare out at the glittering straits.

After a fast glance to see how Mrs. MacAdam was taking a conversation usually reserved for male company only, Marshe continued, "There is a rapidly occurring exchange of wealth in the world . . . and I am a prime example of the phenomenon. My family lost our plantation in the war between the North and the South, and gave our last security to the war effort. With ten horses to our name my father and I supported five sisters and my mother in the only way left to us . . . my father and I with our own hands . . . butchered the ten thoroughbreds, sold the meat, and started a business of it."

Marshe looked at Mrs. MacAdam, a living example of the word feminine, to see how this blunt revelation affected her female constitution. She looked surprised, but not uncomfortable. There was many a southern beauty who had turned away from him in the past at the mere mention of the word "butcher."

Marshe continued, "It took us some twenty years to build up enough equity to raise horses again—rather than butcher them. And now I am making a business in race horses . . . unheard of in my father's day. Recently, I presented my mother a treasured collection of Meissen from an almost moneyless German prince. Yes, I know what it is to be wealthy and powerful and have it all taken away and be redistributed. I know what it is to be old money and new money."

The colonel looked intently at both Philippa and the countess, whose worldly eyes seemed to understand. But it was from Philippa's eyes he drew comfort. He had no idea why. The reappearing scene in Marshe's mind of meeting Philippa for the first time in the stable, witnessing her determination to mount Dude from the floor alone, her lovely form easing down from the sidesaddle, her nearness during the mounting . . . almost wiped away their uncordial words at the Early farm. And he soon learned why he drew such comfort from Mrs. MacAdam. For they had deep loss in common.

"My late husband," began Philippa, "had begun a stud farm some four years when he purchased a horse by the name of Checkmate, claret brown with black points, similar in stature to the colt you just purchased, Colonel Williamson. My husband believed that Checkmate was going to put the Mac-Adam thoroughbred farm on the lips of every horse racer, and often joked that Checkmate's horseflesh was worth more than his own flesh. When disaster befell us in the form of a devastating barn fire, Mr. MacAdam was able to save only one horse, and that was his favorite. Checkmate. But my husband . . . was killed instantly when a burning beam collapsed upon him. The horse ran away from fright."

The countess, Marshe and Richard quietly assumed expressions of sympathy for the untimely death of Mr. MacAdam.

Philippa added, "I did not send anyone out to look for the horse, and the animal came back two days later, after my husband's funeral, in the middle of the night. As you know, horses have excellent memories and can find their way home in the dark, so I was not surprised to learn he had returned. However, the horse had been as devoted to my husband as my husband was to him, and he refused to eat . . ."

Marshe interposed with an encompassing kindness noticed by all, "As you yourself, the animal was indeed grieved at the loss of your husband, Mrs. MacAdam . . ."

"So grieved . . . Colonel . . . that in spite of my spending night and day with Checkmate . . . the horse died of starvation."

No one said it, but they all thought that the horse had committed suicide.

But no one, except for Marshe, sensed that Philippa's

sympathetic participation in the experience of the horse's suicide—had prevented her own.

And as if coming out of the effects of a verbal purge, Philippa's brightness of expression resurfaced. She returned to the subject of horse racing, and praised the ardor and vehemence and struggle for victory that excites the energies of horse and man.

The countess supported Philippa's resurgence and added, "I have seen horse races without riders in Italy. At one such race I saw a horse hold his rival back by seizing him with his teeth."

"I should love to paint such a scene," exclaimed Philippa.

Marshe, full of spirit, falling in love with Mrs. MacAdam, exclaimed. "My favorite painting is *The Horse Fair* by Rosa Bonheur. Whenever I am in New York I go to the Metropolitan Museum to see it. Mrs. MacAdam are you familiar with the painting?"

The countess smiled warmly and answered for Philippa, "Colonel Williamson . . . why . . . Mrs. MacAdam studied painting with Rosa Bonheur in Rome . . . and one of Mrs. MacAdam's paintings is hung at the Women's Building at the world's fair . . . ."

Surprised, the colonel graciously replied, "I have been told by John Fuller that you are painting his Dude this summer. But I did not realize, Mrs. MacAdam, that you are an accomplished painter of horses." Marshe imagined Philippa standing next to an easel in the bluegrass of his Kentucky farm, painting Armande. Then he imagined pulling her lovely form down to the thick bluegrass and before he could imagine the rest, Mrs. MacAdam addressed him, and he fantasized that she had undressed herself instead.

Philippa smiled at Marshe and admitted, "Compared to Rosa Bonheur, I am a beginning artist, Colonel. And if I have come a long way in a short time, I attribute it to learning the anatomy of horses. A subject about which I am sure you are an expert, Colonel."

Marshe noted that Mrs. MacAdam said the statement in a matter of fact tone without a trace of society lady affectation or sense of the distastefulness of butchering horses.

"Philippa continued, "Of course I did not learn anatomy from butchering horses . . . I dissected them . . . ." Philippa enjoyed the reaction of utter astonishment on the faces of Marshe and Richard and the countess.

The countess looked at Philippa who smiled at Marshe who looked at Richard who smiled at the countess who smiled back, and all broke out into a round of laughter. The worldly group shook off the insecurities of their untraditional, uncertain lives and the untraditional, uncertain lives of others, by releasing belly laughs and expelling stale air. Layers of forced formality fell off the men and women, like veils falling from harem dancers stripping.

Marshe Williamson decided then and there that he was going to invite Mrs. MacAdam to his Kentucky farm the first week in August, on the pretext of painting Armande. Enroute to Kentucky he planned to meet the Director of the Government Stud from Beberbeck, Germany, on a mission from Kaiser Willhelm to study horses at the Chicago World's Fair. After this initial meeting, the studmaster had been invited to Marshe's farm to visit his thoroughbreds. And to buy at Colonel's Thoroughbreds. Marshe could not think of a more charming horsewoman to sit as hostess across his fifteen-foot mahogany dining table, one of the few pieces of "old" furniture his family managed to keep after the Civil War.

Realizing that he had not aided Richard in a discussion of himself, Marshe stated, "When it comes to horse racing, Mr. Anders is quite the swashbuckler. I've heard he bet his whole life savings a few years ago and made himself a fortune in one fast swoop."

Richard smiled openly and answered, "What I made for myself was a name. A name so infamous among respectable people . . . such as my father, who swears that all 'respectable folks' will have to give up the sport of horse racing altogether because of gamblers like me . . . that I changed my name."

The countess asked, "May I inquire as to how your father responded to your changing your name?"

"Countess Gianotti, my father never said anything. He was undoubtedly . . . secretly relieved. I washed his hands for him, of a son he prayed would walk in his same weighty footsteps. You see, my father is a well-respected trial lawyer turned judge.

"I changed my name when I heard he was up for nomination for the state supreme court. We were not in correspondence at the time. I kept his name, so to speak, out of the local papers a year before they were to make the appointment . . . but he did not win it. He did not achieve what I know was to him . . . one of the greatest honors any American could achieve in a lifetime. Whether or not I was responsible . . . and whether or not he holds my disreputable reputation responsible for his loss . . . I cannot shake the feeling that I lost my father, I mean, lost my father's appointment."

With brawny resignation, Richard quickly added, "You see Colonel Williamson, you are not alone when it comes to receiving criticism from the old-fashioned among us . . . who are bitterly nostalgic for a lost age of innocence. For a time when great men dedicated themselves to honor . . . not money. For a time when gentlemen raced horses for the fun of it."

Anna felt the sting and loss implied in Richard's words. She imagined that Richard's old-fashioned father saw his modern son as a race-runner for advantage, a man with short finite aims, a foolish egoist without prospect. But Anna sensed Richard as a man instinctively masculine, who was bound and determined not to sit in a stuffy office behind a desk for the rest of his life. She smiled warmly at the younger man, whose eyes clearly adored her.

Richard smiled in return and felt Anna as a woman instinctively feminine, whose softness absorbed his hard truth without recoil, drawing it away from his troubled self. He asked himself what magnetic phenomenon the countess possessed, for he had feelings of inseparable association with a woman he barely knew, who did not talk about herself. Yet he could not help feeling, he had known the countess his entire life.

Richard's revelation of the trouble with his father was but a small explanation of a much larger problem, which would explode because of the countess before the end of the summer. The trip to Sault Ste. Marie was the calm—before the storm.

"I see one of our hotel's exquisite songsters, the yellow warbler, dining placidly from fresh horse apples. Isn't that the most? How can such beautiful music come from a creature that dines on horse droppings?"

No one needed to look up. Even if they had not recognized Rutherford Haverhill's voice, only Rutherford would have made such an observation public. And only Rutherford had no new admirer to steer his need away from gaining the attentions of others, through one of the many riveting statements he articulated in a day.

Perhaps because the group felt Rutherford's loneliness, or because they were so energized from their new alliances, they all looked to him kindly and made little comments on the other beautiful birds they had seen on the island, like the purple finch and red-breasted nuthatch and black-capped chickadee and purple martin. And if Rutherford had not been looking over the side of the longest porch in the world at the yellow warbler dining on golden horse apples, and had not looked down upon the empty lawn vacant of guests playing croquet and lawn tennis, no one in the group would have heard or seen the commotion below. The bagpipers approached playing another schottische but twenty feet away.

"There's a cow on the front lawn looking up at me," Rutherford stated.

Everyone wondered what remark he was going to come up with next.

"Now she is throwing her neck about. Now she is bucking her hind feet. . . I say. . . what a display. You must all come and look. Sully, perhaps you should inform proprietor Hayes that he has a cow with a star on her forehead bucking about on the front lawn of his Grand Hotel." Rutherford laughed in his jerky way. So rustic, he thought, this would never happen in Newport.

Faster than herring gulls darting for food, the Big Four fairly flew to the side of Rutherford Haverhill, who felt quite pumped up having the entire admired group of four women suddenly flocking around him. They recognized a much thinner Glendora on the lawn below, mooing in alarm about something, kicking her heals about as if a swarm of wasps were stinging her hooves.

The countess shot a questioning look at her three friends. They answered without words. And before anyone could imagine what all the fuss was about the Big Four hastened two hundred feet down the veranda, followed by little Frederick and Monica Venn, who had just joined their MaMa. Lifting up their skirts, they walked briskly down the hotel's entrance steps, darted between the carriages in the porte-cochere, bounded down the whitewashed stairway leading to the lawn, and hurried over to Glendora.

By this time, resorters who had not been alerted that the Big Four had left the veranda in haste were either sleeping or deaf. For some five hundred guests gathered at the veranda's edge, hearing the bagpipers play and watching the four high society women and two children running like gazelles into the wind, after a cow with a clanging bell that was heading into the dark and fragrant pine woods beyond the lawn.

In the late afternoon breezes, which were turning cool and invigorating, the four women's gorgeous afternoon costumes fluttered and filled like colorful wind driven sails on a sea of green grass. One by one their hats of ribbons and berries and flowers fell off of their heads, littering the velvety green lawn, and looking ever so much like fanciful jars of flowers from afar. Little Frederick's four-year-old legs could barely keep up with the spirited women, but not a whimper was heard on the veranda above.

Every resorter watching the excitement from the veranda that late Sunday afternoon wondered where the women and children had gone to and what they would find and what they would do. But no one wondered more than Richard Anders, Philmore Calhoun, Sydney Froilan, and Marshe Williamson; and no one wanted to run after the four high-spirited women more than these four men.

A half-hour passed, and when the women and children did not come back, Rutherford suggested that Jimmy Hayes should send someone out to look for them. Professor Bellamy immediately volunteered, followed by a chorus of male voices eagerly awaiting the chance to form a search party and join the chase.

No sooner had the gentlemen volunteered to go after the women and children, when the Big Four showed up on the lawn below. A chorus of chatter, near all thirty-four doric gossip columns, crescendoed into a flattering finale when they saw the aristocratic countess walking beside a newborn calf, and the other high society women and children walking next to the calf's mother, Glendora.

And when the nosy resorters found out that the Countess Gianotti and Mrs. Venn and Mrs. Gilbertson and Mrs. MacAdam had pulled the calf out of a bush on the side of a cliff, endangering their lives to save it, even taking off their gloves and making contact with the farm animal with their bare hands, they could barely believe their ears. But they could believe their eyes, for the ladies' couture costumes were muddy and the Countess Gianotti's was torn.

Alerted to the latest Sunday excitement, Jimmy Hayes grabbed two coachmen from the porte-cochere, hurried down the steps to the approaching women and greeted them like prodigal daughters returned. He instructed the coachmen to take Glendora and her new calf back to the public pasture across Cadotte Avenue nearby. Jimmy seemed to enjoy the ruckus. No doubt he felt his guests had enjoyed quite a show.

The Big Four, beaming with radiance at the thought of having saved the newborn calf, forgot about their new gentlemen admirers, and retired to their rooms for the evening—where they began to think about nothing else but their new gentlemen admirers—and set themselves to writing thank you notes to them to be delivered promptly by bell-boys.

The gentlemen admirers remained on the veranda until dinner talking about boxing and the money panic and the revolution in Nicaragua. Having received the thank you notes, they dined together in the gigantic dining room, which was some two hundred feet long with twenty-seven-foot ceilings and with a balcony filled with musicians who serenaded the privileged diners. Passing up an elaborate meal, the gentlemen chose only what was "necessary;" which meant a simple meal of soup, one entree, a salad, a bottle each of burgundy, coffee. And a pony of brandy—to restore equilibrium.

At dinner they talked about the Big Four and what they said, what clothes they wore, how they wore their hair, the age of their jewels. They swore the four women had bewitched their hearts. And they made final plans, with great enthusiasm and controlled passion, for the trip to the Sault where they could woo the women of their choice without five hundred sets of eyes watching.

"Good evening, Colonel Williamson."

The men looked up to see a stunning woman painted with red lip rouge. They all rose from their chairs to greet the reckless horsewoman.

"Please do not get up gentlemen. Colonel, I have a message for Mrs. Clare Gilbertson. Would you please give it to her?"

Philmore Calhoun wondered why the rather loose looking woman knew Clare, and why she had asked the colonel to give Clare the message. Then he remembered that the colonel had escorted the woman into the ballroom last night. And he really began to wonder.

Not knowing quite what to do, Marshe replied, "Forgive me . . . but I do not remember your name . . ."

"Mrs. Vivian Larron."

"Mrs. Larron, perhaps you would get your message to Mrs. Clare Gilbertson more quickly if you asked a bellboy to deliver it."

"That is impossible. The front desk will not give me the number of Mrs. Gilbertson's room. And not one bellboy has agreed to deliver it, no matter what I offer him. Don't you find that curious?"

The gentlemen did find it most curious. That Marshe

Williamson was obviously annoyed with the intrusion, and that his attitude did not seem to phase Mrs. Vivian Larron, was noted by all.

"Mrs. Larron, if this message is so urgent, I suggest you turn the matter over to Jimmy Hayes. I am sorry to keep you from your meal because of my inability to be of service."

Each gentleman thought that Marshe handled the forward woman well. When Marshe told them about Kentucky Jean, and his odd coincidental meeting at the ball with the reckless horsewoman who nearly killed John Fuller's horse, the gentlemen's curiosity diminished, and they dismissed the woman in their minds as if she did not exist.

Mrs. Vivian Larron felt that the men were instinctively and unknowingly protecting Clare. She began to hate all-too-good Clare Gilbertson even more than before, and began to lay plans to wedge herself more dramatically into Clare's privileged life.

Luckily for Clare Gilbertson, she was to have three days of peace before confronting the ruthless Mrs. Vivian Larron.

9

Great Pipe With Kneeling Figure

"Good morning, ladies . . . good morning," boomed bronze-faced, pewter-haired Philmore Calhoun standing at the gangway to his 144 foot-keel schooner sailing yacht, with its crew of sixteen, with a main mast of sixty-nine feet deck to hounds and a main-boom of eighty-two feet, destined for a two-night stopover at Sault Ste. Marie for the enjoyment of shooting the rapids and getting in a little fishing—that is a little fly fishing and a whole lot of bait fishing.

The countess, Clare, Beatrice, and the Cudahy wives, somehow beaming in spite of the ungodly hour of six o'clock in the morning, and wishing Philmore merry morning greetings, arrived in a launch and were handed to the decks.

"Welcome aboard *Calla*. Delighted to have you on board," Philmore repeated graciously to each one of his guests in a tone that meant what he said.

Like a hunter stalking game—the first shot must be decisive—Philmore seized the opportunity to grasp Clare's hand and assisted her to embark upon his "boat" with captainlike bravado.

He stole a quick look at Clare's smart yachting suit of white linen duck with a short jacket sporting full sleeves of leg-o'-mutton shape, and her white straw sailor hat high in the crown, narrow in the brim. He thought Clare looked particularly fetching, but refrained from saying it because the other ladies dressed in sailing costumes of crimson serge and pale blue serge and white flannel and navy blue and black, wearing American man-o-war caps, English midshipman's caps, regulation white yachting caps, all looked equally lovely, if less alluring to Philmore.

As he led the group to comfortable white wicker lounge chairs on his expansive deck, embellished with a large and handsome Turkish rug in pale rose and deep emerald green and royal blue, he stated, "In summer I'm semiterrestrial and I'm exceedingly happy on the water. But I am happiest to enjoy the sensations of the sea with such a beautiful group of ladies and all the fine gentlemen to come." He smiled handsomely, his eyes lingering upon Clare. All the ladies smiled back charmingly, but none more so than Clare.

"Please make yourselves comfortable. Until the launch arrives with the rest of our party, I will leave you to enjoy the view of Mackinac Island from the harbor, and to accustom yourselves to the motion of the sea."

Everyone thanked him for his consideration, sank into the leather cushions on the fanciful wicker chairs, and obligingly set their sights on the picturesque view veiled in the mists of early dawn.

The ladies gazed through layers of cool morning air past ring-billed gulls soaring and dipping among gently rocking Mackinac sailing vessels and row boats and steam and sailing yachts, to the quaint little island village at the left, to the lush fort garden straight ahead flanked by the Indian dormitory, to the white fort sprawled upon the bluff above the garden, to the cozy looking cottages on the east bluff. The scene appeared to float out of focus and fade in more distinctly with every minute nearer to sunrise.

Mrs. John Cudahy eased into early morning conversation

by remarking, "I have asked Mr. Cudahy who *Calla* might be named after . . . but he has never thought to ask Mr. Calhoun."

All the ladies commented that they were unable to enlighten her on the subject.

Mrs. Michael Cudahy added, "Undoubtedly, Mr. Calhoun's love of people extended to his departed wife . . . a loss which deeply wounded him. Perhaps his yacht is named after an endearment he conferred upon her."

Without trying to appear boldly interested Clare responded, "Mr. Calhoun told me he lost his beloved wife in an accident . . . but he did not explain."

The Cudahy wives, having noted the attentions paid to eligible Mrs. Clare Gilbertson by eligible Mr. Philmore Calhoun, understood Clare's statement and obliged her with the unhappy story, bringing the group of ladies into sympathetic discussion.

"Mr. Calhoun lost his wife when the great steamship of the Cunard line, the Oregon, sank off of Long Island's coast a few years back."

"How shocking for him," commented the countess.

"Yes, Countess Gianotti, but it was the shock to his wife's nervous system that killed her. Perhaps you will recall that all passengers and crew were rescued just before the ship sank."

"Ah yes," the women sighed in unison.

"His wife had an attack of typhoid fever right after the near fatal accident. She could not fight off the fever because of the shock. She died not long after."

The women remained silent until Beatrice Venn mentioned carefully for the sake of Clare, "I noticed that he does not wear a wedding ring."

"He has never remarried, though his name is linked to many a grande dame."

Beatrice asked, "Has Mr. Calhoun any children?"

"None that I know of. There might be truth in the rumors that Mr. Calhoun's wife was pregnant some five months at the time of the accident."

A quietness blanketed the group of women until Clare practically whispered, "How tragic for him . . ."

"He is a man who embraces life no matter what comes. He married late, after he had become one of the wealthiest mining barons in the Great Lakes region. I understand he adores children. He has always been exceedingly kind and jovial with my children."

Clare's heart sank. For one of the many sorrows in her life was that she could not bear children. And clearly, she was more smitten with Philmore Calhoun than she let on.

Deep voices trading jolly morning greetings were heard by the ladies, and soon Sydney Froilan, Richard Anders, Rutherford Haverhill, Professor Bellamy, Eugene Sullivan and the Cudahy brothers joined the group of beautiful ladies. Taking their yachting caps off, the gentlemen bowed to each one of the ladies as he greeted her.

Ineligible Sydney and eligible Beatrice exchanged smiles concealing excitement at the prospect of the short trip together, which Professor Bellamy could not help but notice.

Eligible Richard smiled adoringly at the ineligible countess, to whom she responded with a warm if formal smile, noted by curious, envious, Rutherford Haverhill.

Although it was so early in the morning, with sunrise still some twenty minutes away, the fun loving group managed, without obvious forcefulness, to effect an atmosphere of almost juvenile gaiety; not at all difficult for ladies and gentlemen cultivated to look for the enjoyable and beautiful in life. Even stuffy Rutherford almost relaxed at the prospect of enjoyment with his high-spirited new friends.

While a couple of deckhands in immaculate whites brought tea and coffee and sparkling water to the guests, Philmore introduced a Mr. Gibson of Toledo, Ohio, a well-known comic banjoist, as well as a guitar, mandolin and yacht organ player, whom he engaged for the sole purpose of entertaining his guests to and from Sault Ste. Marie. After Mr. Gibson was introduced he left the group.

A young skipper, a brawny physical Titan of a man, was heard ordering the crew to weigh anchor. *Calla* was towed out into the straits, and in no time the skipper ordered the hands to set sail. *Calla* caught the westerly winds and drifted out into the straits. The lively group watched the village and fort and east bluff houses gradually recede.

Professor Bellamy mentioned, "Back in the '40s when my wife and I came up to the island, our first view from a similar vantage point was upon thousands of red-skinned aborigines camping in teepees on the shoreline, where they waited to receive annual money from the U.S. government. And when the money came by sea, the captain set off rockets which set off wild cries from the excited Indians on the shoreline. It was a sight . . . ." The old professor seemed to drift off for a few moments as he stared at a shoreline tamed away from such wild, if inglorious, scenes.

Philmore, lingering near Clare, pointed out to his guests legendary Arch Rock, a natural limestone bridge some fifty feet wide and one hundred forty feet above the water on the eastern side of the island.

And one by one Philmore's guests commented most enthusiastically, at the early hour of half past six, about Arch Rock. Even argumentative Rutherford Haverhill, struck with the almost instant relaxation and camaraderie of the diverse group, kept to himself his contrary opinion that he preferred the shape of the arch at Natural Bridge in Virginia.

"Arch Rock looks as if it is hanging in mid-air . . ."

"It's rumored a lady rode a horse over it . . ."

"Too dangerous . . ."

"The chasm below the limestone Arch Rock was produced by the falling of rock, which you can see below on the beach."

"The Indians revered the rock formation, because they saw it as bridge upon which passed away souls crossed over to island caves, where they dwelled forever in their last resting places . . ."

"I recall a legend about Ojibway Indian lovers connected with the creation of Arch Rock," commented Professor Bellamy.

Philmore announced that sunrise was approximately five minutes away, and if everyone were willing to remain on the deck for its viewing, he would in the meantime ask Professor Bellamy to entertain the group with the legend.

Everyone of Philmore's privileged guests said they would happily remain on deck for the sunrise, and encouraged the professor to tell them the Indian love legend. And Sydney and Beatrice, and Philmore and Clare, and even Richard and the countess, without realizing what they were doing, though everyone else noticed, smiled spontaneously with unguarded eyes at each other.

Honored to be asked to share his knowledge, Professor Bellamy began in a voice deep and compelling, "In a round topped lodge of elm bark and saplings, on the shores of Lake Huron, lived an Ojibway chief and his daughter named 'She who walks like the mist.' The Mist Woman was beautiful and many young braves came to their lodge bearing gifts for her.

"But one day, the young braves found her welcoming smiles faded, and her father found her paddling in her canoe alone at night. He demanded to know of his daughter if she had come under an evil spell that she rejected the young braves. For he was impatient and he told her that soon she would grow as old and wrinkled as the Mez-he-say turkey, and that she must marry one of the admiring braves soon. But his daughter would not respond to his questions nor his pleas, and he became angry."

Professor Bellamy assumed voices of a great Indian chief and an Indian maiden, " 'Though I have never beaten you, I will do so if you do not answer me.' His beautiful daughter finally responded, 'I am bewitched by a spell. Two moons ago, paddling back to the shore of our village after gathering wild rice in the evening, a handsome brave dressed in white deerskin and a robe of shining light appeared to me. My father, suddenly I could not paddle my canoe and drifted away from the shore. The brave told me he was a sky person and son of the chief, Evening Star. He told me he had fallen in love with me from above and had come to earth to ask me to join him in his sky home. My father, I told him I would marry him.'

" 'No! You will not marry him. It is forbidden,' yelled the chief. Then he siezed his daughter and dragged her to his war canoe. With mighty strokes he plowed through the waters to the island resembling a giant turtle, to the island of Mackinac. On shore, he dragged her to a great rock hanging above a precipitous cliff-side, and tied her to the rock with deer sinew. 'You will stay here until that day you reject your sky lover and become a loyal daughter once more.' And he left 'She who walks like the mist' alone in the wilds of the island exposed to the beating sun and rains.

"The Indian maiden cried tears upon the rock below her and gradually these tears melted the limestone until a bridge appeared beneath her. Through the chasm beneath the arch one night, the rays of the evening star appeared. And upon these rays strode her lover, the son of the Evening Star chief. He cradled the poor Indian maiden, still of great beauty, in his arms and lovingly carried her up to the land of the Sky people upon the star rays.

"The tears of 'She who walks like the mist' had melted the stone of Arch Rock, but could not melt the heavy heart of her father . . . .And ladies and gentlemen, I believe the rays of our daytime star will appear any moment."

Philmore thanked Professor Bellamy for relating the love legend and all the guests' relaxed eyes turned from the professor, and Arch Rock now quite small, to face east in anticipation of the sunrise. At quarter to seven, as if hushed by the presence of a godlike form, the lively group grew quiet and gazed at the luminous sun rising in the direction of Marquette Island.

Aligned with the great lake swells, *Calla* and her passengers rolled gently from side to side, and Mr. Gibson, appearing from nowhere, plucked the melody "Greensleeves" on his mandolin. As if in a colossal cradle soothed by the gentle motion of the sea and the sound of a mandolin lullaby, a short period of utter calm lulled the guests' early morning senses.

Minutes passed. Professor Bellamy broke the verbal silence with a spoken thought, that the glorious scene looked as if the Roman god of fire and metalworking, Vulcan himself, had poured hot molten silver onto the cool gray green waters.

Everyone liked the professor's poetic perception. And as the silver blobs of Vulcan floated like giant sterling fishing bobs in a line from the horizon to the schooner, they bounced and mingled and divided themselves into a million parts, catching the light rays from the white sun and throwing them back at the viewers' gleaming eyes. Radiance from the new light of day shot invisible, alluring auras around everyone in the yachting party.

Abruptly the winds changed, and the swift schooner *Calla*

began to cut sharply through the silver waters of Lake Huron bound east for the Detour Passage, but seemingly bound for the sun.

Sydney Froilan ached for a canvas as he watched Beatrice Venn's sun shot auburn ringlets of hair flutter around her illuminated grecian face.

Richard Anders wanted to grasp the countess' shining pale blue silk scarf, flying up and down, flirting with the wind, and with Richard.

Philmore Calhoun wanted to lift the white veil from Clare Gilbertson's eyes so she could see the irradiated scene more clearly, and so he could see her unclothed face.

Professor Bellamy wished to recite a poem about sunrises aloud but said it to himself and dedicated it to his late wife.

Rutherford Haverhill had a vague sensation of feeling, of loneliness, made all the more unbearable at the sight of the light intense feminine faces and forms so nearby. He cursed his emptiness and could have fallen in love with any one of the women—had any one of them showed the least inclination to fancy him.

The Cudahys and Eugene Sullivan quietly discussed the beauty and how much Jimmy Hayes would have enjoyed the trip.

No one raved or pretended that the northern sunrise was grander than anywhere else in the world. And as the trip got underway, the magical moments of sunrise faded as most of Philmore's guests became preoccupied with getting their sea legs and avoiding *mal de mer*, or secretly regretting that they did not get up every day to experience the sheer beauty of the sunrise.

"Ladies and gentlemen . . . please feel free to wander about the boat to your hearts' content. A buffet breakfast will be served in the cabin at eight o'clock. There will be vinegar and water, mustard pickles, and garlic and fat pork for those of you unable to get your sea legs."

Everyone laughed, but many felt a dull ache.

"And for those of you who are aboard *Calla* the first time, if you would care to join me, I will show you . . ."

Philmore Calhoun showed his guests the ladies' cabin, the library, the pantry, the staterooms, the middle cabin, the smoking room. But it was the yacht pet that really impressed the moneyed guests.

"What a funny creature." Clare giggled, accompanied by all the other amused ladies and mildly interested gentlemen, who watched the little wooly creature, similar in appearance to a raccoon with a monkey's tail and large ears and eyes protruding from its sockets, climbing about a gilded needle-point chair.

Philmore explained, "It's a black-handed lemur from Africa. Belongs to my first steward. He's given to picking up all kinds of oddities in foreign parts." And Philmore picked up the lemur by the tail, causing the ladies to look exceedingly sympathetic. He smiled and said directly to Clare, "Do you think me cruel? The creature loves to be picked up this way."

Clare replied, "He certainly does not object . . ."

"I am surprised he is up this early. He usually comes out to pester us at night." Philmore reached for a banana, from a nearby solid gold eighteenth-century tray from Ceylon piled high with polished fruit, and handed it to the little mammal. The lemur grabbed the banana, skedaddled around the ladies' skirts in figure eights, and disappeared around the corner much to the ladies' delight and consequent great amusement to Philmore.

Philmore announced, "It is nearly eight o'clock, ladies and gentlemen, please follow me to the cabin." To Clare he added quietly, "Mrs. Gilbertson, would you kindly meet me after breakfast in the library. I have something to show you."

Philmore Calhoun led Clare Gilbertson to a bureau—in his seven-by-nine foot yacht library with about five-by-five feet of space to move about—filled with every manner of pipe from every corner of the globe.

"I recognize the meerschaum from Mr. Fenton's Indian Bazaar . . ."

"If it were not for this meerschaum, Mrs. Gilbertson, I would not have the pleasure of showing you my prized collection. Why . . . my pipes mean more to me than *Calla* herself. There is nothing like a good smoke to puff care and sorrow far away. After all, man is but a pipe and his life is but smoke." Philmore moved his Falstaffian body closer to Clare, whose lovely scent in the small library was refreshing to him.

Clare did not step away from Philmore. She replied warmly, "I possess my late father's meerschaum."

"Do you now . . ."

"I take it with me wherever I go. Its weight is of no consequence. I carry my mother's silver hairbrush as well. I use the hairbrush . . . but not the meerschaum."

Philmore grinned.

"Mr. Calhoun, I am very curious to know the origins of your pipes . . ."

Philmore's face lit up and he pointed out to Clare his Cornish fisherman's pipe of crab's claw, his slave woman's pipe from Peru, his gourd pipe from Africa, his Chinese pipe of human bone, his opium pipes from Borneo, his Nile valley pipe with a human head bowl, his Sumatra battack pipes of brass, his Polynesian shell pipe, his tomahawk pipe, his mound pipe with a heron totem . . . .

Philmore rhapsodized, "From pipes such as these . . . the breath of man has ascended to the gods for millennia."

Looking directly at Clare for reaction, Philmore saw the corners of her mouth draw up into a whimsical smile. He liked it. Then and there he decided to open a drawer in the bureau. He looked expectantly at Clare and asked, "Would you care to see my great pipe with a kneeling figure? I do not display it because it is offensive to some . . . ."

In fact, Philmore showed the kneeling figure pipe to every woman he had ever been interested in since the death of his wife. He judged the woman of his current interest by her reaction to this pipe; it separated the girls from the women from the disguised whores all out to marry rich Philmore Calhoun. With twinkling eyes, he lifted the pipe, swathed in satin, out of the drawer and unwrapped it slowly.

When Clare saw that the kneeling figure on the pipe was an Indian, she was not surprised. What surprised her was that the Indian had an orifice in the buttocks used for the insertion of a stem.

Feeling that Philmore was deliberately testing her with the embarrassing pipe, Clare responded carefully, "The Indian character, in the carving of this great pipe with a kneeling figure, is not as spirited or lifelike as the heron totem on your mound pipe . . ."

Disappointed with her all too evasive and intelligent answer lacking humor, Philmore began to wrap up the unusual pipe.

Smiling ironically, Clare continued, " . . . and Mr. Calhoun . . . in the case of this particular kneeling figure . . . it is not the breath of the man alone, which is symbolically ascending to the gods."

Large Philmore Calhoun let out a laugh so long and hard the nymphs and sirens of the sea must have heard it 750 feet to the bottom of Lake Huron. Never had women in the past answered so well when he had shown them a pipe that caused—most older-looking young ladies to blush, most mature ladies to gracefully turn away their faces, and disguised whores of all ages to laugh loudly. Philmore thought Clare's intelligence and humor a rare quality in a woman, and decided then and there he would arrange to go fishing with her—alone—at the Sault. He knew the other sportsmen would understand.

When Philmore got back his breath he showed Clare his seventeenth-century old Dutch clay pipe, his Bavarian carved pipe bowl, his Staffordshire bisquit-ware pipe, his coiled porcelain pipe by Pratt, and finally his favorite meerschaum.

"Did your father ever tell you, Mrs. Gilbertson, that the meerschaum was named after its likeness to petrified sea foam?"

Philmore once again moved nearer to Clare. Once again Clare did not move away from him.

"As the story goes, the first pipe was made by a Hungarian shoemaker. When his fingers touched the bowl, the meerschaum turned a golden brown color. But it was not his fingers alone which caused this . . . it was the cobblers wax on his fingers . . ."

Philmore handed his prized possession to Clare, his brawny fingers lingering upon Clare's hand. Slowly he withdrew his large hand, which Clare noticed resembled that of a working man.

" . . . not only did the Hungarian cobbler wax the entire pipe, he found out that the wax caused a sweeter smoke than before."

In a voice which sounded sweeter than the taste of any pipe Philmore had smoked since the death of his beloved wife, Clare said, "Mr. Calhoun, can you keep a secret?"

"I am known for a loud mouth, Mrs. Gilbertson, not a loose one . . . ."

"Then I will tell you confidentially . . . I tried smoking a pipe myself . . . twice."

"No . . . really . . . what possessed a lady of your refinement to pick up the pipe?"

"Youth. I saw my father smoke from the day I could remember. He smoked Yale mixture, a brand I fell in love with . . . in fact . . . the same brand you smoked in Fenton's shop on the day we met."

Philmore politely asked Clare to sit down on the one sofa-bed in the library, and not so politely sat down right next to her without asking permission, after lighting up the Yale mixture tobacco in his favorite meerschaum. He made no effort to close the door to the library, setting Clare at ease.

"When I smell the tobacco you are smoking, Mr. Calhoun, I grow quite nostalgic, almost grieved actually . . ."

"Mrs. Gilbertson . . . do you wish me to stop smoking if such aromatic memories grieve you?"

"Oh no, Mr. Calhoun, please continue. Admittedly, I sometimes find my emotions more awakened through grief than I care to admit . . . ."

Surprised at such a candid statement coming from a high society woman he had known less than a week, Philmore did not know quite how to respond to Mrs. Gilbertson's remark. If the same remark had been made to Sydney Froilan or Richard Anders, Clare would have had a response immediately. But Philmore was no polished bohemian or overeducated gambler. He had to work physically hard to get where he was in life. And instant answers to such surprising statements were neither in his blood nor his ready vocabulary.

Clare continued, noting Philmore's kind eyes but lack of verbal response, "When I was fifteen, I lost my father because of a tragic accident. His carriage rolled over on a stormy night. When I learned of his death that dark night, plagued by the inability to sleep, I tiptoed down to his library and made a fire in his fireplace. I so longed for him, though he had left my life only a few hours before, that I went to his desk, picked up his favorite pipe, filled it with his favorite tobacco in the same manner I had seen him perform thousands of times, lit the pipe, and put it to my lips . . ."

Far away in spirit from the cozy library on the schooner *Calla*, which floated upon Lake Huron bound for the Sault, Clare did not notice that Philmore sat at the edge of his sofa-bed. Nor did she immediately notice that he had placed his huge hand over hers.

Philmore wondered what rare sort of woman, with the spirit to smoke a pipe, graced herself so close, so very close, to him. Yes, he thought, Clare is sweeter than the taste of any pipe I have smoked since my wife.

In a voice disconnected from the moment, Clare related, "The scented smoke of the tobacco . . . rising phoenix-like from the ashes of his pipe . . . seemed to resurrect the spirit of my dear father and bring him back to me. My bereaved mother, smelling my father's tobacco smoke . . . as if fleeing an imagined nightmare . . . dashed into the library . . . madly expecting to find my father sitting at his desk as he had for their twenty contented years together. When she saw me through the smoky haze of her hope, she remained silent, left the room, and never reprimanded me for my rash act."

Philmore observed Clare unconsciously inhale the ignited tobacco he expelled from his favorite pipe. He liked the idea of Clare vicariously sharing the vaporous fumes of flavored air. Like his pipe, consumed by slow combustion, Philmore felt the same desire for Clare he had felt after the grand ball at her bedroom door.

Heady from lack of oxygen, Clare suddenly realized Philmore's hand covered hers. In her fingers she felt heat from his embracing hand that, like a newfangled electrical generator, shot jolts of warmth up her slender arms to her white neck and red ears. In a voice suddenly breathless, Clare's flushed lips somehow iterated the sounds, "In fact, Mr. Calhoun, about a fortnight after we buried my father, my mother and I were sitting in his library together . . . and . . . you might be taken aback . . ."

"Nothing about your past would take be aback . . . ," Philmore declared gently. Prematurely.

Clare saw Philmore's eyes glowing like lighthouse beacons in the Mackinac straits on a pitch black night. He drew a few long puffs from his pipe and filled the air around his head with semi-sweet smoke. Clare's eyes sought his. And even through the thick air, as if through patchy fog, she saw his eyes gleaming like dual beacons signaling safety and winking desire.

She wondered if what he said, "nothing about your past would take me aback," were true. She wondered if she could ever tell the direct and spirited Philmore Calhoun, a man who was what he appeared to be, the whole truth about herself. A truth that she did everything possible to keep from the public.

For the "truth" was that Clare Gilbertson had been the wife of a distinguished man—murdered by his mistress before he turned forty—allegedly killed by the blow of a heavy sterling silver candelabrum.

Clare wondered if Philmore Calhoun would not be "taken aback" by the shocking events in her life. That right before Mr. Gilbertson's mistress had murdered him, Clare learned that her husband had a child with his mistress—the heir Clare could never give him. And that a few days before his murder back in 1890, Clare, a Catholic, had quietly suffered a divorce from Mr. Gilbertson.

Yes, Clare wondered if Philmore would not be "taken aback" by the fact that at that very moment, Clare was financially supporting her murdered husband's mistress and illegitmate son—blackmailed by the mistress who had murdered Mr. Gilbertson. And all this did not add up to the "whole truth" of Clare Gilbertson's life.

And before she could wonder any more, her face glowing with the rush of heat and conflicting thoughts of hate and love, Clare saw Philmore gazing at her lips and heard him saying in a voice deep and soothing, something about an "ideal mouthpiece is made of amber," and that if he could "find a woman as soothing" as his pipe, with as "fine a shape" as his pipe, with "blissful kisses which burn" like his pipe, well, he would give his life to have such a woman as his wife. And he gently pulled Clare close and kissed her well-formed brow and flushed cheeks and burning lips and without thinking she relaxed against his body as he placed a protective arm around her shoulder.

Almost overcome with the heat and smoke and emotional excitement, Clare managed to let go of her fears for a few moments in the welcome arms of Philmore Calhoun. For the first time since the death of her father, Clare sat in a room with a man so unlike her father in stature and personality, and somehow as comforting in spirit as her father had always been to her.

After years of living lies with her husband in life, like the curse of a disease passed on, Clare continued fighting his corruption beyond his death. How she longed to replace her shameful past. How she longed to be free of protecting the distinguished Gilbertson family name. How she longed to banish the name Gilbertson in connection to Clare.

"Mrs. Gilbertson . . ."

"Clare . . ."

"Please . . . Clare . . . allow me to be taken aback by your unusual story."

In the eye of the wind of impartial truth, trying to control her breathing set off by the excitement of Philmore's lovemaking and fear of her secret past, Clare continued in a voice tender to Philmore's ears, "As I mentioned . . . a fortnight after we buried my father . . . my mother asked me to light my father's pipe for her. She said . . . just this one more time . . . she wanted the room to be filled with the sweet smoke of his memory. We stayed in the library together from night until early morning, taking turns puffing the sweet smoke, filling the library with the resurrected phoenix of his memory."

Clare paused. And Philmore imagined himself smoking his other favorite pipe . . . his St. Claude made of briar root . . . smoking in his home library . . . and watching lovely Clare through the hazy smoky air . . . lounging voluptuously near his fireplace . . . without a stitch of satin or lace upon her naked body . . . a fire roaring and splashing hot highlights upon her chestnut hair and fair face and soft breasts and . . . .

"And from that time, my father's meerschaum disappeared as well as his entire pipe collection. I assumed my mother gave them away. In spite of our close relationship, I simply could not bring myself to ask her what had become of the pipes . . . perhaps because our pipe-smoking bereavement had been so intensely secretive and indulgent. Mr. Calhoun . . ."

"Philmore . . ."

"Yes . . . Philmore . . . it was a mystery to me as to what happened to the pipes until I found out on the day she died."

"Had she kept them, Clare?"

"Yes, the doctor had asked me to find a change of linen for my mother after her death. Since it was Sunday and the servants were out, I had no idea where to look and accidentally came across the pipes in her . . ."

Clare laughed in low soft tones and continued, "She had kept them for twenty years in her bedroom bureau drawer . . .

and . . .," Clare leaned away from Philmore, looked him directly in the eyes, flashed a charming smile and spilled, "each pipe was wrapped in one of her most intimate pieces of lingerie. There my mother was lying in bed, dead but fifteen minutes, and I was overcome with the touchingly comical sight of the pipes in her bureau drawer or should I say . . . drawers."

Philmore loved that kind of naughty innuendo from a fine lady whom he wanted to take to bed with him—perhaps for the rest of his life.

"I was so overcome, I could contain myself no more and broke out laughing in the room of my dead mother. The doctor thought I was in shock. And to this day I wonder if my mother, who had the dearest sense of humor, meant for me to discover this and remember fondly the contented life that my parents had shared. She always asked, 'Clare, do you think God has allowed your father to smoke a pipe in heaven? I live to see that day.' They were a very close couple." Clare added wistfully, "I had a false sense of life because of their happiness . . . ."

Once more, Philmore did not quite know what to say when Clare added that last bomb of a statement. He could not instantly reply something witty in response to Clare's too serious revelation about herself.

Reluctantly, Philmore moved away a respectable distance from her on the sofa. And perhaps, gladly, moved away from an underlying sadness in Clare he did not wish to entertain. Continuing to cover Clare's hand with his own warm hand, he began to tell her briefly about himself.

With an energy Clare rarely saw in a gentleman in those days of financial panic, Philmore just about broke down the walls of the library with the bare unembellished facts of his life.

Born to a Great Lakes' captain of bulldog tenacity, who

owned his own cargo schooner, which he sailed loaded with lumber or grain or coal from port to port, Philmore grew up as a hand on his father's schooner.

" 'If the clouds seem scratched by a hen,

Better take your topsails in.

When the wind shifts against the sun,

Watch her, boys, for back she'll come.' "

Philmore recited the seafaring rhyme without a wave of nostalgia in his voice.

"Yes, I worked as a hand on my father's schooner through cold frontal storms and squalls I thought we'd never live through. But by the mid '70s I could see there was no future in following my father's footsteps as a Laker captain. I saw that the times were rapidly changing. There was talk of monster steamers taking over. My father, having been a wooden ship sea captain, swore up and down it was not fitting that a steel ship could stay afloat. He said the steel ships would spring their rivets and bolts in stormy weather."

Philmore paused, enjoyed a few puffs on his meerschaum and a few quick glances at Clare's lustrous eyes and shapely bosom and delicate hands, and continued, "So, without my father's blessing, I left his employ. I will never forget my father saying to my mother, in reference to me, 'What a big and promising boy Philmore was, strong as me Daddy and smart as me uncle the priest. But now that he chooses not to be a sea captain, he's adopted the ways of the everyday world and in no way tries to rise above its level.'

"He might have simply said, 'The boy dashed all me exalted hopes to bits.' And although my father never would have admitted it, he bought the American idea that everything could be done here in the shortest and quickest way . . . ."

Clare sized up big Philmore Calhoun as he told the story of his rough and tumble life in a spirit as magnanimous and individual as a folklorist who believed the tall tales he told. And in the case of Philmore Calhoun, the larger than life stories were true and therefore all the more unbelievable.

" . . . There were few things open to me other than going down into the mines or going into the woods. I became a lumberjack. And when they saw I could think on my feet they made me a timber cruiser. One thing led to the next and I was sent to the upper peninsula of Michigan to buy timberlands. I purchased some eight thousand acres for some $23,000 . . . was to have one third of the profits from the resale of the timber. Never found out what price the timber did bring.

"You see . . . Clare . . . the land under the timber I bought . . . was solid iron ore . . . and twelve million tons were mined out even before the mine started rolling. You've heard of Iron Mountain? Well, after that fortunate discovery I put away my compass and axe and never went cruising for white pine again. Last year I sold my interests just as they were installing the largest water pumping engine the world has seen. And now I plan on spending the rest of my life sailing and speculating."

Philmore did not feel the need to add that the very mine he sold his "interests" in, back in '92, recently folded due to the current silver "Panic" of '93.

"What an exciting and fortunate life you have led, Philmore," Clare said, disguising her own sadness in ill-fortune.

"My parents never lived to see my ultimate success. I am sorry they could not share in all the luxuries my good fortune buys. My father saw his own Laker . . . bought from William Bates in Manitowoc, Wisconsin, and sold to a nameless man in a company I do not remember . . . taken apart before his very eyes. He likened it to watching a pet dog butchered alive by cannibals. He watched the masts torn down and saw his once-proud cargo schooner reduced to a dirty little tow barge run by steam. Why he watched this, I don't know to this day. But when it was over, he was finished with life.

After forty years of fighting cold frontal storms and gale winds at forty miles per hour and blizzards and fog so soupy no ship dared sail through, my father died in his sleep. Knowing my father all too well, he would have rather sunk the laker and gone down with her, than see his proud schooner reduced to a tow barge. But in respect to my mother, who was ill at the time and needed expensive medical treatments, my father, one of the saltiest old sea dogs of the saltless Great Lakes, sold his ship into what he called slavery."

Philmore and Clare heard a knock on the open door.

"Captain . . ."

"Yes . . ."

"You had asked me to inform you of the hour."

"Thank you. Clare . . . I want you to know . . . our time together has meant so much to me . . ."

Philmore . . . I am all too gladly keeping you from your guests . . ."

Philmore Calhoun wanted nothing more, at that moment, than for Clare to have said, "Dear we must join—our—guests."

And Clare wanted nothing more, at that moment and all moments of her adult life, than to cancel her cruely overbearing past. A past she already knew many a well-off gentleman of her former acquaintance could not accept in a future "good wife," when she had honestly revealed it to him. A past she was not sure even generous Philmore Calhoun could accept in a wife.

For Clare knew all too well that the old-money, and even the new-money gentleman of 1893 with Philmore Calhoun's newly arrived sophistication, wanted an idealized woman as a wife without a hint of scandal to her name. He wanted a fine lady in public, a madonna mother in private, a first class whore in bed. Clare was acutely aware that if few women were capable of pretending the lady-mother-whore role, it was also true that few men really had it in them to match up to their idealized triune woman—with the possible exception of eligible, bigger than life, Philmore Calhoun—a not-too-refined gentleman, so like in spirit to Clare's beloved father.

Clare smiled warmly at Philmore as he offered his strong hand to help her up. And Philmore wondered what it was about Mrs. Clare Gilbertson, beyond her shapeliness and intelligence and humor, that made her so instantly special to him.

10
Shooting the Rapids

"Is it true, Froilan, that you have a tattoo on your chest like a common sailor?" Rutherford was careful to ask this out of earshot of his host Philmore Calhoun, and stared at slightly tired looking Beatrice Venn—as if she should know the answer about the tattoo on Sydney's chest.

Although the unmarried gentlemen had slept on *Calla*, and the unmarried ladies had slept at the Chippewa Hotel at Sault Ste. Marie, Rutherford had the sneaking suspicion that Sydney Froilan and Beatrice Venn had not slept at either place. Or had not slept at all.

After the first day of the relaxing Sault excursion on *Calla*, interrupted only by cynical remarks between Rutherford and Sydney, the countess caught Rutherford staring down Beatrice. After that she had no patience for listening to any more intentional feather ruffling. Trained to avoid all unpleasantness as a lady-in-waiting at the court of Queen Marguerite, the countess instantly replied to Rutherford's question about the tattoo, before Sydney had a chance, "The Earl of Cranar has his coat of arms emblazened on his aristocratic shoulders."

Although thoroughly impressed by this noble tidbit of information, Rutherford, feeling the unwanted rogue, bit his tongue while tempted to ask Countess Gianotti, have you been in a position to see the earl's shoulders? Instead he replied, "It is a painful process, I hear. The blood must be in good condition so as not to be seriously inflamed."

Both Rutherford and Sydney, like naughty children put in their place, received the countess' early morning "stop your relentless fighting" message. But whether they would have stopped their mutually enjoyed bickering out of respect to the Countess Gianotti, it is hard to say. For just at that moment, Richard Anders arrived with the Indians whom he had hired to take the party through the rapids.

Rutherford, nervous about shooting the fearsome rapids guided by "American peasants"—why, to himself he considered the Indians were not even peasants, but landless drunkards subsisting on government handouts—noticed that Richard was on overly familiar and friendly terms with the poor Indians. Although Rutherford calmed down, thinking that his precious life was in the more trustworthy hands of Indians who obviously favored Richard, he grew wary of Richard.

Rutherford formed the rash opinion that Richard Anders was a suspicious man, because he pretended equality with the Indians where none existed. But Rutherford Earle Haverhill V, of the oldest and wealthiest money in the group, had the most to lose if untrustworthy Indians had been hired to take him through the fearsome rapids. Rutherford was secretly grateful to Richard for his suspicious association.

Richard addressed the yachting party with the reassuring words, "Our guides are Bush Buscher's sons. I learned to row and fish from their father. When I crossed the North Sea in an open rowboat, it was not my father I thought of when the going got rough . . . it was their father. We are in good hands if Bush Buscher's sons take us through the Sault rapids."

It is no use denying that even Philmore Calhoun, with a nature like the sea god Neptune himself, who had seen violent Great Lakes' storms he was lucky to have lived through, was somewhat uncertain about putting his life into the hands of a poor Indian "crew" he did not know. But so great was his trust in young Richard Anders, his uncertainty turned into excitement at this first time adventure. He remarked to Clare with gusto that he would "very much like to be in the same boat with her." He did not add, in more ways than one.

With worldly carefreeness Richard explained, "Shooting the Sault rapids can be as risky as desirable. If you should have an upset near the shore, there is the possibility of bruises. If the boat should rush into the center of the rapids it means certain death. I suggest we take the middle course, as near center as possible for an exciting ride."

The yachting party laughed anxiously and each adventurer, male and female alike, harbored second thoughts about actually fulfilling their liking for dangerous excitement.

Sydney and Beatrice and Professor Bellamy and Eugene Sullivan gathered in one boat. Richard and the countess and Rutherford and Philmore and Clare went in the second boat. The Cudahys and their wives headed straight to the fishing site where they were all to meet later.

Everyone smiled bravely at each other as they climbed into the canoes and covered themselves with oilcloths as make believe protection against the spray of wild waters to come. The women especially tried to ignore the untamed fright they felt in the wilderness and the real possibility of upset and even possible death in the rapids. Only the Indian canoe men felt no fear—because they had nothing to lose except their lives. Lives that were really ghosts of former self-contained lives. Ghostly lives made subservient to the white man's ways.

The Indian canoe men paddled through the water and began to ascend the river. Stationed at bow and stern, they each grabbed a stout pole and drove it into the river bed as if driving a spear into a white cavalryman. Tugging with great force against the current, the Indians' contorted faces mirrored taut unseen leg and arm muscles, struggling to pull the heavy canoes with man power alone, bearing weight upon the stout poles as they slowly ascended the river.

Barely moving through the dark and rushing shallow waters, the canoe parties passed great gray boulders exuding coolness, worn and rounded by water and weather, strewn in the river like the stepping stones of giants. Masses of dark green moss covered the banks, from where lightning-felled evergreens formed random bridges to river rocks. The faint scents of pine trees and fresh water and wet wood and old oilcloth and manly perspiration mingled and set off their olfactory nerves.

Richard Anders watched the sons of his Indian teacher sweat blood as they pulled down hard upon their poles with calloused hands. Like beasts of burden, they uttered subtle grunting noises with each laboring pull. Beads of sweat soaked their shabby white man's shirts.

As if struck with the Indians' exhaustion and the challenging tug of war between water and man, Richard motioned to the Indian in the bow. And before the countess or Clare or Philmore or Rutherford, who had his oilcloth tucked about his neck as if it were a security blanket or great napkin, knew what was happening, Richard began spearing the waterbed with the pole and tugging upstream with all his power.

After five minutes passed, wet with perspiration, the sun beating upon his brow, Richard stripped to his waist to the utter astonishment of everyone in the boat—including the Indians. He continued moving the canoe, which dragged along the jagged rock filled river bed, until they finally neared the end of the ascent. And if Richard Anders did not realize it, every gentlemen in both canoes saw that the ladies did not bother to hide admiring eyes full of wonder at his physical prowess.

The countess wished she had not seen her young admirer

standing so tall at the bow of the canoe, his strong arms and tough spirit alive with energy. She purposely looked away from his half-naked laboring form and tried to concentrate on the form of a nearby boulder instead. She failed. The boulder looked phallic. Her mind rushed back to the grand ball and the waltz with Richard, his powerful arms hidden beneath a dignified swallow tail coat, holding her and whirling her about the floor . . . . Her eyes rushed back to the all too robust sight of half-naked Richard at the bow.

And Rutherford Haverhill, observing the countess' every bat of the eye, figured that Richard Anders had begun to do some serious fishing at the Sault, and might very well have a noble nibble on his most substantial young bait.

The canoe parties finally arrived at the beginning of the descent. In Richard's boat, the Indian half-smiled at Richard and took his rightful place in the bow. Richard put on his shirt.

Everyone's blood beat accelerated when they finally saw the death defying rapids before them. Stretched from shoreline to shoreline roared seething cascades of whitewater foam rolling wildly upstream, the darker water breaking into massive waves. One canoe after the other entered the descent and at first stabilized, calming the fears of the passengers, until the current grew faster and faster and the sunlit waters, as if tumbling liquid crystals, began to drag them into the rapids' fearful course. Yelling out cries of warning before they struck the big waves, the Indians handled the poles expertly to keep the canoes from upsetting.

Dashing headlong into the descent like a downhill locomotive off its track, they shot into powerful whirlpools and hurled over steep cascades, tossing up and down and back and forth. Reeling from side to side in mighty eddies, foam and flying water hit the bow, sprayed their faces and oilcloths with cold water and filled the canoes with a half-foot of the rapids.

Water lashed and bashed itself in fury, dashing the canoes against rocks. Their adrenalin gushing, the unnerved passengers panicked, sure they would turn over. But somehow they rushed past the rocks, down slopes dark and deep, in and out of the shallow white foam.

As if shrieking and struggling from a savage power seizing and carrying them away by rapine force, the Indians cried war calls as their canoes lurched in violent defiance of the seething big waves. They tore past trees and houses and a small island at the head of the rapids. Wet and giddy and breathless after the mile descent, the passengers glided calmly and quietly into the smooth waters below, which rippled and sparkled in the gentle breeze.

A round of cheers broke forth from the exhilarated passengers. The men noticed that the women were filled with such explosive vitality they could only imagine that same physical dash with them in their beds. The women wondered if anything in their lives would ever be that exciting again. And everyone noticed that Rutherford Haverhill was the wettest of all. For during the excitement, in trying to keep his feet dry, Rutherford raised his feet and in doing so threw all his weight upon his wooden seat which broke, and set him in seven inches of water at the bottom of the boat. But in keeping with his personality, Rutherford announced that his shirt bosom was still dry.

As arranged, the Indians paddled the canoes to a nearby shore and met with the Cudahys and fishing guides in canoes filled with the party's gear. Philmore and Clare climbed into one boat. The countess was quickly guided into a boat which she soon learned, with some embarrassment, was to be occupied only by younger Richard and her married self. Rutherford and Professor Bellamy and Eugene Sullivan sportingly ignored the obvious pairing off, and with great spirits united in a boastful declaration that they were going to catch the most fish. Though it was obvious to all, that the threesome did not even have a nibble on the line.

Beatrice, claiming dizziness and a need to change her wet clothing, asked to be taken back to the hotel. Sydney, looking as amorous as ever, volunteered to escort her and asked to be taken back to *Calla* for a change into dry clothing.

Rutherford figured that Beatrice and Sydney would help each other change clothes.

Professor Bellamy ignored the implications in Beatrice's actions; though Beatrice and Sydney did not look all that wet to his unsuspicious old-fashioned mind.

In high spirits, the fishing party broke up and headed into various streams divided by numerous islands at the foot of the rapids. The stream's dark and deep holes and lively pools and whirling eddies seemed to promise a successful morning of fishing for speckled trout and black bass and sturgeons and white fish—considered by Philmore the daintiest fresh water fish in the world—next to lake herring, which Rutherford considered better tasting than white fish.

"Countess, we are fishing for lake herring. It is pleasant sport for ladies." Richard ventured into conversation with the quiet countess as their canoe conveniently turned into a different stream from the others. He continued carefully, "In early July, lake herring collect here by the millions. The Indians told me we have a good chance to catch some though it is late in July. Are you fond of fishing?"

"Mr. Anders, I am very fond of fishing in larger groups," Anna replied in her full and mellow voice, seasoned with the firm tones of a married woman tricked into a possible compromising position in the eyes of others, if not herself.

"Will you forgive my obvious manipulation, Countess?"

Anna smiled with a knowing look, "As long as you do not take off your shirt . . ."

They laughed quietly, intimately. The kind of immediate intimacy kindred spirits share; a kind of intimacy few long-married couples experience. Anna and Richard were both struck and puzzled by their deep feelings of closeness.

"I promise not to take off my shirt . . ."

Anna could not help but think of Richard at the bow of the canoe, half-naked, tugging the heavy boat with all his might. She changed the subject, dropped her formality, and leaned over the boat in a most undignified and becoming fashion. In a voice melodious and fun-loving she spoke, "Look at the fish below us. They appear to be playing. Ah . . . a couple leaped out of the water. Wouldn't it be a nice sentimental thought to believe that fish couples tumble about in the water because they are happy?"

Richard loved her sentimental thought free from the tight-assed intellectualism he usually heard from the educated, intelligent women to whom he was usually attracted. Women who were afraid to drop their veil of knowledge for even a moment. Yet coming from an unintelligent woman the idea would have seemed unbearably sweet. Richard sensed that the countess was consciously rebuking her intentionally careful, intelligent, well-informed observations and opinions. He noticed a slight change in the pitch of her voice. It was less deep, more breathy.

Although Richard knew that lake herring seldom take an artificial fly, he attached a small brown one to their lines, almost as if he did not want to be bothered with catching anything, except Anna.

Anna watched Richard cast expertly and did likewise, if not as smoothly. She felt her spirit flying free with the line. And as if diving into the crystal waters right along with the fish, Anna dove into youthful feelings from long ago. She let go of her secret cares and gave in to the free moments away in the north woods wilderness, away from overbearing formality and prying eyes at the Grand, at the court of Queen Marguerite, really, wherever she went. Free moments made possible by all too attractive Richard Anders. Anna's surprising carefreeness, almost childlike gaiety, was more of a compliment and an enticement to Richard than she would have imagined.

Richard, who could sing the "Songs of Solomon" by heart, who knew *The Scented Garden* by heart if not by practice— wasting himself because of no luck in finding a partner to suit his fantasy—wanted nothing more than to take his hands off his damned full-rigged fishing rod and put them on full-bodied Anna sitting so close. He imagined her wrapping her full nourishing passion—and legs—around him in unlimited surrender to physical good times, responding to his every caress, her form undulating beneath his, and he suddenly felt a wave of psychic kick new to his experience. And on top of all that, he had a fish on his line.

While reeling in a fish, with a break as determined and vigorous as a trout, he addressed Anna, "Countess, I do not want to dampen the delight in your idea of happy fish, but usually fish leap out of the water with a careful eye to what food may be swimming ahead. Yet . . .," Richard's eyes twinkled, "I've seen female and male carp delighting in sportive glee . . . leaping and chasing each other about playfully . . . uh . . . I imagine . . . that . . . if I may say it . . . sexual instinct is responsible . . . ."

"So . . . Mr. Anders," Anna replied lightheartedly, "you do not think that fish play for the sake of playing?"

"Perhaps they do, Countess . . . after all . . . what convincing proof do we have that they are not playing . . . as you say . . . for the sake of playing . . . ."

Anna and Richard understood each other perfectly. For ineligible Anna—too perfectly.

Eligible Richard, wishing for the first time in his sporting life that a fish had not been on the line, looked away from the fish struggling for freedom, and stole a quick glance at Anna's blue eyes, suddenly stripped of formality's residue, looking warm and wet, aglow with reflective intelligence, alive with the desire to love.

The Indian guides pretended not to listen in on the white people's strange talk as they watched the fish fight bravely for its freedom from the painful hook. It jumped and jumped. And although Richard had much empathy for the red men, he wished to throw them over the side of the canoe so that—just for once—he could be entirely alone with the countess. To Richard's romantic mind, the countess was a woman of nature. No, a woman of refined nature. A refined woman, he felt, who desired love in all its forms as much as he did.

It did not matter much to Richard Anders that the countess was eight years older and married. He knew that her husband, Count Gianotti, was some twenty years older than the beautiful Anna sitting so near to him in the gently rocking canoe.

Richard knew that the once debonaire count suffered a sickness some gossiping guests at the Grand Hotel had politely termed as a malady of the spirit; but which European educated Richard Anders guessed to be an inability to enter the modern age. A failure on the part of the count to rise above what overeducated Richard called the modern psychoses of cold mental over-tension and palsied feelings, so opposite to an old world Italian like the count, whose psychoses had until recently been likely penetrated by sensual warmth.

Richard had young friends, sons of nobility in Europe, who watched their mothers but especially their fathers fade away into mental paralysis from the overbearing realities of the new industrial age; from the demise of their nobility, in all of the word's definitions.

As a man of the world, as a gambler, Richard had found in Anna what he dreamed of in a woman. A woman of the old world and new world. A woman of the country and the city. A sensual woman who behind her formality really took pleasure in the little things in life and in men. He was not about to let the countess slip through his hands. He figured that her husband in Italy was no longer able to appreciate her obvious love of life. Richard conveniently reasoned that an exceptional woman like the countess should not be obligated by law to follow into and nurse her husband's degeneration.

Conveniently ignoring the possibility that the countess loved her Italian husband all the more sympathetically after his cruel downfall, Richard began jockeying for a position in her life. He said to himself . . . as he watched soulful Anna gazing at the pretty lake herring now landed in the boat . . . life is love. I must make the most of my life and my love—now.

And the Indians hammered the pretty fish, which had bitten so freely and played so well, to death.

Everyone stood up and drank to the health of their generous host Philmore Calhoun, while Mr. Gibson played "Auld Lang Syne" on the yacht organ.

Having finished an early dinner on *Calla* of thick wild mushroom soup, whitefish and lake herring, speckled trout and lake bass, sweetbreads with native peas, lamb with mint sauce, corn and new potatoes, canvasbacks and tomato salad, strawberry short cake, accompanied by foreign wines of the best vintage—the countess and Beatrice and Clare and Professor Bellamy and Richard and Sydney and Rutherford and Eugene Sullivan raised their glasses of sweet dessert champagne, in genuine appreciation, to big Philmore Calhoun.

Even Rutherford felt a slight appreciation; and if he had the generosity to admit it, the three-day Sault excursion had been the most fun-filled yachting party he had ever attended. Never had there been a dull moment with all the witty conversation, delicious food, good sport, and sunny weather.

Yes, the yachting party to the Sault on *Calla* had been a great success, long to be remembered. And for three of the Big Four, long to be cherished.

His guests sat down and Philmore got up. Touched by the genuine looks in his guests' eyes, Philmore glanced down at the deep double red carnations and maidenhair ferns on his table, which was laid with Paul Revere sterling and Meissen china and Venetian glassware, and then he glanced over at Clare and again at each of his guests. He spoke with deep voiced deliberateness, "We are a group well-suited to each other . . . a damned delightful and unusual occurrence."

Philmore paused and decided not to add that he thought the freedom of intercourse between the men and women most democratic, because in the case of Mrs. Venn and Sydney Froilan—it could have been taken in two ways. He added, "I hold up my glass to honor all of you . . . my dear guests and new friends. I only wish the Cudahys could have remained with us."

Only one emergency had marred the *joie de vivre* of the yachting party. The Cudahys had to leave early after receiving the message at the Sault that the financial "panic" of '93 had wiped out John Cudahy; the dealer in his family who enjoyed poking fun at the plodding routines of his still rich meat packing brothers.

There was was not one guest, including Philmore, who did not grow clammy when thinking of the "panic" and what it could do to their financial fortunes and resources. They all tried to put it out of their minds.

Rutherford stood up again and proposed, "Let us drink to John Cudahy's return to good fortune . . ."

Everyone thought this very sympathetic coming from Rutherford until he added, "And let's drink to us. If we are rich it is because of our superior biological heritage. Darwin and Spenser will back me up." Eastern bred Rutherford Earle Haverhill V, born to one of the oldest and richest families in America, implied that the western Cudahys had not even arrived before they had lost. But worse, he forgot that not everyone in the group was rich. Professor Bellamy was barely well-off.

Philmore ignored Rutherford, whom he found an amusing if useless man to have around, and invited the gentlemen and even the ladies to the deck for a smoke and after-dinner drink. In the west, it was not the fashion of society to divide up the sexes after dinner, as if they were "girls" and "boys" entering separate school doors.

Although the ladies declined to smoke or drink, they were offered Danziger Goldwasser and Benedictine and Anisette and old Kummel and yellow Chartreuse just like the gentlemen. When the women requested a peppermint drink, the gentlemen thought it most ladylike and fitting. And they were secretly relieved the ladies had declined to smoke cigarettes. Especially Professsor Bellamy. For as liberal as the worldly men were among them, except for young Richard who was turning thirty after midnight, it simply went against their manly spirits to see a female smoke in mixed company.

If the breezes continued, *Calla* would reach Mackinac Island in a matter of a couple of hours. Making the most of the mild weather and fun-loving companionship, Philmore's guests ignored the financial "panic" and plunged themselves into a party spirit. Mr. Gibson began singing and playing popular airs and songs on his banjo. Out came pipes and cigars of every description.

The countess and Clare and Beatrice, gracious guests to the end, entertained the group with charming recitations of "Where Cupid Kissed Her" and "The One-Hoss Shay" and "The Vase." The gentlemen applauded the ladies' contribution to the after-dinner fellowship with great enthusiasm and much eye twinkling.

Philmore and Sydney and Richard wished for one more chance alone with the lady of his conquest, before docking again at the island. For once on the island, all eyes would be upon them again. Between smoking and drinking and singing and listening to recitations and telling jokes, they began thinking of ways to maneuver the lady of their choice into some minutes alone together.

Mr. Gibson exchanged his banjo for his guitar and played Spanish flamenco music, to which Sydney, slightly overcome by Benedictine, stood up, grabbed a tambourine and Beatrice, and induced her to dance a fandango. Throwing the tambourine to Sully, who got up and played it expertly, Sydney began snapping his fingers like castanets and clapping his hands and stamping his feet to the emotional flamboyant rhythms.

Beatrice, willowy in a lovely tight-fitting gown of pale mauve and yellow, her shoulders perfectly bare protected only by garlands of silk Parma violets, her auburn hair fluttering, swayed supply and beat time by tapping her heels. Teasing and pursuing and entreating each other, Sydney and Beatrice forgot the spectators and responded to the throbbing, intoxicating notes.

The countess and Clare began clapping enthusiastically against the seductive rhythms. Beatrice, as if awakening from a trance, realized her friends protective call to calm down. She turned splendid and dignified, much to Sydney's disappointment and Professor Bellamy's relief. For if her friends had not brought Beatrice Venn to her senses, the professor would have.

Mr. Gibson wound down the ecstatic dance, and world

famous Sydney Froilan, playboy of the western world, snatched the tambourine from Sully and played it. Beatrice watched as he expertly shook the shallow hand drum and the metallic disks danced. She watched his thumb rubbing the hand drum and her heart pounded like the tic tac of heels, as she thought of the morning they had spent together in her hotel room at the Sault.

Professor Bellamy, angry with Sydney for his obvious seduction of Mrs. Venn, stood up and purposefully upstaged Sydney by announcing that he would recite a Vedic creation hymn in relation to the sea and dance. Clever Mr. Gibson began playing plucked notes vaguely east Indian in nature, while the old professor recited: "When there, O gods, ye stood in the primeval sea, holding each other by the hand, then rose from you as dancers clouds of dust." And he sat down, satisfied that if he had not stolen the show from Sydney, he had broken the spell married Sydney Froilan wielded over his new friend, Mrs. Venn, with the two lovely children and a reputation to uphold.

Tipsy Sydney, another drink in hand, lifted it above his head and blurted out, "I am not the polygamist you think I am, Professor Bellamy. I support monotony . . . oops . . . I beg your pardon . . . I meant to say . . . monogamy. Never went wrong on my wife because I felt the need for independence. When she saw me getting away she said . . . go on a fishing trip . . . and that's exactly what I did . . . ."

The party, except for the old professor, chuckled at Sydney's complex joke, with some reservation in respect to Professor Bellamy.

If the sun had not begun to set, casting orange light upon the guests' faces, everyone would have noticed Beatrice's face burning scarlet. For Beatrice came to her senses and realized that everyone on the yacht, except Professor Bellamy, knew that Sydney's excursion to the Sault had nothing to do with fishing for fish. They also knew that Sydney had not only caught a rare catch at the Sault, but he had supped on it too.

A gracious host to the end, Philmore changed the subject and asked Mr. Gibson to play and sing gondolier songs. And with less than an hour left until they reached the island, the yachting party quietly gathered into smaller groups.

Professor Bellamy, with one ear listening to Philmore and Mrs. Gilbertson and Sully and Rutherford telling fish stories from the Sault and adding up some thirty-five white fish, lake herring, speckled trout, and black bass among them, he strained with his other ear to overhear Beatrice telling that rogue Froilan something in a rather earthy tone nearby.

". . . somehow . . . instincts . . . failed me . . . I . . . never . . . able to escape . . . ego . . . or rise above . . . ego . . . I . . . failure as . . . mother . . . I only . . . interested in . . . children . . . when they . . . old enough . . . interest me as persons . . ."

But no matter how hard he tried, the old professor heard words only here and there, and could make no sense out of the mumbo jumbo. Beyond Sydney and Beatrice, quite a distance from the group, Professor Bellamy observed Richard and the enchanting countess standing a respectable distance from each other, perhaps admiring the setting sun together, he thought.

If the professor had a question about the countess, it had nothing to do with Richard Anders. It had to do with why the countess was staying at the Grand Hotel such a long time when her husband was ill in Italy. He heard it had something to do with her family business. He heard she was waiting on the island until her family estate was sold. Something like that. Or something about accompanying Queen Marguerite's laces back to Italy after the Chicago World's Fair.

Yet . . . though the countess enraptured the old professor,

he told himself, the women of today do not even have time to stand still for illness. What have we men done to the woman of today that she has to stand in the world alone . . . .

As *Calla* approached the Straits of Mackinac, sailing west as if into the sunset, Richard gazed at the orange star and turned to watch it set on Anna's radiant face.

"Countess . . . I find fishing contemplative amusement . . . a gentle art . . . I have faith in the skill of a great fisherman as opposed to good luck only. Yet . . . if finding love is similar to fishing . . . I would say that plain good luck is as necessary as skill . . . in finding love."

Richard, who had studied philosophy, surprisingly did not waste any time in coming to the point. "You see, Countess, I have not had luck in finding the woman of my dreams . . . before . . .," he paused and did not finish his sentence. "You see . . . I have found that the modern women of today cannot love."

Anna skirted Richard's disguised declaration of finding the woman of his dreams—herself. She quickly replied, "Mr. Anders, I know women, many at the Grand Hotel, desirous of love they cannot find. In place of love, they look to their rights for equality, like the New Woman college girls. Or they turn to outward satisfactions, like travel and reading, and allow their longings as women to become unattractively silent and wither away. Like many of the so-called old maids of faded beauty promenading the veranda with books in hand."

Anna thought of intelligent and pretty Cynthia Price, and decided then and there to encourage Richard to see more of her.

She continued, "I often think, in relation to these women, that perhaps men are not loving women well enough. Perhaps, Mr. Anders, that is why you find that the modern women of today cannot love."

Richard found Anna's answer so wise. He looked away from her intelligent beauty to the sun finally sinking below the horizon of St. Ignace.

Intending to remind ardent Richard Anders of her married status, Anna added wistfully, "Unlike most women, I learned from my husband what lovemaking is about. It's delicious foolishness. And somehow our hearts grow noble through the experience."

Richard could have listened to the countess talk until sunrise. Preferably in bed together. But he did not want to hear her talk of her husband. He felt he was losing control of the discussion. And that if he was not careful, the older woman would take over, overwhelming him with her infinite knowledge. He could not let the countess feel he was younger. He decided to challenge her experience of love.

He spoke quietly, seeming to caress the words as his eager lips formed them; desiring to caress Anna's face with his lips instead. "I have found that women do not give their bodies, hearts and souls in love . . . as men do. A woman gives herself . . . because she finds it enjoyable to be loved by a man. To me love is the pleasure I feel with a woman. But to women I've been interested in . . . love to them is the enjoyment of giving pleasure to a man. I don't want that kind of love.

"I am looking for a woman who feels pleasure in a man . . . the way a man feels pleasure in a woman. One needs great luck in finding such a rare woman. Though I believe such a woman exists . . . ."

Anna understood Richard's feelings. And Richard knew it. The fresh cool wind of twilight both invigorated and tired their bodies as they swayed gently on *Calla*. Like the mixed feelings from the wind, Anna and Richard aroused and soothed each other at the same time. The intensity of these instinctive . . .

connubial feelings . . . tightened the muscles in Anna's chest. For she knew there could be no future in sharing these feelings with Richard, who was so ready for them.

Richard spoke with a maturity Anna had not expected from the romantic man too near to her, "You must miss your husband and family in Italy . . . ." He noticed Anna's upper lip tremble slightly.

"Yes . . . but my late father's business brings me back to Michigan. I must settle his estate . . . ."

"Countess, would you keep a confidence?"

"Of course, Mr. Anders."

"Right after midnight . . . it is my birthday . . . my thirtieth . . . and for the first time in my life . . . I have never enjoyed the time around my birthday more. I have Philmore Calhoun . . . and you . . . to thank for that."

"Mr. Calhoun has provided us with great pleasure. I shall always cherish the memory of this excursion. And please . . . Mr. Anders . . . let me be the first to congratulate you on your birthday." Anna's warm smile all but embraced the worldly athletic gambler.

"I have never found it a day to celebrate. Although my father, with forced cheerfulness, always insists on celebrating it with a dinner."

"I must admit, Mr. Anders, I always enjoy the presents and attention paid to me on my birthday. In fact, I even enjoy other people's birthdays as much my own."

Richard allowed himself the indulgence of flattery and thought, how like the countess to share her happiness. "Then perhaps . . . Countess Gianotti . . . you would consider joining my father and me for dinner tomorrow evening? Though before you reply, I must warn you that my father will tell you how he was a farmer's son who attended district school . . . and had to work his way through college and then on to state university . . . ."

Richard's handsome face, in transition from youth to middle age, grew taut. " . . . My father will tell you he spent a good part of his life in his own law firm before becoming a judge of late. He will tell you he did not need fancy eastern schools or European universities in order to practice law . . . and that he won more than half of his cases . . . and has never been ambushed into a false position . . . or taken by surprise."

The worldliness in Richard's face and intelligent eyes appeared to grow more intense when he admitted, "Can you imagine a life where you never allow yourself to be taken by surprise? I could never follow in my father's footsteps. I could never go through life without surprise."

Anna did not admit to Richard, that in her own life, she had suffered too many surprises.

"Countess . . . would you honor us with your presence at my birthday dinner tomorrow evening . . . in spite of my frank warning?" He flashed a longing smile.

Something about Richard's smile unsettled her. Was it so very much like the Count's smile? In vain she tried to remember what her husband's smile looked like, but she could not remember and her face clouded. Suddenly it came to Anna.

"Mr. Anders . . . your smile reminds me very much of someone I used to know."

"I hope it is someone you have fond memories of . . ."

"Very handsome and . . . perhaps . . . too good for this world."

"Being too good, in some cases, is a vice. I know a virtuous, passionless man who is too good. He has set himself up in an impenetrable fortress and judges harshly those . . . who cannot afford to set up castles real or imaginary . . . who cannot manage to get through life unscathed. Frankly, I overlook a judgmental nature in a woman . . . but I despise it in a man. And that man . . . is my father."

"Perhaps you judge your father too harshly?"

"Then I would be guilty of the very charge I despise in him." Richard took a deep breath and continued, "Countess . . . please honor me with your . . . if I may say . . . enlightening presence . . . at my birthday dinner tomorrow . . . and judge my father for yourself?"

Anna glanced away from Richard's eyes, so full of admiration, so full of new love.

Alive to her buried feelings of youthfulness, with great pain in her spirit, Anna knew she must discourage Richard's invitation, his disguised declaration of love. She knew she must wound the younger man's affections for her and outrage his pride by coming right out and telling him, his attentions must stop or they will grow obvious to all. For she was not free to accept his love. And their love was ill-fated.

But instead she asked him if she could bring a friend along to accompany her to his birthday dinner. Assuming that the countess would bring one of the Big Four, Richard grew quite excited thinking what a delightful evening it was sure to be.

The countess decided to bring Cynthia Price along as a surprise. A choice Richard would not have made. Having asked Richard to describe his father's cottage in the annex, she tried to convince herself, there could be no moral wrong in meeting his father and celebrating Richard's birthday. For Anna intended to interest Richard Anders in Cynthia Price. Intended to bury Richard's subtle and crude appeals which played rhapsodic duets upon her heart strings.

"Thank you, Countess, for accepting my invitation. But there is something I must reveal to you. I had not mentioned it before, because I did not want to extract your sympathies and influence your answer. Yet it must be said to give you an opportunity to weigh a change of mind."

Anna and Richard saw the first twinkling lights of the village and the east bluff cottages of the island in the distance. It was both a welcome and sad sight. For they wished to extend their precious time together away from prying eyes.

"You see . . . at some time during my birthday celebration . . . my father will suddenly insist we stand up and drink a toast to my mother . . . as he has at every one of my birthday dinners since I can remember."

Anna looked up at him inquiringly.

"You see, Countess . . . my mother . . . died the very moment I was born."

Like an anchor let go, Anna's heart fell to her stomach. She pictured Richard as a little boy suffering the loss of his mother and imposed guilt from his father, on a day that should have been joyful. Even if the dusk had not shielded her gesture, Anna gently grasped Richard's broad hand and held it firmly, as they gazed at the village lights and pale white fort and shadowy buildings of Mackinac Island growing larger and larger as they entered the harbor at dusk.

For the first time in his life, Richard found someone who understood. He felt he had known Anna his entire life.

It is often spoken of the sacrifices parents make for their children. But as Anna held Richard's hand in hers, she pondered why it is that the very real sacrifices children make for their parents . . . are never mentioned in the holding together of families.

"Stand by and lower the anchor," yelled the skipper.

"MaMa! MaMa!"

Allowed to stay up late and greet their returning mother at the launch, little Frederick and Monica Venn, lifted out of the carriage by Owen Corrigan, ran to greet Beatrice as she was helped out of the launch by Sydney. Before shrinking back from the family scene, Sydney whispered something to Beatrice and walked to a nearby Grand Hotel carriage with Eugene Sullivan and Professor Bellamy.

After a rousing welcome, the children bolted over to Professor Bellamy without permission. The old professor was tickled pink when the children hung on to him as if he were a favorite blood related grandpa.

Philippa MacAdam and Nanna, waiting in Owen's carriage, greeted Beatrice as she entered the hack. They explained that the children begged till they were blue in the face to be allowed to go with "Owney" to meet their MaMa at the boat.

Looking somewhat transfigured, Beatrice tried to jerk herself away from fantasies of worldly Sydney Froilan and concentrate on reentering her summer life on the island. She kissed the children cuddling next to her, feeling so warm and secure next to their mother. But Beatrice felt no further acclimated than when she had first seen little Frederick and Monica running happily to her.

Philippa asked, "Beatrice, do you think Clare will be long in coming? I have been given a message to deliver to her. An 'urgent message' I have been told. From a Mrs. Vivian Larron . . . you know the woman in red who entered the grand ball at half past two . . . ." Philippa's voice cracked noticeably, as she pictured Marshe Williamson with Mrs. Larron at the ball.

"But what should that woman want with Clare?"

"I do not know. But I did not like her attitude when she gave me the note. Instinctively, I do not trust this Mrs. Vivian Larron. While you were away, I saw her for the first time in the dining room. She wore diamonds to the breakfast table . . . ."

"Well, I overheard Mr. Calhoun say to Clare that he needed, I repeat needed, to show her something before she left his yacht. I assumed he wanted a few minutes alone with her.

He is a marvelous host, Philippa," said Beatrice, her zesty voice laced with innuendo.

"Oh . . . really . . . ." Philippa smiled in genuine regard for the possible feelings ignited between eligible Clare and eligible Philmore Calhoun on the excursion.

"The trip was a great success and ever so much fun. I have so much to tell you. However, dear Philippa, we missed you."

"Thank you, Beatrice. But you know my aversion to the sea. Why even the ferry ride from Mackinaw City to the island is too much for me."

"Leddies," Owen Corrigan spoke up, "me Charley is an impatient one tonight. Should we wait fer the other fine leddies, seein' thare is no earthly room fer them in me fine hack? Or should we head up back to the grand palace and get the wee ones tucked into their comfy beds?"

Against Philippa's better judgment, they decided to go on ahead. After all, Clare and the countess could accompany each other back to the Grand. Mrs. Vivian Larron's urgent note, sticked before it had been sealed, would just have to wait. And Owen was right, it was way past the children's bedtime.

Before the countess, Richard and Clare left the yacht, Philmore led Clare to his stateroom and showed her the bathtub underneath his sofa. Clare laughed to herself mistakenly, thinking that the bathtub was what Philmore had "needed" to show her. Above the bathtub-sofa, she noticed a finely wrought, even elegant-looking ax with a gleaming metal blade, hung in an artistic manner.

"Clare . . . this is what I needed to show you."

Philmore held up a small oval portrait on ivory of a beautiful looking woman.

"My late wife always said that this portrait of herself was over idealized. I never thought so. She was gentle, refined, beautiful and unassuming. Just as you see her here. A true lady with a clean slate. I knew her for only three years. I . . . I . . . just wanted you to see this now. For I plan on locking it up in a drawer . . . ."

"As you have locked your beloved wife in your heart, Philmore . . . ."

"Yes, Clare. You understand."

Clare may have understood. But she had never known how it felt to be beloved by a husband. And if it was in Clare's nature, she would have grown envious of the dead woman in the portrait. Instead she felt a deep sadness.

Philmore locked the small portrait in a small desk drawer. Then he silently held Clare's arm and accompanied her to the gangway. Clare tried to forget his words, "true lady with a clean slate."

Having handed her down to the sailors in the launch, Philmore boomed, "By the way . . . *Calla* is named after my lucky ax . . . the ax I carried in my timber cruising days . . . the magic ax that led me to Iron Mountain."

To Clare, Philmore sounded and looked like a folk hero incarnate, standing so tall on the yacht above her. Clare called back good naturedly, "What does *Calla* mean?"

Philmore boomed back so loudly that the fort soldiers and east bluff cottagers and even the Grand Hotel guests leaving the veranda after the nightly outdoor concert might have heard, "Beautiful . . . Clare . . . beautiful!"

The Big Four, without planning it, timed their arrival back at the Grand Hotel perfectly. Old Stinkweed had gone to bed, so few crafty crackpots were still around after the veranda concert to take notes that three of the Big Four had indeed come back in one piece. But the spys who were around noticed with disappointment on their faces that Mrs. Venn, and

Mrs. MacAdam accompanying her, were not on the arms of gentlemen, but with the children and their nanny who had stayed at the Cudahy cottage during Beatrice Venn's absence.

Fifteen minutes later, the countess and Mrs. Gilbertson arrived accompanying each other without a trace of a gentleman nearby. No, the group of four women did not look tired from late hours. No, the spies concluded, there was nothing in the rumors that three in the group of Big Four, absent from the hotel for three whole days, were partying past bedtime on a sugar daddy's yacht.

Back in her room, Anna immediately wrote a note to Cynthia Price, explaining Richard's invitation and asking Cynthia to accompany her to his birthday celebration.

Anna sent her Italian maid to the Prices' room down the hallway to deliver the note. Then she changed clothes quickly and popped into bed for a needed full night's sleep. Though her mind wrestled with conflicting thoughts of Richard Anders and Count Gianotti, she fell asleep content that not only had she conducted herself properly, she had enjoyed the liveliest yachting party of her life. And never would she forget the exciting ride at the Sault rapids.

Rutherford Haverhill would never forget the yachting party either. In fact he could not stop thinking about Sydney and Beatrice's obvious enjoyment of each other. About Clare and Philmore's obvious budding romance. About the countess and Richard's obvious conflicting passion. He could not stop thinking how utterly left out of life he felt even into the early hour of three o'clock in the morning. Gulping eighty proof toasts to each of the three couples, it occurred to Rutherford to drink to Philippa MacAdam and Marshe Williamson as well, just for the hell of it. Because it looked to Rutherford that Marshe was the type of man who got what he wanted. And it looked as if Marshe had his sparkling eyes set on lovely Philippa.

Rutherford Earle Haverhill V could handle his hard liquor as well as the next man with a wooden leg. But four shots of the finest brandy within an hour's time would souse even the most dedicated drunk come back from a trip to the desert.

Yes, Rutherford was pickled when he woke up his valet and told him to find his gold monogrammed black velvet slippers, which matched his gold monogrammed black velvet robe lined with cashmere from Kashmir, which covered his gold mono-grammed black silk pajamas. His velvet slippers were right next to his bed. He had tripped over them enroute to waking up his valet in a room next to his. He told his valet to open the door to his balcony and to wrap a "common wool blanket" around him.

His valet complied unwillingly, realizing that his master could easily fall off his private balcony and land on the longest porch in the world—with one of the richest broken necks in the country. But the valet knew it was no use correcting Rutherford even when he was drunk. Like a spoiled brat from whom life had not yet knocked out the bull-headed spirit at forty, Ruther-ford would have his way at whatever cost.

Looking like an Indian come into money, Rutherford stepped out onto the small balcony overlooking the veranda, and stepped into the chilly darkness of a Mackinac Island summer night. The cool air slapped his hot face as his parents should have but never did. Drinking in the coolness and another shot of brandy like a thirsty thoroughbred lapping down water, Rutherford pretended to shiver, railing against the fifty-five degrees with three layers of silk, cashmere, and heavy wool protecting him from the cold, if not buffering him from the need to feel the cold. The need to feel less comfort-able, less passive. The need to feel more earthy, more passion-ate. Simply, the need to feel at all.

Dizzy, Rutherford grabbed the spindle carved balustrade, and plopped down on a brown wooden chair. To him the air seemed perfumed with a fragrance foreign to the island. He dismissed the scent and for no apparent reason thought about his extensive collection of Japonaise art and crafts, all the rage in New York and Paris.

Floating images, bathed in shadows, paraded as if in procession past his stoned mind's eye; images of *netsukes* and *ukiyo-e* wood block prints and ornamental swords and bronze Buddhas and old *kosode* costumes and kimonos and gold lacquerwork and tea ceremony utensils and picture scrolls and folding screens and toys of fancy and folding fans for batons on battlefields and pottery and porcelain and . . . the images started colliding and transforming themselves . . . his shiny swords sliced through kimonos . . . folding screens opened and closed on their own . . . bronze Buddhas whisked pea green tea to a froth with his tea ceremony utensils . . . .

Feeling his mind sinking deeper and deeper into his body, like a rock falling hundreds of feet to the bottom of the Mackinac straits, invisible but there, Rutherford smelled the perfumed air once more. It reminded him of the scent of sandalwood, suggesting oriental splendor and sumptuous so-phistication. His body swayed as it had on *Calla* but six hours ago. He liked the feeling and decided to commission a yacht twice as long as Philmore Calhoun's. Turning slightly he sniffed another whiff of sandalwood carried on a westerly breeze and looked over to his right. Rutherford tried to focus his eyes on a neighboring balcony, some fifteen feet away, bathed in soft light from the hidden bedroom beyond.

For onto the little balcony floated a woman with black hair wearing a resplendent trailing black robe with deep reverse décolletage. Gracefully she lifted her hands to her shoulders, and dropped the black robe, which fell elegantly around her feet.

As if a radiant adolescent Venus emerged from her bath, the woman stood totally nude in the fifty-five-degree air—simply for the sensual pleasure of it all. She stared out at the darkness beyond the hotel and thought:

Oh! life you are the cryptic light
From darkness in the womb,
A comic tragic interlude
To darkness in the tomb;
Think not of this foredoom!

Like a drunken Peeping Tom, Rutherford sat perfectly still staring at her nakedness—simply for the sexual pleasure of it all. He refocused in on the graceful woman's long slender waist and thighs and swelling pearlike breasts and short calf. So unlike the women he had known with long legs and full bosoms, from whom he had so little real pleasure; because those women, in spite of full form, had not possessed the personality to love men.

Someone hiccupped way down the veranda below the balconies. Rutherford froze.

The comely woman bent down as gracefully as a willow bent in the breeze, gathered the black robe about her, slipped it on her well-formed shoulders, rose up, turned to Rutherford, and bowed fifteen degrees with slight indication of head and shoulders in a disarmingly simple and straightforward fashion.

Intoxicated with the liquor and the sensuous sight, caught in the act of voyeurism, not knowing what else to do and being the fine gentleman he was, Rutherford staggered up from his wooden chair and bowed back. Notwithstanding his lustful curiosity or the woman's former nudity, the thought struck him that an atmosphere of modesty and purity surrounded the fleshly vision so nearby on the balcony next door.

Rutherford refocused on the woman's face, three-quarters lit by the light from her bedroom. He made out a magnificent widow's peak darting on and off a forehead above slanted oriental eyes looking out from a round face featuring a cherrylike mouth. If he had been closer, he would have seen that the Japanese woman had soulful eyes, so unlike his own.

The oriental woman turned slowly and seemed to float off the balcony into her bedroom, her black robe trailing behind.

Rutherford staggered back into his bedroom, wondering if he had had an erotic dream. And wondering who the hell was hiccupping nonstop on the veranda below.

11

This Storm Shall Never Pass

If Sunday was a difficult day of the week for the resorters at the Grand Hotel, rainy days were worse than the Lord's Day for troublemaking. For if rain fell on any day of the week but Sunday, resorters felt no holy obligation to refrain from petty quarreling and downright dirty gossiping.

In the morning, trouble had already broken loose all over the hotel as families and friends, obliged to stay indoors because of the storming weather, were forced into perhaps too much togetherness.

Hungover Rutherford Haverhill did not even bother to get out of bed. Since it was his valet's day off, he argued all day with himself whether or not he had hallucinated the bare skinned woman on the balcony next door, and had hiccupped himself, causing the woman to bow to him. The more he argued the more he thought of her graceful unadorned body.

Little did Rutherford know that Jimmy Hayes was suffering the final leg of a forty-hour bout with the hiccups.

Yes, stirring up trouble was the unstated agenda on a rainy day. Belinda Gaines gushed and giggled openly with every college girl's beau she could find, as well as a few young married men, infuriating every intellectual flirt and young married woman attached to Belinda's receptacles of coquetry. The men flirted back out of boredom or a need to "get back" at their young loves for reasons they could not even remember.

Old Stinkweed, waiting for something scandalous to happen, was grumpier than ever having to keep his tight shoes on in the parlor. Even he could not take the smell of his feet in a closed room.

A lancet-tongued old maid spread the rumor that another oriental pagan besides Ibrahim the lecturer, and this time from the far east, had entered the grand hotel scene that summer. She had seen the oriental's kimono-clad figure exiting the parlor early in the morning. The old maid figured it was the oriental who had set up the exhibition of Japonaise embroidery in the parlor. The jealous old maid would not admit aloud that she had only seen such exquisite handwork at the Chicago World's Fair. Little did she know that the same woman, Aki Shima, was the producer of the beautiful embroidery at the world's fair and at the Grand Hotel.

Even the old Muldoon sisters-in-law became bellicose with each other as the rain drenched Mackinac Island and their usually effusive spirits. One Muldoon went so far as to say to the other, "Aren't you enough to make a stone shed tears today."

But few seemed as deeply troubled as Clare Gilbertson and Cynthia Price.

"Cynthia dear, please reconsider your rash acceptance to this Richard Anders' birthday dinner tonight."

"Mother . . . I am sorry you do not approve. But I wonder if you are upset that I answered the countess without your approval . . . or because of the fact Mr. Anders did not ask me personally."

"Cynthia . . . you have failed to address my real concerns. After many inquiries I have learned for you that he is a race horse gambler . . . but this information seems not to have affected you in the least. In addition, I found no one by the name of Anders who owns a cottage in the Annex. In fact, I entirely question the motives of Countess Gianotti in accepting

the invitation and inviting you along as a surprise guest."
Mrs. Price did not mention to her daughter what she really
suspected.

"Forgive me, Mother . . . but I am twenty-eight years old
. . . and I have sent the countess my acceptance and will not
. . . like a child disciplined . . . go back on my acceptance."
Cynthia fidgeted with a stray ringlet of her mouse brown hair,
remembering the highly charged look in Richard's eyes when
she had seen him with the honey haired countess on the
veranda after tea a number of days ago. Cynthia did not know
that Richard and the countess had traveled to the Sault together.
"I have found Mr. Anders the complete gentleman. And
certainly if the gracious countess thinks to include me, she
must reason that Mr. Anders has an interest in me."

Suspecting that someone might be listening at the hotel
room door, though whenever she looked no one was there,
Cynthia lowered her voice, "When I contemplate a life alone
or a life with a gentleman of education and worldliness such as
Mr. Anders . . . no matter what his profession . . . I would
prefer to spend my life with such a man."

"Cynthia . . . whatever happened to your talk of marrying
a man like your father . . . a hard working man content with
the simple things in life and . . ."

Cynthia interrupted her MaMa, "Mother, please . . . you
are lucky to have PaPa . . . I am lucky to have him as a father
. . . but I have not been lucky in finding a man like him. I
cannot wait for the rest of my life!"

For the first time in Mrs. Price's life she did not go to her
daughter, when Cynthia broke into terrible sobbing. With deep
reluctance, Mrs. Price turned away from her daughter's shaking body and uncontrollable tears. She knew that no good
would come from a race horse gambler. She would not comfort
her daughter's guilt with her decision.

For the first time in her life, Cynthia told herself that she did not care if her MaMa comforted her or not.

As pounding rain assailed the island, Beatrice Venn felt like sailing into her children as well. Right on their little behinds. It was no wonder they misbehaved at lunch and would not eat. In the rotunda before lunch, Beatrice and her children had approached Belinda Gaines flirting with Sydney Froilan—or was it the other way around—Beatrice was not quite sure; and while Beatrice chatted with Sydney, shrewd Belinda passed little Frederick and Monica six chocolate bonbons with cherry centers. Hiding behind Belinda's mold-green dress, the children managed to gulp down three bonbons each, while their mother, gazing deeply into Sydney Froilan's eyes, did not suspect a thing.

Since Nanna was off for the day, Beatrice had her hands full with two usually good children turned naughty at lunch. Finally, the last straw was played when Monica threw an olive pit under the table at Frederick and it landed on Beatrice's white napkin instead. Had the olive pit landed on the lap of the countess or Philippa or Clare—strangely absent, the children knew their adopted aunts would not have breathed a word and probably would have winked, as had happened in the past.

Beatrice dismissed Monica from the table rationalizing that she had caused Frederick to act even more naughty than was usual to the naughty side of his nature. She should have blamed Belinda Gaines. Beatrice personally took Monica up to her room where a maid was told to look after her and ordered the little girl into bed. Beatrice returned to the dining room, passing Sydney's room on the way. In a second she forgot about Monica and cursed the rainy weather. For she had planned to sit for Sydney that day. Or whatever position he would require of her.

Ten-year-old Monica Venn was not unaware of her mother's "moods," though her Nanna did everything she could to cover them up. And since fearless little Monica Venn was walking in her mother's footsteps and developing some "moods" of her own, she decided to sneak out of her room and visit Professor Bellamy some five hundred feet down the hallway from her room. She knew the professor would not be taking lunch on a rainy day he could not take exercise. She figured he probably felt lonely all alone in his room and would welcome her company.

In fact, Professor Bellamy was relishing the moments of conversationless peace in the privacy of his room. A highly social man, even Professor Bellamy could not be "on" all the time. The excitement from the trip to the Sault was exhausting, and the witty conversation was hard work. So when he heard a light knock on his door, interrupting his reading the first volume of Henry Schoolcraft's *Algic Researches,* full of Ojibway Indian tales and legends, he almost told what he figured to be a maid, to go away.

"Come in."

"It's me, Professor . . ."

"Well, well, well . . . good afternoon, Monica . . ."
Professor Bellamy found Monica a bright and fun-loving little person. He looked for Beatrice behind the little girl and was surprised she had come alone.

Little Monica Venn burst into tears.

"Why are you crying, dear Monica?" Professor Bellamy graciously bent down to Monica's level; cursing his cracking bones all the way.

"I am not allowed to eat lunch. I was sent to my room. But I escaped when my maid was not looking."

"But your maid will be worried that you have run away."

"I don't care."

"She could be let go and be without work and money."

"So what."

"Do you mean that?"

"No."

"Well then . . . let me take you back to your room."

"No, Grandpa, no!" Monica turned red with embarrassment, "I mean . . . Professor . . ."

It was only natural that after Monica's spontaneous burst of sentiment, the old professor would find another way to comfort her. "Will you let me send a note to your mother?"

"Only if you promise not to send me back to my room."

"I cannot promise that, Monica. I do not know what your mother will say." Loral Bellamy wrote two notes and rang for a bellboy.

"My mother is mean."

"Do you mean that?"

"I mean that she is mean to send me away from the table without food and I played so hard this morning and suddenly I'm so hungry." Monica looked around the room and noticed food next to the professor's reading chair. "I see that you have cheese and crackers, Professor . . ."

"Yes, we were beginning to eat them," the old professor's eyes twinkled with merriment and his stomach groaned with hunger.

"We?"

"Yes, my pets and myself."

"You have pets in here?"

"I'll tell you about them later."

"Ok. Professor . . . may I have some cheese and crackers?"

"Normally I would have offered you some. But since you

were naughty and sent away from the table to be punished, I cannot go against your mother's wishes."

"Pretend you don't know. You always tell us to play pretend."

"This is a different situation."

"Well then, don't you eat your cheese and crackers when I can't eat anything." Monica looked intently up at Professor Bellamy who was by this time standing up because his legs were getting stiff.

"But I haven't been naughty and I have quite an appetite," he said kindly, trying to hide his amusement and a drop of impatience.

Without uttering a sound, Monica turned her face away from the professor and cried silent tears. She thought for sure the grandpalike gentleman would have taken her side, whatever may have come.

A bellboy knocked and walked through the open door. Professor Bellamy handed him a note for the maid down the hallway. He gave the bellboy a second note and said, "Please deliver this note to Mrs. Beatrice Venn in the dining room and bring back her response. And . . . please . . . take the cheese and crackers with you." He sighed, his stomach grumbled, and he sat down thinking how easily he collapsed to the tyranny of this child, when he would not submit to any form of tyranny whatsoever.

Before the old gentleman knew what happened, little Monica Venn climbed onto his lap and hugged him with all her might. The scene was a bitter-sweet moment he would never forget.

And that was the day that Monica Venn learned to keep a secret for her "best friend" the professor. For right after that two darling little mice scampered up his leg. Not only were the mice pets of the professor's, but to little Monica's utter delight, especially on a rainy day, she learned that the mice could actually—sing.

With much trepidation, Philippa MacAdam knocked on Clare Gilbertson's hotel room door after dinner.

"Mrs. Gilbertson's not in, Mrs. MacAdam. Can you think on it, my mistress ordered a carriage and went out into this violent weather!"

"May I ask where she went?"

"Not sure. But she looked white-faced she did."

Philippa's suspicions grew. For after having delivered the "urgent" note from Vivian Larron to Clare in the morning, Philippa had not seen Clare the entire day. And when Clare, uncharacteristically, had not sent word of explanation for her absence, Philippa grew alarmed.

Noting Philippa's concern, Clare's maid blurted, "Mrs. Gilbertson did say something which didn't make any sense . . . about a crack in the island."

And Philippa recalled that Vivian Larron rode Kentucky Jean on the day of the accident from Crack-in-the-Island. Was Clare meeting Mrs. Larron there? Then she thought about the legend and superstitions attached to the natural curiosity. That it is haunted by a giant demon, who back in time had tried to descend through the crack to the Spirit of the Dead. But rejected from the abyss, the demon now clings despairingly to the edge of the crack. Anyone who steps on the demon's giant fingers will suffer loss of wealth or misfortune in love or sickness or a host of other common everyday calamities.

As if warned by the old legend, Philippa tried to resist even stronger suspicions about Clare and Mrs. Vivian Larron—and about Marshe Williamson. For she had seen Mrs. Larron approach Marshe in the rotunda that morning. Philippa had even ventured near them, hoping to overhear their conversation. But could not pick up a word. When they had walked off together toward a private room, Philippa needed to go out for a ride as she never had since the death of her husband. But she did not ride because of the rain. Instead she rushed out onto the longest porch in the world and strolled it back and forth, denying to herself that Marshe had anything to do with Mrs. Vivian Larron, who painted her lips red.

But her doubts had continued to plague her. And when Marshe had approached her after his meeting with Mrs. Larron, Philippa found excuses not to be in his presence—all the time wanting so very much to be with the southern gentleman, who could have been her late husband's brother.

While her three friends had been at the Sault, Philippa had met with Marshe—alone—but once, accidentally in the corral where she painted Dude. Marshe had shown genuine appreciation for Philippa's work and asked her to stop at his horse farm on her way back to Virginia. He had asked her to paint his Armande. Philippa had told Marshe she would consider it. But the couple's relationship did not progress further than it had at the Sunday tea. And Philippa kept asking herself why two people, who felt such excitement in each other's presence, could not seem to come together.

By seven o'clock the rain had not stopped. Though it was no longer pouring, the evening was so damp that the countess, going to Richard's birthday dinner against her better judgment, and Cynthia Price, going against her mother's wishes, felt the dampness deep in their bones as they nervously rode along the west bluff in Owen Corrigan's carriage, enroute to the cottage of Richard Anders' father.

Thick fog obscured the usually breathtaking view to their left of the straits from the west bluff. To their right they passed recently built palatial wooden cottages of Queen Anne style, faced with fancifully cut siding shingles, defined with chateau-like towers translated into wood and spacious verandas and small porches. The misty air softened the cottages' outlines darting up and around curved corners and abrupt angles, like juxtaposed eccentricities.

Even though the countess lived in a grand palazzo with too many rooms to count, she always startled herself at the sight of the new big cottages on rustic Mackinac Island. They seemed to try so hard to be noticed, seemed to say, look at me—how big and bold and new money am I.

Anna longed for a time twenty to forty years past when money really did not show on Mackinac Island, populated with Indians and fisherman and lumberman and sailors and soldiers and few summer tourists staying in modest hotels. For a time when those who visited the island, with money, did not make a big show of it in front of others less fortunate.

Soon Owen drove them into the Annex, a gentle wooded area of the island where the oldest cottages of modest size, many built in the 1880s, were located. Anna recalled the humorous explanation Richard had given her on *Calla*, about the friendly rivalry between those who lived on the west bluff, and those who lived on the east bluff. It was actually his father's version about whose expansive bluff view and location was better.

Richard had explained his father's version like this. The east bluff cottagers claimed their view was full of visual entertainment and a cozy intimacy with the town below and Round Island beyond the straits, which no west bluffer could boast of. Why many an east bluffer could see the harbor clearly and watched the comings and goings and unloading of Arnold's ferries and other maritime vessels. Not to mention the sun-rises, and proximity to the fort and Arch Rock, and the bird's eye view of the main street and church steeples.

Yet it was the west bluffers who could and did lay claim to expansive water views rivalling any seen from the Riviera, "uncluttered with the details" the east bluffers boasted about. The west bluff cottagers revelled in the open watery expanse and did not care if they knew what size the ship or yacht or whaleback passing through the Straits of Mackinac really was in relation to its surroundings. They did not care if they saw the comings and goings of "strangers" in a busy harbor. After all, the Grand Hotel was in their "own backyard" and if they wanted to see "strangers" they could go and eyeball them face to face there, not through periscopes from some east bluff porch.

Richard's father often said that the west bluff cottagers were really in the "Grand Hotel's backyard," but they never recognized this.

Yes, there was a bit of friendly rivalry between the east bluffers and the west bluffers, whose cottages were on government property.

And there was yet a third group of cottagers, generally set apart from this rivalry, who lived in the Annex without water views, surrounded by trees, and who owned their land. Richard's father called it Gordon Hubbard's Annex. And he accused Hubbard of being the first man to exploit Mackinac Island by bringing in well-off summer nomads, like himself, to build residences on land better left alone. Like all the capitalists of his day, Hubbard had not thought of leaving nature alone, because he had been in financial trouble and he needed to exploit something to get out of it.

Richard's father perceived that the cottagers in his own section, the Annex, were indifferent as to whether an east bluff or a west bluff view was better, or whose cottage was bigger and more lavishly furnished. The Annexers were at Mackinac to get on with the enjoyments of summer life. Certainly they enjoyed, even loved the views from the east and west bluffs, from Fort Holmes and Fort Mackinac, from Arch Rock and Lover's Leap, but they equally enjoyed the view from their protected cozy cottages, which overlooked nothing more than trees and flowers.

Richard's father pointed out, it was not that the Annexers were the sort of people to be easily satisfied. In that case they could have built a summer house anywhere. No, to the Annexers, like himself, there was no place in the world to compare with Mackinac—with or without water views from their residence.

Yes, in terms of location, the only detail which united the rivaling east bluffers to the west bluffers—was that they both were not Annexers.

"Whoa, Charley."

When Owen Corrigan stopped in front of a quaint little white cottage, with a railed porch, gabled roof, shiplap board siding, and carved wooden trim fitting the description given to him by the countess, he felt an uneasiness in his fingers which had nothing to do with holding the reins. He could not figure out what ground him up inside. He saw someone with a broad umbrella running out of the cottage in order to accompany the two ladies in one by one.

After Countess Anna left the carriage, a realization hit Owen like the kick of Charley's hoof upon Owen's own forehead when the old horse was a young lucifer so many years back. But it was too late to warn Countess Anna about it. Owen thought, perhaps she knows already. He felt a wee let down that the countess had not mentioned the least thing about it to him . . . if she knew.

Owen Corrigan drove Charley into the small barn behind the cottage, placed a pile of hay near him, and went into the kitchen where he had been invited to take dinner and wait until the ladies were ready to go back to the Grand Hotel.

So overjoyed and honored with the countess' presence,

Richard Anders overlooked his disappointment with the surprise guest accompanying Anna. Richard had expected the charming Clare or Philippa or Beatrice. And in order to cover his small letdown Richard overplayed his welcoming attentions to placid if pretty Cynthia Price—utterly convincing Cynthia of his unstated affection for her.

He led them to a small parlor, masculine in feeling, filled with books and overstuffed chairs and antiques and oriental rugs and landscape paintings. Richard's father, looking ever so much like Richard from behind in the act of tending cheerful flames in the fireplace, turned around and smiled. His unconscious magnetism was obviously handed down to his son; his middle aged facial features were not. And to say which man appeared the better looking was a matter of taste—and age.

"Countess Gianotti . . . Miss Price . . . may I present my father Arthur Andryer . . ."

Silence bred of loss and rediscovery merged with the crackling of the tamarack flames.

"Can it be Elizabeth Anne . . . ." Arthur Andryer, paralyzed by conflicting emotions, could not make himself move to welcome her.

Dumbfounded, Richard shot a look at the countess. A smile unsure and vulnerable and warm cast an expression of sad surprise upon her radiant face. He saw her lips tremble slightly, her eyes moisten just enough to make them gleam in the firelight facing her. He saw that she was too moved to speak. His father addressed him in a tone of voice so gentle, so unlike his usual defiant courtroom voice, that Richard looked over at him, startled.

"Richard . . . son . . . do you remember . . . Anna?"

Suddenly shared visions of a summer twenty years ago filled the memories of Anna and Richard and Arthur. The carriage rides to British Landing and Sugar Loaf and Skull's Cave, the ball games, the boating, the dances, the first passion, the marriage proposal, the birth of a calf, the blissful happy days shared by all three which followed until . . . .

Richard remembered that if Anna had been true to her answer and true to his father, she would have been his mother. He remembered how both he and his father suffered upon learning that Anna would not honor the marriage proposal she had accepted before obtaining permission from her parents. He remembered praying to God in the sky that fun-loving Anna would come back to them. He had even prayed to the Indian gods, in case the Christian God would not come through for him as had been his experience.

Arthur Andryer abruptly blocked his bitter sweet memories from twenty years ago. He could not help himself and gazed openly at the woman Anna had become. Her quiet grandness, her manner and bearing so dignified so fresh, her face so worldly so soft, her full form so . . . .

Anna pulled her eyes away from Arthur Andryer, her first love, and thought of her mother insisting upon a long European trip, pushing her to marry the debonaire Count Gianotti, her second love, her second passion, who made dear Arthur look small town and middle class. And Richard . . . who grew from the memory of age ten to the reality of age thirty in a second . . . Richard . . . so like his father . . . so like the Count . . . so unlike both of them.

"Please forgive us, Miss Price . . . I welcome you to the Andryer cottage." Arthur finally broke the wave of emotion riding on the silence.

Cynthia Price did not know what to think. Though she was poised enough not to appear curious, she was dying of curiosity. Looking over at Richard she observed him gazing into the fireplace, his young-looking face strangely contorted.

"Miss Price," Arthur addressed her, "we have rediscovered an old island friendship quite by coincidence . . ."

"Is it coincidence . . . or is it fate?" asked Richard quite jovially. He turned from the fire, his eyes aged by the discovery, and gazed directly at the woman he planned to take back from the count, who had stolen dear Anna away. Then Richard changed his thinking. He thought, no, the count had not stolen Anna. The Count had preserved Anna. For it was not meant for Anna to be my mother. To be my father's wife. It is meant for Anna to be my wife.

Cynthia could see that unmarried Arthur Andryer, a man in his late forties, of good form and graying temples, was quite taken with the married countess and began to think of her mother's warnings about the birthday dinner of Richard Anders. In fact, she noticed with some embarrassment, that provincial Arthur Andryers, so unlike his worldy son, could not take his eyes off of Countess Gianotti sitting splendidly in a princess evening gown of yellow crepe de chine made over silk, her trained skirt caught up in festoons with rosettes, her left shoulder ornamented with a yellow velvet rose and brown velvet leaves, her bronze slippers catching the glow of the fire.

Unattached Cynthia Price, in a gown of white net over white satin with trails of white roses, so taken with Arthur Andryer's attention to the countess, failed to see that his son Richard had steaming eyes for the countess as well.

Only Anna in the foursome could not gather her energies for some time. The surprise had been too great. As had so many of the surprises, and so many of the secrets, in Countess Elizabeth Anne Gianotti's life. She finally spoke in her expressive melodious voice, "Storms pass in time . . . ."

Cynthia answered naively, "It seems this storm shall never pass," and she listened to the thunder from clouds banging and crying out in the night.

"Time allows new storms to gather . . .," Richard said with quiet forcefulness.

Arthur questioned what his son meant by the disguised

answer to the countess' disguised talk. He wondered what sort of intimacy existed between the two of them. He wasn't born yesterday. He decided to counter Richard's private statement to the countess with one of his own.

"Mission Church is closed, Anna . . ."

"It has been for some time, Arthur . . .," she answered gently.

"But Anna . . . do you think it will ever open again?" Arthur alluded to the night the Mission House hotel held an outdoor dance by the light of the full moon over Round Island. The night he whisked Anna away from prying eyes to Mission Church nearby. The night he had asked her to marry him as a young widowed lawyer with a ten-year-old son, and she had answered "yes." The night he had held her and kissed her more passionately than he had any woman in his entire life.

Anna understood Arthur's disguised talk as well. She felt like collapsing from the exhaustion of dealing with what was unsaid. She smiled carefully at Arthur and replied, "I understand that Mission Church has been closed for such a long time . . . there appears no possibility of reopening it in our lifetime, Arthur . . . ."

Richard thought the questions and answers terribly suspect. He grew immediately guarded, almost jealous of the probable passionate memories his father and the Countess . . . Anna . . . shared which he knew nothing about. He could still feel the softness and warmth of her hand around his on *Calla*. And he laughed inside for the joy of their reunion, and the answer to his feelings ever since he first saw the countess— of having known her his entire life.

"I have told Anna all about you, Father." Richard might have said, don't bore Anna with the details of your life. Worldly people like the countess do not care about such details. They want to be entertained by conversation, not monologues.

"But Richard, you have told me so little of Miss Price," Arthur said in his usual courtroom voice.

Touche! Richard thought, you know damn well I never spoke to you of Cynthia Price, nor any woman for that matter.

From then on Arthur Andryer seized every opportunity throughout the evening to focus Richard's attention on pretty and intelligent, if wooden, Cynthia Price. Really, Arthur was quite taken with the similarities of Cynthia's nature and physical features to Richard's mother; a woman Arthur had known for a mere two years before her death at Richard's birth. A death which took place that very day exactly thirty years ago.

And like a lawyer for the plaintiff, himself, extracting information from the defendent, Anna, Arthur Andryer forced aside his emotions and seized every opportunity to find out in a round about way, what his second love Anna, so unlike his late wife, had really become behind a facade so tempting as to be ideal.

"Dinner is served," announced Arthur Andryer's immigrant cook.

"We do things very informally here Anna, not at all what you are accustomed to in Europe among royalty, I would imagine," Arthur spoke up needlessly as he offered Anna his arm and led her into the dining room. To have Anna on his arm again was as shocking as if his dead wife had come back to life, on the anniversary of her death.

Anna had everything she could do to keep herself from tears on the arm of Arthur Andryer, her first love ignited the last time she had been on her beloved island.

Arthur helped Anna to her seat and Richard did likewise with Cynthia Price. The dining room table was set with simple American china and sterling and glassware. Four cloisonné candle holders, surrounded by wildflower wreaths of yellow birdsfoot trefoil Arthur had spotted on the beach below the Annex, decorated the understated table.

"I am looking forward to food cooked in a family sized kitchen, Arthur. It will be a delightful change to be served in your cozy dining room. Living in grand palaces and hotels, I find it a relief to dine in more peaceful surroundings."

Everyone accept Arthur was convinced the countess meant what she said. Because for once, Anna's vibrant energy seemed slightly depleted. Arthur, who had never seen Anna on the veranda or at parties or at dances, had no idea of the charming continental capabilities of the countess in a crowd.

"Well, Richard can tell you that I seldom set foot in the Grand Hotel. The island has never been more overrun since that caravansary, which holds up to 1,000 loud voiced tourists, was built on this once idyllic escape. However, if I had known that soft spoken ladies, such as yourselves, graced the Grand Hotel's premises, I think I would have managed to attend a few more outdoor concerts and hops through the years."

Anna was struck by the provincial honesty of Arthur.

Richard thought his father's honesty too small town.

Cynthia accepted the compliment with a sweet smile.

Arthur continued, "We hear the cry of hard times, yet the Grand Hotel set has never been more elaborately entertained, I hear from Richard."

"How lovely you have everything," Anna countered gently.

"No . . . I am not wanting either. But I am not making a fuss over the hard times in between swallows of the best champagne and mouthfuls of pheasant. I do not serve game with the feathers on here."

"I have never acquired a taste for feathers, Arthur," Anna responded, much to Richard's smiling approval. With notice-able irony in her voice Anna told them about the fancy dress ball of the Baroness Koenigswarter and the stuffed peacock with jeweled eyes and gilded beak, feathers and all. She even mentioned, for the sake of disdainful Arthur, her role as a lady-in-waiting to the queen of Italy, without the slightest degree of pretension in her voice.

Arthur enjoyed her quickness and rebutted her acquired aristocracy in a friendly fashion, "I do not pretend to be impressed with your noble title, Anna. You will forgive my candor . . . but how many of your royal friends have done anything extraordinary in their lives. Did Dante and Michel Angelo and Shakespeare have blood royal? No. But I believe it is those men who have the true royal blood."

Anna thought of her own Queen Marguerite, so beloved and extraordinary for what she did for her people without anyone knowing it. Talent and genius alone did not impress Anna the way it obviously impressed her first love Arthur Andryer. The way it obviously impressed most Americans who could never seem to see beyond people's over achievements or under achievements—and see the people themselves.

"Please tell me Anna . . . how can your American spirit hob nob with all that foreign royalty . . . and how can you be a subservient lady-in-waiting?"

"It came with my marriage to Count Gianotti."

Arthur's face clouded. For Anna had chosen the count instead of himself—with much encouragement from her mother unknown to Arthur. Trying to control his emotions Arthur suggested, "Then it is your legal duty . . ."

"This will come as a disappointment to your independent American spirit, Arthur. It is my privilege to serve the queen. I do not disdain my relationship to royalty."

"All that bowing and curtsying to human flesh whose blood is no bluer than yours or mine. It would go against my American pluck. Wouldn't it go against your American spirit, Miss Price?"

Cynthia had no ready answer and murmured, "It is possible, Mr. Andryer."

The countess replied, "There are a great many jokes about Americans in Europe who disdain to learn the manners and etiquette of the country they visit. Why there is a story about the American ambassador to Italy who would go out into the street upon learning of the king's approach, and instead of saluting the king as he passed by in his carriage, he would crow like an old cock."

Everyone laughed.

Arthur stated knowingly, "He was crowing his independence . . . good for him."

"Like a little rooster he was loudly crowing his miniature nature. For the king, of generous nature, bows to all passersby so often, including the peasants, that the poor royal gentleman seldom has a chance to put his hat on or enjoy his ride in peace."

Arthur reluctantly noted that Anna's intelligence and experience was much surpassed from twenty years ago. But he was too proud to admit to himself that Anna's experience, like his son's, far surpassed his own.

Richard thoroughly enjoyed watching his father, the invincible lawyer who claimed to never have been taken by surprise—be taken by surprise—and be taken by a female. It was only Richard's generous nature that prevented him from the enjoyment of watching his old-fashioned father tripping over himself.

The countess glanced at Richard as if asking him why he did not contribute to the conversation.

Richard spoke up, "I have noticed that Americans in Europe are generally impolite. Especially regarding the fair sex."

Anna's eyes sparkled, "Your travels abroad were most enlightening on the subject of the fair sex?"

This continental talk in the confines of the modest little cottage on remote Mackinac Island was too much for conservative Arthur Andryer and even Cynthia Price, who stared at Richard and Anna as if they were foreigners. To Arthur and Cynthia it sounded as if Richard were a bohemian and had women in his rooms at night. It sounded almost as if the countess were a lady of the night encouraging such talk.

Cynthia pictured her mother mouthing warnings about the race horse gambler in particular and bohemians in general. Cynthia Price questioned if Richard Anders was really a bohemian. Mrs. Price instructed Cynthia that bohemians were to be avoided at all costs. She said they falsely dedicate their giddy brains to an art or science for the betterment of mankind. They devote themselves to grand themes in life. But life is not a theme. What they really do is despise convention and trade. They do not want to work. They call people who do work— moneygrabbers. But can their high ideals put bread on the table? They sacrifice material comforts to high ideals.

Cynthia came to the conclusion that Richard was not a bohemian because he was rich and spent a lot of money. But she could not figure out just what Richard was. And without realizing it, she felt comforted in the strange setting knowing that Richard's father was a respected lawyer, and of late a judge. Needfully she attached Arthur Andryer's obvious respectability to his free-wheeling son—the son she had fallen in love with.

Arthur Andryer countered his surprise with the continental talk, by deciding he was not about to let Anna . . . the countess . . . think him entirely unsophisticated. After all, he had had some dealings with foreigners as well. "I am tired of hearing how rough around the edges we Americans are. I have only been abroad to London on business once. The English made me feel like a gorilla in a deciduous forest."

Everyone chuckled.

" . . . I refuse to crawl on all fours before the English. Now is that politeness, etiquette and refinement . . . to make me feel so uncomfortable that I had a knot in my stomach the whole time I was there? To make me feel that I cannot speak English? I am not an actor like you, son . . . able to wear fancy clothes like I was born into them . . . and remember where every finger should fall every waking moment of the day. I'm a simple man," Arthur claimed, and masked his cynicism with a magnetic smile.

Richard shot back, "Father . . . if you would travel more you would get rid of your international prejudices. You are so proud of your position as a simple independent man that you are as arrogant as those English who are so proud of their complex and imperialistic natures."

"The Englishman's greatest joy is to let the world know that Americans cannot speak English." Arthur Andryer was thoroughly enjoying the opportunity of showing the expatriate countess that he did not buy the anti-"Americanisms" from abroad. "English critics should spare themselves the rigamarole of discussing our noncomformity and imperfect use of the English language. Because the language of our great country is not English . . ."

Anna, Cynthia and Richard looked inquiringly at Arthur, who knew he had the "jury's" undivided attention.

"Legally, our language is called the 'language of the United States.' The congress which named our language as such, spelled public with a 'k' at the end, and added a 'u' to honor. In changing the spelling of many words, we emphatically stated to the English our free right to spell and use our 'language of the United States' as we Americans see fit!"

It was quite a speech Arthur served to impress his charming female guests during the split pea soup. He began to grow quite grateful to Richard for having invited such delightful company on a rainy evening. Richard's father, who did not socialize much, even forgot that it was his son's thirtieth birthday—and the thirtieth anniversary of his young wife's death.

The countess remarked with a renewed energy exotic to Arthur, "Your frank discussion makes me feel quite at home. Perhaps I have missed America more than I realized. My life in Europe is so far more controlled, allowing little opportunity for such debate."

"Yes, that I would imagine." Arthur introduced a related subject, "About Europe . . . not everyone is possessed by a feverish craving for travel like my son Richard here. Why is it that for most of my professional life I was content to go to my law office every day and vacation on this island for two months every summer? Where do you think my boy got his yearnings to travel and gamble his time away?"

"Ah ha!" Richard exploded with carefree abandon, gazing at the countess with adoring eyes. "It was you, Anna. My god it was you. I remember it as if it were yesterday. You are the person who talked to me about traveling to Europe with your parents. You told me about where you were going to tour, what you were going to see. The Alhambra and bullfights and Michel Angelo sculptures and palaces and cathedrals and castles. You told me you wanted to travel as a female adventuress to China and ride across the Sahara on a camel and explore the Amazon jungle in a dugout . . . and I begged to go with you . . . do you remember?"

"That could have been any young woman fantasizing aloud about . . ."

"No it was you. I remember your eyes, your voice . . ."

Embarrassed, Anna interrupted, "I am delighted to hear of this. But I am fearful that your father will never forgive me for putting such impractical ideas into your head."

"I had no idea you wished to see the world, Anna," Arthur's voice trailed off."

Richard said to himself, did you ever think to ask her, Father?

Anna responded, "I am sure . . . way back then . . . I realized that adventurous travel was a childish fancy no woman could pursue. So I shared it with a ten-year-old child. At eighteen, one does not want to be laughed at or patronized, so I probably did not tell an experienced widowed man of twenty-nine such as yourself, Arthur, about my childish dreams." She smiled gently.

It became obvious to Richard, if not Arthur, that twenty years ago Arthur had recognized Anna's beauty but hardly regarded her dreams, and consequently her mind.

It struck Anna as she sat in a dining room, which might have been her dining room if fate had been different, that Arthur remembered her youthful sweet nature and never realized her adventurous spirit and thirst for knowledge.

Anna realized if she were eighteen in the world of 1893, she would probably be a college girl, who discussed art and politics and read Ibsen. Instead of picking wildflowers and plopping them in a vase helter skelter as she did in the '70s, in today's world she would have arranged orchids in a vase artistically. Instead of that girl in the '70s, who plucked daisy petals and whispered, "he loves me he loves me not," in 1893 she would have spouted out cynical opinions about romance.

If Anna felt nostalgic for that lost innocence of twenty years ago, her former lover Arthur Andryer was overcome with nostalgia for it that stormy evening.

Anna continued picturing her many remembrances . . . eluding her chaperone . . . allowing Arthur's arms to embrace her and his lips to kiss her fervently. He was no saint . . . he had taken enormous liberties with her and Anna had felt as if she had known him all her life.

Arthur was the first "mature" man at twenty-nine who had

ever kissed her passionately. Sitting in his dining room twenty years later, she could not decide whether she had responded to the waking passion inside herself or to his passion or both. She asked herself if Arthur had sought passion from her or simply manifested his own? What had he seen in her? Had he seen the innocent sweetness of his first wife, alive in a face and body so young to look upon that the manifestation was irrestible? There was no doubt that she loved Arthur Andryer wildly that summer of 1874. She said "yes" immediately upon his asking her hand in marriage.

It was too late to debate whether her parents were right to prevent the marriage to the rather poor widowed lawyer, by keeping her abroad so long. By arranging a marriage with nobility in a year's time. But there could be no doubt as to one important fact. The truth is that Anna also fell in love with Count Gianotti at first sight. It was no wonder. The count was thirty-five and in his prime.

Never mind that Count Gianotti could talk someone into loving him. If a trifle short, he had a pleasant face, was of robust health, of excellent education and perfect manners. He lived in a palazzo full of Italian masterpieces. They sold the masterpieces as the years went by. Yet the palazzo retained its charm because it was a happy place, despite the loving couple's one dooming problem. No children were conceived.

Yet the palazzo halls were filled with lively little nieces and nephews—one of whom would someday preside over the palace. Count Gianotti was not an arrogant man. If he did not have a son, someone of his own blood through his brothers or sisters would continue in the role of count in the family palace. He saw the times changing and wondered what noble blood would mean in the future. All in all, sitting in the little dining room with Arthur again, Anna did not feel regret in her choice twenty years ago.

One can only wonder what Anna would have thought in Arthur Andryer's cottage, if she had known that Count Gianotti had kept his Italian masterpieces many more years than he had anticipated, because of the generous marriage settlement provided for Anna by her father, a rich Michigan lumber baron.

Unfortunately Anna's parents reaped but a few years of affiliation and enjoyment with the noble Gianotti household, which they bought so dearly. Anna had been married but a few years when her father came down with cholera while in Italy and died. Her mother went back to America to oversee the business her retired husband left behind to his brother and found it floundering, a victim of the financial crash of 1879. Anna's family lost their millions—and unknown to Anna—the count lost his income from America.

Had Anna known the details of her marriage settlement to the count, one can only wonder if her feelings in Arthur Andryer's dining room might have been different. Yet Anna's count never mentioned the gain or loss of his income from her father's great wealth.

While Cynthia Price chatted about the city she called home and the Chicago World's Fair, the countess suddenly remembered a time, about five years into her marriage, around 1879, when the count seemed even more in love with her than their first year together, which had been a whirl of grand parties and early morning lovemaking. She remembered being warned by her MaMa that eventually passion dies in the best marriages. Yet, her noble husband had ravished her as if it was their first months together. To Count Gianotti, after the discontinuance of money from America, Anna became his by a choice that did not depend on the great wealth of her parents. A choice few noble men and women were free to make. A choice, had he been a commoner, the count would have made freely.

The renewed passion lasted six months. Until her count became ill. No physical ailment could be found. His spirit simply left him. Anna and the Count's mother were the only people he would see. They fed and clothed him and little by little servants left because there were no balls or dinners. A year later the count was up and about. His arrival back at the court of Queen Marguerite was cause for great celebration. Yet his former health never came back. It deteriorated steadily for a decade and the count, at age fifty-five, had been bed-ridden for three years. And Anna's mother had died in Italy one year ago.

Anna wanted to tell Richard and Arthur the partial truths of her life since they parted. That she was back in the states to oversee her mother's will. That her uncle had run her family's business into the ground. That she could not sell her shares of the company because they were not worth anything. But she thought it safer to keep details to herself. Especially one secret.

The only facts Richard knew were that Anna accompanied the queen's laces to the world's fair, and that she was trying to sell her parents' mansion. And until the sale was completed, Anna stayed at the Grand Hotel for a respite from the demanding life of an aristocrat and lady-in-waiting.

Cynthia ended her enthusiastic comments about the world's fair; a "trumped-up" sight Arthur Andryer had not felt the need to experience.

Richard wondered at the countess' silence, figuring that this reunion overwhelmed her usually attentive company.

Arthur rekindled his opening statements, "When so many people have been ruined by the financial crisis, I see it as bad form to make any display of wealth."

Richard shot back, "Are we all supposed to act as if we are not enjoying life because others have it hard?"

Arthur, intending to include Miss Price in the discussion and his son's life, asked her to offer an opinion.

Cynthia stated, "Perhaps, Mr. Anders . . . one can enjoy life without making a show of it." Mrs. Price would have been proud of her daughter's practical answer. Cynthia could not have answered Richard's father with a more astute opinion. Nor could she have answered Richard with a more boring one.

There could be no doubt in anyone's mind that the birthday dinner of Richard Anderss was one of the more . . . stimulating . . . birthday dinners they had attended in quite some time.

Between the soup and entree Arthur led discussions about the economic depression in America, degradation of the poor in America, increasing trusts and combinations of great wealth in America, the overworked farmers raising mortgaged crops on mortgaged land in America. He declared that boxing created more excitement than the presidential election in America and this fact sustained the theory that "man has descended from the monkey."

During the entree, the countess described her shock at the careless waste she witnessed in America upon her return, and the nervous strength, the Europeans call "Americanitis," of the men and women who needed lessons in relaxation.

Before the salad, Richard spoke of the recent death of one of his favorite authors, Guy de Maupassant. He claimed that the author's characters seemed real and the public called attention only to the sensual parts of his work.

During the salad, Arthur proclaimed that de Maupassant belonged to the filthy school of literature, and that he catered to the perverted tastes of a public craving for filth.

Richard replied with controlled politeness, "My father is currently reading *The Works of Washington Irving*. I am reading de Maupassant's *Sur l'Eau*. Is it no wonder that we do not see eye to eye on many subjects? What are you reading, Anna?"

"*The Complaining Millions of Men* by Edward Fuller . . . ."

Richard and Arthur, and even Cynthia unnerved that Richard read "filthy" books, laughed.

During dessert, Arthur offered a curious toast to Richard on his thirtieth birthday. "Richard, my son . . . happy thirtieth birthday . . . and may I quote from Shakespeare:

'To you your father should be as a god;

One that composed your beauties: yea, and one

To whom you are but as a form in wax,

By him imprinted, and within his power

To leave the figure, or disfigure it.' "

Waiting nervously for his father to ask them all to rise for a toast to his dead mother, Richard did not sense the purpose in Arthur Andryer's quote. And to Richard's utter surprise and relief, the toast to his dead mother never came.

For the first time in some thirty years Richard did not have to rise and drink to the woman he had murdered through his birth. Richard did not know whether to jump for joy or take this as a sign that Arthur had his mind—on the woman he still desired as his second wife. Anna.

Only the countess instinctively felt something ominous about the lines Arthur chose to recite.

Although Richard felt his father taking control of the gathering, there seemed to be nothing he could do about it without seeming disrespectful to his father in front of their guests. And Richard knew—that his father knew it. But when his father asked Cynthia if she played chess and she replied in the affirmative, Arthur practically ordered his son to play with her. Richard was bound and determined to get his father back for that sly trick.

And on top of that Arthur cleverly maneuvered the two "young" people, as he purposefully called them, into the parlor, keeping Anna to himself in the dining room. Clever Arthur Andryer was a successful lawyer despite his lack of worldliness. He could plainly see that his son Richard was infatuated with the countess in Anna. But Arthur could not see into his son. For Richard had no regard for self-indulgent infatuation and was more than ready for commitment to love.

From the parlor nearby, Richard strained to hear the conversation between Arthur and Anna as he played chess charmingly with pretty Cynthia Price. So excited to be alone with swashbuckling Richard Anders, Cynthia had no temptation to listen to the conversation in the dining room.

"Anna . . . may I ask why you came back to Mackinac Island after all these years? I admit the question has been on my lips this entire evening. But in deference to your privacy . . . I felt I dare not ask."

"Why, Arthur . . . is it not natural that I should want to visit the happy environs of my youth after all these years?"

"That's not fair, Anna . . . answering a question with a question." His judicial mind figured that Anna was covering something up.

"I came to Mackinac in part because it is to my mind the best health resort in the world." Without the slightest affectation the countess added, "I have been to every resort from the Isle of Wight to Biarritz . . . yet none of them compares with this island. I feel here . . . an insensibility to pain without loss of consciousness."

In awe of Anna's verbal abilities, Arthur sat silent for some moments. He simply did not hear women talk in such a fashion in his home town. Not sure if he liked thoughts like that coming out of the weaker sex's mouth, he decided if Anna were not so beautiful he would find her speech unattractive. Overcome with Anna's style, Arthur failed to catch the disguised meaning in her words.

"Anna . . . after I lost you . . . I stopped looking for a wife and devoted my life to my son and my work. I have been fairly successful in my work, but I failed with my son. No doubt you know after years of fancy eastern and European schools . . . he has become a good for nothing race horse gambler who spends April in London and May in Paris. He lives on instincts . . . during a time of the highest enlightenment, highest education, highest consciousness."

"Arthur . . . would you discredit and repress these instincts? Would you have him become too refined resulting from his overeducation?"

"Overeducation?"

"I see in this country such systematic overeducation that it is producing spongy youth with pale faces and dull eyes. They look overburdened and must develop into unhealthy adults. Yet in spite of his overeducation, I see in Richard an individual who remains instinctive. I have seen few Americans with this nature in the months since I have been back."

"Do you mean to say . . . masculine . . . nature?" Arthur asked almost jealously.

Anna answered firmly, "Instinctively masculine."

Arthur tried to change Anna's focus way from Richard as the instinctual man he had become at thirty, to the boy he had been at ten. "Twenty years ago . . . did you ever think that ten-year-old Richard would throw his life away as a race horse gambler?"

"It is my understanding he has become quite a judge of horseflesh and immensely successful."

"He made more money in a year than I have made in my entire life as a trial lawyer. He bets his money and other gamblers' money. If that is considered success these days then so be it. Nowadays the unfeeling moneymaker is the flower of manhood. My son's values are not mine . . . ."

Anna knew that Richard was anything but unfeeling and responded neutrally, "Richard loves the sport of horse racing."

"Twenty years ago racing was considered a sport of moneyed gentlemen. Now it is a means of acquiring wealth rapidly. People of respectability have quit racing. Twenty years ago a stake valued at $5,000 attracted attention from abroad. Now the stakes and purses have increased by ten times that number. There are three races a year worth $50,000 each."

"Perhaps it is a passing fad, Arthur."

All I hear from the young men is talk of the turf. I never thought my son would devote his life to it." Arthur looked directly into Anna's eyes and stated, "To the young men today . . . duty . . . is an unfashionable word. Those daily duties which give peace to my spirit make my son feel as restrained as a race horse behind the starting line."

"I remember you telling me that you devoted much of your youth to steeplechasing."

"There was beauty and skill. Now the only thing treasured is betting on speed."

"I do not mean to disagree with you, Arthur . . . but I enjoy both very much."

Arthur changed the authoritative tone his voice to one of such gentleness, Anna felt chilled in the memory of his soothing voice back twenty years in time.

"Anna . . . in one way you have not changed . . . you are still able to see the beauty or whatever in everything and everybody. I do not possess that ability. I had hoped to learn that from you twenty years ago."

Arthur Andryer talked through his hat. At twenty-nine he was not capable of seeing in Anna's nature what his son Richard, at the same age, saw in Anna immediately. At twenty-nine, the arrogant young lawyer Arthur did not realize he had anything more to learn from anybody. At forty-nine Arthur romanticized himself as a deep feeling man. He was not a deep feeling man. He was sentimental, simple, sincere, a small town wit, molded by tradition with a strict sense of personal morality, but he was not deep feeling.

Arthur noticed that Anna held back response from his reference to their love affair. He quickly changed the subject.

"My son totes around that ridiculous bamboo walking stick loaded with a heavy steel bar. Have you seen it? The handle is polished black steel with his monogram in pure gold. In gold!"

"It is the most recent craze among the younger men in Paris."

"You mean the most recent affectation. He'll become a prig if he continues like this. He imagines himself superior in intellect and experience to everyone."

Anna ignored Arthur's judgment and answered, "I hear the younger men carry it for the purpose of tightening and strengthening the sinews of their arms." She pictured Richard's half-naked body and sinewy muscles powerfully pulling the boat up the shallow river at the Sault.

"I imagine the fair royal sex in France regards this with favor," Arthur shot back too politely.

"I would not know. The duchesses, marchionesses, comptesses and dowagers I know in Paris did not speak of it last time I was there," Anna answered with equal politeness but more irony.

"If you find me one of those contemptuous, narrow-minded middle class Americans with a disposition to criticize aristocracy and our American upper classes . . . you are absolutely right. Our young people who could be doing good are watching horse races, galavanting all over Europe, picking up affected ways, especially in Paris, coming back and polluting our country with them. The immorality today is shocking. And I am not talking only about that which happens between the sexes. The fraud, usury, false witness and the like are shameful. I am angry at the way our country is going, and my son is contributing to its demise."

Arthur continued speaking in what Richard would have called a small town monologue, "I wanted my son to inherit my thoughts and values. Instead he casts aside my ideas as old-fashioned, and chooses to be like all the other American offspring who enter adulthood without so much as a trace of inherited values. Instead he turns to literature and newspapers and magazines. He moves from place to place. He lacks belief in anything, even himself. My son looks like the man of the world living the good life. But I doubt whether he can keep up with accommodating himself all the time. I have witnessed too many lives shattered within, in my law practice, to believe he is the invincible son who can keep up to the pace and way of life he has chosen. What do you think, Anna?"

From the other room Richard overheard his father and realized that the man nineteen years his senior cared little about his son's inherited values—at that moment. Richard knew enough about sportsmen to realize when they were stalking game. And Richard knew that his father was doing everything in his power to shatter the image of a younger man of the world, who happened to be his biological son, in Anna's mind. He wanted Anna for his old-fashioned self.

Anna answered, "Then you shall have to see to it, Arthur, that your son does not shatter."

"He will not listen to me. Perhaps he would listen to you. After all, at one time I had hoped you would be his mother. He respects and adores you. He would listen to you."

"Should I tell him to resist adapting to modern times?"

"Exactly. We must find something nourishing to give to him."

Anna thought, we? and replied, "I have not been able to resist this adaptation . . . for many reasons . . . .How can I encourage him?"

"Because it takes power to adapt. Both of you have it. And both of you must save yourselves from your own power. A power which could shatter you both."

Anna tried to cover her shock. Did Arthur realize the

entangled feelings between Richard and herself after a mere two hours together? Quickly she remarked, "If I had not known you before, Arthur Andryer, I would say that you are a man of affected superior virtue. But behind your remarks, I think there is a man sincerely outraged." Trying to steer Arthur Andryer away from talk about his son she brought up politics, his favorite subject. "But when you referred to America before, which America were you talking about?"

"What do you mean, Anna?"

"Your America, the miner's America, the chambermaid's America, the factory worker's America, the stockbroker's America, the industrialist's America?"

"I want a lean America based on the principles of our forefathers."

"Well, Arthur, you know very well that most new immigrants have no idea about our forefathers' ideas of democracy and want jobs. To them democracy is jobs. America is jobs."

"A nation simply cannot stand united when everyone is of a different mind."

"And neither can a family, Arthur."

Richard's father understood the countess' implication. And once again that evening Arthur was overcome with a feeling of painful loss. Loss of his son. And loss of Anna.

He lowered his voice, "Anna . . . there is so much in my heart . . ."

"Perhaps it is better left unsaid . . ."

"Is it? Why didn't you write to me? Did you think I merely wanted a wife?"

Gently, Anna admitted, "At that time in my youth I had little to offer other than wifely love and duties . . . so I could not have known what you wanted or what else you may have seen in me other than . . ."

"A beautiful young woman . . . so full of life and . . ."

Arthur was too old-fashioned to say . . . passion. And as he gazed at the unusual woman Anna had become he realized she was entering some sort of second youthful time in her life. He tried to ignore his own feeling of barrenness in her presence. And as if bewitched he felt driven to somehow find a way to share in her second youth though he was past his own. Or to absorb her second youth like a well-worn sponge soaking vintage champagne.

When Arthur learned after many careful questions that Anna's husband was an invalid, Arthur Andryer asked God to forgive him, but he wished the count dead; he wished Anna in his life and in his bed with him. Sitting in the soft candlelight of his cozy dining room, looking upon the nourishing full-bodied woman of old manners and new spirit so near at the table, it occurred to Arthur that perhaps his son was beyond infatuation and—longed for the same woman.

Another storm, born from thirty years of birth coupling death and pent-up longing coupling abstinence, broke out on Mackinac Island that instant. An emotional storm between father and son that tore at their souls and all but ripped out their guts.

"Miss Price has won the game," announced Richard as he walked into the dining room, having excused himself for a moment from Cynthia. It was no wonder he lost. Richard had been listening to his father and the countess without a thought to the dull action on the gameboard.

Cynthia Price figured that Richard might have had too much dinner wine. She never would have imagined a Harvard graduate and philosophy student at Heidelberg so deficient in strategy. But she adored Richard for his many magnetic smiles and his complete lack of excuses in his loss of the game.

Cynthia Price had no idea that Richard was thinking of nothing but strategy during the chess game. How to capture the queen, really being the countess. And then he maneuvered his father into showing Cynthia some moves on the chessboard, and told the countess there was something he would like to show her.

Richard led Anna into a small dark greenhouse attached to the other side of the cottage. The air was warm and moist and smelled of earth and sweet fragrance. He showed her his father's orchids, then quickly changed the subject.

"Countess . . . I mean Anna . . . I overheard everything my father said to you. And everything you said to him. Thank you . . ."

Anna smiled. When she finally spoke her voice barely rose above a whisper. "Richard . . . I am quite overcome and confused . . ."

Richard's mouth and eyes and cheeks smiled back. "I have been overcome and confused ever since I first saw you on the veranda. I felt I had known you my entire life . . . and tonight I learned why I felt so instantly close to you. And lately . . . I feel the need to possess another human being. I never had that feeling before."

Trying to avoid Richard's disguised meaning, upset with herself for allowing Richard to lead her into the green house, Anna answered in low soft tones, "That feeling usually comes and goes. It wears itself out because it is essentially selfish. None of us can be selfish for too long. Eventually we lose our selfish needs and simply become indifferent to that which we possess."

"How is love kept alive between two people if what you say is true?"

"Thinking about love every day of our lives. Giving some love away every day of our lives." Anna put her jeweled hand in her pocket. "Richard . . . I have something for you . . . for your birthday . . ."

She lifted Richard's broad hand, took out a piece of jewelry and placed it on his palm. He gazed at the opaque green stone set with flawless diamonds and was about to utter he could not possibly accept such a generous gift.

"Please accept it . . ."

"Dear Anna . . ."

They were two words quietly uttered, but they made Anna start. Trying to gain control of her breath she explained, "The stone is a chrysoprase of the Revelations . . . it is found in Silesia . . . it brings good luck to all who keep it."

"I shall treasure this for all my lifetime. Thank you."

"Happy Birthday, Richard . . ."

"Anna . . . it feels so good to call you Anna . . . I . . . am overjoyed to find you again . . ."

"Richard, please . . . you shall cause me to lose my control . . ."

That is when Richard Anders lost his control in the moist greenhouse of his father's cottage, away from prying eyes, finally alone with Anna. He wrapped his arms around her . . . and felt as if his heart left his body and entered her breast.

And that is when, from a room nearby, hidden from view, Arthur Andryer saw Anna lift her face to Richard and saw them kiss with a passion he remembered from a summer night twenty years past . . . and felt as if his heart had been pierced with two knives.

Owen Corrigan noticed even in the darkness and rain that Anna looked pale as he and Arthur Andryer helped her into the carriage at midnight. He glanced at Arthur also looking pale and gazing longfully at Anna, as if he wanted to follow her into the carriage. Owen reckoned that the Countess Anna and Arthur Andryer had not known each other existed, and that the meeting was too great a surprise after all those years.

It just never occurred to old Owen, until Charley pulled up in front of the wee cottage, that it was Arthur Andryer who was so in love's embrace with young Countess Anna so many years ago. That the meeting did not go well in spite of all the fine gab he picked up now and then, when he was not flirting with the cook in the kitchen, was obvious. To Owen, it appeared that only Cynthia Price had a heck of a good time.

"Go lang, Charley."

"Whoa whoa, Charley!"

A carriage whipped past them out of the ornery storming darkness as if it were chasing lightning. Owen caught a glimpse of a woman driving the carriage and saw the skirt of another woman inside with her. He thought this plenty oddish and mentioned it to the Countess Anna and Cynthia.

But neither the countess nor Cynthia paid much attention to Owen's reckonings about the reckless carriage driver, a woman at that, or his good-natured jokes on the way back to the hotel.

As they headed down the rain drenched carriage road on the west bluff, Cynthia saw no one's face but Richard's. Pumped up and excited after the stimulating evening, where for one of the first times in her life Cynthia's opinion—not her mother's—had been asked for and listened to, Cynthia could not wait to tell her mother just how wrong she had been about Richard Anders.

Anna stared out into the dark rain. She tried to control her guilt, having given in to her appetite for expression. Having given in to her love of love. These appetites she knew her beloved Italian husband would forgive in her. What the count would not forgive was that she had opened herself to something beyond the physical magnetism of Richard Anders, to the penetration of his spirit.

At the cottage, Richard tried to control his ecstasy and his father tried to control his raging anger. It ended in a vicious fight over Anna—without mention of Anna's name.

" . . . What you call brilliant intelligence . . . I call confusion. You seem to need all that is unusual and unconventional . . . you are as decadent as the French novelists you read!"

"I'm not listening to your disapproval any more. I am moving into the Grand Hotel . . . tonight. By the way . . . I wonder, Father . . . regarding your unneccessary comment about not liking the hotel to the two fine ladies who graced us with their presence here tonight and who stay at the Grand . . . I found it suspicious . . . after all . . . the architecture represents everything you admire . . . simplicity, sanity, proportion. Or are you too beginning to see that perhaps behind this facade and even your own lies complexity, disorder and imbalance—"

Arthur began to lose his temper, "You see confusion in everything because you are confused. You think yourself so intelligent and experienced. The only intelligence you have is born from book learning. The only experience you have is born from money. You have had no experience in life that you cannot buy. You delude yourself in dreaming that you can have her—"

"Then in your crude terms, Father . . . in terms of buying . . . hear me . . . I will not pay for your two losses once again. For thirty years I paid for your first loss of Mother . . . the love of your life whom I murdered during my birth. Cruelly . . . I paid for your loss as you reminded me of it every birthday of my life. Hear me . . . I will not pay for your second loss of twenty years ago. Your second loss—will be my gain."

"Spoken like a true gambler . . . and counterfeit man of the world."

Richard rushed to a table near the fireplace, picked up a cut glass decanter reflecting light from the roaring fire nearby, poured two brandies, rushed back to his father, and handed one to him.

Arthur could not look at his son. Without saying a word he did not accept the drink.

Richard held up both glasses and exclaimed, "I offer a toast. To Mother . . . I offer a toast to her . . . since you failed to offer her one this evening for the first time in thirty years." Richard gulped down the brandy, pushed the other glass into his father's face and uttered with extreme force, "Drink to Mother, Father. Drink!"

Arthur Andreyer slapped the drink out of Richard's hand with his left hand. With his right hand he swung at Richard's face, but Richard was too quick and broke the intended blow.

In a voice wracked with a pain Richard had never heard, his father yelled violently, "Get out! Get out of my house before I . . . get out!"

Richard left the room . . . almost broken.

Arthur turned to the oil portrait of his wife on the thirtieth anniversary of her death. Fate would have it that the spirits he had knocked out of his son's hand had spattered upon the painting of his dead wife.

Arthur stared at her pretty face and thought, I have hurt your son more than I realized. But I will not . . . I will not . . . let him cause a second loss . . . no . . . a third loss for me . . . .

Arthur poured himself a double and drank it down in two swallows. He gazed at his wife's posthumous portrait. And as the drops of spilled spirits rolled down the canvas, Arthur Andryer hallucinated his dead wife shedding tears—he himself could not produce.

12

The Hen Feeding

It was one of those life avowing "Mackinac days" when the straits glistened below a deep blue sky, and life seemed carefree and happy and bright to the well-adjusted resorters. They fancied their animal spirits feeling as fresh and renewed as the plant spirits of the trees and grass and wildflowers along the scented carriage roads, which before the two days of rain, "practically suffocated" from a blanket of gray dust.

After two long days of "foul weather" and an overdose of unimaginative gossip—there was even a rumor that lovely Clare Gilbertson, one of the Big Four no less, was seen rushing from the hotel alone looking pale—and after two rainy days of too much indoor togethernesss, most resorters bounded out of the hotel after breakfast, skipped their morning constitutional on the veranda, and headed for the natural curiosities on the island.

Monica and Frederick Venn, itching to play outside, talked Beatrice and the countess and Philippa and Clare into taking them on a picnic to Fort Holmes, the highest point on the island, with a stop off at "scary" Skull Cave on the way back.

But the children were disappointed when Jimmy Hayes, having heard them begging, offered to send big picnic baskets full of goodies for fifty people or more up to Fort Holmes. Arrangements were made and before the children could protest, the entire matriarchal group including the New Woman and intellectual flirt daughters and the Prices and the Gaines, and some popular old maids, and the Muldoons, and the oriental woman new to the Grand Hotel scene who hoped to sell her embroidery and promised to bring her shamisen, were scheduled to meet together at Fort Holmes at one o'clock for a gala impromptu picnic. Most would have called it a hen feeding.

The children could not understand why they could never be alone with their mother and pretty adopted aunts—without a whole crowd around them all the time. After Jimmy Hayes' generous offer, they wished simply to go into the village with the professor and climb up the long steep ramp to Fort Mackinac. At the fort the children liked to stand around for awhile scanning the glorious view and watching all the action going on in the harbor and village below, while listening to the professor tell legends about the island.

Although Monica and Frederick liked Jimmy Hayes a whole lot, they did not appreciate his interference with their plans. When Jimmy Hayes was asked by one of the old Muldoon ladies, so happy to be included in the outdoor affair, how such "heroic" last minute picnic arrangements for such a large group of people was possible, the children purposefully did not listen to his usual bombastic reply.

"Mrs. Muldoon, in my lifetime I have fed between 13,000 and 15,000 people in two days. We consumed 2,200 pounds of turkey, 2,000 pounds of roast beef, 1,500 pounds of beef tongues, 1,500 loaves of bread, two barrels of crackers, 250 pounds of coffee, 400 gallons of milk, 2,500 finger rolls, 350 pounds of butter, 30 barrels of oranges, 10 barrels of apples, one barrel of loaf sugar, 25 gallons of cream, 150 gallons of ice cream, 200 pounds of beef tenderloin, 100 pounds sweet-breads, 350 squabs, and 300 dozen eggs. The buffet dinner was held in a new building a quarter mile long, where I placed two tables the entire length of the building. 1,240 people could stand at these tables at one time. So you see Mrs. Muldoon, a last minute picnic for fifty will be of no difficulty for me." Jimmy Hayes smiled broadly, amazed at his own achievement.

It took quite some time for the Muldoons and some fifty other ladies and girls flocking around hale Jimmy Hayes to comprehend the numbers he reeled off.

While Jimmy Hayes talked on and on entertaining the women with the food story, Monica and Frederick moved a distance from the group and began pinching each other, ever so lightly just for fun, out of sight of any adult who could reprimand them. And that is when they overheard a woman nearby say to a man: "Clare Gilbertson is not cooperating."

Even little Frederick was struck by the remark and they planned to tell their MaMa about it as soon as they could find a moment alone with her. That moment alone was not about to happen as soon as they liked. For Nanna appeared and gently reprimanded them for leaving her side. And then they watched their MaMa accompanying world famous Sydney Froilan with easel, paints and canvas in hand, stroll out of the rotunda doors and onto the sun-filled veranda.

Other female resorters observed that Sydney Froilan was undoubtedly commissioned by Mrs. Beatrice Venn to do her portrait, and they could not wait to see the results. Just to think that a world famous artist who painted royalty and aristocracy and American high society was at the Grand Hotel on remote Mackinac Island, sent shivers through their livers. Only Belinda Gaines among them, with the instincts of Delilah, gathered that there was more to the sitting than met the naked eye.

At the upper edge of his palette Sydney squeezed out one inch dabs of rose madder, raw umber, and yellow ochre, burnt sienna, viridian green and titanium white, cadmium red, ivory black and Naples yellow, cerulean blue and earth green.

Quickly he combined the colors into subtle gradations and off-key mixtures.

"I want to show character, Sydney."

"Whatever do you mean, dear Beatrice?"

"Wrinkles show character . . . ."

"I warn you, Beatrice . . . your portrait shall be ideal." Sydney Froilan's flirting eyes penetrated Beatrice Venn's bodice.

"Sydney . . . what shall I do when you leave here and I have no one around to flatter me?"

"Perhaps I will stay the entire season. But Beatrice . . . you are flattered constantly . . . simply in the looks people give you. You shall get along without my flattery no matter what our future brings. But I am not sure how you will get along without my . . ."

"Hush, Sydney . . . people are approaching us . . ."

"Ah . . . as usual." He whispered, "By the way . . . anything unusual in your room last night . . . after I left?"

"Do you mean the miniature obelisk I found upright on my bed?"

Sydney's eyes gleamed and he boomed for the benefit of passerbys, "Science is killing poetry. Science is killing art. Science is killing our love of the beautiful. What do you think, Mrs. Venn?"

"But Mr. Froilan, that very science made possible the beauty of the Columbian Exposition . . . which was made possible by electricity and the use of cheap materials."

"Ah yes," Sydney mixed dabs of colored oils into a rose pink hue to match Beatrice's rose pink gown and answered, "thousands of dabs of roseate light have painted our mechanical age softer than it is. And with all the newfound prosperity in this mechanical age . . . there has developed a sudden explosion of human spirit . . . and no one but us artists around to express it for the prosperous." He wanted to say, talentless rich. But instead he began sketching the general outline and masses of Beatrice's face and neck and shoulders and chest with a thin wash of raw umber.

Some lancet-tongued old maids—a few hypocondriacs among them sniffling from allergic reactions to the imagined odor of oil paints, turpentine, and linseed oil on the veranda—passed by ineligible Sydney and eligible Beatrice. After a few once-overs, they were convinced that there was nothing more going on between the world famous artist and the high society New Yorker than an innocent sitting for an oil painting, and alot of high-faluting rhetorical talk with no depth and no modesty. In other words, harmless nonsense.

Painting brushstrokes furious and free, Sydney began to capture a sense of Beatrice's lovely three-dimensional form and weight and texture. He violated academic laws of composition as readily as he violated the laws governing his marriage.

Beatrice loved the charade she played with Sydney Froilan. Her marriage to her "departed" husband, had been so boring that when he made the least allusion to bed, she yawned with uncontrollable passion. The kind of passion based on sufferable distress. She blamed this state of affairs on her mother. For Beatrice's mother had taught her never to resist distress, never to preoccupy herself with herself, and not to use the word "I" too often because overuse of the word "I" causes nervous distress.

As a result, Beatrice accepted the distress of a husband she grew to dislike. She forgot that the "I" in her existed. She became a bored nervous wreck. But worst of all she never lost her buried ego in spite of it appearing dead on the surface.

When she told Sydney, their first morning together at the Sault—"My mother and then my husband always wanted me to have the temperament of a prize cow . . . but I could not moo to that tune for my entire life . . . really my husband should have married my mother"—Sydney laughed loud enough for passersby in the hotel hallway to hear and began mooing "The Wooing" by Sieveking.

For the first time in her life Beatrice had found a man who understood what it meant to be raised in a sentimental fashion by a mother devoted to "culture." She felt free to tell him— almost—everything about her life. Having been tutored by a governess, her mother sent her to Europe, and after the grand tour of Europe, Beatrice was expected to be educated and prepared fully for life.

Without any idea what a pair of gloves cost or how to run a kitchen or do any other domestic chore, having dabbled in literature, philosophy and theology, having experienced a short-lived feeling of freedom, having developed flares of impulsive and abandoned behavior—Beatrice Venn imprisoned herself in a marriage with a man who did not understand a woman who had tasted bits and pieces of life. Somehow with this boring man she bred two children, whom she did not know the first thing about bringing up.

As the years went on it seemed to Beatrice that the more she resisted her buried ego the more it resurfaced. Eventually, she felt as if she had lost her instinct as a mother.

Beatrice had admitted to Sydney on Calla, "I have never risen above my ego and fear myself a failure as a mother. It is well understood that letting go of one's ego is the basis of true motherhood. Why, I almost gave up my children in order to have freedom . . . before my husband departed from me. But it was Nanna who somehow made me see . . . in that old world way of hers . . . in terms much simpler than I will relate to you . . . that the freedom I craved was not from the children, but from the oppressive ordinariness of a husband who mirrored society in general."

Yes, Beatrice Venn turned from the cool and clever and

irreproachable wife and mother, into an egotistical woman with temptations and appetites just like any man might have.

If Sydney realized that Beatrice was pushing her new personality too fast since her husband "departed," he did not say so. It was obvious to him that Beatrice Venn really needed right then to love a man. He simply laid back and enjoyed the fruits of her escape and experimentation. And never did he push her to admit the truth which he suspected; Beatrice's husband was not "departed" in the sense of dead, but in the sense of divorce.

When the crafty crackpots were one hundred feet away, the illicit couple spoke again while Sydney rapidly slashed the paint and daubed and scumbled and carressed the paint, depicting his lover onto the canvas. And trying to suggest his thoughts and his lover's thoughts onto the canvas.

"Beatrice?"

"Yes . . ."

"Would you consider posing for me like Renoir's "Nude in the Sunlight?""

Beatrice blushed and gushed, "But I have, Sydney . . . if not in the sunlight . . . whenever we can!"

They laughed with abandon, forgetting that anyone in the world existed on the veranda but themselves.

"Seriously, I mean for a painting, Beatrice . . . we could get an Indian to row us out to the golden sand beaches of Round Island . . . where we would have complete privacy . . ."

"Sydney, I could never pose like that . . . for a painting. I will not deny I have fancied myself an artist's model . . . I have read all about the bohemians in Paris . . . but if my secret disregard for morality were ever recognized in one of your paintings, by those society friends of mine in New York who hate bohemian ways, my children would suffer too dreadfully . . . oh . . . good morning, Professor Bellamy."

Good morning pleasantries were exchanged as the old

professor questioned what Beatrice meant by her children suffering.

Sydney quickly tried to cover up what Loral Bellamy might have heard. "Professor Bellamy . . . I have been here almost two weeks . . . and first today, perhaps inspired by the glorious weather, I feel the primitive creative power to paint."

The old professor noticed Sydney said this with a bear-like force that made Beatrice Venn's eyes come alive. He wondered what primitive procreative power Sydney might wield over Mrs. Venn before the season's end. He was more bound and determined than ever to protect the lovely Mrs. Venn, touched with a streak of vulnerability, from Sydney's polished bohemian nature. Little did the old professor know—he was too late.

For Sydney Froilan, man of the world, had instantly opened Beatrice's mind and body to new levels of emotion. No eligible woman with an ounce of instinct left in her would have passed up the opportunity. And nearing forty, Beatrice gave in to her fears that this might just be the first and last time for such expression in her sheltered life.

Professor Bellamy answered, "I should very much like to see your portrait, Mrs. Venn, when it is finished. I only hope that Mr. Froilan will not capture you and make you over at the same time as artists with a great range of painterly experience as Mr. Froilan . . . are wont to do." The professor really wanted to say, "are wanton to do."

Sydney failed to understand the protective old gentleman's statement; which meant that world famous Sydney Froilan should lay off sheltered Beatrice Venn—figuratively speaking.

The professor excused himself and went to find Nanna and Monica and Frederick.

Beatrice did understand the old-fashioned professor's disguised protectiveness of her femaleness and spouted after he left, "More than ever I feel that women should have as much liberty as men. I do not intend to be a slave to the house or cradle like my mother and grandmothers before her."

Sydney, concentrating on drawing the line of Beatrice's delicious-looking mouth, unimpressed by her typical New Woman talk, answered absent-mindedly, "Aren't you afraid of making yourself valueless?"

"In what way, Sydney?"

"Why, by denying the highest natural duties of being a woman."

"I have contributed to those duties. I have two children. I give as much as I can regarding motherly duty. I try to create little motherly tendernesses whenever I can. And in between my duties and tendernesses . . . I want my liberty."

"And you . . . came to me . . . to prove to yourself you have liberty," Sydney said carelessly.

"I was not aware that I . . . came to you . . . Sydney."

Sydney immediately caught the hurt tone in her voice and damned his unfeeling remark. He did not want to lose pleasurable Beatrice Venn over a trifle.

Beatrice continued with a slight tone of high society in her voice Sydney had never heard, "I responded to you because you are an artist. You," she looked to see that no one ventured near them on the veranda and continued, " . . . you make love only the way an artistic human being can make love. If I have . . . come to you, Sydney . . . it is because I have fallen in love with your ability to make love."

Suddenly the vertical quality in the portrait bust of Beatrice Venn alluded to an effect of smartness Sydney had not intended. He repainted one eyebrow—up. He painted over Beatrice's mouth from relaxed and tempting to firm and fine.

Sydney felt a small portion of the sting from Beatrice's tone that he had felt with Rutherford Haverhill's upper-class accent, the first day he had met him on the magnificent veranda. In spite of having seen more of the world than Mrs. Venn . . . in spite of having met most of the world's outstanding human beings in contrast to Mrs. Venn's sheltered and untalented New York society . . . Sydney felt from Beatrice's slight upper-class tone like a Vermont farmboy once again. Specifically, like a hick stud made good in high society.

What is more, Beatrice said these words consciously. She stung from Sydney's nonchalance about her need for liberty. She had not expected such lack of feeling from the man she thought the most sensitive male animal she had ever met in her life—back at the Sault. Visibly disturbed, Beatrice Venn wondered if they could ever go back to the Sault.

Sydney thought, just like a spoiled rich woman to jump at one slip of the tongue. But he assumed his devil-may-care attitude and asked charmingly, "Beatrice . . . you say you have fallen in love with my—ability—to express myself . . . but what about me? Do you love me?"

"I have known you for two weeks . . . one week really," she paused, her heartbeat accelerating as she thought of their first time together in the hotel at the Sault—the first time she had ever . . . . "How can I answer you?"

"Well," Sydney's face imitated the look of an all-conquering man, "would you ever consider marrying a man like me?"

Beatrice smiled forgivingly and quipped, "Would you ask?"

That closed the subject.

And Sydney quickly repainted her eyebrow in its normal friendly curve, and repainted her lips tempting and slightly ironic.

"Oh! How breathtaking . . ."
"Oh! How beautiful . . ."

"Oh! How magnificent . . ."

Before the hen feeding began, standing on a twenty foot high wooden look-out platform, every lady but one commented in a rather animated fashion and unusually loud voice at least three times, how "sublime" et cetera, the panoramic view from Fort Holmes, the highest point on the island, "really truly honestly" was at one o'clock. They were not exaggerating.

Miles and miles in every direction, clear skies and glittering water and island forests formed a round sea of scenic vastness. Blue-white atmosphere encircled the horizon and climbed gradually from one subtle color variation to another, like a crescendo in blue, until a deep sky hue filled the firmament above the ladies' heads.

In the distant south the deep green shoreline of Michigan stretched east past Cheboygan and west passed Mackinaw City until it fell off from view as if off the earth. To the south just beyond Mackinac, the densely forested Round and Bois Blanc islands, like geological invaders in the Straits of Mackinac, with uncontinuous shores of golden yellow sand, appeared to harbor semi-hidden coves. In the distant north and east the Les Chenaux islands, resembling giant alligators surfacing for air, hosted numerous white fishing boats near their shores. In the distant west, St.Ignace, a town settled in 1671 by Father James Marquette, lined the shore.

Dressed for the al fresco lunch in serge or flannel outing suits with cheviot or silk shirt waists, topped off with sailor hats or close-fitting toques or turbans, and carrying silk or satin seamless parasols, the ladies and girls and children gradually sat down upon heavy picnic blankets after inspecting the view. They conversed with gay animation until the black Grand Hotel waiters, dressed in white, passed out the picnic goodies.

Perhaps it was the constant, fresh Great Lakes wind at Fort

Holmes blowing in the ladies' ears, like heavy breathing most true ladies seldom heard, which caused the group grown to seventy-five to speak louder because it was harder to hear; and induced most of them to youthful giddiness.

Even the countess, Clare, Beatrice and Philippa found themselves commenting about the view to everyone in a slightly excited sort of way. But none of the ladies at the picnic would have suspected that the delightful group of four high society women were excited over events—that had nothing to do with being transported by the sheer glory of the Fort Holmes view. Their excitement had to do with Richard Anders and Arthur Andryer and Philmore Calhoun and Mrs. Vivian Larron and Sydney Froilan and Marshe Williamson.

Only one woman, the oriental, did not comment over and over again about the view. Most ladies and girls thought that the comely Japanese woman—simple elegance personified in a light silk leno-weave peach kimono, wearing no ornamentation on her body except for two long hairpins and a comb of pure amber colored tortoise shell in her blue black hair, done up in the classical way—did not say anything because she could not speak English well. They thought wrong.

If Aki Shima were not transported by the panoramic view, because she was jarred by all the giddy exclamations around her, she revered the natural scene with great tenderness of feeling nevertheless.

Although she enjoyed viewing the vast distances, and the Grand Hotel's roof top porch, Aki particularly liked the Mackinac Island view directly below her. A narrow clearing, used as a rifle range, led to the bright white Fort Mackinac a half mile away, which was framed by bluish water and green grass. Aki watched the fort's U.S. flag curling and unfurling in liberty and spontaneity, contrary to the restraint and regulation associated with the garrison of soldiers stationed there.

She also liked the little clearings below that seemed carved out of the pine and beech, and tamarack and sugar maple, and red oak and cedar, and balsam and fir, as if in relief to woody dominance. At one time these clearings were gardens cared for by American soldiers and possibly Indians before them.

But Aki received greatest pleasure from the curved and angular forms of two pines standing together nearby, which reminded her of two lovers. She called the pines, to herself, the giant bonsai trees of the island's giant fairies.

As the ladies and girls and children conversed carefreely, they ate cold broiled chicken, pâté de foie gras between light flaky biscuits, sliced grouse between fresh baker's bread, pickled water melon rinds, Saratoga potato salad, raspberries, peaches, pineapples, watermelons, oranges, green grapes, and drank lemonade, white wine, fresh milk and sparkling water.

It mattered to no one, except a few New Woman college girls, that the site upon which they placed their privileged behinds that sublime afternoon had historical significance. They could not have cared less that Fort Holmes was built after the British captured Fort Mackinac in 1812. Or that each islander was told to give three days of labor to its building. Or that it was probably blown to pieces some time after the Americans regained the island. Or that the fort was originally called Fort George after the king of England, and changed to Holmes in honor of Major Holmes, an American who was killed by the British trying to recapture the island for the United States in 1814, out at the Early Farm.

Instead of the history of Fort Holmes they talked about recipes, though few of them cooked.

Instead of history they chatted about furs at the world's fair.

"The highlight of the collection was the cloak made of Imperial Russian sable tails."

"The tails were so well-matched that it took ten years to gather them."

"The sable coat cost $17,500."

"The sable coat was lined with cloth of gold."

"I could have used the royal ermine bedspread edged with lace and lined with velvet on a cold Chicago night."

"I absolutely need the ermine parasol for winter in Detroit."

"I would be tickled to find a simple little ol' pair of royal ermine slippers under the Christmas tree in Charleston."

"I heard in New York that Mrs. John Jacob Astor had a shrewd eye for furs. She sorted out the finest pelts for her husband and demanded $500 an hour from him."

Instead of history, if the ladies were not talking about recipes or furs, they talked about jewels.

"I will never have a turquoise in my collection. I should live in such mortal fear of seeing it suddenly turn color."

"Yes . . . but turquoise relieves headaches . . . protects one from contagious diseases . . . appeases hatred and most importantly—reconciles lovers."

"Amber has electrical properties."

"No . . ."

"It is a living thing."

"I declare."

Little Frederick, running around with Monica and some other resort children who had gulped down their food in record time, called out at the top of his lungs, "Look there's a flying flower!"

Monica called back in her most adult voice, "Freddy, you mean a butterfly."

To which he shouted back, "Look I'm a flower. The butterfly landed on me!"

All the ladies and girls laughed merrily at little round faced Frederick, who as yet showed no sign of feminization in spite of spending most of his time with women. Even the countess and Beatrice and Clare and Philippa forgot for some moments the confusion in their lives. But only for some moments.

Philippa was to meet Marshe Williamson and John Fuller after the picnic, for her last hurdle jumping lesson before the big annual Field Day competition and festivities scheduled for the next day if the weather held up. Jumpy about jumping for an audience, Philippa wondered how she would perform. She told herself that she wanted to be her best for John Fuller who had spent so much time with her; although she was to reciprocate the use of Dude by painting a portrait of the horse. The truth was that Philippa MacAdam really wanted to be the best for Marshe Williamson. The dashing black-haired, black-bearded southern gentleman she so very much wanted to trust—but could not.

Unknown to Philippa, John Fuller needed her to make his Dude the highlight of the Field Day competitions—because of the secret betting that just about every gentleman interested in horseflesh at the Grand Hotel had already participated in. Much to John Fuller's dismay, only Marshe Williamson had refused to bet on Philippa. The southern gentleman did not think it was fitting "unbeknownst" to Mrs. MacAdam.

In a rare moment, when not one of the admiring ladies or girls was talking to her, Philippa thought over the short time since she had met Marshe. She scolded herself for expecting anything to come of chance meetings at a Grand hotel. She tried to forget the suspicions concerning Mrs. Vivian Larron and Marshe Williamson.

The ladies and girls finished their delicious picnic and were entertained by the Japanese woman who played her shamisen and sang lilting haunting melodies of Japan in a voice which astonished them. They spread the news that the Japanese woman had come to the Grand Hotel as a respite from the Chicago World's Fair and to sell her outstanding embroidery. They had not expected her to be an accomplished musician as well—no matter how odd she sounded. Generally they accepted the foreigner as a novelty, though they held reservations about her. She had traveled to the Grand alone.

The Muldoons immediately befriended Aki. That they thought the oriental graceful and humble had little to do with the attraction. They loved her accent, a mixture of Japanese and French translated into English. The Muldoons learned from Aki that she traveled to Paris in 1889 to show her embroidery at the Exposition. And she had never returned to Japan since. The Muldoons had so many questions, but decided to wait to ask them on the veranda. They did not want to learn too much too soon. Immediately, the kindly ladies invited her to join them on the veranda the next morning after breakfast, and if she wished, to accompany them to the Field Day activities.

Aki accepted graciously and gratefully for she felt quite alone, and then promised to demonstrate the folding of origami paper figures for them after breakfast tomorrow.

The old Muldoons wanted to assure Aki that her company, without such entertainment, was most welcome. But not knowing if this paper folding was customary among the orientals at first meeting, they did not want to insult the comely foreigner they believed to be around thirty-years-old.

Meanwhile, all was not relaxing among the Big Four, the most popular ladies at the picnic, whose company was sought in every little group that formed at Fort Holmes. The countess was even more invisibly nervous than Philippa.

For at that moment Cynthia Price informed Anna excitedly that Richard Anders had moved into the Grand Hotel. She confided to the countess that she reasoned Richard had moved into the hotel to be closer to herself. Cynthia told the countess feelings about Richard she had not shared with her own MaMa.

Cynthia described Richard as a young man with a character few possess, with true Christian desires and motives, with nobility and humor. But she had a hard time reconciling his gambling career with the man she saw before her. And if Richard asked her to marry him at the season's end, she would have to ask him to change his profession.

Anna looked away from Cynthia and caught Mrs. Price's eyes all but glaring back at her.

Cynthia thought the countess' looking away a rather indelicate response from the usually delicate countess; especially after she had just poured out her heart to the older woman who had set up the budding romance for her. Then Cynthia reasoned that the view at Fort Holmes was too tempting even for the grand countess, who had seen the most gorgeous views in all of Europe.

Anna gazed at the dark green bushes nearby with orange and red berries, their waxy leaves lustrous in the sunlight. From her viewpoint on the ground, she watched the wild flowers set against the sky swaying and bobbing in the fresh wind, like color itself taking life and moving about. When Anna finally collected herself, she looked Cynthia straight in the eye and asked her if she had fallen in deep love with Richard Anders.

Cynthia replied that she never loved a man more.

Weakened by the twist of events in her life, yet again, in a matter of twenty-four hours, it took all of Anna's energy to place her hand upon Cynthia's and say, "Dear Cynthia . . . I will keep your confidence close to my heart . . . and I feel for your feelings regarding young Richard Anders. He is an exceptional gentleman. But I must mention . . . he is a gambler . . . he takes chances most men would never dream of . . . are you sure that aspect of his nature can ever be tamed?"

Cynthia answered naively, "Look at his wonderful father, Countess Gianotti . . . certainly with the proper guidance and encouragement Richard will turn out like him, with a decent and conscientious career."

Anna graciously excused herself from Cynthia Price. With a smile on her face and a chest as tight as if she had sprinted a mile, Anna escaped from the hen feeding with measured quickness and climbed up the steps to the Fort Holmes platform. There she saw the oriental woman, as if in a trance, staring down at the scene before her.

Standing a short distance away, Anna did not disturb the younger woman's privacy. Indeed, confused Anna needed some privacy of her own having learned about Richard Ander's deliberate move to the Grand to distance himself from his father. But more seriously, Anna knew in her heart that Richard moved to the hotel to be closer to herself.

It was not long before pale-looking Clare Gilbertson, who could not force down even a chicken leg, joined the countess high upon the wooden platform, away from the jolly picnic below. The women smiled at each other faintly, and slipped into their private thoughts.

Clare saw *Calla* out on a run in the straits. She imagined Philmore Calhoun on the deck enjoying the speed and the sun and view. She imagined herself standing next to big Philmore, sailing around the world, stopping at ports so far from Chicago, so far from the realities of her life . . . that those realities would seem like dreams. And her only reality would be the exotic sights and smells of foreign places.

Clare had had to cancel two meetings with Philmore because of the note from Mrs. Vivian Larron. She feared that Philmore would wonder if she were losing interest in him. Because if that were the case, she knew he would leave Mackinac Island bound for the next port of call. Philmore had made it very clear to Clare that he never moored more than a week at the island. And Clare sensed that if she did not show more interest in him, he would cut his losses and move on.

Anna sensed that something was urgently wrong with Clare and asked her if she were feeling well. Clare replied honestly that she felt a bit weak. She did not tell the countess what was really wrong. She could not tell anyone that her very life had been threatened yet again. By Mrs. Vivian Larron last night at a secret meeting far away from the hotel, near Crack-in-the-Island.

For Mrs. Larron was the mistress—who had murdered Clare's husband. She was the woman who hated high society Clare and who was blackmailing Clare into supporting both her son sired by Mr. Gilbertson and herself. She was the ruthless horsewoman who had come to the island to demand even more money of Clare . . . than Clare was able to provide.

At the secluded spot of Crack-in-the-Island on the rainy night of Richard Anders' birthday dinner, the blackmailer demanded a note for thirty-three thousand dollars immediately or Mrs. Larron would spread the sad story of Clare Gilberton's murdered husband like manure spread on the veranda floor; and send her own version of the manure to Philmore Calhoun out on his yacht as well. Only Mrs. Vivian Larron did not use the word manure. She used a four-letter word instead. In fact, most of her words at Crack-in-the-Island had four letters. Clare did not even recognize some of them. Nor could she recognize the masked accomplice with Mrs. Larron who had roughly grabbed Clare and held her back from choking Mrs. Larron to death.

That very moment Clare Gilbertson held back her tears and anguish and contemplated jumping off the platform, which was stationed near a precipice of Fort Holmes. Then she felt a small hand in hers and looked down at Monica and Frederick Venn. Standing next to Monica were Beatrice and Philippa staring at her with inquiring, concerned eyes.

Little Frederick and Monica had finally found a moment alone with Beatrice at the picnic and told their mother what they overheard in the lobby about dear Aunt Clare. That she was "not cooperating." The children had demanded to know of their mother what this meant. When Beatrice had mentioned this to Philippa, both women surmised it must have something to do with the note Mrs. Vivian Larron insisted that Clare receive.

Clare gently told the children how grateful she was to them that they should be so concerned. Slightly shaking, Clare even managed to bend down and hug and kiss each one of them. To calm their fears she told them it was nothing for them to worry about. The children felt that Aunt Clare did not want them to worry, but that there was something very wrong. Yet when their mother suggested in that lovely way of hers to go down and play, they obeyed immediately, though they would have rather stayed to comfort Clare.

And as some seventy-five ladies and girls and children below drank in the beauty of Fort Holmes and lemonade or white dessert wine, as they ate up the goodies Jimmy Hayes provided for them, as they chatted about the city they called home or the

Chicago World's Fair or had their palms read by the Muldoon ladies in true Romany fashion or played "riddle of the Penny," Clare Gilbertson quietly, desperately revealed the bare facts; her inner open scars burning from the salty residue of crushing recall. Beatrice, Philippa and the countess forgot about their love troubles and formed a protective circle around Clare.

For the first time in three years, Clare told the truth about her life with a husband . . . who was from a distinguished and respectable family, a family Clare loved dearly and who loved Clare in return . . . a husband who became mentally sick . . . who demanded sexual acts from her she found unbearable.

Detailed images Clare prayed to forget raced hidden behind the raw words spoken to her friends. Images . . . of a doctor mouthing "sterility" and her husband mouthing "your fault" . . . of whips and ropes and empty beds on sleepless nights . . . of imagined whorehouses and willing victims. Images . . . of stunning mistress, Vivian Larron, bounding out of a beautiful house given to her by Mr. Gilbertson . . . of depleted bank books with the name Clare Gilbertson engraved in gold . . . of Mr. Gilbertson staring and walking away, always walking away . . . of divorce papers served to her by her husband's attorney three days before his murder.

Prayers hung unanswered and the pictures of the past never left Clare's mind. Frightening pictures clung to her startling words like blood suckers cling to flesh. Pictures . . . of a note in black ink demanding "come to the house of your husband's friend—alone—if you want to avoid scandal." Pictures . . . of her husband's dead body in Vivian Larron's bed . . . of Mrs. Larron's red tinted lips mouthing, "I murdered in defense from his cruel sexual torture by striking him on the head with this candelabra,"—though no bruises existed. Pictures . . . of flashback wedding scenes and the gift of that same candelabra to Clare by her mother . . . the same candelabra that her husband declared stolen from the Gilbertson mansion . . . that he placed in his mistress' bedroom.

But it was the images of the red tinted lips of Mrs. Larron that almost drove Clare to madness. Red tinted lips . . . mouthing threats that she would tell the police and the newspapers about defending herself against Mr. Gilbertson's sadism . . . mouthing threats of revealing a son she bore him . . . mouthing threats that large sums of money must be paid to ensure that she would keep her mouth shut for the sake of the distinguished family name and for the support of Mr. Gilbertson's son. Red tinted lips . . . swearing four letter words and curses and "I will kill you like I did him if you do not cooperate . . . . I will dispose of the body . . . . You will tell the police he is missing in a couple of days . . . ."

Clare told her friends that although Mrs. Larron had been accepting the blood money without much todo the past three years, that she had even showed Mr. Gilbertson's son to Clare a few times in a park . . . basically she had left Clare alone. But now the murderess had followed her up to the island, demanding a $33,000 note from Clare accompanied by threats once again. Clare confessed that she lost all control and stupidly tried to choke Mrs. Larron at Crack-in-the-Island, but an accomplice of Mrs. Larron's with a masked face and black hair jumped out of the darkness and had held her back forcibly.

Philippa pictured the black hair of . . . and gasped to herself . . . it cannnot be . . . it cannot be him!

Caught up in the torment of Clare's tragic story, Anna and Beatrice and Philippa failed to take into account that the oriental woman, who could speak English, had undoubtedly heard the whole story. When they did notice her, the Japanese woman turned to the Big Four, bowed forty-five degrees, held the position for some moments, raised herself and said with an air of soulful compassion: "I have heard nothing."

From that time on Belinda Gaines called the group of four women, "the Big Four and the oriental." And from that time on ruthless Mrs. Vivian Larron was to be handled by five women instead of one.

13

Field Day Frolics and Folly

"It will be the greatest show on earth!" called out Jimmy Hayes.

Excited resorters hustled and bustled about the Grand Hotel's rotunda before breakfast, talking each other into competing or accompanying them to one Field Day activity or another sponsored by the hotel.

"It is a great big jumbo day of sporting contests meant to satisfy every taste and give pleasure to the resorter as well as the villager," shouted Jimmy Hayes, who, along with John Fuller and Eugene Sullivan cheering people into action, had his hands full luring active resorters into last minute signing up—for the ropewalking contest, the running contest, the three-legged contest, the tub race, the boxing, tennis, rowing, dog swimming, sack race, croquet, greased pole climbing, baseball, tug-of-war, egg race, and horse jumping competitions. The regatta and Mackinac boat race were closed to new entries.

After breakfast Rutherford signed up to compete in his favorite sport—croquet—along with the Muldoons and Monica and Frederick Venn and a number of the other hotel children.

When Sydney Froilan, who had enlisted for the baseball game and the ropewalking and the greased pole climbing and tub race and sack race and tug-of-war and three-legged contests, read that Rutherford committed himself to croquet, he called out to Rutherford, "Haverhill, croquet is not a sport, it's a social diversion. First you aim, then you hit the ball, and then you gossip. Aren't you going to sign up for a real sport, old man?" Sydney noticed the two pink roses Rutherford carried and added, "Or would a floral show contest be more to your liking, Haverhill?"

Rutherford shot back, "Froilan . . . you lazy dog . . . I see you have not signed up for the canine swimming race . . . or isn't your pedigree up to snuff? If you should enter, do not expect me to bet on you. My bet is on Jimmy Hayes' . . . purebred . . . English Setter, Donny. And before Rutherford had a chance to see how his snotty remark affected Sydney, his attention was drawn to perfectly attired Richard Anders, and a handsome middle aged man dressed "in spite of fashion" who was new to the Grand Hotel scene, as they both approached the countess at the same time from different directions. The men took turns smiling at her lovely face and subtly glaring at each other.

Instead of needling the expectant Sydney still further, Rutherford asked him to identify the new face admiring Countess Gianotti. Sydney guessed that the striking similarities between the two men meant that the man was Richard Anders' father. Considering the fact that Richard had moved from his father's cottage to the hotel, Rutherford decided to seek out the intriguing little triangle that day, curious to watch the countess and Richard and the new face, who turned out to be Arthur Andryer, interact.

Then Cynthia Price entered the group, without hesitation and without her MaMa, and this little action aroused Rutherford's curiosity to an almost feverish pitch.

He also noticed Marshe Williamson hovering around Philippa MacAdam and John Fuller. As he walked over to them to find out if any female other than Mrs. Larron was going to compete with Mrs. Philippa MacAdam for the hurdle jumping competition late in the afternoon, he noticed "that striking parvenue," Mrs. Larron, walk directly to Marshe Williamson in a most seductive manner. He remembered that she had approached the colonel at the sportsmen's dinner table before the trip to the Sault. A quick glance at Philippa told all.

Rutherford observed that usually smiling Philippa shot daggers through Mrs. Larron, while Colonel Williamson treated the parvenue with his customary southern gentleman politeness. Never guessing that Philippa was a jealous type, Rutherford feared his power of character analysis slipping. There was no doubt that Mrs. Larron was stunning. But certainly no more so than Philippa. And she certainly was not the blue-blood Philippa obviously showed herself to be. Rutherford inched near the group and overheard Mrs. Larron telling John Fuller to officially sign her up for the hurdle jumping contest in direct competition to Philippa; though the entire Grand Hotel set knew a week ago that Mrs. Vivian Larron was jumping against Mrs. Philippa MacAdam. And then Mrs. Larron announced that she would be riding a bay mare. "One of Colonel Williamson's former bay mares."

Rutherford watched lovely Mrs. MacAdam's fair facial aspect turn milky pale and curdle, ever so slightly. And although Rutherford had betted on Mrs. MacAdam winning, no matter who challenged her, he had second thoughts after noting Mrs. Larron's willful attitude and athletic body; and her pink cheeks and red lips—so fake, so artistic, so enticing.

Looking over to the veranda doors, Rutherford saw the big form of Philmore Calhoun almost spilling over the borders of the open entrance space. He watched Philmore stride over to the check-in counter, figuring that he was collecting Clare Gilbertson for the festivities. Rutherford knew that Philmore's "boat" was going to be the flagship for the yacht race late in the morning, and that he had probably invited Mrs. Gilbertson to accompany him on *Calla*.

Then he saw Mrs. Larron standing next to Philmore Calhoun at the counter and astutely observed the countess, Beatrice Venn and Philippa MacAdam staring at Philmore Calhoun . . . or was it Mrs. Larron? No one surpassed Rutherford's attention to detail, nor his nose for alliances, and misalliances.

Thinking over Sydney's challenge about Field Day competitions, Rutherford decided to sign up for tennis although it was played on clay courts at the Grand; and he played the game in the only way it should be played—on the grass in Newport.

Then Rutherford signed up for baseball on what he thought was the opposing team to world famous Sydney. Little did he realize that the men were going to play the women—or was it the other way around; and he would have to team up with cock of the walk Sydney. Nor did he realize, at that moment, that Sydney was the only person who had bothered to talk to him in the rotunda that morning, overflowing with the familiar faces of seasonal guests he could name with their faces turned. Why, even Belinda Gaines ignored the elegant, if fussy, eastern born Rutherford that morning, in favor of a middle-aged millionaire new to the scene from Hot Springs, Arkansas.

Stepping out onto the sun-filled veranda, Rutherford glanced quickly at the sparkling view of the straits, which meant to him that the weather was perfect for the "corny" Field Day activities to come, (which he was secretly looking forward to), and strutted along the veranda in the direction of the Muldoons. If Rutherford had been honest with himself, he might have admitted that he had never felt quite so alone as in the veranda crowd that morning.

From his distant viewpoint he could see the white-haired

sisters-in-law and he grew annoyed. Sitting with the angelic faced old ladies, who reminded him so much of his own dear mother, was a dark-haired intruder.

Since Rutherford had received a long letter from his mother in Newport, and looked forward to reading it in his most anglophiliac voice to the Muldoons, who had finally owned up to enjoying his accent immensely, he damned the intruder. As he walked nearer, arguing with himself to turn around and avoid the "spoilsport," he stopped in his tracks. Could it be she was not an erotic dream . . . he asked himself . . . and misfired a heartbeat.

For beneath the dark hair, that blue-black hair, was the same golden skinned face marked by a magnificent widow's peak and slanted eyes, which Rutherford reasoned he had hallucinated on his balcony a few days ago. Since he had not seen the oriental anywhere in the mammoth hotel, since he had not gone into the parlor for days and had not seen her Japonaise embroidery, and since he had not heard a word of gossip about her, he did not ask if anyone had seen an oriental woman.

Rutherford quickly observed the studied casualness of the oriental woman's perfect coiffure, with one stray hair, and the erectness of her pose in a cedar bark colored kimono. Even fully dressed, Rutherford sensed a subdued eroticism in the exotic woman he had seen without clothes.

He did not know whether to approach the Muldoons or turn away. One of the Muldoons noticed him and waved. He had no choice but to greet them. Besides he wanted to present two of the most beautiful pink roses extant on Mackinac Island, which he had personally chosen, to the two Muldoon ladies that morning.

Rutherford strode slowly to the Muldoons and once again smelled the faint scent of exotic sandalwood—and met the bright dark-eyed gaze of Aki Shima. For the first time that summer . . . Rutherford Earle Haverhill V had nothing to say.

He certainly could not tell the old Muldoon ladies that he had already, sort of, met the splendid oriental woman, who had dropped her robes and stood deliciously nude on a neighboring balcony in the fifty-five degree cold, while he wore three layers of clothing and pretended to shiver.

Rutherford tried to cover up his excitement as he wondered if Aki recognized him as the drunken next-door neighbor voyeur.

"Miss Shima, this is our dear veranda friend, Mr. Haverhill."

Aki bowed fifteen degrees and Rutherford did likewise.

"I am honored to . . . finally . . . meet you, Mr. Haverhill."

The Muldoons noticed that a red hive-like patch broke out on Rutherford's forehead. They figured he was drinking too much coffee again. They had warned him, in a kind motherly fashion, time and time again about drinking too much coffee at breakfast.

Rutherford smiled almost sheepishly at Aki, realizing that she recognized him. But he revved up his anglophiliac accent to such high speed, he sounded hopelessly arrogant and replied, "Miss Shima, I do not deserve your honor but I accept it most humbly."

The Muldoons exchanged loaded glances at the idea of Rutherford being humble, and one of them explained, "Miss Shima is folding papers for us. Look, Mr. Haverhill. She made three monkeys. See no evil . . . hear no evil . . . speak no evil. They are delightfully precious. As is Miss Shima . . . if we may say."

Aki Shima smiled radiantly, bowed, and with deliberate

gracefulness, folded white paper until it resembled a flower. She handed the flower to Rutherford.

"Please accept my humble gift, Mr. Haverhill." Aki Shima said this with such modesty as she handed the origami flower to proud Rutherford, she might have been the Virgin Mary handing Oscar Wilde a paper lily.

"Thank you, Miss Shima. But please enlighten me . . . what flower have you folded for me?"

In a soft tone and thick accent Aki said, "I would very much like to enlighten you, Mr. Haverhill. I believe you call it . . . narcissus . . . ."

The Muldoons could not help but smile.

Rutherford broke out with another red patch on his forehead, but clearly enjoyed the self-possessed exotic woman, whose quiet subtlety matched his bold arrogance like a black kimono lined with red. Then he gently handed the two roses to the two Muldoon ladies.

"Rutherford," they both exclaimed and one of them continued, "these pink roses are more beautiful than the roses that grow on my graveplot."

Aki thought Rutherford's affection for the old Muldoon's—an exquisite act of politeness and kindheartedness.

Rutherford and the Muldoons resumed their morning *tête-à-tête*, including Aki whenever possible. They talked about kissing babies. Rutherford said that he did not believe in "unnecessary osculation" because of spreading disease. They talked about dogs in Paris. Rutherford said that poodles and Brussels terriers were "out" and tailless Dutch schipperkys and hairless Chinese terriers were "in." They talked about servants in the drawing room car of trains. Rutherford said that he could not abide the servants because they felt uncomfortable with their betters, and that only one's own class should occupy the car.

They talked about ship tea. Rutherford said it was the "most wretched slop" he has imbibed and brought his own tea and utensils. They talked about resorts in Europe. Rutherford said that Deauville and Trouville were out and Biarritz was inhabited by Spaniards and English—at separate times—and that few Frenchmen of prominence went there.

When they asked Aki what she thought of Mackinac Island, she told them how much she liked the limestone formations, which Countess Gianotti, Mrs. Venn, Mrs. Gilbertson and Mrs. MacAdam and Owen Corrigan had showed her yesterday after the picnic. Of all the natural rock curiosities on the island, she favored the view of Sugar Loaf from Point Lookout, and understood the bold form was inhabited by a great Indian spirit. But it was Arch Rock that she found most to her liking. She told them that the round arch and vacant space below the bridge framed the green-blue waters of Lake Huron, much like a picture frame around canvas; and the natural bridge vaguely reminded her of a man-made bridge in her beloved Kyoto.

One of the Muldoons pointed out the lovely parasols of some intellectual flirts passing by.

Rutherford stated in his most know-it-all voice, "The women are unusually beautiful this summer. I think it is because of the parasols they carry. Look at the light cast upon their faces from the transparent pink or mauve chiffon parasols."

"Is it the light cast upon them . . . or is it the softly tinted shadows that beautifies their faces?" asked Aki sweetly.

The Muldoons watched Rutherford's face. His dull filmy eyes lit up like pools reflecting the sun. They watched him open his mouth and suddenly close it again.

Aki continued, "I think it is the softly tinted shadows from the parasols that light up into loveliness the faces they so graciously shade. Like coffee lit with cream."

Rutherford instantly recognized that Aki Shima, like himself, knew how to look at things. But he was totally struck with the way she said it, the softness of her expression, as if she felt her words. She was similar to the Countess Gianotti in her ability to feel, he thought. Her opinion did not smack of conceited knowingnesss or blunt American matter of factness. That Rutherford realized these vices in others, but not himself, was much to his discredit and others' chagrin. And that Rutherford gazed with glistening eyes at Aki Shima was noted by the observant Muldoons.

Aki guarded her eyes from Rutherford, who had just stood up and whose figure towered over her. She felt thrilled in the presence of Rutherford, whose form she found flawless. He was like a god manifested and she understood why such a man exhibited arrogance. She did not see his manners and insights as emasculated, as Americans did.

The Muldoons noticed Rutherford smile at Aki in an almost intimate way. They raised their eyebrows at each other. To the Muldoons, Aki was a cute and modest person. Never in their long sheltered lives would they have thought that Aki had turned on Rutherford's taste for things foreign and strange. Never would they have imagined that obtrusive and unseductive Rutherford Haverhill would find Aki Shima unobtrusive and seductive.

And never, never would the Muldoons have dreamed that Aki Shima found Rutherford Earle Haverhill V—the most exquisite western male form she had ever laid eyes upon. To Aki, Rutherford's overbearing manner and attention to detail and obvious old money ways, likened him to the Japanese feudal prince she instinctively felt she had been married to in a former life many generations ago. She was truly stunned and honored to, perhaps, have found her lord's spirit in Rutherford Earle Haverhill V.

Rutherford, noting every angle of every fold in the white paper narcissus he held, was determined to find the most beautiful orchids on Mackinac Island and send them to Aki Shima's room before nightfall. He instantly decided to attach a note stating that he would very much like to be "enlightened" by her presence with him on a carriage ride around the island to sights she had not seen, like Lover's Leap. Also, Rutherford could not wait for Sydney Froilan to see the lovely exotic female that he had attracted.

Yes, Rutherford Earle Haverhill V would never forget that he found his exotic "treasure" on "rustic" Mackinac Island among "mish-mash society people," on the morning of the "corny" Field Day festivites. And Aki Shima dreamed, beyond reality, that she had found her "lost feudal prince."

(From that morning until the end of the season, the Muldoons and Rutherford and Aki Shima met every morning after breakfast; and whenever Aki was not with the Big Four, she was seen with Rutherford morning, noon, and night.)

Bang! The preparatory gun fired for the big "three cornered" yacht race, with a triangular course of two and one-half mile legs, at 10:30 for the sloops. Bang! The sloops got under way at the 10:43 gun at which time the schooners got ready. Bang! The schooners took off at 10:53. Aided by the Great Lakes' breezes and accompanied by a fleet of steam yachts and small sailboats decked gaily with colorful flags, the yachts raced from one buoy to another, creating a delightful maritime scene for a large crowd of excited spectators basking in the sunshine and breathing in the bracing lake air. Each onlooker wondered which yachts were to win one of the two costly silver cups, to be presented by Jimmy Hayes at the end of the Field Day.

The spectators, made up of resorters and island villagers

and daily tourists and villagers from the mainland, dressed in their nattiest frocks and festive headgear, stood watching the regatta on the dock, along the harbor, on the edges of the bluffs, along the Grand Hotel's veranda, or sat in their handsomest equipages from any vantage point available. The officers and soldiers watched from Fort Mackinac. The island children, barefooted and full of cheek, dressed in their playclothes, watched from anything they could climb.

Standing next to Philmore Calhoun on *Calla*, Clare Gilbertson watched the fastest sloop pass the first buoy at 11:01, the second buoy at 11:25, the finishing stake at 11:44. She heard the crowd cheering from the island and watched the fastest schooner pass the first buoy at 11:13, the second buoy at 11:22, the finishing stake at ll:57. Then she watched Philmore in action, ordering the crew to make ready for the big marine parade to follow the regatta. Steam yachts, schooners, sloops, naptha launches, dinky boats, Mackinac boats, all taking part in the parade, lined up east of *Calla*, and soon they began heading up the straits toward St. Ignace in the wake of Philmore's grand yacht.

Next to the ride on the Sault Rapids, Clare never felt so exhilarated in her life. Knowing that Mrs. Larron was somewhere on shore, Clare, weary with relaxed tension, drank in the pleasure of the moment as if it might be her last on *Calla*, and moved toward Philmore.

Even with all the excitement surrounding him, Philmore noticed Clare's action and relaxed face and moved toward her. He offered her his arm in an intimate manner, as *Calla* passed the Grand Hotel and the steamship *Algomah* cruised past in the opposite direction on her afternoon trip to the island. Captain Boyton of the *Algomah* opened up the steamship's great whistle with a stirring salute to *Calla* and every vessel in the parade line as he passed by, and each vessel answered him back with a rousing greeting.

Philmore shouted an order and *Calla* made a majestic sweep to the port and then to the starboard drawing up in position to review the procession of vessels, which glided by like mammoth butterflies on the lake and eventually headed back to anchor in the harbor below the fort.

Again, Clare heard the crowd of thousands cheering from the island and looked up at Philmore. She wondered if she would ever share such moments again with the magnanimous gentleman, whose first wife had a "clean slate."

"Clare, I have missed your company the past few days."

"And I have missed yours, Philmore."

Philmore believed Clare Gilbertson's words, but wondered neverthelesss why she had not found time for his invitations, despite the politely written explanations for her inability to accept. Never would Philmore have believed that utterly feminine, seemingly helpless Clare, had meetings at all hours of the day with blackmailers at secluded Crack-in-the-Island. Although he did notice that an exquisite seven-carat diamond, which Clare had worn since they had met at Fenton's Indian Bazaar, was missing from her finger. But he did not think twice about it.

"Philmore, I want you to know that the thrill of this moment does not surpass our time together in *Calla's* library."

Philmore Calhoun beamed from ear to ear for the first time since the trip to the Sault. He had known few women who would make such a distinction. "Why Clare, against all my hopes I have told myself these past days . . . that perhaps you no longer cared to repeat those private moments."

Oh Philmore . . . I can only dream to repeat those moments . . . ." She felt his arm gently encircle her waist. Clare decided she was going to have this Field Day with Philmore no matter what Mrs. Larron might do to destroy the relationship after tonight. For Clare had not given in to Mrs. Larron's demand for $33,000, though she had given her a ring worth half that value to keep Mrs. Larron from talking . . . especially to Philmore Calhoun. And Clare supposedly had until midnight to give the blackmailing murderess and her accomplice a $33,000 note, or else . . . .

Back at the dock, Beatrice Venn, giggling to the point of breathlessness, watched red-faced, world famous artist Sydney Froilan, dressed in a bold red and white striped bathing suit, try to walk a rope from one dock to another nearby in the rope walking contest. Splash!

For some moments Sydney did not resurface from the clear water and Beatrice wondered if he was putting on a show or really was in trouble down under. Then his head popped above the surface, and Beatrice saw his cocky smile and wet teeth gleaming in the sun, and she felt ever so much like jumping in with him. It suddenly struck her that never had she enjoyed the summertime more. Even Professor Bellamy, who disapproved entirely of the illicit "friendship," would have melted somewhat at the sight of Beatrice's smile and youthful looking face when she met Sydney Froilan's twinkling eyes.

For the first time in his life, Sydney wished he possessed a camera to preserve Beatrice's face that very moment. Even his fastest painting technique could not have captured Beatrice's look of pure joy. He damned his married status as he swam to the dock. He damned his French wife who had modeled for him and supported him when he had no money for food in Paris; and for whom he felt no soulful connection in spite of five children—and to whom he felt great gratitude. Yet Sydney's married status was not to get in the way in the hay later that delightful evening. Yes, Sydney and Beatrice were to have one unforgettable field day—during the Grand Hotel's annual Field Day.

On the other side of the dock, Frederick and Monica, holding Professor Bellamy's hand and jumping up and down as wildly as the village children, cheered on Donny in the dog swimming contest at the top of their lungs.

Owen Corrigan was there alternately rooting for his friend Jimmy Hayes' English Setter calling out, "Donny Hayes ye son of a bitch show us what yer made of! Go fer it!" and booing the St. Bernard who had sat in his carriage path once too often. "Ye mug-faced hippo, why don't ye submerge!"

Donny, lithe and quick, did not win. The St. Bernard, faster than the rest, swam in the wrong direction. It was a little West Highland terrier named Malcolm who swam past the finishing line first and won the grand prize: a dish of corned beef and cabbage and a blue ribbon. Frederick and Monica noticed that Malcolm wolfed down the obviously delicious corned beef, but looked away from the cabbage with an air of disgust; they did not blame the perky little fellow. Cabbage was even below spinach on their list of hated vegetables.

Standing at the farthest edge of the dock, the countess and Arthur Andryer and Cynthia Price stood waiting for the rowing competitions to begin. And Richard, who had rowed across the North Sea in an open boat, was about to row the mile or two to little Round Island and back.

Only Cynthia felt excited from the exhuberant energy of the lively and cheering crowds around her, as she watched her secret undeclared love, Richard Anders, maneuver his rowboat into position for the start of the race. She noticed that Richard had "only an Indian" to compete with in the solo rowing race. But there were twenty other rowboats full of college girls, Helen Newberry among them, or college boys, Marshall Field Jr. among them, and island villagers, and villagers from St. Ignace, and Indians from the Les Chenaux Islands located north of Mackinac, who were competing with each other.

Pop! A band from Island House hotel played "Explosions

Polka" near the shores of the harbor, and the rowers dug their oars into the saltless sea over and over again enroute to Round Island, where an official boat anchored in the choppy waters was there to greet them and send them back for the final leg. Soon the boats full of rowers, college girls in the lead, pulled ahead of Richard and his sole competition, the Indian.

Arthur and Anna, standing next to each other again on the dock after twenty years, felt each other's presence intensely.

And a sentimental thought rattled Arthur's self-possession. That this scene might have been enacted in much the same manner. That Anna would have held his arm as they cheered their—son—Richard on to victory. If the marriage had taken place. Instead silence hung between them and their arms remained at their sides. Dry pangs . . . sensations of utter loss and wasted years . . . prodded Arthur once again as he thought that his life without Anna was like a fountain without water; no source to draw comfort, no origin of inspiration, no wetness to cool him.

To Anna . . . Arthur's nearness, her first love once again so close . . . intensified the unholy reality that Arthur and his son fought for her love . . . while her invalid husband in Italy knew nothing of this uncanny triangle. Anna's emotions, struck with the pain of conflict, pulled taut within, as a hooked fish in striking pulls desperately from pain.

Simultaneously hit by the remembrance of Arthur's revenge on his son, and by his lovemaking twenty years ago . . . almost feeling Arthur's arms embracing her . . . she wanted to run from the festive scene, somewhere into the scented recesses of the wooded island . . . and simply be lost to Arthur's obvious longing for her and his bitterness within himself. Arthur's sad bitterness, strangely enough, did not turn off Anna's youthful feelings and adulterous temptations standing near to him. For in spite of Arthur's righteousness and small town ways, Anna's first love still held some unexplainable magnetic attraction for her. She did not even try to understand. Nor did usually controlled Anna do the practical thing, and try to shut off her emotions toward him.

When she finally tried to get her mind off of Arthur standing too close, and concentrate on Richard far away who was struggling against the rough waves, Anna tried to relate to the champion rower's toil. But she could not relate, and her emotions took off and replayed the youthful sensation of Richard's lips upon hers in the greenhouse on his birthday, and the feeling of his spirit entering herself, like sunlight penetrating a window.

Anna finally came to her senses and decided she had better break the deviant trinity of passion mounting by the minute . . . and in the next second she lost her fleeting sense of reality and longed to be with Richard who had so recently reawakened her passions . . . longed to be with him out on the pure water, away from the island always reminding her of time past, away from her first love Arthur Andryer, who still had the capacity to arouse her, as if the time in between never happened, as if they picked up from where they had left off.

She asked herself if her life had become a requiem to youth until she had set foot on this island again . . . and felt youthful once more due to Richard. She accused herself of suckling old nostalgic memories like a newborn at its mother's breast; for acting as needful and selfish as an infant. She suspected that her uncontrolled emotions might be due to the recent death of her mother, and her husband's slow expiration from life, and her childlessness. She even admitted her loneliness, in spite of seldom having a minute alone at the Grand. And that the strain regarding the—real reason—she had come back to the island, might be contributing to her seemingly irrational attraction to father and son. Simultaneously.

To herself she said, I have caused hatred between father and son. It is my fault . . . what they are doing to me . . . with their obsessive love . . . making me feel alive and desired and pursued again . . . .Oh damn . . . why does it feel so exciting . . . why doesn't it feel unnatural . . . .

It is difficult to know if Countess Elizabeth Anne Gianotti could not let go of the feeling "to feel young again," to feel pursued and desired by two men before her fountain of youthfulness completely dried up . . . or . . . if she was losing all sense of reality, because of suddenly being back in America again carrying her many burdens . . . or . . . if she were seriously affected by two men who believed she was the most desirable and important woman in the world. It is difficult to know, because the countess herself did not know.

In her thirty-eight years, Anna had neither indulged herself nor accidentally got mixed up in such emotional entanglements; she did not know how to handle them. So she did the next best thing. Chastised herself.

Glancing at Cynthia Price, whose face seemed filled with imagined love for Richard, Anna realized with a sinking feeling that she never should have brought the sheltered Price girl into worldly Richard's life.

Unaware of the fresh smell of the glistening harbor water surrounding her, or the merry sounds of Field Day activities near her, or the warmth of the sun upon her face, troubled Anna began to question the sincerity of her own intentions with Cynthia Price, wondering if she had somehow misused the young old maid, without conscious manipulation, but nevertheless misused the former sleeping beauty.

Suddenly a cheer exploded from the crowd on the dock. Sydney Froilan had won the tub race, and the large and lively group of spectators moved en masse toward Anna and Arthur, and separated Cynthia from the latent couple. Arthur grabbed Anna around the waist before she almost fell off the dock.

"Arthur . . . thank you!" Anna lost her composure and smiled as lovingly as from twenty years past. For a moment her body, aglow with energy, instantly responded to the closeness of Arthur, whose resilient body did not show the bitterness of his heart.

He did not return her smile or remove his arm from her waist. He held her to himself. Covetously.

Anna feared his eyes, turned bloodshot and glassy, in an otherwise handsome face. She tried to make light of the incident, but Arthur would not let her.

"Anna . . . please . . . could we arrange some moments alone—"

"Time has passed, Arthur . . ."

"Richard has always told me I should live for—now. Dear Anna—"

Cynthia rejoined them, "Why, I almost fell off the dock! Mr. Andryer, may I indispose you for the use of your field glasses? I should like to see if Richard is ahead of the Indian. Oh, I hope he wins. Don't you, Countess?"

"Of course, Cynthia . . . but you know that Richard is a champion rower . . . it is most likely," began Anna, trying to cover up her excitement.

Arthur interrupted, "It is unfair to the Indian is what it is. Why my son thinks to show his strength against a poor red man is beyond my imagination."

Anna shot back carefully, "But Arthur, as Richard explained it to me, if he had not competed no one else would have, and the Indian might not have had a chance at the thirty-dollar prize."

"Isn't that just like Richard," Cynthia said with utter sincerity in her voice.

"Really too big of him," Arthur stated without emotion. He looked at Anna's troubled eyes as she asked for the field glasses from Cynthia, and he smiled to himself for the first time since the birthday dinner. For Arthur had not overlooked the fervent response in Anna's body when he saved her from falling off the dock. He knew there were memories buried deep inside Anna about her cherished Mackinac Island . . . and her first love . . . and those memories were more connected to himself than to his son. He planned on appealing to Anna's one vulnerability—her memories. Arthur knew it was a weak position to be coming from. But against his worldly son, provincial Arthur Andryer realized he had to use whatever position he could.

Yes, caught by the surprise of his own jealousy while watching the impassioned intimacy between his son and Anna in the greenhouse, Arthur dropped his small town rationality, and baited his line for a catch in waters where, like his son, he should not have been fishing.

"Ah . . . the parade is lining up below Fort Mackinac. Ladies, shall we go and watch the festivities?"

Cynthia replied quickly, "But Mr. Andryer, we shall miss Richard's return."

Arthur looked directly at Anna and said, "If I am not mistaken, Anna, you said you wanted to be at the egg race on Main Street before the parade because you promised a . . . Mrs. MacAdam . . . I believe . . . that you would be there to watch her."

Anna had promised Philippa to watch her during the race and meet her after the short parade. "Cynthia, I had quite forgotten my promise to Mrs. MacAdam. I am sorry to disappoint you. I . . . too . . . would like to see Richard row in . . . and since I am chaperoning you . . . feel unhappy that I should take you from your preferred activity . . . ."

"Countess, thank you for your consideration. But I shall most happily accompany you. We shall cheer for Mrs. Mac-Adam instead," Cynthia replied with friendly politeness.

And on top of everything else in Anna's entangled life, she was beginning to grow exceedingly fond of Miss Cynthia Price; a young woman whose romantic life was now somehow linked with her own. But in spite of Anna's questioning of her own intentions in trying to match Cynthia with Richard, she seriously wondered why Cynthia did not notice that Richard had no romantic intentions for her; only the most cordial friendship. She asked herself why Cynthia Price did not feel this instinctively.

Anna had no time to answer herself that Cynthia Price, practically raised to sexlessness, had little instinct in her; like so many of the protected well-off girls in the world who could have been her clone.

Before the countess and Arthur and Cynthia left the dock, they joined Beatrice and Professor Bellamy and Frederick and Monica, who held their breaths as they watched Sydney in his red and white bathing suit, inch up a greased pole. Higher and higher husky Sydney pulled himself, his hairy arms and legs wrapped around the slippery pole like a monkey climbing a wet liana vine. Just as Sydney reached out for the ten dollar bill on top, the crowd gasped. He slid, lost control, and fell some fifteen feet shouting, "Free bath!" and hit the water in a belly flop that splashed the excited onlookers.

Beatrice laughed with abandon and kissed Monica on the forehead, and lifted little Frederick up and hugged him with all her might—much to the four-year-old's delighted surprise. And even more to the professor's delight.

To old Professor Bellamy there was nothing more beautiful in the world—than a loving mother embracing her children. Especially when the mother was as comely as his new friend Beatrice Venn, and the children as special and cute as Frederick and Monica. In spite of despising Sydney's ill-placed seductive nature, the old professor, moved by Beatrice's elation, joined in the noisy applause when world famous Sydney Chase Froilan resurfaced looking dazed, but smiling broadly.

Crack! Those horses frightened by the noise, broke from the starting line for the egg race down Main Street—and broke their riders' eggs pronto. And those riders in control of their horses—like Philippa riding Dude, and John Fuller riding Kentucky Jean, and Eugene Sullivan riding Mackinac Belle, and Marshe Williamson riding one of his bay mares, and cottagers riding thoroughbreds, and island children riding bareback—had no trouble getting started. The crowd lining the street chuckled plenty, while watching the racers trying to balance their eggs on spoons and attempting to get to the finish line before their rivals.

One by one the Grand Hotel swells on the fanciest horses dropped their white eggs on Main Street. The cottagers, young John and Joe Cudahy and Guy Irwin dropped them past the half way point. As steady as Philippa's painting hand was, she could not make it to the finish line without watching her little egg roll off her spoon, as Frederick and Monica cheering her on commented to Professor Bellamy, "Like Humpty Dumpty having a big fall . . . ."

Philippa noticed Marshe Williamson pass her and just before the finish line, he dropped his egg as well, his friendly laugh acknowledging the appreciative clapping on the sidelines that he got as far as he did. She heard many lively spectators call out to Marshe on the parade route, and was thoroughly surprised that he was so well known by the merchants and islanders and resorters.

And then she saw a little half breed islander, riding a frisky quarterhorse, pass the finish line to victory. The islanders in the crowd roared approval and the little boy turned his horse around, galloped up and down Main Street at breakneck speed showing off, and stopped back at the finish line to pick up his prize—five dollars. The eleven-year-old boy just about burst with pride.

Philippa, still smarting from the news that Mrs. Larron would be riding one of the colonel's bay mares at the hurdle jumping contest . . . and still suspicious about Clare's description of Mrs. Larron's accomplice with black hair and beard at Crack-in-the-Island . . . and picturing the colonel following Mrs. Larron into a private room during the storm . . . and still trying to decide if the colonel had buried his face in Mrs. Larron's red panties on the balcony that Sunday morning . . . and not quite believing John Fuller's story about the colonel following Mrs. Larron into the ballroom at 2:30 a.m. . . . and wondering how the colonel could have built up his stud farm so successfully in such a short time . . . and in spite of all these disheartening suspicions about the colonel who awakened her libido in the stable so recently . . . she smiled ruefully to herself. Because Philippa could not help but think that Marshe dropped his egg on purpose, so that the rather poor islander could win the substantial prize.

But when she mentioned this to Marshe, who drew up next to her, he smiled charmingly, looked knowingly, and said, "Mrs. MacAdam . . . the islanders are proud . . . they would see through such a ruse. The better man won."

And again Philippa supposed clashing judgements about the southern gentleman who had delayed his journey to the Chicago World's Fair by a day, in order to lend a hand to his new friend, John Fuller, for Field Day competitions. After the hurdle jumping competition, John was going to put on a show with his high jumpers. And Marshe had promised to jump as well.

"Mrs. MacAdam, would you care to wait here with me until the parade passes? I should enjoy your company."

"Of course, Colonel. Thank you."

"It has been quite some time since our tea on the veranda. I remember that afternoon with fondness. It seems we have been working so hard on conditioning Dude for the hurdle jumping contest this afternoon, and conditioning John Fuller's other high jumpers, that I have not had the pleasure of your company except near a horse."

Marshe recognized Philippa's bright expression but troubled eyes. He wondered what had happened to Philippa since their first meeting in the stable . . . since the tea. He damned his bad luck with her, and figured that Mrs. MacAdam was one of those New Women who had no time for men in between her painting and her riding. He found this shocking in a southern blue blood, but at the same time her consuming interest in horses excited him. For horses were his life. And he was looking for a woman of like spirit to share his life. Philippa MacAdam more than qualified.

For all Philippa may have known, Mrs. Vivian Larron, excellent if ruthless horsewoman, murderer and blackmailer with stunning looks, might have qualified just as well for Marshe Williamson. And just as Philippa was about to answer Marshe, she turned to see Mrs. Larron on the Colonel's matching bay mare.

Mrs. Larron, speaking a little too loudly, and right past Philippa, said, "Why, Marshe, I thought for sure that you would win the egg race. Oh my, will you look at what's coming down Main Street."

Marshe, surprised that Mrs. Larron used his first name, noticed Philippa staring down at the ground, her lips compressed. Hell! Why haven't I thought of it before, he asked himself . . . .

A small band playing woodwinds, brass, cymbals and drums blared rousing happy-go-lucky Sousa marches as they sat on a dray pulled by two horses that sent the spectators into loud waves of giggles. For pulling the dray was a horse wearing ribbons—and a horse wearing a pair of blue jean overalls and a straw hat.

Following the band was a hay wagon loaded with local beauties dressed in gala attire, who waved and greeted the crowds and showed themselves off in anticipation for the beauty contest to come. They were greeted back with much appreciation—especially by the men.

Following the beauties was Jimmy Hayes, standing in a Grand Hotel chariot decked with flowers and a banner boasting the words "Grand Hotel's Field Day." He threw cigars and illustrated remembrance souvenirs of the festivities into the crowd and shouted, "Come one, come all to the Grand Hotel for the afternoon and evening competitions to come!"

Owen Corrigan called out to him from the sidelines, "Jimmy Hayes ye rascal . . . ye would follow the beauties instead of the band!"

Jimmy called back, "Owney Corrigan . . . if ye could . . . ye wouldn't follow the beauties . . . ye would sit with them!"

The crowd laughed. Old Owen grinned at Jimmy's joke and attempt at brogue. He waved, with pipe in hand, at his hale young friend who ran the grand palace up on the bluff.

Behind Jimmy, children and adults rode bikes of every description decorated with colorful crepe paper, their wheels making clicking noises from playing cards attached to the bike frames and flapping against the spokes. Some wore signs advertising various shops on the main street. Several children pulled a wagon with a barking pet dog dressed in a funny hat and shirt.

A couple of cows, stray cows, mooing to beat the band, their bells clinking and clanking in offbeat rhythms, followed the bikers. The parade watchers had no idea that the cows were not officially part of the parade and clapped loudly when they passed by.

A small group of bagpipe players followed the cows and blew a grand Scottish folk song as if introducing John Fuller on horseback, who wound up the short parade atop his white stallion high stepper, Rosebud. It was the women's chance to enjoy beauty. Yes, many a feminine heart fluttered when handsome John Fuller, costumed in dashing Russian officer garb, a heavy red cape fluttering behind him, sat tall and majestically as he pranced his spirited Rosebud down the main drag to resounding applause.

The parade over, Mrs. Vivian Larron went her separate way after mentioning to Philippa that they were the only two signed up for the hurdle jumping competition at half past four. And dropping, that if Philippa knew what was good for her, she would bow out of the contest.

Philippa replied carefully that if Mrs. Larron had understood her competition she never would have dreamed of entering the hurdle jumping competition. But Philippa's stomach turned. For the sake of Clare, for the principle of it all, she meant to beat the murderer and blackmailer in the competition—because she could not do it with her own bare hands. She said to herself, the hurdle jumping to come will be the first step in getting wretched Mrs. Vivian Larron out of dear Clare Gilbertson's tragic life.

The countess, Arthur Andryer, Cynthia Price, and Beatrice, Sydney, Professor Bellamy, and the children, who had easily found Philippa in the crowd high atop Dude, overheard the bantering with Mrs. Larron. They all assured Philippa that she would win against "that Larron woman" and watched Philippa dismount with the gallant help of Marshe. They all thought the two eligible southerners would make a lovely couple. And they all knew that the relationship was sadly "not jelling." But they did not realize Philippa's worst suspicion—that Marshe Williamson might be secretly involved with Mrs. Vivian Larron.

John Fuller, leading Dude and accompanied by Marshe rode back to the stable, promising to join the group later.

While walking back to the hotel for an outdoor buffet lunch before the afternoon contests, the men wondered aloud as to what "surprise uniforms" Jimmy Hayes had come up with for the baseball game after lunch. The men questioned aloud as to how they had been talked into participating in the "unusual" baseball game, which was to be played for thousands of Field Day revelers. They had fogotten that the Big Four practically begged them.

During lunch they were also joined by the Muldoons and Rutherford and Aki Shima and Clare and Philmore, and Richard Anders—exhausted and trying to rise above his disappointment that Anna had not been on the dock for his victorious return from Round Island. He had passed the finish line one boat length ahead of the Indian. And he was sure he would have lost, if he had not anticipated Anna watching him win.

Initially, Cynthia Price was the only person at lunch who showed any real interest in his hard won victory; and who had won in the group races. He told Cynthia, who hung on his every word, that the Indians from the Les Chenaux islands came in first, followed closely by three boats of college girls, followed by some islanders, and in the rear a group of ivy league college men. And while Cynthia praised him strongly for his victory, he tried to make contact with Anna's eyes. To Richard it seemed as if Anna, although perfectly charming, was purposely trying to avoid him, as he purposely tried to avoid Cynthia's adoring eyes which were beginning to annoy him slightly.

When Cynthia finally left the Big Four with the excuse she

must pay respects to her MaMa sitting with the matriarchal group on lawn chairs a distance away, Anna approached Richard.

"I am sorry I missed your victory, Richard. I was obliged to attend the parade—"

"If I had not thought of you . . . I would have lost."

"Richard—" Anna was not at liberty to say what was in her heart, and looked down at Richard's hands deformed with calluses from the oars, "your hands . . ."

He lowered his voice and carressed his words, "Every stroke I thought of you . . . wishing . . . instead of the water . . . it was you . . . ."

Right after lunch, Rutherford, the Muldoons, and Frederick and Monica, and some fifteen others competed in croquet. Rutherford would have won hands down if he had not, for perhaps the first time in his life, selflessly let the children get the better of him.

Aki Shima, who also played modestly, noticed that Rutherford made the game quite fun for the children. Even the Muldoons, who tried to play their best game and lost, noted that Rutherford was uncommonly generous in not hitting the children's croquet balls very far out of bounds—though he hit their croquet balls "to kingdom come!"

Professor Bellamy even asked Rutherford if he was not feeling well; until he took a good look at Rutherford's bright eyes. It did not take long for the wise old man, observing Rutherford with Aki Shima, to realize that the "eastern" man was fascinated with the "far eastern" woman and that she returned his interest with almost regal discretion.

After the croquet contest, won by a precocious-twelve-year old girl, the Salisbury orchestra set up on the lawn below the hotel in preparation for the baseball game to come. At the same time, hotel guests and cottagers moved their chairs to the edge of the longest porch in the world, and villagers and daily tourists gathered along the road leading past the Grand, or sat near the players on the great lawn. No one had to worry about getting a hard ball in the face, because it was announced that the baseball game, "Ladies vs. Gentlemen?" was going to be played—with a large elastic ball and a tennis racket for a bat.

"Ta-ra-ra Boom-de-ay! Ta-ra-ra Boom-de-ay! Ta-ra-ra . . .," the crowd of thousands sang along with the orchestra as the nine members of the ladies' team, dressed in natty tennis outfits, bounded down the white steps to the improvised playing field. Every hotel guest gossiped that the "Big Four, no less" numbered among the players, and that Countess Gianotti carried the "bat."

The tune abruptly changed to, "He'd fly thro' the air with the greatest of ease, A daring young man on the flying trapeze; His movements were graceful, All girls he could please, And my love he purloin'd away." And the spectators sang along, until down the white stairs stumbled the motliest team of "gentlemen?" baseball players—ever to be seen on Mackinac Island before and since the summer of '93. In a flash, the fun-loving spectators stopped singing and started laughing.

For out onto the field the nine gentlemen? players either punched, skipped, rolled, pushed, leaped, flipped, kicked, sprinted or long-jumped their way past the umpire to their respective places.

The umpire was Jimmy Hayes dressed to perfection—in an old sugar barrel. With fringes of mollasses at his bare knees, and a bodice with cutout décolletage and demi-sleeves of dark blue serge, and a sash of sky-blue cheesecloth and yellow ribbons above his shoulders, and an immense poke straw hat, and white linen cuffs worn at half mast—at the ankles, and an immense hatchet tied with a blue scarf for a fob, well-known Jimmy Hayes was cheered wildly.

The catcher, Richard Anders, wearing a modest bathing

suit, a bird cage mask and a pair of boxing gloves, his face partially blackened, punched his way past the umpire.

The pitcher, Rutherford Earle Haverhill V, wearing a full dress suit with white lined lapels and trousers of curtain material, a salt cellar fob around his neck, his right eye blackened, skipped his way past the umpire.

The first baseman, Eugene Sullivan, wearing a calico suit padded with fat pillows, rolled his way past the umpire.

The second baseman, big Philmore Calhoun, wearing a combination yachting, tennis, and humpty dumpty suit with spots of blue and red on the left leg of his trousers, pushed his way past the short umpire.

The third baseman, Sydney Froilan, wearing a Renaissance tennis shirt with Etruscan trousers and a mustache done up in curl papers he claimed were once owned by Mme. Recamier, his legs padded with Grand Pacific champagne bottles, leaped his way past the umpire.

Right, left, and center fielders and shortstop, played by ivy league college men, wearing shirts bearing the crests of their alma maters, and green paper skirts resembling masses of paper ivy vines over bare legs, either flipped, kicked, sprinted or long-jumped their way past the umpire.

Mr. John B. Drake, Judge Gary Higginbotham and Honorable Hempstead Washburn, all from Chicago, were score-keepers. Professor Bellamy was the surgeon. The game began with the ladies up at bat and five innings later—the surgeon suggested the game come to a close for fear that the crowd would die of laughter. The ladies claimed victory at 27-17.

Highlights included—Jimmy Hayes, umpire, was mobbed twice during every inning, and could only be bribed to change his unique decisions with the inspiring aid of a beer. Professor Bellamy, surgeon, set the umpire's bones with tidy dispatch. In the fifth inning, the ladies administered whitewash to the "perfect gentlemen" who had throughout the game physically held them back from running base to base on obvious home runs . . . carried them from base to base for the sake of the ladies' "health" . . . got down on bended knee and proposed marriage to them when a lady tagged them out . . . and a hundred other gentle tricks that caused the crowd to roar.

The crafty crackpots' tongues wagged in triple time . . . when big Philmore Calhoun picked up Clare and ran with her instead of the ball . . . when Richard Anders, catcher, caught the countess around the waist before she could touch home base . . . when Sydney Froilan grabbed Beatrice Venn's hand and with gentle force ran with her from base to base, in the wrong direction, on a home run . . . while the matriarchal group and even the old maids laughed generously, wishing they could be in on the harmless fun.

Arthur Andryer, standing on the veranda, envious of Richard's fun-loving show-off maneuvers with Anna, damned himself for declining Jimmy Hayes' invitation to join the team. He had thought, I am not going to play the court jester for Jimmy Hayes and the Grand Hotel's purse. Provincial Arthur Andryer was not yet a true sportsman.

Even high society Rutherford Haverhill, when asked by a fellow sportsman to join in something, would think twice before declining. The only reason that Rutherford had not joined in the "corny" cigar and umbrella race weeks ago was because—no one had cared to ask him.

"Ladies and gentlemen!" Jimmy Hayes, holding up his sugar barrel, called out, "As umpire of this most illustrious baseball game, I decree that the gentlemen losers must give a supper to the victorious ladies after the hop and beauty contest tonight. All of you are most cordially invited to the hop and to vote for the beauty of your choice in the casino at eight o'clock this evening." The spectators applauded.

"For those of you interested . . . there will be a glove fight sure to ignite your contesting spirits, between my maître d' Bludsoe and my waiter Big Jack, to be held in the casino right after my announcements. The three legged race and sack race and all running races will be held on the road in front of the hotel at the same time. The tennis matches will be played at the same time on the Grand Hotel's new courts. All those gentlemen signed up for the tug-of-war, please meet on the great lawn in two hours. After the tug-of-war, you will not want to miss a moment of the ladies' hurdle jumping contest which promises to be a fine show of feminine skill . . . followed by an exhibition of master John Fuller's hugh jumpers. Thank you ladies and gentlemen and continue to enjoy the Field Day!"

The crowd roared approval and at least one hundred of them ran down to the lawn, armed with Kodaks, to take a picture of the outrageous-looking gentlemen's? team hovering among the fine ladies who beat them. The baseball teams graciously obliged the picture takers. They stood perfectly still, and on the count of three, one hundred snapshooters clicked Kodaks in chorus.

Jimmy Hayes thundered thanks to all the "fine sportsmen and sportswomen," who were aching and thirsty; and quietly announced a gala champagne supper at midnight and on the house, for all players and spouses, to honor the victorious ladies' team, and to be followed by a moonlit serenading party "whether the moon shows its fat face or not."

Little did the Big Four know . . . that they would be late for the midnight supper . . . .

"The tug-of-war will take place in five minutes! Come down to the great lawn and cheer the team of your choice on to victory!" announced Jimmy Hayes.

This time Arthur Andryer had volunteered when Jimmy asked the gentlemen to join in . . . and grabbed the rope, facing in direct opposition to his son.

Behind Richard stood Sydney and Philmore (at the very end) and Jimmy Hayes and fifteen other muscular Grand Hotel swaggers and college men and cottagers and villagers. Behind Arthur stood Rutherford (wearing monogrammed leather gloves) and Eugene Sullivan and Edward Cudahy and fifteen other brawny resorters and villagers to match their opponents.

Anna and Beatrice and Clare and Professor Bellamy and the children and Aki Shima and the Muldoons and Cynthia Price and Belinda Gaines and a host of New Woman college girls, (angry that their feminine natures prevented them from competing), and intellectual flirts and MaMas and old maids, and hundreds of other cottagers and villagers, surrounded the men on the lawn.

"Heave!"

Thirty strong men seized the stout rope, dug their heels into the ground, cast their weight back, and tugged with all their power. Red faces contorted with strain, muscles bulged beneath pastel colored shirts, and the self-made he-men struggled to pull some three thousand pounds of muscle and fat, inch by inch, over the line on the lawn. They turned on their strength and the women watching. No wonder the feminine voices cheered lustily.

Anna, not knowing which side to root for, overheard Arthur wisecrack to Richard dryly, "A struggle for supremacy . . ."

Richard, his shirt wet, his teeth clenched, managed to shoot back, "I'm hellbent on winning . . ."

Throwing his weight back and gaining an inch for his team Arthur blasted, "I'll be damned if I'll lose . . ."

And no one on the sideline, except Anna, knew what the

hot-blooded father and son really meant, as the rope stretched taut and tense and the opposing teams barely yielded to each others' brute force.

"Drag! Haul! Pull! Tug! Drag! Haul! Pull! Tug!" chanted the excited onlookers half wondering why they cheered such coarse efforts; the women half horny at the sight of "male animals" struggling.

Suddenly, Philmore Calhoun yelled, "Heave ho!" Clare flushed as Philmore, the rope tied about his waist, pulled back with a force like a draft horse, while Richard and the rest strained inch by inch to support him.

Arthur's team held tight, but his feet inched closer and closer to the white line until he could no longer hold out and Richard's team pulled victorious.

"Yea! Bravo!" cheered the onlookers.

Richard looked his father straight in the eye . . . and said nothing.

With surprise bordering pride, Arthur realized his son was too much of a sportsman to gloat over his rival's defeat, even in a trifling tug-of-war. But Arthur was suddenly uncertain whether he could take credit for this virtue in his son. And the uncertainty nagged the hell out of him for the rest of the Field Day.

Both men sought Anna's face in the crowd . . . but saw her walking with Clare and Beatrice toward Philippa, who was being expertly mounted on Dude by Marshe Williamson not far away.

Philmore and Sydney and Rutherford and Richard and Arthur, and Professor Bellamy who had just turned the children over to Nanna, decided to find a good vantage point for the hurdle jumping competition to come. And discuss their bets on who would most likely win. Mrs. Philippa MacAdam or Mrs. Vivian Larron. Both had earned reputations overnight as unbeatable horsewomen on Mackinac Island; due to John Fuller who had stirred up enthusiasm to a pitch of wild, covert speculation the past week—and who had much to win . . . or lose . . . in the contest.

John Fuller told Karl the groom to remove the top bars of a white five-barred gate set up on the great lawn. He looked over at Philippa nervously.

"Well, Mrs. MacAdam . . . I am afraid you are going to disappoint a lot of gentlemen this afternoon—"

Philippa glared at Mrs. Larron, but did not answer her. She observed that John Fuller looked as if he could have killed the "parvenue" just to shut her up. But he did not say a word to support Philippa. And Philippa knew that John Fuller needed Vivian Larron for his hurdle jumping show.

And Vivian Larron knew John Fuller needed her. She continued, "I would say you have tens of thousands on your head, Mrs. MacAdam. When you lose . . . you will let down alot of admiring gentlemen. Isn't that right, John Fuller?"

John could not look at Philippa's face. He had wanted to tell Mrs. MacAdam from the beginning that heavy secret betting was going on for the hurdle jumping competition. He had thought that, perhaps, they would become intimate and then he would tell her. But when Philippa showed preference for Colonel Marshe Williamson, John felt he could not tell the high society sportswoman, who had so graciously obliged him with her talents, that he was using her to make a few extra bucks. Tens of thousands of "extra bucks," depending on whether or not Philippa jumped with Dude to victory.

Flustered over the news that heavy betting had taken place on her—and not to have at least been accorded the respect of being told—Philippa tried not to show her surprise and answered, "I plan on making a lot of gentlemen very happy, Mrs. Larron. Haven't you heard the odds? Your chance of winning is one in a hundred."

Marshe, who had been holding Dude steady and talking softly to him, looked up at Philippa after Mrs. Larron spilled the news. He sensed that Philippa, usually plucky and full of nerve, had become seriously nervous. He led Dude away from Mrs. Larron, who was mounted on his former bay mare called Clementine.

Quietly, Marshe said, "Mrs. MacAdam . . . as I understand it . . . John Fuller did not want you to be aware of the betting. He knew that once you promised to participate in the contest, being the fine sportswoman that you are . . . you would not back down from the competition . . . in spite of such knowledge. He was concerned that this knowledge would cause you strain . . . knowing that money was placed on your generous efforts. I . . . myself . . . have made no wager . . . I . . . I am looking forward . . . with great respect . . . to enjoying the graceful sight of your skill on Dude."

Struck by Marshe's kind and carefully spoken words of support, feeling a common sympathy with him as she had felt at the Sunday tea too many days past, Philippa smiled warmly. But before she could reply, Mrs. Larron rode up beside her once more. To herself rattled Philippa said, if only Mrs. Larron were not riding one of the colonel's horses. What kind of man is he? Kind words one minute . . . the next minute dealing . . . or mating . . . with such a dangerous guttersnipe as Mrs. Larron . . . .

No one knew better than Vivian Larron that when a woman felt vulnerable, and when a horsewoman lost her nerve—she could not win at anything in life, especially jumping horses. And she intended to break Philippa's nerve before the competition. She wanted Clare Gilbertson's dear friend to make an utter fool of herself, in front of the two thousand spectators standing on every available square foot in view of the Grand Hotel's great lawn. She wanted Clare Gilbertson's friend to lose her nerve ever to jump a horse again. She even imagined Clare Gilbertson's friend tumbling on Dude—and breaking her pretty blue-blooded neck.

Mrs. Larron hated all spoiled, blue-blooded, rich high society women whom she pretended to emulate; and for whom she had suffered their husband's sexual perversions.

"See here, Mrs. MacAdam . . . I performed as a school rider with the circus in Paris for many years . . . I jumped flaming hurdles sidesaddle . . . so high . . . you could never dream to jump . . . ."

John Fuller nearby, looked as if his stomach were about to come up. He wondered if Mrs. Larron would say more . . . .

Philippa shot back, "Then you jumped your poor horse digging spurs into the animal's side. I have seen the cruel circus in Paris . . . and what hidden tortures are inflicted on the animals in the name of entertainment."

Mrs. Larron laughed at Philippa's righteous reply, peered narrowly at her and clamored, "Not only that . . . they used to tie me to the sidesaddle! Does that shock you?"

Philippa knew from Clare, that a sidesaddle was not the only thing Vivian Larron had been tied to—when she had been paid to perform. And if Philippa did not hate and loathe Vivian Larron as murderous blackmailer for the sake of Clare . . . she would have pitied the woman.

Clare—overhearing Vivian Larron's dangerous talk to Philippa . . . sensing that her dear friend Philippa had suddenly been struck down with nervousness . . . knowing that a rider's loss of nerve could be felt by the horse and even cause fatal accidents—ran to the side of Philippa to attack Vivian Larron verbally, just as Mrs. Larron rushed her horse past Clare within a foot of knocking her down. Frightened, Clare jumped back.

"Clare!" Philippa rode Dude over to her.

Anna and Beatrice moved quickly to Clare's side.

Seething, Philippa said in low tones, "I swear to you Clare . . . that woman will pay . . . one way or another . . . ."

And Anna and Beatrice, boiling with anger, added to Philippa's biting threats.

Even Philmore Calhoun, gazing at lovely Clare from quite a distance . . . daydreaming about taking her to his boat after the midnight supper . . . knowing she would gently refuse to bed with him, making his fantasies with her all the more tantalizing . . . noted the recklessness of Mrs. Larron's action from afar.

And Aki Shima, watching and understanding the callous scene from the veranda with the Muldoons, who did not notice the near accident off to the side, asked the dear old ladies if they would so graciously excuse her humble self. Dressed in a kimono printed with swimming trout, the Japanese woman walked gracefully and noiselessly along the veranda, her hips swaying with gentle and natural rhythm. She entered the hotel and learned from the clerk the number of Mrs. Vivian Larron's room.

A sudden idea had occurred to her when she witnessed the ruthless Mrs. Larron's latest, veiled attack on Clare. An idea that could help the lovely, but frightened, Mrs. Gilbertson, who had instantly befriended her. Astute Aki knew that now, while everyone attended the Field Day festivities, was the perfect time to enact it.

As Jimmy Hayes announced the contest, Aki Shima— having explained to a trusting maid that she had been asked to deliver a piece of embroidery to "my dear friend's" room—

skillfully managed to gain access to Mrs. Larron's room. And gain enough time to search . . . .

"Ladies and Gentlemen! The ladies' sidesaddle jumping competition, which you have been waiting for this fine Field Day, is about to begin!" called out Jimmy Hayes. "The lady contestants are Mrs. Philippa MacAdam from Charlottesville, Virginia, jumping John Fuller's . . . Dude . . . and Mrs. Vivian Larron from Chicago, Illinois . . . home of the World's Fair," the crowd clapped noisily, "jumping . . . Clementine . . . of 'Colonel's Thoroughbreds' owned by Marshe Williamson of Lexington, Kentucky. These formidable horsewomen are to be given three tries for each raising of the bar in the gate, to which their fine jumpers must clear the hurdle without so much as tipping the top rail. Our judges this afternoon are Judge Gary Higginbotham and Honorable Hempstead Washburn. Our first contender jumper . . . is . . . Mrs. . . . ."

Vivian Larron mercilessly dug the spur on her boot, hidden beneath her heavy skirt, again and again into Clementine's side. She flourished her whip and the pained horse bounded like a fury onto the great lawn during thunderous applause from an audience in awe of such sweeping speed—from what they assumed was a genuine lady on a naturally spirited horse. Mrs. Larron, with perfect form and handsome face, performed like a professional and immediately won over the spectators, (except for the Grand Hotel set), charmed by her obvious skill even before she jumped.

"Our second contending jumper is Mrs. Philippa MacAdam . . ."

As if in studied contrast to Mrs. Larron's dramatic entrance, Philippa walked out showy shining Dude. His easy stride, his head carried so proudly, and Philippa sitting him so regally, caused the Grand Hotel set, in love with Philippa as it was, to break out into a cheer above the polite clapping of the other less impressed spectators . . . who had no idea that Mrs. Philippa MacAdam was one of the Big Four . . . nor would have understood what almost . . . royal . . . loveliness the idea of the Big Four represented to the cultivated Grand Hotel guests.

"The competition will begin!"

Vivian Larron rushed Clementine at the jump, wielded her whip, dug her hidden spur, and flew over the three-foot-six-inch bar with a good deal to spare. The crowd applauded. It was obvious to the experts on horseflesh, that Clementine, a wonderfully careful jumper, had not needed the whip of Mrs. Larron over such a relatively easy height. The experts did not know that Mrs. Larron wore a spur hidden beneath her heavy skirt, and used that as well.

Philippa, trying to hide her nerves, patted Dude's neck and set off for the same gate going slow at timber. Dude sailed over the gate with ease—until Philippa heard the fatal click of his hind legs tipping the top rail.

Jimmy Hayes announced she had two more tries, and some forty gentlemen, who had stakes up to one thousand dollars on her performance, cheered her. Noisily.

Rattled, Philippa could not believe that Dude, a grand fencer with an extraordinarily fine snaffle mouth, had not managed to clear the first bar. She spoke softly to the horse and took off once more for the white obstacle seeming higher to her than before. Dude threw a fine leap and managed to land safely. But Philippa did not believe her own ears until the judges nodded that Dude had not hit the bar. And the Grand hotel set clapped like mad.

Vivian Larron knew she had the competition in the bag when Philippa had not managed Dude on the first jump. She knew that both rider and horse had been flustered by their inglorious first attempt. Smiling conceitedly at the specators, she dug her spur and raced Clementine to the four-foot jump, dug her spur again, snapped her whip and cleared the hurdle amid thunderous applause. Clementine pranced about excitedly much to the spectators' vocal delight, and did not want to turn around until Mrs. Larron wielded the whip again.

Philippa, concentrating on her next jump, paid no attention to prancing Clementine and encouraged Dude in a soothing voice before attempting the four-foot bar, in a style of fencing the expert spectators called "temperate"—in contrast to Mrs. Larron's rushing and "punishing" Clementine with her whip and "jobbing" Clementine's mouth upon landing. Most of the audience had no way of knowing that the judges, and the experts, did not approve of Mrs. Larron's jumping style . . . as successful as it was. And the Grand Hotel set sighed when Mrs. MacAdam could not jump Dude successfully over the four-foot bar after two attempts.

"Mrs. MacAdam and Dude have yet one more try, ladies and gentlemen. Please . . . can we have complete silence!"

John Fuller noticed Colonel Williamson patting Dude on the neck and speaking to Philippa. Pale and beginning to count up his losses, John could not even watch when Philippa and Dude . . . sailed over the four-foot hurdle with room to spare.

The Grand Hotel set went wild.

Mrs. Larron could have spit venom.

Karl set the bar at four-feet six-inches, feeling so nervous for Mrs. MacAdam, knowing that she had managed to jump Dude at that height but a few times in the past weeks of training. And still angry as hell at Mrs. Larron for getting him in trouble over Kentucky Jean. Karl tried again and again to figure out why Colonel Marshe Williamson sold Clementine to the reckless, ruthless horsewoman. And if Clementine had not been one of the colonel's horses, Karl would have wished the bay mare to break a leg and fall on top of "that Larron woman" who caused him a terrible tongue lashing from John Fuller and almost lost him his job . . . he with ten mouths to feed . . . .

Vivian Larron atop Clementine flew over the four-foot-six-inch hurdle with ease and the crowd clapped boisterously—until at the very last moment the horse's hooves upset the bar causing it to tumble to the grass. Vivian came around to give it another try, dug her spur—but Clementine lifted her legs up and down, and would not run. Feeling the whip repeatedly, Clementine finally raced toward the gate, jumped it, and again knocked down the bar.

Never had most of the lively crowd seen such fine jumping by a high society lady such as Mrs. Larron, even if the bar fell down. And never would they have believed that Clementine was cut and bleeding beneath Vivian Larron's heavy skirt.

Philippa, calming down and regaining her pluck, noticed that Mrs. Larron rode with too short a rein and when the horse landed, threw undue weight upon Clementine's forelegs. She wondered how long the horse would put up with Mrs. Larron's painful demands, especially rushing the gate and being punished by the whip at the jump. Philippa figured that Clementine had never received such rough treatment, even at the hands of the suspicious Colonel Marshe Williamson.

And just as Philippa wondered, Clementine, in pain from the spurring, finally showed her equine temper and just as she reached the gate—balked violently—sending Mrs. Larron over the fence without her horse. The crowd screamed. Great was Mrs. Larron's mortification upon finding herself on the wrong side of the fence . . . especially after having lived a life on the wrong side of the tracks.

John Fuller ran to her. But Mrs. Vivian Larron got up, turned to the crowd, waved, and just about brought the house down before he could be of service. No one noticed the horse's blood on her navy blue riding habit.

Marshe caught Clementine and immediately noticed that the horse's side was pierced and bloodstained. He threw a blanket over her, grabbed Karl and ran Clementine to the Grand's stable.

Few saw Marshe leave, except Philippa, who at that moment needed his advice. For she too had just attempted to jump the four-foot-six-inch bar twice, and had brought it down both times.

Instead, John Fuller approached her. "Mrs. MacAdam . . . do you really think you should attempt it?"

"Why, Mr. Fuller, I plan on doing just that!" And she thought of Clare and decided just this once to use her whip lightly on the jump.

Dude trembled with excitement. Surprising the spectators, Philippa raced him to the jump, and just as Dude steadied himself for a moment, she lightly cut him with her whip and he cleared the gate by a hair's breadth and no more.

"Brava! Brava!" shouted the crowd along with the Grand Hotel set, who were almost near tears at the sight of "our brave and beautiful Mrs. MacAdam!" And a wave of onlookers bearing Kodaks rushed at Mrs. Philippa MacAdam. But no one rushed to her faster than Clare and Anna and Beatrice . . . and no others beamed more proudly.

Philippa noticed John Fuller looking pale and morbid. She thought, certainly he must have gained much money through Mrs. Larron's defeat. And while Jimmy Hayes, exhilarated at the sight of the Field Day audience so highly entertained, handed her a sterling silver goblet . . . Philippa noticed John Fuller walking back to the stable.

14

Blue Blood Brigade and Blackmail

"Well . . . I declare . . . your sister Cynthia certainly has no time for us since the Big Four took her under their wing. Look at her dancin' with that Richard Anders fella. Between him and his handsome father and the other gentlemen admirers of the Big Four, I do believe she hasn't missed one dance all evenin' at this lively Field Day hop."

"I noticed that your dance card is not entirely full this evening, Belinda." Fifteen year old Priscilla Price had learned a few feminine tricks from Belinda, and was beginning to make use of them.

Mrs. Price, sitting behind the girls, was pleased to overhear that her Priscilla's ill-sorted association with Miss Gaines that summer was paying off.

Belinda ignored Priscilla's quick response and answered sweetly, "I would imagine there will be an announcement soon . . ."

"Announcement?" asked Priscilla innocently.

"Why Cynthia's and Mr. Anders' engagement announcement!" Belinda Gaines said the news loud enough for everyone sitting nearby to hear. And by starting a rumor, felt she "got back" at Cynthia Price for the talking down and tongue lashing she received from Cynthia on the day of the first outdoor Sunday tea with the Big Four.

Priscilla looked bewildered while Mrs. Price, horrified at the thought of her Cynthia marrying a race horse gambler, turned pale and instantly decided it was time to take her girls back home, even if it was three weeks before the season ended. Mrs. Price figured that sly Miss Gaines had somehow found out that Cynthia and Richard were secretly engaged, and that her suspicion about the countess using Cynthia as a camouflage for her love affair with young Richard was not true. It was worse!

Mrs. Price surmised that the countess was helping Cynthia shield her secret engagement to Richard Anders, "gambler!" from her own MaMa. Mrs. Price promised herself that before she left Mackinac Island, she would tell the Countess Gianotti just what she really thought of her. And the fact that Cynthia admired, why quite adored, the countess seemingly more than her own MaMa, just about drove the rational Mrs. Price to jealousy.

"I have no earthly idea why the crowd voted that village girl as the most beautiful girl in the beauty contest, have you Priscilla? Her eyes are small and her nose is big. Did you know surgery can change the shape of your nose? Julia Marlowe changed her nose, and now instead of comedy—she plays tragedy. But you can't change the shape of your eyes. Priscilla honey, your nose is awfully big. Really darlin', you ought to pinch and stroke it faithfully. I know it can be tedious labor, and it takes so long to produce effects. It might take ten years or more. And by then you'll be an old maid. And you'd always have a red nose. Red noses and red ears are the worst malady a lady can suffer and . . ."

"MaMa says women have red noses and ears because their corset lacing is too tight and so are their shoes." Priscilla had also learned to interrupt sweetly from Belinda Gaines.

"Why Priscilla, my dearest friend, your ears have a reddish

tint. You had better bathe them in a solution of borax, water and a sprinkle of cologne. Or your ears will become as red as Owen Corrigan's nose!" Both girls giggled gaily.

While Belinda Gaines lectured Priscilla Price she failed to notice the Big Four and Aki Shima leave the hop—without their gentlemen escorts. When she finally looked over at their box, she saw Cynthia Price, minus the quartette of beauty and the oriental, surrounded by the Big Four's gentlemen admirers (except for that "dashin'" Colonel Marshe Williamson), and just about burst her algae green gown at the bodice with envy.

And then Belinda and the entire gallery crowd saw Mrs. Price approach Cynthia, lead her back to the matriarchal group where she collected Priscilla, and murmur polite departures to the other MaMa's and chaperones; the threesome promptly left the casino ballroom.

Belinda's envy turned to puzzlement. She had no idea why Mrs. Price ruined the utter glory of having such highly repected and rich gentlemen surrounding her eligible old maid daughter pining for a husband. Belinda decided then and there that she just never would understand "northern" MaMa's and thanked God she had been born a "normal southerner." Then her puzzlement turned to satisfaction, as she realized that Mrs. Price must be highly upset with her idea of an engagement between Cynthia and Richard. A smug smile curled the corners of Belinda Gaines mouth, and she rose to take the arm of her middle-aged millionaire gentleman admirer from Hot Springs, Arkansas, for the next waltz.

"Did you bring the 33,000 dollar note? Just hand it over and I'll give you back your precious ring, Mrs. Gilbertson. And don't try any tricks like you did last time around my throat, 'cause my accomplice is beyond me in the dark, and this time you won't get away without a beatin' if you should try somethin'. Fine time you'd have explainin' black eyes and face to the fancy swells in your Grand Hotel set."

Clare shuddered in the cool black woods surrounding Crack-in-the-Island. She held up her kerosene lamp and looked Mrs. Vivian Larron straight in the eye. "I do not have the note. Nor will I continue to be blackmailed into paying support for the son you swore my husband had with you . . . in addition . . . to paying you to keep your mouth shut. You had never given birth to a Gilbertson . . . as you have claimed the past three years!"

Mrs. Larron, stunned by Clare's confident words, heard footsteps in the woods. She figured her accomplice, late because of the hop, had finally come. And as she blasted Clare, she listened for the signal of an owl.

"The son I gave your husband is the spittin' image of his father . . . you saw him . . . you wept when you saw the little lad . . . how can you deny the little lad is not a Gilbertson . . . how can you abandon the fine Gilbertsons' flesh and blood now. You society women are all alike . . . disloyal and selfish. When your husbands ask a few unusual sexual favors of you, you are all too afraid and send them to us. We perform their perversions and then they go back to you fine ladies, who are too religious or too good or too high and mighty to soil yourselves with your husbands' animal natures," Mrs. Larron paused listening for the signal, "I told you . . . without that money I can't get out of the country . . . and if I can't get out of the country your husband's son will be killed along with me . . . you are not the only one bein' blackmailed, you know."

In spite of her fright, Clare broke out laughing at that last statement. Suddenly the strain and ludicrous meaning of Vivian Larron's words seemed unreal and ironic and downright funny. She noticed Mrs. Larron sweating. And when the blackmailer kept talking, Clare knew that for some reason Mrs. Larron was stalling for time.

"I need that money to start my own horse business in Paris. I assure you, Mr. Gilbertson's son will be well provided for."

"Where is your accomplice, Mrs. Larron? Or are you alone in the woods tonight?"

"He is here but I have no need of him yet and instructed him to stay in the dark, unless you do not cooperate. Now make your decision, Mrs. Gilbertson . . . hand over the $33,000 note . . . or I will leave to inform every gossip at the Grand Hotel before notifying every newspaper in the country about your husband . . . and if you anger me any more, your face will be disfigured the way a young friend of mine was by a fine gentleman thirty years ago . . . when she and I first started trickin' . . . when she and I was ten."

Mrs. Larron failed to notice Clare's change in facial expression. She was too nervous wondering what had happened to her accomplice and listening for the signal. She continued stalling, "I've noticed that you and your fancy Chicago Women's Club fought to raise the legal age of consent from ten to sixteen . . . it's good you did that . . . I can tell you from experience, at ten it's too rough on a girl. But I was lucky . . . I knew a girl from the Everleigh Club who was whorin' since the age of six . . . ." Mrs. Larron paused, listening and hoping to hear the signal. "This is the last time I'll ask you . . . now what do you say!"

"I say . . . I feel my heart sick for your tragic life, Mrs. Larron . . ."

"Bitch! I don't need your high falutin' sympathy. I need your money!" Mrs. Larron heard the owl signal and feeling reassured pushed Clare to the ground and kicked her in the ribs.

Her accomplice, with black hair and masked face, carrying a kerosene lamp, leapt to Mrs. Larron's side as she struggled with Clare. He put down his lamp next to Vivian Larron's lamp, pulled her off of Clare and in a muffled voice yelled, "Stop beating her, woman!"

And four kerosene lamplights lit the surrounding darkness.

"Don't move! We have guns. Don't try to run away from us. In the dark you will stumble to your death in Crack-in-the-Island."

Clare looked up to see the countess and Philippa and Beatrice and Aki Shima appearing like heavenly apparitions made flesh. Philippa walked unsteadily nearer to Mrs. Larron's accomplice and said, "Move away over here. I will shoot you if you run . . . ."

Trembling, the countess spoke up, "I have made arrangements for both of you to leave the island tonight. Owen Corrigan is nearby and he will drive you to British Landing. There you will embark a Mackinac boat manned by Indians who understand you are dangerous. Who understand that if you attack them, they will make sure your bodies drown to the very bottom of the Straits of Mackinac, never to be found again." Anna almost swooned from her own words. Emotional residue from her love troubles with Richard and Arthur vanished, for the time being.

Beatrice moved to Mrs. Larron and demanded, "Don't move. For the sake of my friend . . . I would kill you . . . ."

Clare got up off the ground slowly and moved away from the blackmailers.

Aki Shima, dressed in a black robe, holding her kerosene lamp to her face, looking as if her lighted face alone floated in the darkness, moved nearer to Mrs. Larron. She bent over, opened a satchel, and threw a bundle of letters onto the ground near the blackmailer.

In a voice firm and laced with incrimination, Aki explained, "Today . . . during the jumping competition . . . I entered your room Mrs. Larron and found these letters you had hidden. Letters from men you lied to that you carried their babies in pregnancy. Letters from Mr. Gilbertson. Why you even kept Mr. Gilbertson's last words to you . . . his suicide note. He killed himself after you told him you would not marry him . . . after demanding he turn his entire fortune over to you or you would expose him to his family . . . after you showed him the photographic pictures you have of yourself with him in the acts of sexual perversions . . . after telling him you miscarried his baby . . . after showing Mr. Gilbertson this . . . ."

Aki bent over the satchel once more and took out an object covered in a purple cloth. "And this is what you showed Mr. Gilbertson and all your men to shock them, along with your other threats about exposing them . . . .This is what you showed Mr. Gilbertson before he wrote his suicide note to you . . . ."

Slowly Aki pulled the purple cloth off the object. A kerosene lamp nearby eerily lit up the large jar—containing a baby boy floating in formaldehyde, eight months old.

Clare Gilbertson closed her eyes then forced them open. Knowing of the danger her loss of control would mean to her friends, who were risking their lives for her, she swallowed the violent cries within her and expelled the air quietly that rose to support them.

Aki Shima, in a voice compassionate but firm, said, "Please forgive me . . . forgive me . . . but there was no other way. If I had informed you of this evidence in addition to the letters, all of you might have suffered so from it that we could not have functioned with the strength we need this sad night. I have two maids as witness to this . . . this innocent . . . in Mrs. Larron's hotel room."

And Mrs. Larron stood as speechless and still as Lot's wife, who had looked back at Sodom and Gomorrah and turned to salt.

Only the masked accomplice saw that all the women were in a state of near shock and exhaustion. He made his move. He grabbed Philippa's gun and held it to her head.

Philippa glanced fearfully into the accomplice's eyes, recognized him and fainted. Without hesitation her sisters turned off their lamps in unison, as planned if an emergency arose.

Bang!

And once again a bullet, foretelling a contest to come, exploded that Field Day.

Silence fell upon the black wooded recesses of Mackinac Island, only to be broken by the distant echo of "Go lang, Charley!" and the belabored beats of an old horse's hooves.

"Clare?"

"Yes . . ."

"Beatrice?"

"Yes . . ."

"Anna?"

"Yes . . ."

"Get off of me!" Mrs. Larron's voice thundered.

"Aki?"

"Hai . . ."

"Philippa?"

" . . ."

"Philippa!"

Bravely or stupidly Clare managed to switch on a lamp, and rolled away from it immediately into the shadows. The lamp she switched on revealed all. Slumped over Philippa was the masked accomplice. Beatrice held her gun to Mrs. Larron while Clare and Anna and Aki approached the two bodies slowly. Carefully they pulled the masked man off of Philippa.

Aki pronounced him dead while Clare and Anna, holding back wrenching sobs, cradled Philippa's head and felt her pulse.

"Countess Anna? Leddies?"

"Owney! Find the path to Crack-in-the-Island!"

Mrs. Larron yelled, "One of you killed him! This will not be on my head! I have no gun! I am not a killer! Whatever I am I am not a cold-blooded killer! I did not kill Mr. Gilbertson! I am not a cold-blooded killer!

Aki answered, "No, Mrs. Larron . . . I believe you have neither the courage nor the skill to kill with your hands. You kill with your heart. That is worse. It is more honorable to kill with your hands out of defense or passion of love . . . than to pretend to kill as you have done to frighten Mrs. Gilbertson. You even pretend to be strong. You are the weakest of us all."

St. Patrick himself, miraculously transmogrified into old Owen Corrigan, could not have arrived sooner. Owney hobbled up the path with the speed, if not form, of a youngster, arriving out of breath. If anyone had looked or could have seen in the dark, the twinkle left Owen Corrigan's eyes and he wondered, in his old age, how many more tragedies he was to add to his long lifetime list . . . before he kicked off to purgatory. And the old island jester helped Anna and Clare carry Philippa, in a state of shock, along the narrow path to State Road, to the old dilapidated carriage.

Beatrice and Aki led Mrs. Larron at gunpoint to the carriage and had her lie down at the bottom. Anna gently told Clare, white and trembling, to stay with Philippa, and suddenly filled with a surge of negative energy, asked Owen to return with her to the body. When they got there, they noticed something different about the man. A black wig had fallen off his head. Owen pulled down the mask revealing a black beard. Anna gasped and thanked God that Philippa had not seen him, for it might have been the death of her.

But Philippa had recognized the masked accomplice's eyes. And it was not only the shock—that almost caused the death of her at the recognition of John Fuller—it was the simultaneous relief that the masked accomplice was not Colonel Marshe Williamson.

Owen searched John Fuller for any sign of a gun but could find none. Next to him was Philippa's gun . . . warm.

Old Owen dragged the body to his carriage. Old Charley snorted and threw his head back and forth as if implying, oh you humans, if you would act more like us horses these tragedies would not happen.

Aki told Mrs. Larron to get off the floor of the carriage, and Owen laid John Fuller, who had no visible bloodstains anywhere on his body, carefully down, and pulled off his fake black beard. Owney shoved the black wig and beard and mask into a satchel, which he promised to burn later in his fireplace.

Aki ordered, "Mrs. Larron, get down on the bottom of the carriage."

"You can't make me . . . I won't do it!"

Clare seethed, "Mrs. Larron . . . you had no problem dealing with my dead husband's body . . . making up the vilest lies that you killed him . . . in order for me to live in fear—that you would murder me as well and besmirch the Gilbertson family name these past three years, if I did not pay you blood money for the rest of my life. Now lie down. And if a carriage should pass us . . . if you so much as move . . . I will knock you out with my gun!"

Owen threw a tattered blanket that concealed dead John Fuller and very much alive Mrs. Vivian Larron—lying on top of him. As she had positioned herself many times before. Under different conditions. And the Big Four and the oriental placed their muddied boots upon the blackmailer.

"Go lang, Charley."

The women rode in silence to the Grand Hotel stable; except for an escaped sob now and then . . . from one or another.

One-half hour before midnight, Jimmy Hayes met the group in the stable. His bird dog Donny greeted him with lively tail wagging, but no barking, as if sensing something was wrong. And of all people, Ibrahim J. Kheiralla walked in along with Jimmy. Not only was the little Egyptian a lecturer, he happened to be a doctor. Of what—no one was sure. But Jimmy Hayes was not about to get a local doctor—or police— if he did not "need them." He explained to a doubtful Ibrahim that John Fuller was found dead in the stables by Mrs. MacAdam.

After examining Philippa, the little Egyptian blurted, "Mrs. MacAdam is as strong as an Arab."

Everyone stared a hole through the "little Islamic."

"Ah! You wonder . . . I mean an Arab horse, of course. She will be fine. Get her some brandy what's your name you?"

"Just call me . . . Colonel."

After riding expertly in the high jumping show with John Fuller, Colonel Marshe Williamson explained that he had stayed in the stable with Clementine, who was fast developing an infection from Mrs. Larron's cruelty with her spur. He had attended the hop only a short time to receive Field Day honors, which Jimmy Hayes had handed out for the show of John Fuller's high jumpers, and then had left the hop with John and walked back with him to the stable.

When Owen Corrigan had driven into the stable, the ladies had seen Marshe sitting next to Clementine and Donny sitting next to Marshe. They had no choice but to include the colonel in their secret plan. It was Marshe who had left the stables to find Jimmy Hayes, dancing up a storm with an old maid at the Field Day hop. After Marshe had whispered the shocking news, Jimmy had marched up to Ibrahim, who had the nerve to attend the hop, and brought him back to the stable as well.

Marshe explained, "I was surprised when John Fuller saddled up Kentucky Jean and said he was heading into the village. He seemed under a strange influence." As Marshe said this he noticed Philippa coming back into consciousness. He felt a protective urge to put his arms around her and comfort her.

From a corner of the stable, Ibrahim emerged smiling. As if beginning a lecture, his arms flying about like a traffic policeman in a jam, the little Muslim reported, "Genteel ladies and men . . . you told me that Mr. Fuller might have committed suicide with a gun . . . yet there was not one bullet in his body. Mr. Fuller died . . . because he had a case of walking typhoid. You see people . . . a man may be dangerously ill for many days but may walk around minding his own business . . . as if nothing is new . . . as if no bad eyes exist . . . and then suddenly . . . pshhhhh . . . boom . . . he falls down dead. Like a dead bird from the blue sky."

Jimmy Hayes, utterly relieved that his "season" had once again been saved—knowing full well that if people knew of John Fuller's death, whether or not it had been murder, suicide, accident or disease, they would leave his colossal caravansary as if the plague had reappeared on the island—immediately asked Owen Corrigan to kindly fetch Dr. Bailey and the police. Jimmy knew that they would promise not to release the news to the local papers . . . until the end of the season.

Until then it would be said of master horseman John Fuller that he was struck down with illness and returned to New York to be taken care of by relatives. There was nothing untrue about this statement. Then Jimmy told Ibrahim that he could have his old hotel room back and continue lecturing at the Grand.

But Ibrahim, most popular at the Island House the past

weeks, declined. And then he dropped that the Shah of Harremajarra was staying at the most excellent Island House hotel—incognito—on his way back to Persia from the Chicago World's Fair.

Jimmy Hayes ran his hand through even fewer hairs on his head than he had had at the beginning of the "season," tried to ignore that the shah had come after all, assured himself that the little Egyptian was lying, and reminded Ibrahim that on his honor, as a member of the most honorable medical profession, he would be expected to keep Mr. Fuller's last moments and inglorious death a secret.

Ibrahim answered with a droll look and ironic eyes, "Of course, Mr. Jimmy . . . as a doctor . . . I belong to a most honourable profession . . . ."

Ibrahim might as well have stood with his arm out and his greasy palm up.

Jimmy said, "There will be payment for your services in my office tomorrow. And if you keep your mouth shut until the end of our season . . . there will be a reward. But if I hear any rumors . . . you will pay retribution, Ibrahim. Now get out of here."

And Vivian Larron, hoping for mercy, told all in her semi-finishing school accent, after Owen and Ibrahim left. She explained that John Fuller had started the secret betting for the hurdle jumping competition, after he learned, following Kentucky Jean's accident—that she had been a school rider and professional circus jumper—who could jump five-foot hurdles sidesaddle . . . and after he learned that Mrs. Larron had "dealings" with Clare and could get a $33,000 note temporarily from her.

Then he placed his secret bets with some forty swagger resorters, at one thousand dollars, against Mrs. MacAdam. Gentlemen gamblers all, John's surprising wager against Philippa MacAdam was kept quiet. Especially since John had asked them, as "good sportsmen," to keep his private wager "under their top hat."

When John had told the colonel that he was involved with a little private betting that Mrs. MacAdam knew nothing about . . . and asked the colonel to wager just to feel him out . . . the colonel had declined. But Marshe Williamson also promised to keep the betting a secret, never imagining that John Fuller betted—against—Philippa MacAdam.

Mrs. Larron admitted, "You see, Mrs. MacAdam, John Fuller betted against you because there is no doubt that I would have won, if that fussy horse had not got it into her head to defy me at the very last minute. John and I knew that you would not have even attempted a five-foot hurdle . . . for the sake of Dude more than for yourself.

"You see, John would have earned $40,000 in winnings . . . $33,000 which he would have given to me . . . to give to the colonel in cash for his two bay mares. That's all that John wanted . . . the two bay mares which I had bargained for him, from the colonel."

Marshe spoke up, "Then why didn't John simply come to me . . ."

"Pride. John Fuller was a proud man. Too proud. John didn't want you to know that he was speculating heavily to get the money to buy your horses . . . that he didn't have enough money of his own. You know a man's head gets turned 360 degrees at fancy watering places such as this . . . where every man or woman but himself is rich. Anyhow, John figured that you would not take kindly to selling your bay mares to him, especially for me to jump with after the accident with Kentucky Jean. And John knew what you felt for Mrs. MacAdam.

"Colonel, you see, John Fuller reckoned that you would think him a low-down heel knowing that he was using your

horses and betting on me to win the jumping competition—
against Philippa MacAdam who was doing him the grand favor
of jumping for his contest, and whom John had been training
for weeks. Yes, John Fuller was a proud man. His pride held
him back from simply going to you."

Philippa smiled weakly when Marshe gazed at her across
the dark stable where they had first met.

Clare asked quietly, "So why did you torture me yet again,
Mrs. Larron?"

"I did what I had to do. We never planned on keeping the
$33,000 we tried to get from you. We saw it as a loan. John
would not have heard of keeping it . . . in the beginning. He
was not a professional extortionist, not an outright thief. He
was even too proud to be a thief, until he lost his head tonight.
You see, I bought the horses from the colonel, with a type of
gentleman's agreement . . . with the promise that I would pay
him with a $33,000 note by the end of the week.

"That's why I threatened you yet again, Mrs. Gilbertson; I
needed the note for that amount from you. But you did not give
in. And I could not give the note I promised to the colonel in a
week's time. Nevertheless, the colonel let me train with
Clementine for the jumping competition . . . when I gave him
your diamond ring, Mrs. Gilbertson, as a show of good faith."

Everyone watched Marshe take the seven-carat diamond
ring out of his vest pocket and walk over to Clare. He lifted her
hand and placed the ring, which sparkled even in the dim light
of the stable and once belonged to a royal European family,
into Clare's hand, which was black and blue from protecting
herself when Mrs. Larron kicked her in the ribs. Slowly,
Marshe bent over Clare's bruised hand, and kissed it.

Mrs. Larron put her eyes up in her head at the sight of the
colonel's "sugary high society gallantry" and continued, "But
tonight . . . things got out of hand . . . John seemed to have

lost his mind . . . he suddenly demanded that we get the money from Mrs. Gilbertson and keep it . . . because he owed $40,000 to the Grand Hotel swells . . . and because he could not escape his payments.

"He was too proud to tell the swells he didn't have any money . . . and he could not escape the island with a stable of his horses . . . could he? I told him that the swells would forgive his debt to them . . . but he was too proud. And he forced me to go through with this tonight, or he would turn me into the police. He said his word would be trusted over mine at the police station."

Marshe declared, "John Fuller must have been out of his mind with this insane scheme . . . it must have been his illness . . . ."

Mrs. Larron continued, "You are too kind, Colonel. John turned on me like a snake in the grass . . . he threatened me."

Jimmy Hayes interrupted, "Never mind! What were you to get out of all of this?"

"The Colonel . . . a true gentleman if I ever saw one . . . had agreed to sell the bay mares to me for $33,000 though the horses might have fetched thousands more in a good market. Between John Fuller and myself . . . I was to pay the colonel $33,000 out of our $40,000 winnings, and keep the $7,000 for myself.

"And in this way, without putting out a dime, John Fuller was to have the Colonel's bay mares that he coveted . . . and I was to have the $7000 dollars to get to Europe. I know Mrs. Gilbertson will not believe me. But we were going to return her $33,000 dollar note, and when I left the country with the money from our winnings, I was going to stop blackmailing her."

Mrs. Larron paused, glared at Clare and said, "You see, Mrs. Gilbertson, I really do need to escape the country. That's why I followed you up here to the island in the first place. To get a large amount of money from you. I have spent all the other money you have given me the past three years. My mistake was in thinking I could win the money with John Fuller . . . a man I thought might marry me in the end if I helped him . . . and even leave the country with me."

Marshe added quietly, "She told me she was sorry for hurting Kentucky Jean, that she did not know that the horse had thin withers, that she was all alone, that she was being blackmailed, that she had been a paramour since the age of ten, that she wanted to change her life and escape prostitution . . . and to start her own horse business in Paris . . . I believed her story . . . I believed that she wanted to start all over again . . . until I saw how she had dug cruelly with her spur into the side of Clementine." He turned to Mrs. Larron and said, "It was your cruelty with Clementine, a horse that never knew such ill treatment, which lost you and John Fuller your dirty dealings."

"It was my future I was spurring, Colonel. But then most men worry more about the horses in this world . . . .than the women."

Everyone fell silent.

Until Philippa spoke gently, "Without knowledge of Mrs. Larron's past, I might have believed it too, Colonel Williamson. In fact, most of what she told you, she confessed to us in the woods." Philippa had broken the silence, and secretly chastised herself for her own cruel incriminations about the character of Colonel Marshe Williamson.

The colonel gazed at Philippa as she spoke her kind words with such deep sadness; he felt all over again, as on the day of the tea, that she was a soulmate in the understanding of pain. Philippa's gently spoken words helped lift the guilt and embarrassment off the colonel, for having been taken by the stunning blackmailer Mrs. Larron—at the expense of Clare Gilbertson.

Clare supported Philippa's remark, realizing the southern gentleman's sense of utter shame. "Colonel Williamson . . . you are not to blame. And if it were not for your generosity with Mrs. Larron . . . I might have been held in her power for the rest of my life. You . . . and my dear friends," Clare paused, exhaled trapped air in her throat, and continued in a thin voice, "all of you have released me, and words will not express the gratitude in my heart to you . . . Philippa . . . . . . Anna . . . Beatrice . . . Aki . . . ." Clare's voice broke and she could not continue.

The women were so moved . . . not one of the Big Four and the oriental could have formed a word or found the breath to support it, even if their lives depended on it.

A rush of relief energized Philippa's body as she realized that John Fuller must have set up the scandalous entrance of Vivian Larron and Marshe Williamson to the grand ball—at half past two in the morning; hoping that Mrs. Larron could perhaps seduce Marshe . . . and bed with him . . . in exchange for privileges with his horses.

Philippa figured that when that rendevous failed, John Fuller, smitten himself with the stunning Mrs. Larron who wore pomegranate red, walked unrecognized through the Grand Hotel to Mrs. Larron's room disguised in a black wig and fake black beard (as described to Philippa by her sisters when she came to), and sealed their conspiratorial intercourse with sex. (Which apparently was very good—for it was John Fuller who threw Vivian Larron's red panties off the balcony that Sunday morning.)

Philippa even surmised that Mrs. Larron had been checking out Crack-in-the-Island as a remote setting for her own further blackmailing of Clare, that fateful day she had met John Fuller during the accident with Kentucky Jean. Sometime between the massacre lecture and the grand ball, Vivian Larron must have told John Fuller that she had been a school rider and circus performer. And they had fallen into each other's snare.

But Philippa wondered curiously, why John Fuller donned a black wig and beard styled after the colonel. Was it unconscious admiration? Or had he meant to somehow besmirch the colonel's name with Vivian Larron? Philippa shuddered to think that at one point she had actually favored . . . and even trusted . . . the attentions of master horseman John Fuller over Colonel Marshe Williamson.

"I have committed much wrong in my life. But in this case I swear I never planned on keeping that amount of money from Mrs. Gilbertson. I swear! Please . . . if I sign something . . . if I leave the country . . . anything . . . I will get out of Clare Gilbertson's life forever. Just don't turn me over to the police!"

"Mrs. Larron, what proof do you have that all you say is true?" asked Jimmy Hayes.

"I have saved letters from John Fuller . . . letters even that shrewd businesswoman . . . that oriental . . . could not find in my room. Letters of agreement regarding the jumping competition and the wagering and the horses.

"And I'll tell you, Mrs. Gilbertson . . . if you put me in jail over this . . . I'll still spill the beans to the newspapers about your husband. His suicide and photographic pictures would provide some juicy scandal for the *National Police Gazette*. For my letters will be needed as evidence against me and you can't destroy them. And your precious Gilbertsons will not be able to show their faces in public again."

Clare shouted, "Then tell the horrid tragedy we share, Mrs. Larron. I can no longer live with this secret." Defeated, she quietly added, "I cannot fight this anymore. You have dug your spurs into me for so long I am used to the pain. But I am no longer fearful of you. You are not the cold-blooded killer you pretended to be, with your threats to me.

"But whether you are in jail or out, I can never be assured you would keep my tormenting shame a secret from the Gilbertsons nor the newspapers. You have won the bitterest contest this Field Day, after all."

No, Clare had no strength left—since Vivian Larron had not given birth to a boy with Gilbertson blood—and she surrendered her role as protectress of the Gilbertson family name.

And . . . Clare gave up all her hopes about . . . Philmore Calhoun . . . whose departed wife had a "clean slate."

Jimmy Hayes broke into a cold sweat, thinking of his guests' broken illusions regarding the undefiled beauty of Mrs. Clare Gilbertson, and her membership in the Big Four, once this "scarifying news" was made public by the whore Vivian Larron. Thinking that his guests might leave before the "season is over" because of utter disillusionment with the Big Four in general, and because of Clare Gilbertson specifically, he sputtered, "Now Mrs. Gilbertson, let us not be hasty. Let us think this out."

The countess jumped up off a hay bale. "I have an idea . . . as to how to dispose of Mrs. Larron forever! And we will need little Ibrahim."

Everyone, including Mrs. Larron, looked uneasy . . . .

15

Dui-du

Pop! Pop! Pop! Pop! Pop! Champagne corks hit the supper room ceiling when Jimmy Hayes, accompanied by Marshe Williamson, ordered Bludsoe to open the Grand Hotel's finest champagne as the clock struck one in the morning. Exquisitely pale, the Big Four and the oriental glided into the supper room seconds later.

Decorated with huge bunches of white ox-eye daisies and yellow black-eyed susans and brown common cat-tails gathered from the island, the room was filled with the ladies and gentlemen? baseball teams and other participants in the Field Day, dressed in peasant frocks and priceless jewels and sporting suits and silk socks, who had just finished the "most delicious midnight supper" each had ever eaten in his or her "gastronomic life".

A string quartet rushed into a gypsy melody. And Sydney and Richard and Philmore and Rutherford and Professor Bellamy and Eugene Sullivan and Arthur Andryer, and college men, and all the other female Field Day revelers, full of fizz, rushed to gather around the five women, greeting them grandly and inquiring as to why they were late.

The merrymakers all fell into a hush as the countess answered, with a dramatic charm to rival Sarah Bernhardt, "You ask us why we are late? You never would believe it! We have been in the black woods at midnight near Crack-in-the-Island, tracking down a blackmailing murderer . . . .Didn't you hear the gunshot? No you couldn't have. The champagne corks popping make too much noise!" And the beautiful Countess Gianotti raised her glass and toasted, "Alla salute!" And shot a quick knowing glance at each of her accomplices, who raised their glasses to her in return.

The tight revellers roared at the tall tale—the wild idea of such refined ladies chasing a murderer to Crack-in-the-Island tickled their funnybones—and they all but lifted the countess above their shoulders. While Jimmy Hayes saw to it that the champagne flowed freely, he marvelled, that no one but the Big Four could have pulled it off.

Exhausted but beaming, Clare thought, how lovely is the feeling in this supper room. How cheering to be surrounded by admiring new friends. How lucky to feel free for the moment. How wonderful the champagne feels warming my body and tickling my nose. How deeply grateful am I to have these light moments to wipe away life's ugliness. How good it feels . . . to feel again!

Not one of the Big Four, not even Aki Shima, could have slept that night, or faced the violent dreams they were bound to have—alone. So when Jimmy Hayes announced the serenading party to follow, the four women were the first to exclaim, "How delightful!" and all but flew out to the hay wagons followed by their gentlemen admirers.

The men imagined that youth itself must have poured forth from the champagne bottles, as they happily observed that the four women were never so free from composure. But Sydney and Richard and Arthur and Philmore and Rutherford suspected that something unusual had happened with the ladies, during their absence, to have sparked such vulnerable childlike merriment.

When they piled on the hay wagons and noted Marshe Williamson's hand covering Philippa MacAdam's hand, they knew for sure something unusual had happened. But did not waste much time thinking about it. Instead they made the most of the women's high-spirited hoopla as they positioned themselves on the hay wagon.

Never was a homely hay wagon filled with such bonny beauty and money and jewels and smiles and one ventures to say—lust.

Clare Gilbertson allowed Philmore Calhoun to place his arm around her waist, and she placed her (gloved and bruised) hand on his other hand.

Beatrice Venn, because of crowding of course, could not help but lean against (married) Sydney Froilan (as a prelude to leaning—against, under, and over him—in the hay after the hayride). On the other side of Beatrice sat Loral Bellamy, and she held the old professor's arm in a gesture of the warmest friendship.

Aki Shima (who had spent much of the day with the easterner she thought her prince), allowed Rutherford (who fell in love at first sight with the exotic far easterner), to sit behind her, so very close, she felt his warm breath on the cool nape of her white neck. So very close, he sensed her subtle sandalwood scent.

And the countess . . . with two (obviously adoring) men at her side approaching the hay wagon? The regal countess all but threw her curvaceous body down on a cushy little hay mound, landed in a deliciously compromising position, and announced she was going to "hog all the space."

"Oink oink!" squealed Richard going haywire at the tempting horizontal sight of her, and stretching out near Anna's right side, without touching her, of course.

"Oink oink oink!" grunted Arthur hog-wild for the first time since his youth . . . under the influence of spirits of one kind or another . . . wanting to land a haymaker on his son's jaw . . . and stretching out on Anna's left side, without making physical contact, of course.

Yes, provincial Arthur utterly surprised worldy Richard (and Anna) with his loose behavior.

Everyone chuckled and secretly thanked them for "hogging" the space. Because they were obliged to move closer to their heartthrobs.

The only time that Anna or Richard or Arthur may have lightly touched each other was to drink from the champagne glasses they held steady on their stomachs.

Before the musicians boarded a special wagon with seats, Rutherford astounded the entire high society Grand Hotel set when he proclaimed, "As a rule I do not have to drink. But when I am in a prohibition state . . . I must have wine or beer . . . if I cannot have champagne!"

Everyone stared at Rutherford. It was the first funny statement they heard him make all season. They were so surprised they failed to laugh, until Aki covered her mouth with her hand and giggled lightly, and then they laughed right along with her.

Aki said softly, but loud enough for her new friends on the wagon to hear, "Mr. Haverhill, you are impolite . . ."

Rutherford, who had been drinking lightly in order not to be forward with the ladies, especially Aki, as he was known to be when drunk, asked politely, "Miss Shima . . . why am I impolite?"

"You are sober, Mr. Haverhill. I am not. When other people are intoxicated . . . it is entirely impolite to be sober."

Everyone laughed again, and Rutherford almost felt overwhelmed at the warm response in his direction, which he knew was caused by gracious and soft spoken Aki Shima. She turned to him and smiled. He looked into her soulful eyes and almost said right out loud as was his custom, that eyes are everything in a woman. That women can change the shape of their nose or ears in surgery, but there is no science that will make peepholes into soulful melting orbs. But he kept his know-it-all opinion to himself. He thought, Aki Shima's eyes are like the countess' eyes, soulful. And they make everyone else's eyes, except for the eyes of Clare and Beatrice and Philippa, look like ox-eyes.

Yes, Rutherford Earle Haverhill V, after forty years, was learning to keep his know-it-all opinions to himself up on "rustic" Mackinac Island, full of a "mish-mash" of society people and "God knows what hoi polloi."

The musicians' wagon, with the addition of soloist Herr Max Heinrich singing Austrian operetta, pulled ahead, and the other five wagons, loaded with hay and some ten revelers each, headed for the village slowly along quiet Cadotte Avenue.

Into the cool night air of peaceful Mackinac Island, the powerful baritone voice of Herr Heinrich released a melody of pleasure and words of universal brother and sisterhood:

" 'Bruderlein, brother mine
and sister mine.
I have pledged thee in wine,
and I am thine.
Bruderlein, brother mine
and sister mine.
Dui-du is now our greeting
that will mean to me we're in sympathy,
and our hearts as one are beating.
I to you, you to me,
du, du, du always you!
I take you, you take me,
du, du, always you, always you,
always, always you!
It seems to me that we all agree
so each to each say after me—
Bruderlein, brother mine
and sister mine . . .' "

And those revelers who knew the words sang along in rounds, and those who did not listened dreamily. And everyone on the Big Four's hay wagon wondered if brothers and sisters of like disposition and culture and sympathies would ever gather like this again. Especially on a hay wagon.

Yes, they asked themselves, would there ever be a field day like this again in their lives . . . .

The hefty draft horses pulled the five hay wagons through the quaint village streets where Field Day activities had not yet ceased in the beer shops, which were packed with contestants guzzling cool bubbly alcohol malted and hopped, competing to swallow the most mugs full of brew. As the revelers rode through the village streets lit by the leaping flames of gaslights, they serenaded and drank toasts and wished "Dui-du" to new lovers and old lovers renewed, who were having field days of their own while strolling the streets and the docks arm in arm, seeking out cozy nooks for spoonological purposes.

They drove past Mission Church singing: "Let Bachus to Venus libations pour forth, Vive la compagnie . . . And let us make use of our time while it lasts, Vive la compagnie . . . ." They turned around and drove past Mission Church again singing: "Oh! Vive la vive la vive l'amour . . . Vive la compagnie!"

And each time they passed Mission Church the hearts of Anna and Arthur, lying too close to each other, ached for their lost youth and remembrance of proposal and passion. While Richard not knowing their memory, lying too close to Anna, ached for her to be wrapped in his arms et cetera

Passing the crescent harbor Philmore Calhoun requested the driver to stop, jumped off the hay wagon, and lifted Clare off. Sydney jumped off as well and lifted Beatrice down to the road. The entire wagon load had been invited to the "boat," but the rest had declined. The two couples bid "Dui-du!" to their brothers and sisters, walked down to the harbor, and boarded a launch to *Calla*. And the old-fashioned professor comforted himself with the thought that Clare would take care of her sister Beatrice, against seductive Sydney Froilan.

Nothing could have been further from the truth. For when the couples embarked upon *Calla*, Clare had only one thought, to lead Philmore into the library for a long talk. And Sydney had only one thought, to lure Beatrice into a stateroom for dessert.

After Philmore's disguised words of love on *Calla* at the Field Day maritime parade, Clare had realized that even if Mrs. Larron dropped dead, she could not live with the secrets between herself and Philmore should they begin a serious relationship.

And it was in the stable at midnight, that Clare had decided to tell eligible Philmore Calhoun—a gentleman who smoked the same brand of tobacco as her dear dead father, a gentleman who was obviously taken with her, a gentleman who had a beloved wife with a "clean slate"—the whole truth about her own unclean slate. And in spite of those eligible, serious, wealthy gentlemen who had abandoned her the past three years after hearing only parts of her slimy story . . . Clare seized the bull by the horns and told all to the sailor cum lumberjack cum mining baron, while he smoked his meerschaum pipe and sat so close to her on the sofa-bed in the library.

Philmore could barely believe his ears and wondered if he was punch-drunk, while lovely Clare told the tragedy of her married life and aftermath.

She quietly explained about her husband's shocking death that ended up being a suicide, about Mrs. Larron's blackmailing, claiming a Gilbertson son, and extorting some two hundred thousand dollars from Clare over the past three years, about the melodrama at Crack-in-the-Island some four hours ago.

But Philmore really figured he had misheard Clare, when she told him the part about John Fuller falling over dead on top of Philippa MacAdam and everything that followed at Crack-in-the-Island . . . . Then Philmore remembered that the former riding master owned him $1,000.

"Dear Philmore, I will understand . . . after my scandalous past . . . if you should decide to unlock your desk drawer and take out the portrait of your wife . . . a fine lady . . . once more."

Philmore had battled the elements all his life. He had lived through forty-mile-an-hour Great Lakes gale storms as a sailor, freezing cold in the north woods as a lumberjack, the sinking of the ship *Oregon* causing the death of his beloved pregnant wife, but he had never been victimized into battling blackmail and alleged murder and defending a family name. The realization struck him that he had finally met a woman with a will strong enough to match his own brute strength. And he liked this idea.

"But Clare . . . I cannot unlock that drawer ever again . . . I have thrown its key into the straits. There was only one key to that particular drawer." Hoping to use a different key to unlock Clare's drawers, Philmore placed his brawny hand on Clare's soft pale face and pressed his lips to hers. And when he placed his other hand on Clare's breasts he held himself back from ripping her bodice, and she held herself back from letting him.

Clare gently placed her hand on Philmore's warm forehead and said engagingly, "Why, Philmore . . . your temperature is up . . ."

"Dear Clare . . . that's not all that's up . . ."

Philmore leaned back and Clare laughed charmingly.

"Should I bring you a cool cloth . . . for your warm forehead?"

"If you leave this library my . . . temperature . . . will go down, and I shall have no need for a cool cloth . . ."

Again they laughed and kissed and he held her against himself. And soon Clare and Philmore, deeply in love, exhausted, intoxicated, and blissfully happy, exchanged "Dui-du," lay down on the sofa-bed . . . and simply fell asleep in each others arms.

Meanwhile in a stateroom nearby, Sydney and Beatrice also held a most revealing conversation, during dessert:

"Dui-du."

"Same to you."

"Darlingest."

"Dearest."

"Sugarboobies."

"Bottomkins."

"Erectus."

"Erotikos."

"Open season . . ."

"Open up . . ."

"On top of me?"

"Or under you?"

"Too naughty . . ."

"Too too . . ."

"Oh!"

"Ooh!"

"Ah!"

"Oooh oooh oooh oooh . . ."

"Ahhhhhhhhhh."

"Oh yes again!"

" . . . Really?"

But soon Beatrice and (middle-aged) Sydney, in love with love, intoxicated, exhausted, blissfully guilty, lying on *Calla's* sofa-bed, the yacht rocking gently in the harbor waters, fell asleep in each other's arms.

Meanwhile, back at the hotel, after the hay wagon drivers dropped off some fifty resorter revelers, old guard Professor Bellamy wished "Dui-du" and "pleasant dreams" to his fellow revelers, and sat up waiting for Beatrice in the rotunda. He did not trust Sydney Froilan, probably "pie-eyed," to accompany the ladies back to the hotel from *Calla*. He scolded himself for not accepting Philmore Calhoun's invitation. He could have escorted Beatrice and Clare back properly. Yes, if the ladies did not come back within a reasonable time, he would go back to *Calla* to accompany them. No, there seemed to be no one around to protect the ladies these days.

Colonel Marshe Williamson accompanied Philippa Mac-Adam to her room, all the way explaining that he had to leave the Grand in the morning for the Chicago World's Fair because of horse business with Kaiser Wilhelm's stud director. Although he had to journey back to Lexington, he would try to make it back to the hotel for the last week of the season. Then Marshe kissed Philippa lightly on the lips, and reluctantly left the woman he planned on marrying as soon as possible.

Tessie, Philippa's maid, stayed up all night listening to Philippa's euphoric talk about the colonel and frightening story about Crack-in-the-Island. Tessie thanked God that Philippa came back in one piece. She thanked God that Philippa seemed alive once more . . . as she remembered her. Then she thanked God that . . . the colonel was a southerner . . . for Tessie knew that she and the colonel would have an immediate understanding.

Meanwhile . . . Aki Shima astounded Rutherford when she told him she had "no attachments in this world" and asked him, with an air of innocence, to do her the honor of pillowing with her and sharing a sunrise tea. She mentioned, when Rutherford looked hesitant, that everyone should live for now because . . . life is shorter than a snowflake melting.

Yes, Aki saw that Rutherford was a gentleman of fine ancestry and perfect form, whose attention to detail indicated he had all the makings of a brilliant lover. Never had a western mind, in America or abroad, thought thus about know-it-all, fussy if handsome, Rutherford Earle Haverhill V.

Rutherford, up for the occasion, did not want to let Aki Shima down. He thought he understood Japanese culture enough to know that it would be highly impolite and insulting to plead a headache. He realized that Aki Shima had an erotic love of form. His form. And he understood why. In return, Rutherford was crazy about every detail of Aki's. Hadn't he ogled her sensuous details in the flesh, during their first meeting on the balconies after the trip to the Sault? Really, her bold invitation was too tempting to be true. He wondered if he were dreaming the soft spoken Japanese woman, who in one day made him feel it was worth being alive.

A half an hour after receiving the most humbly elegant and risqué invitation of his life, Rutherford entered Aki's room lit only by candles. He noticed she wore the same black robe he had seen her drop to the balcony floor, and that she held its hem gracefully in her left hand. He took off his shoes.

Surprised at his thoughtful gesture considering there were no tatami mats on the floor, Aki bowed to Rutherford a most respectful forty-five degrees. She helped him into a yukata robe and led him to sit on the floor near a sparse flower arrangement and a scroll she had attached to the wall, both near an unadorned corner of the room. When Aki saw Rutherford sitting on his legs in an oriental fashion, her eyes watered, for she was convinced that her prince's spirit was in Rutherford.

Without explaining, Aki asked Rutherford to take three sips of sake from a laquered cup. She sipped likewise.

"We have performed a solemn and deep bonding between two persons," Aki said softly and bowed almost to the floor.

Rutherford, who owned the most extensive collection in the world of Japonaise art and objets d'art, (outside of the orient), was also versed in Japanese custom. He knew that the ritual Aki had performed was used in the marriage ceremony.

As if appearance created reality, he answered in a voice almost absent of anglophiliac accent, "So be it. Our destinies are tied." Rutherford bowed almost to the floor . . . almost humbly.

And something here to fore unknown tugged inside of Rutherford for the first time in his adult life. And that something was a sense of bonding. The first step to—feeling.

Softly, Aki began playing "Chin-Chin-Chindori" on her three-stringed shamisen, with its ivory pegs and gold fittings and cat-skin belly. The last note of the haunting melody plucked, Aki gracefully laid down the musical instrument and looked into Rutherford's excited eyes.

"You show me the flowing eye . . ."

"My eyes are flooded . . ."

And some time later, in the early morning hours before the moon faded from the night sky, Aki guided Rutherford's hand under her black kimono lined with red.

He felt . . . she wore no underclothes.

She sensed his excited response and began to disrobe slowly . . . with studied suggestiveness . . . and spontaneous sweetness.

Rutherford ravished by the sight of her unclothed body, savored her sensibility to the beauty of graceful action. He laughed easily at the recognition of a red tattooed sun setting between the fleshy parts of her upper derriere. But for some moments, he sank back into his old argumentative self. He argued to himself, if Aki were so enticing because she had performed this scene too often, or if she was naturally and sensually fresh.

He could not decide. So he decided . . . for once . . . not to decide. He stopped thinking. And it was when he stopped thinking and began to sense the tugging within him, began to sense the mystic instinct in his nature, and stopped performing the role of Rutherford, that for the first time in his adult life— he sensed what it meant to feel.

In the next dream-like hours of making love and after-love and sunrise tea, Rutherford Earle Haverhill V forgot his name and forgot himself . . . by bonding to Aki and giving himself to her.

Yes, Rutherford received more than he would have dreamed possible in giving himself to Aki. Because for the first time in his life . . . he loved during the act of love.

Never was the eastern man's life to be the same.

And never had Aki Shima, from Kyoto to Paris to Chicago, dreamed that she would again find the spirit of her pure love the prince, on a remote island in a great saltless sea in a wild North America. Truly her instincts about Rutherford Earle Haverhill V were true. His perfect physical form and sensitive action as a lover proved it.

Early that morning, after their sunrise tea, after wishing each other "Dui-du," Rutherford quietly dashed to his room but could not sleep. He wrote immediately to the closest person in his life, the only person he had ever felt any connection to as a child, and a remote connection to as an adult, his dear mother.

He wrote to his mother to relieve himself of his utter happiness. He wrote to his mother to let her know that he had finally found the love of his life—a woman of cultivated elegance and gentle wit—like herself. He wrote to his mother to let her be the first to know he planned on asking Aki Shima to marry him at the end of the season.

Meanwhile . . . Anna, having discouraged intoxicated Richard and intoxicated Arthur from escorting her to her suite . . . having refused the entrance of either of them into her sitting room . . . having encouraged both of them to lower their voices and leave her sitting room immediately . . . having threatened both of them with calling hotel security to get them out of her sitting room . . . having come between them when they started a fist fight . . . having tried to revive them when they knocked each other out . . . finally threw up her hands and threw a blanket over the father and a blanket over the son lying on the floor . . . and eventually climbed into her bed, exhausted.

Anna's only comfort in their presence was she did not have to face a morning full of dreams—alone. And when she half awoke by a scream, her own, hours later . . . Richard half awake and hating Arthur, and Arthur half awake and hating Richard, forgot their hatred momentarily during the early morning hours and were there to comfort Anna . . . though they knew not what provoked such a violent dream . . . and knew not what they were all doing when they woke up hours later . . . in Anna's bed.

16

Women of the World

"What the hell . . ."

"I don't believe it . . ."

"I believe it . . . is too late to suggest that you both slap a steak on your black and blue eyes. Do you remember knocking each other out?"

"Vaguely . . ."

"Vaguely . . ."

"But I don't remember how I got . . . here!"

"Neither do I . . . oh yes . . . now I remember . . . ."

The countess laughed softly at the rumpled sight of father and son on either side of her, fully clothed in sporting outfits, and looking ever so foolish sitting up on her bed wearing shoes and—hats.

Anna said sweetly, "May I suggest that you two . . . uh . . . gentlemen depart from my rooms pronto, with as little ado as possible. And please check the hallway before you sneak out of my door. Or I am afraid my well-regarded reputation will never be the same. And, Arthur . . . neither will yours . . . ."

"What about my reputation . . . don't you care in the least what the gossips say of me?" Richard half smiled.

Anna returned the half smile and said, "The world expects such behavior from young gentlemen, Richard. But not from gentlemen of your father's stature, not openly. And never, ever from a lady such as myself . . . ."

Arthur quipped, "Go ahead, make fun of me . . ."

"Oh may I? Really Arthur? It would be such fun. Then you can make fun of me . . . and then the two of us can make fun of Richard and then . . ."

Richard, bloodshot eyes gleaming, pretended to sulk and said, "Young men like me are always being made fun of."

"Ah! Richard." Anna smiled ironically. "Young men like you? If it is worth being born at all, it certainly is for the young men of society, even those who are not half so well off as yourself. You happy-go-lucky creatures go through life sought after and invited and petted and courted. A hostess orders her best dinners for you and dresses her daughters in their loveliest gowns. The young woman? She will receive a few invitations for which she probably does not have the proper frock, while her brother, with one set of tailored dress clothes, goes through life socializing with the richest and prettiest girls, eating at everybody else's expense and having fun."

Anna looked at each man on either side of her and concluded, "To the young men, everybody opens their drawers . . . ah excuse me . . . doors . . . . And then everyone wonders why he does not marry . . . ."

Even Arthur half smiled at Anna charmingly spouting such an observation in bed with two strange bed fellows, with their hats on, at seven o'clock in the morning. He figured that any other woman, except generous and enchanting Anna, would have undoubtedly caused a scene. If Arthur had not been so stunned waking up in Anna's bed, he would have been thrilled. And if he had read of such a situation in a French novel, he would have called the book "dirty."

With regret, Aurther said, "All right, Anna . . . we'll leave."

And just as the embarrassed father and half-embarrassed son strolled into the sitting room—about to leave with their tails between their legs, not sure if they were embarrassed because they woke up in Anna's bed . . . or woke up fully clothed in Anna's bed . . . each wishing to stay and be between Anna's legs instead—they heard rapid knocking on the door. Father, son and Anna whispering "Holy Ghost!" glanced at each other excitedly. Who could be knocking at the door at seven o'clock in the morning?

Anna whispered spiritedly, "Quickly, into my bedroom. Lock the door. Don't make a sound. And don't fight!"

The men gazed lustily at Anna as she leaped, like a graceful gazelle with soft lustrous eyes, to a gilt framed mirror. She looked in the glass and almost uttered "ugh," but managed to ignore the truth and tidy her honey colored hair. Then she straightened her pale yellow silk nightgown and tied the loose golden strings of her robe. What a robe. Cascades of cobwebby old Flanders lace flowed around and behind her in an elegant train. She looked as if she had lain the night in a bed full of magical spiders, which had spun figured webs of fantasy fabric around her full form.

The insistent rapid knocking commenced again. The men reluctantly slammed the bedroom door to the lovely sight of Anna half undressed and running around.

Anna knew that Richard and, needless to say, Arthur, had never been in a predicament like this before or they would not have—slammed the bedroom door. In fact, as Anna flew to the hallway door, the luscious lace train flying behind her as if calling daintily, "wait for me," she realized excitedly that she had never been in such a predicament either. Anna took a deep breath, steadied herself, and said, as if she were greeting someone on the veranda in her most melodic sounding voice, "Good morning . . . who's there?"

A voice urgent and flat responded, "Please, Countess, I must speak with you. It is Cynthia Price."

Anna opened the door and Cynthia, red-eyed and red-nosed, all but charged inside.

"Countess, something terrible has happened."

"Cynthia, what is wrong?"

"My mother heard that Richard Anders and I are engaged."

"Well, did you tell her it is not true?"

"No . . ."

Anna sighed and heard something fall to the floor in her bedroom.

"What was that noise, Countess, coming from your bedroom?"

"I believe it came from the hallway, Cynthia. Perhaps your mother found out you came to my room and has followed you?"

"Oh no! Please let me hide in your bedroom!"

Anna's quick ruse did not work. She admonished herself for trying to get Cynthia's mind on her mother and—off the bedroom hiding Richard and Arthur.

"No . . . no, Cynthia. If your mother should come you must face her."

"I will never speak to her again!"

"Well, then you will never speak to her again . . . on my balcony. She will immediately suspect you are in my bedroom. Do you understand?"

"Yes, yes, dear Countess. Oh . . . I need your help."

"How can I help you Cynthia?"

"Convince my mother not to leave the Grand before the season is over. She overheard that conniving little coquette Belinda Gaines announce to my sister Priscilla, at the hop last night, that Richard and I are secretly engaged. That little snake Belinda—who bubbles and hisses and foams all at once, who is as effervescent as soda water and can be bought for the same price—guessed my intentions with Richard, and made up a wonderful lie I can only wish to happen by the summer's end. But MaMa says she will not allow me to to marry a race horse gambler . . . not even over her dead body. My mother never makes such trite statements . . . so I know I cannot convince her. But you might . . ."

"But Cynthia, certainly, you must tell your mother that you are not engaged to Richard Anders."

"I intend to be engaged . . . and she must get used to the idea. But it will never happen if we leave the Grand now. I could kill Belinda Gaines!" Tears of anger rolled down Cynthia's flawless dry complexion; the kind of complexion that makes youth beautiful and old age intolerable.

Again, a noise, muffled yes, but still, an indefinable noise seemed to come from the countess' bedroom. If it were not so early, and if she had not been up all night crying and coaxing her MaMa to remain for the rest of the season, Cynthia Price would have suspected that Countess Gianotti was holding something back from her, something or someone, in the bedroom. But never in her wildest imagination, would Cynthia have guessed that someone was her intended fiancé Richard Anders—and—her intended's father.

If the lighter moments of the hayride and the morning awakening had not happened and had not restored Anna's humor, she too might have shed a few compassionate tears for Cynthia's obvious loneliness. Anna sensed that Cynthia felt unwanted by any man to the point she imagined love where none existed; and Anna knew that love affairs could not be easy for the sheltered young woman, dealing with an overpowering if well-meaning mother.

Yes, those lighter joyous moments on the hay wagon, had somehow lifted the heaviness hanging upon Anna the past days since meeting Arthur again . . . and dealing with Clare Gilbertson's tragic plight. And Anna did not want to let go of those few joyous moments. She did not want them erased with yet more heartache. Wishing she had never introduced Cynthia to Richard, she felt partly responsible for Cynthia's pain. Anna wished her soggy conscience and subsequent guilt to dry up. And she longed for, perhaps, just one day of peace. Fat chance.

"Cynthia, how do you know that Richard Anders will ask you to marry him?"

"I just know it, Countess. I feel it."

"Sometimes what we think is genuine feeling, is really fleeting emotion." Anna sighed. "To me . . . feeling is like the earth itself, the grounding for the roots of our body, mind and soul. Many people do not understand this grounding, they do not even have it. To me . . . emotion is like the rain or the sun or the snow which conditions the earth. The earth is there to receive the weather. But the weather changes from day to day."

Anna sat down on a forest green settee with lion claw legs, wondering if the men in her bedroom were snickering at this little conversation, moved by it, or startled by it. Anna figured that Richard would relate with the earth and Arthur would relate with the weather.

Anna asked Cynthia to sit next to her. She continued, "Few of us are of the earth. And most of us are of the weather. I am talking very mysteriously this morning, am I not? Well, that is what happens when one tries to talk about feeling . . . an instinctive sensibility in the human being, which in this mechanical age, seems to be . . . dying.

"What you say merits thought, Countess."

Anna suppressed a smile. Really, she did not know what to say to Cynthia Price. "Cynthia, you think you feel love for Richard. But what do you think he feels for you?"

"I do not know, Countess. He certainly shows much warmth . . ."

"Like the sun?"

"Countess, I understand your point about the weather. Now please understand me. There is only one thing which holds Richard back from being an excellent match for me . . . his career as a race horse gambler . . . which is really not a career but a youthful indulgence. Do you think it would be such a price to pay if Richard gave it up for me? If I could convince him by summer's end?"

"Ah . . . I see we are no longer talking about feeling, but about matching and giving up and a price to pay . . .," interposed Anna.

"Countess . . . you are as honest with me as my mother. I thought I could come to you for a different point of view . . . a more romantic one . . . considering that you brought Richard and me together . . . ."

"Why did you really come to me, Cynthia?" Anna asked gently.

"Because you are a woman of the world . . . because most every gentleman who looks upon you, looks upon you again, seeks your company, why . . . if I may say . . . even desires you. I want to be that kind of woman. I want to stay on at the Grand. I have money of my own. I want to stay on and learn from you how to be attractive to a gentleman of today's world. My mother prevents me from attracting the kind of man I desire . . . a sophisticated man who knows how to love.

"Please. Please tell me you would chaperone me, if I should stay on against my mother's wishes. She stayed up all night packing our Crouch and Fitzgeralds and is ready to leave this morning after breakfast. Even Priscilla begged her to stay. If I could stay, perhaps, by summer's end, with your help, Richard will fall in love with me . . . as I am in love with him."

"And ask you to marry him . . . and change his profession for you. . . ."

Before Cynthia could reply to these improbabilities, there was loud knocking on the door in much the same rhythm as Cynthia's soft knocking. No wonder. It was Cynthia's mother.

"Oh no! She mustn't know I am with you! Please promise . . . please do not tell her I have come to you!"

"Out to the balcony then . . ."

Anna glided slowly, regally to the door, her Old Flanders lace flowing behind her. "Who is it?" she practically sang.

"Mrs. Price. I apologize for the intrusion at this hour . . . but it is urgent."

"Of course, Mrs. Price." Anna opened the door. "What has happened?"

"Cynthia is missing. I . . . I wondered if you had seen her?" Mrs. Price gazed about the lavish room, noting photographic pictures of Anna with the crowned heads of Europe, and noting the door to Anna's bedroom was—shut tight.

"Missing!" Why I will ring for a bellboy immediately, Mr. Hayes must be told. We must get a search party!"

"No, no, Countess," Mrs. Price looked suspicious, "You misunderstand me. We are leaving today. And I believe . . . that my Cynthia . . . would prefer to stay. She is enacting a childish prank, I am forced to admit. A prank that I had never expected from a Price. But then I never expected that a daughter of mine would not be married at the age of twenty-eight. And that the man she would finally choose to marry would be a race horse gambler."

Anna maintained her lady-in-waiting composure—in other words, a pleasing poker face—much to Mrs. Price's annoyance.

"I am referring to Richard Anders, of course. Your young friend. Countess, I had no idea when you put the two together the first time, at the grand ball, that he was a gambler. Or I would have forbidden Cynthia to dance with him the first time.

I notice you are with the handsome young man, most of the time."

Anna caught the inference in Mrs. Price's almost leveling tone. "Mrs. Price, perhaps you are unaware that Richard's father and myself were engaged to be married on this island some twenty years ago. Richard was ten at the time. I am sure you are also aware how these summer engagements disentangle practically overnight . . . ."

Mrs. Price caught the inference, (her Cynthia having suffered many matrimonial engagements that never materialized). She sniffed and nodded.

Anna continued, "You can imagine my joy in discovering Richard and his father again on Mackinac Island after all these years."

"Cynthia has mentioned all this to me. My first reaction was the emotional pain it must have caused you after all these years . . . in addition to the pain of a husband sickly and bedridden in Italy."

Anna had met her match in Mrs. Price. And the momentary lightness of the hayride and the humor of the morning awakening—Richard and Arthur half-smiling and perhaps lessening their malice towards each other, because of the comical common experience the past hours—all faded because of Mrs. Price's curt and cutting words.

"Countess . . . I must be frank. I feel you led Cynthia into the arms of this gambler. I also have my reasons why you might have done it. It has not been so long since I passed the fortieth year of my life. But to use Cynthia in the way you did I find vulgar and common."

Anna, so regal, so full of love and life, sat stunned. On top of it, a reaction came from the bedroom. A muffled sound of God knows what. She could have killed Richard and Arthur.

Mrs. Price eyed the door to Anna's bedroom—convinced that her Cynthia was hiding there.

"Mrs. Price . . . I answered my door to you out of courtesy and respect. You have entered my premises, at an hour that no friend of mine would think to impose upon me, and you have added insult to your imposition. I must ask you to leave. And I will put out of my mind this highly unpleasant conversation. I understand that your nerves are stressed due to Cynthia's absence."

"If my nerves are stressed it is because Cynthia's head is turned because of women like you. You pretend to old-fashioned manners but your minds are from untraditional molds. You live fantasy lives full of freedoms I cannot imagine functioning within. Freedoms with consequences I shudder to think upon. Not only does your type charm the men, you charm the women. Everyone seeks to act like you and dress like you . . . so sophisticated . . . so worldly. But I wonder, Countess Gianotti . . . what your life really is about . . . ."

Anna's stomach turned. Mrs. Price was a highly insightful, if old-fashioned woman. Anna wondered if Mrs. Price somehow had guessed why she was really at the Grand . . . .

Mrs. Price continued, "Especially my daughter is impressed with you and your friends. She adores and wishes to emulate women like you with all the manners of our class, and all the magnetism of women of the night. She is too young to discern your clever manipulation of language and gesture. She does not see how you build invisible walls around your vulnerability, and escape unwanted passion in your union, as Miss Belinda Gaines named it, of the Big Four."

"I beg your pardon . . ."

"The Big Four. That's what the resorters call your band of merry women."

"I see."

"I must say, Countess, that as an example to young women, you should realize your responsibility."

"And I must say Mrs. Price, that you have failed to prepare your daughter for the sophisticated life you expect her to lead."

Mrs. Price arose from the settee, marched over to the bedroom door and tried to open it.

Anna froze.

Luckily Richard or Arthur had remembered to lock the door. If they had not managed to keep still. On purpose.

"So, Countess . . . I see you have deliberately deceived me." She called, "Cynthia I know you are in there. Come out this minute. We must hurry if we want to eat breakfast before the morning ferry leaves the island."

Crash!

Mrs. Price jumped back from the door. "Cynthia! I have never known you to throw things! Come out this minute!"

Crash! Crash! Crash!

Mrs. Price whirled around, stared at Anna and uttered, "Your influence is responsible for this unseemly continental behavior."

Anna, supressing laughter and anger, replied, "Mrs. Price, your daughter is not in that room." And then Anna decided to hand Cynthia over. It was something Cynthia had said. Something about Richard having to "pay a price." It made Anna realize why Cynthia had not found the kind of gentleman she fantasized—a man capable of love. She had no idea what loving a man was about.

Since there was no future for Cynthia with Richard, Anna thought it better to end the charade no matter how disappointed Cynthia would feel. In fact, Anna wondered how truly affected the Price girl would be. And concluded that a woman of Cynthia's intelligence and rationality certainly could not have expected a worldly man, like Richard Anders, to give up his freedom as a race horse gambler and go to an office everyday for her sake.

In fact, Anna became instantly suspicious that Cynthia was really one of those women who only hunger for a man obsessively. Who really does not want her hunger satiated. Who wants to feel the miserableness of hunger pains. Who even makes sure she unconsciously causes events to prevent any real commitment to a man.

Anna saw no point in sticking her neck out in sisterly support of Cynthia and said, "Mrs. Price . . . your daughter is out on my balcony. She begged me not to tell you. I made no promises to her that I would not tell you. And . . . I apologize for misleading you when you arrived. Everything happened so fast and I have since drawn some conclusions for myself. Frankly, at this point, it is better if I do not become involved in your daughter's life, though I must admit to having become quite fond of Cynthia. And I also admit to having hoped that Richard Anders would have taken an interest in her.

Mrs. Price walked near the window to the balcony and recognized her daughter's skirt showing itself between the slightly parted curtains. Again, she looked suspiciously at the countess' bedroom door. Then she walked up to Anna.

"Pray tell . . . are you saying that Cynthia and Richard are not secretly engaged?"

"In my opinion, Mrs. Price . . . even if Richard Anders loved your daughter and wanted to marry her, he would not have given up his profession as a race horse gambler, as Cynthia would wish him to do. You see, Mrs. Price . . . your daughter's price . . . would have been too high."

Sighing in utter relief, Mrs. Price said quietly, almost apologetically, "I am leaving, Countess. I will not offer apologies for my bad behavior. I continue to feel you have misused my Cynthia in some way you may not even realize in yourself. Nevertheless, you have been honest with me now. But please send Cynthia to me. And now I must admit to you . . . my weakness. My husband warned me about bringing Cynthia to a summer resort for the sole purpose of finding a husband. I should have heeded his warning.

"As for your own husband, Countess," Mrs. Price peered at the bedroom door with a knowing look, "I can imagine the strain of caring for an invalid . . . the longings you must feel as a woman for a man with health . . . but a word of caution . . . do not be too modern, Countess . . . for you too will pay a price."

I have already, Anna said to herself as she walked Mrs. Price to the door, wondering who Mrs. Price thought was behind her bedroom door. And wondering if the father and son had heard the mother's angry words against her.

Having opened the hallway door, Mrs. Price turned to the beautiful Countess Gianotti for one long last look. Even in the morning, even under strain, the countess radiated something magnetic, something Mrs. Price could not put her finger on. Truly, the countess looked like a youngish grande dame not even fully dressed. Mrs. Price offered her hand to Anna. The countess grasped Mrs. Price's hand firmly . . . but neither of them spoke again.

After a half hour, Anna finally convinced Cynthia to return to her mother and to relinquish her love for Richard Anders. It seemed to Anna, that when Cynthia left she was somehow relieved. Almost full of childlike gaiety, happy to be going back to her mother. Anna had the feeling that pretty Cynthia Price would remain a companion to her MaMa for the rest of her life. It was a sort of mutual, unconscious pact between mother and daughter.

And out of Anna's bedroom door popped father and son, half grinning.

"Are they both gone?"

Anna smiled ironically. She wondered if the past twenty-four hours had somehow renewed a bonding between father and son, which she had remembered from twenty years past. For their faces looked relaxed and both of them . . . looked a little bit older.

Richard became serious, just for a moment, and admitted, "I never guessed that Cynthia Price wanted to marry me. Today, the young women talk about marriage even before they talk about love."

Arthur added, "Cynthia Price would have made an excellent match for you. She would have made you settle down into something respectable. Someday you will be my age, and then realize you have thrown your life away watching horses race . . . when you yourself could have felt the excitement of being in the race yourself."

"To me, life is not a race to achieve, Father. To me . . . life is sharing love." Richard gazed longingly at the enchanting woman, of old manners and new charms, with whom he dreamed to share his life and love.

Arthur as well looked at Anna, who had not responded to their remarks. As they gazed at her lovely full form and classic profile, each man started laying plans to entice her alone and completely away from the other.

Neither father nor son had any idea that their separate plans were to explode in their faces.

Yes, provincial Arthur was to shock himself. Even worldly Richard was to be stunned by what was . . . to come . . . from his illicit love for Anna.

Thinking of her invalid husband in Italy, the Countess Gianotti stared out of the balcony window. Anna's usually magnificent view of the straits, was obscured by gray fog.

"Professor Bellamy . . . good morning. Let me give you a hand."

Philmore Calhoun grabbed the old gentleman's hand and hoisted him on the yacht. "It couldn't have been too easy rowing out to *Calla* in this fog."

"Forgive my intrusion, Philmore, but Mrs. Venn did not arrive back at the hotel this morning. I fell asleep in the rotunda waiting for her. I did not wake up until an hour ago, when Nanna, after inquiring at the desk if they had seen Mrs. Venn or Mr. Froilan come in, saw me asleep in the rotunda. Nanna shook me awake telling me that Beatrice did not come back last night. Nor did Beatrice send word. Although the night clerk said he thought he saw Mr. Froilan come in. Then we knocked on Froilan's door, but no one answered. Nanna is worried sick, and the children wonder if their mother is all right. I knew I should not have left Beatrice alone with that drunken nincompoop Sydney Froilan last night."

Embarrassed, Philmore replied, "Loral, I must tell you, I do not know where Sydney and Beatrice are. You see, after we arrived on *Calla* last night . . . we . . . ah . . . went our separate ways. Please, Professor, come down to the cabin. It is possible . . . you know, that they may have stayed here.

"And Loral . . . if you should see Mrs. Clare Gilbertson . . . do not think she is any less the lady you had always thought her to be. I must tell you confidentially, that last night Clare . . . and the countess and Mrs. Venn and Mrs. Mac-Adam and Miss Shima . . . when they left the hop . . . had an experience of horror no person, especially with a female constitution, should have to endure. I am not at liberty to relate the events of last night. But as a fellow sportsman, take my word that the women need some manly comfort right now."

The old professor shook his head, wondering what mysterious horror his dear new friends, especially Beatrice, had endured. But he was still nervous that something terrible had happened to Beatrice not to have come back to the hotel . . . and not to have sent word. It simply was not like her. He even reasoned that with all the drinking last night, Sydney had seduced Beatrice and forced himself upon her at Lover's Leap . . . or inside Skull Cave . . . or near Robinson's Folly. He would not put anything past Sydney Froilan's wild and artsy nature.

Philmore led Professor Bellamy below. And sure enough, the first person he ran into was a flushed and totally embarrassed Clare.

"Professor . . ."

Old Loral Bellamy, heeding Philmore Calhoun's information about the ladies undergoing some sort of terror, looked kindly upon Clare. Contrary to his strict morality, he even overlooked what may or may not have happened between eligible Clare and eligible Philmore, between the hayride and the morning. "Good morning, Clare. You are looking well this morning."

Clare glanced at Philmore inquiringly. He shrugged his shoulders slightly.

"I . . . I slept very well last night. For the first night actually . . . in many years. I . . . am surprised to see you here, Professor . . ."

"I am most sorry to intrude upon Philmore . . . but I am looking for Beatrice. She did not come back to the hotel last night . . . either. And she did not send word. Nanna is beside herself and the children have caught on to her worry."

"But Professor . . . I have not seen Beatrice since we boarded *Calla*. I do not know . . ."

The old professor wondered if anyone really looked after anyone anymore.

Philmore spoke up against his better judgement but with consideration for Nanna and the children, "I will send one of my crew to check the staterooms. Please, Loral, come to the cabin."

"Thank you, Philmore."

Philmore led Clare, followed by Loral, through the yacht. As fate would have it, just as Professor Bellamy walked past a stateroom door, Sydney Froilan opened the door, half dressed, and the old professor caught a glimpse of—Beatrice in bed—half naked.

Sydney froze and forgot to close the door. Beatrice and the professor's eyes met. She grabbed her sheet—pulled it over her naked breasts and head—and fell back on the sofa bed in tears. She had not wanted the dear old-fashioned gentleman to know of her secret affair with Sydney. And especially not to learn of it in this shocking way. She knew the old professor would not understand her desires, her needs. Anyway, not her desires and needs—with a married man.

The old professor yelled furiously, "Close the door you idiot!" and summoning up the spirits of his youth, he grabbed Sydney's shoulders and pinned him to the wall.

Sydney tried to make light of it, "Come, come now, Professor, certainly you have indulged now and then in a little refined indoor sport . . ."

Loral kept his voice down and lambasted Sydney, "I indulged with my wife. Not a widow with two children who do not know where the hell their mother is and who are worried sick with her absence."

"Look here my good man . . . there's no harm done . . . come, come now . . ."

"Don't call me your good man," the old man released his hands from Sydney's shoulders and dropped them angrily. He stared past Sydney and uttered, "I don't understand what is happening today. I don't understand."

From beyond the door Professor Bellamy heard Beatrice in a broken voice say, "Please . . . Loral . . . please escort me back to the hotel."

Professor Bellamy answered brokenly, "I shall wait for you

on the deck." He turned to Clare and said, "If you should care to accompany us as well, for the sake of appearances, I will be waiting."

Clare turned to Philmore and smiled sadly. He kissed her bruised hand and before they parted, made arrangements to meet for tea. Clare followed the professor up to the deck.

The old man saw that Clare's hands were badly bruised as she put on her gloves. He again wondered what "horrors" the women had not been protected from.

"Professor Bellamy, please understand, that I am certain Beatrice is highly grieved for your discovery . . ."

"It is her children and their nanny who are highly grieved . . . for much better purpose than an old man's broken illusions. They will be overjoyed to know that their mother is all right. Or thinks that she is. In my day, mothers did not behave in such a fashion. Certain selfish women did. But not mothers."

"If I may say, Professor . . . in your day . . . mothers had little choice."

"In my day mothers did not run off to belong to civic women's clubs, or run to religious meetings without us, or run to feed and clothe the poor leaving us behind to be fed and clothed by paid help. Nor did they play on the stage, nor travel months at a time without us, nor the poor ones work in factories. And irony accompanies their actions as the well-off women claim great success from whatever they throw themselves into.

"Domestic chores . . . mothering . . . is an unexciting profession. But if there are no mothers mothering, daughters will never learn to be mothers. Generation after generation will suffer until, a hundred years from now, the entire fabric of family will unravel . . . ." Professor Bellamy stared down at little waves gently lapping against the yacht.

As if far away from the time in which he spoke, he added, "In my day, rich or poor, we honored our mothers as if they were queens. We felt their nearness day and night. They were like our second selves." He paused. "No, nothing can replace the absent warmth of an absent mother. Nothing."

Clare was too tired to discuss pretty remembrances she also shared of the past. She stared out into the murky fog obscuring the view of the village and the fort . . . and said nothing.

"MaMa . . . MaMa . . . can we go with 'fessor to De-e-e-e-vil's Kitchen to roast marshmallows?" Little Frederick Venn tried to sound scary.

"Freddy, it is not . . . can we go. It is . . . may we go. May we go, MaMa?" begged Monica politely. "The professor has asked us. We did not beg him."

"Beatrice . . . I have promised the little ones for weeks to take them to Devil's Kitchen by rowboat. Miss Shima and Rutherford have not seen the natural curiosity and have agreed to look after the children's safety, since I will be rowing. We would be back after sunset." In quieter tones the professor added, "You see, Beatrice, I am not sure how long I will be staying . . . and I promised the children."

Beatrice Venn could see that old Professor Bellamy had lost the spirit in his eyes. She was deeply upset that her chivalrous new friend had considered leaving early the island he so loved. She knew it had to do with his morning discovery of her on *Calla*. She blamed herself that through her actions, because of her immorality with a married man, she had somehow be-smirched Professor Bellamy's feelings about his island . . . an island he had always considered his escape from a "harsh new world."

Beatrice cursed her lack of care in not sending a note to Nanna. She cursed all men for their over-protectiveness or their under-protectiveness. She cursed Sydney for leaving the state-room when he did. But she mercilessly cursed herself for being the individual to have pushed the old gentleman, who refused to enter the new era, into the black pit of lost innocence. Especially since Beatrice felt that her new friend Loral Bellamy worshipped her, in the old-fashioned way; he put her up on a pedestal as some sort of perfect goddess madonna.

In her heart, Beatrice felt that Professor Bellamy would have died for her and the children, if fate called upon him. But never would Beatrice Venn have thought that she would have been the one to kill—his spirit.

Lowering her voice, Beatrice answered, "Loral . . . you planned on staying the season . . . the children would suffer extreme disappointment if you left three weeks before the season's end. I . . . I would suffer as well . . . I hope . . ."

He could not look directly in her eyes, as was his custom. And he thought to himself, years ago people came to Mackinac Island to cavort with nature. Now they come to cavort with each other. He said quietly, "Please, Beatrice . . . let us live a day at a time."

"Loral . . . that day . . . that 'day at a time' can some-times last years . . . years of loneliness . . . dead years of wasted youth . . . and suddenly someone comes and infuses life into a body, and spirit into a soul . . . Oh Loral . . . please reconsider leaving us . . ."

Frederick pulled Loral Bellamy's hand, " 'Fessor . . . for Pete's sake come on to the rowboat. It will be getting dark."

"Look 'Fesser . . . this dandelion has grown old like you . . . it has gray hair."

Professor Bellamy laughed for the first time that day. He picked little Frederick up and hugged him and put him down again. Then he gave Monica equal time, an affectionate squeeze around her shoulders. The old man thought of his own children, one on the east coast and one out west, both with grown children of their own.

Professor Bellamy and glowing Rutherford helped lovely Aki Shima and Monica and Frederick into a large rowboat in the waters below the Grand Hotel. They passed the sack of marshmallows and green sticks and driftwood, and a surprise bundle Aki brought along, into the big boat. Rutherford volunteered to row, but the old professor insisted that he needed some strenuous exercise. Rutherford had no idea that Professor Bellamy was purposefully rowing himself to exhaustion.

And if Professor Bellamy was not feeling bad enough, a mammoth freighter carrying iron ore, a sight he hated (a sight Philmore Calhoun loved), cut through the waters of the straits nearby.

"Look 'Fessor . . . a floating island."

Rutherford mentioned in his kindliest know-it-all voice, "Frederick that is properly called a pig . . . because they carry pig iron."

The children giggled.

Rutherford continued, "Or you can call it a whaleback. I believe that is the *J.B. Neilson* passing . . . all 308 feet of her. That pig carries some 2,300 tons of iron ore."

Again the children broke up. Aki Shima, giggling as well, covered her mouth gracefully.

Rutherford, thrilled that he made the children laugh, and wondering why he enjoyed the children's company so very much, continued, "But I like to think of the whalebacks, all blackened with coal dirt, as Moby Dick. Can you see the belly and round back and blunt nose of Moby Dick shaking the waves and nosing his way through the Straits of Mackinac?"

Little Frederick, noticing that the professor did not look

happy, tugged at Professor Bellamy's pant leg and said, "Look 'Fessor, look . . . Moby Dick is passing!"

Professor Bellamy spoke up, "I call it a monster."

Rutherford and Aki Shima sensed an anger well up in the old gentleman. For a man who refused to take trains or steamers and came to the island by horse and coach and Mackinac sailboat, it was no wonder. For the ore boats, and all they symbolized, the ugly industrialization of America, galled him every time he set eyes on them. He said to himself, sooner or later some joker will build a bridge to my fairy isle.

"My America, my home, exists no more. I cannot even escape it up here at Mackinac Island," he said sadly while he rowed too vigorously.

Why the professor wanted to escape America, his home, the children could not understand. They were too young to realize that the old professor loved his America more than most and was hopeless for its future. Then Professor Bellamy, thinking of the treeless land and raped bowels of the earth, began telling the scariest tall tale the children had yet heard from him, while he rowed to Devil's Kitchen. He made giant Paul Bunyan shrink to a midget and be buried alive in a mine shaft cave-in. The children loved his terrible sound effects and begged him to make even "creepier" sounds.

Rutherford and Aki Shima exchanged glances. Both realized that something must have happened to the usually jovial professor to disguise his bitterness this way. And for the second time in his life, Rutherford forgot himself, and thought of ways to cheer up the old professor he had become quite fond of.

The group arrived at Devil's Kitchen, located on the island's south western shoreline. To the children, the sight looked like a "mountain of spongy-like rock with little caves."

Rutherford dropped anchor, jumped out of the boat, and assisted everyone to places on the rock. He started the driftwood fire in one of the shallow caverns, and even showed the children how to roast marshmallows. Though he had never roasted a marshmallow in his life—and thought the overly sweet concoction too revolting for words.

The children loved the hot and sweet puffy treats, and thought of Belinda Gaines and all the candy she had sneaked to them . . . and all the trouble they got into because of her.

Considering that Professor Bellamy knew that Rutherford boasted he had never lifted a finger on any of his wilderness adventures from India to Africa to South America, this show of good sportsmanship from the "anglophile from out east," somewhat distracted the old gentleman from his disillusionment with Beatrice.

Regarding Rutherford, the old professor had never seen a man's personality soften so quickly. And then he figured that Rutherford Earle Haverhill V must have been one of the unhappiest and loneliest, though richest, gentlemen in America . . . until Aki Shima. Professor Bellamy wondered if Rutherford's ecstasy was a passing fancy. But the more he observed Rutherford with Aki Shima, the more he thought that for some indefinable reason, the two were like one.

And when Frederick and Monica and Rutherford and Aki encouraged the old gentleman to tell the legend of Devil's Kitchen while roasting marshmallows over the crackling little driftwood fire—its flames burning as orange as the burning sun gradually sinking in the sky over St. Ignace—Professor Bellamy's bitterness began to burn away slowly as well.

In a gentle voice the old professor began, "This place was at one time the abode of the horrible Red Gee-bis . . . the cannibal giants. This Devil's Kitchen is where they roasted men, instead of marshmallows, and ate them. Ate men . . . not marshmallows, mind you."

Ten-year-old Monica shivered. Four-year-old Frederick smiled from cheek to cheek waiting to hear something unbelievably scary.

The old professor continued, "At one time, the Indians camped upon the fairy isle of Mackinac for the summer. When they left the island for the mainland, at the time of the traveling moon, a young and beautiful granddaughter, Willow Wand, stayed behind with her dear grandfather, who was old and blind, and who had been deserted by his tribe. The old Indian told her to leave, that her young man, Kee-we-naw, would seek her out on the mainland. But Willow Wand would not leave the helpless old man. She said that she had put out a white deerskin with vermillion signs on a steep cliff. That fisherman would come along, see the deerskin, and come to their rescue before winter set in.

" 'May Git-chi Man-i-tou protect us then,' the old Indian said sadly.

"The granddaughter took her blind grandfather by the hand and led him to a cave out of sight of the Devil's Kitchen. Away from the caves of the Red Geebies, the eaters of human flesh. Suddenly, a black form moved out of the darkness of the granddaughter's deep cave. 'It is a she-bear! Perhaps I can kill it if I am quick with your bow and arrow.'

" 'No!' said the grandfather. 'Let us have peace between us and this creature. Let her stay in her part of the cave and we stay in ours.'

"Nighttime approached and Willow Wand fell asleep in their cave. The grandfather stayed up listening for any signs of danger. Before long, moans and cries of tortured captives and the horrible odor of roasting flesh was carried in the cool breezes from Devil's Kitchen to their cave. From inside the cave, the old Indian heard his granddaughter call for 'water!' in her sleep. He knew she was thirsty, for they had little water, and it was unsafe to go down to the lake. And that is when the grandfather remembered what Willow Wand's mother had told him, before she died; her girl had magical powers to bring springs of pure water from the earth.

"For seven nights, the grandfather stayed awake guarding the cave, while his granddaughter slept uneasily and cried out for water in her sleep. On the seventh night, the grandfather went into the cave during her cries and Willow Wand leaped up half asleep and struck the cave wall with her hand and cried, 'Water!' A trickling stream escaped from the rocks and they drank gladly. The grandfather told her of her magical gift. And after seven days of guarding, he finally fell asleep.

"Willow Wand stood guard while he slept and a terrible storm blackened the sky. Evil-shaped birds flew over Mackinac Island. And as the winds blew louder so did the cries from the victims of Devil's Kitchen. Suddenly from her viewpoint, Willow Wand saw her beloved Kee-we-naw being dragged into Devil's Kitchen.

"At the same time, the chief of the Red Gee-bis saw Willow Wand, and recognized her as the holder of a wand with magical powers. He tried to capture her and leaped among the cliffs until Willow Wand struck a powerful blow against a rock sending out a powerful waterfall. The rushing water struck the devil chief and carried him to the bottom of Demon's Hole.

"Willow Wand's water also put out the fires of Devil's Kitchen. While the Red Gee-bis tried to ignite their fires again, Willow Wand sent a rainbow mist that formed a bridge for her beloved Kee-we-naw to climb safely to her side. And for an entire day she worked to expel the demons from Devil's Kitchen. Most of the little devils drowned in the lake."

Frederick, looking wide-eyed at the rock upon which he sat and then out into the straits, imagined the little devils drowning.

Professor Bellamy concluded, "The next spring when Willow Wand's people returned to the summer island, they found Willow Wand and her grandfather and her new husband, Kee-we-naw, living in the cave. Throughout the winter, they had survived the cold with the firewood of the destroyed Red Gee-bis . . . formerly from this very site . . . Devil's Kitchen."

Frederick shivered. He even lost interest in roasting marshmallows where Indians had been roasted and eaten by the Red Gee-bis devils.

The old professor figured his legend must have frightened the little boy. So he quickly took something out of his pocket to distract Frederick from the story.

The children laughed with relief to hear themselves laugh.

Aki Shima smiled. Rutherford tried to hide his distaste.

For the professor had brought his singing mice along in his pocket.

"Before I will ask my little pets to sing a recital for all of you, I must receive promises from Miss Shima and Rutherford that they will not tell a soul that I have these . . . ah . . . pets with me in my hotel room. I think that Jimmy Hayes, in spite of his excellent humor, might consider them—rodents."

Aki Shima smiled. Rutherford half smiled. Both of them promised.

Professor Bellamy, becoming more jovial by the moment, announced in the fashion of a circus ringmaster, "Ladies and gentlemen. May I introduce the celebrated musical mice . . . Mousy Enrico Caruso and Mousey Nelly Melba . . . who will now sing for you," he smiled at Rutherford and Aki, "a love song as musical as a lark on a sunny summer afternoon."

The chests of the tiny mice palpitated violently while their little cleft noses moved about, as they sang little sharp notes to the rhythm, "Twit a witter, twit a witter . . .," first in forte, then in dolce piano. They sang C sharp to D to C natural to D then warbled back and forth and winded up with a quick chirp on C sharp and D.

The delighted children clapped and begged politely to hold the little furry creatures. The mice were most docile and did not wiggle out of the children's hands.

Rutherford could not believe his ears and swore up and down to himself that . . . never . . . would he have witnessed such a display in Newport. And watching Frederick's and Monica's faces, Rutherford again felt a tugging inside himself, and without warning, was awestruck by the little children's simple sweetness.

Even Aki Shima, delighted by the small creatures, asked to hold one of them.

Rutherford did not approve of having rodents as pets. Nor touching the disease carrying little pests. Nevertheless, watching Aki stroke the little mouse's head so tenderly, and hearing her say soft words of comfort to the little creature, Rutherford was, again, almost struck down by sweetness. Aki Shima's.

"Ah! I see the sun will set in about fifteen minutes. Please put the mice in my pockets. Come, everyone, we must board the rowboat." And on the way back, Professor Bellamy let Rutherford row.

It was one of those rare evenings when the southwestern waters bordering Mackinac Island were calm and greener than ever. As the boat glided through the tranquil waters, Loral Bellamy felt increasingly calmed by the gentle atmosphere. He looked through the slightly hazy air, blurring the western horizon over St. Ignace, to the setting sun. Instead of the usual orange colored fire in the sky, the sun burned red-orange. The red man's sun, he thought.

Loral Bellamy lived for such a color in the sky saluting the end of daylight. And a great peace came over the old gentleman. He remembered how he and his beloved wife had so often through their years together, shared the simple joy of a red-orange sunset on Mackinac Island. And he thought, perhaps it was high time . . . he joined her again.

Cirrocumulus clouds scattered in the sky, hot pink and orange and yellow from the sun, cast streaks of pink and ochre in the vast green waters reflecting them. The old professor felt the earth pulling way from the sun . . . and felt himself pulling away from the earth. And to himself he recited a poem of R.L. Stevenson's:

I have trod the upward and the downward slope;
I have endured and done in days before;
I have longed for all, and bid farewell to hope;
And I have lived and loved, and closed the door.

Flies flew just above water's surface . . . landing . . . now and then. Fish jumped to catch the flies . . . now and then. Fishing boats nearby barely moved in the calm waters. A single herring gull floated in the distance.

The old professor told the children not to stare directly at the sun too long. They did it anyway. And when the children looked away they saw hundreds of dark and light dots bouncing around in their eyes. It was as if teeny weeny black flies and white flies landed on their wet filmy eyeballs . . . and took off again.

Little Frederick smiled and said directly to the old professor, who looked so lost in thought, "The clouds look like cotton candy."

Monica dreamed aloud, "If the sun would be a big hole in the sky, and if we could somehow pass through its burning mouth, I wonder what would be on the other side?"

Rutherford and Aki exchanged smiles . . . smiles of kindred spirits and utter contentment.

Professsor Bellamy asked Rutherford to stop rowing, in order that they could all sit quietly . . . as the rare red-orange sun sank below the horizon. Strains of music from the Salisbury orchestra playing, "To an Evening Star," touched their ears.

The darkness coming upon them, Aki Shima quickly, gracefully, opened the surprise bundle.

The children "oohed and ahhed" over its contents. Aki took out five little boats with attached candles, which she had made. Rutherford lit the candles and Aki set the boats in the calm water. The children watched enchanted as the little boats with tiny flames drifted out into the now grayish green straits of twilight.

Rutherford, thinking how much his mother was going to love Aki . . . watched gentle Aki watching the little boats drifting. Little did Rutherford know that these moments . . . were to feed his soul for the rest of his life . . . and haunt him with their sweetness.

17
Fate

"How is it possible that only one week is left in the season? My, how time passes . . . ." exclaimed the resorters. And those guests on the veranda eligible (and ineligible) who had not found love, cried just a little inside themselves, and still hoped, just a little, that in one week something surprising might happen to them.

Yes, in retrospect, two weeks since the Field Day had passed faster than the time it takes to say "two weeks." And each day of a guest's life passed as fast as a playing card dealt from a deck; each day imprinted with a memory, like each card printed with a symbol.

The resorters looked back on the season, and their minds played memory after memory, like card after card—of a lively serenading party, a moonlit yacht ride, a romantic walk, a stolen kiss, an afternoon picnic, a midnight supper, an outdoor tea, a dance, another dance, and yet another dance in the casino, a german, a lecture in the parlor, an evening concert, another concert, and another concert, a hayride, a promenade on the veranda once, twice, a hundred times, a rowing to Round Island, a fishing expedition, a croquet game, a tennis match, a sailing party, a bicycle ride, a carriage drive around the island visiting and revisiting again Arch Rock, Sugar Loaf, Skull's Cave, Fort Holmes, Fort Mackinac, Robinson's Folly, British Landing, Lover's Leap—until a whole deck of memories was passed out and replayed.

Every guest on the veranda, waiting to "hear the pins drop," gossiped daily about all the love affairs and possible engagements before the season's end. And many lovestruck women and girls and gentlemen of all ages had one of the Big Four to thank for the introduction to their new love, which had usually taken place at a dance or on the veranda.

Among the celebrities who had arrived throughout the two weeks were Margaret Sangster, editor of *Harper's Bazaar*; and authoress Marion Harland; and Edith Rockefeller, the future Mrs. McCormick; and Baron and Baroness Schutzbar Milching; and P.T. Barnum's sister; and railroad magnate James J. Hill; and Pullman palace car king, George M. Pullman. And among the American queens who had arrived, there was none other than Mrs. Potter Palmer from Chicago, with her children and servants and horses and coach, scheduled to stay until the end of the season.

Although the resorters noted that Bertha Palmer had excused herself from social activities—undoubtedly "fagged out" from her role as manager of the Women's Building at the Chicago World's Fair—the "queen" had managed to stroll the veranda three times a day. And those three times were enough to be seen and discussed in detail.

For a few days after Bertha Palmer's arrival, even the usual talk about the Big Four was put on the back burner. Yes, the swagger couples and the bachelor millionaires, and the eligible millionairesses and matriarchal group members and the New Woman college girls and intellectual flirts and their beaus, and the college men and the old maids and idlers, and Old Stinkweed and crafty crackpots and transients, discussed for hours on end Mrs. Potter Palmer, queen of Chicago, instead of the Big Four.

Belinda Gaines had predicted to the matriarchal group members and their daughters in a merciless tone of voice,

"The Big Four will become old hat now that Mrs. Potter Palmer has been gracin' the Grand Hotel with her almost royal presence. Why her gems alone are only to be exceeded in this whole world by Queen Marguerite of Italy."

And since Mrs. Price and Cynthia and Priscilla had left the hotel—(the matriarchal group missed them sincerely), and were not there to refute Belinda's claim with a cool and rational rebuttal—no one else argued Miss Gaines' snotty contention.

Only a few days of intense chatter about Mrs. Potter Palmer occurred, which included gossip—about her dog collar, the one with 2,268 pearls and seven large diamonds, which she displayed at a casino dance she had attended with her son—about her sister married to a son of the President of the United States—about her biological beauty at thirty-nine years of age—about the fact that she ran the most powerful organization ever to exist among women in relation to the Women's Building at the Chicago World's Fair—about the fact that she was married to one of the richest men in the world.

But after only a few days, the subject of Mrs. Palmer came less and less to the resorters' lips. And the guests' obsession with the Big Four, somehow, grew even more.

Professor Bellamy, (who after two weeks still could not look Beatrice directly in the eye, but had decided to stay on until the season's end, not only because of his prior arrangements with meeting people all over the state of Michigan on his way back to Indiana by horse and coach, but because Frederick and Monica had begged him), figured out why the popularity of the Big Four grew even more.

The old professor thought that Mrs. Potter Palmer's crystal reputation, her genuine devotion to her family, her well-publicized deprecation of gossip and scandal and marital mix-ups, her fetish with self-control, her really all-too-perfect ladylike coolness . . . just could not compete with the mystery and aura and warmth and beauty and fun-loving spirit and open friendliness of the rich Big Four high society ladies, with a genuine countess among them.

Aki Shima had mentioned to Rutherford and the Muldoon ladies, in one of their morning chats on the veranda, that Mrs. Potter Palmer seemed like the kind of grand western woman "burdened by moral prejudice, and one who could not accept weakness in another." The old Muldoons thought this a most interesting statement coming from Aki Shima. They wondered if Rutherford, so relaxed and much less talkative, who was totally impressed with Mrs. Potter Palmer, agreed or not with Miss Shima.

Yes, only a few days after the arrival of Mrs. Potter Palmer and entourage, the Grand Hotel seasonal guests got back to some serious gossiping about what had become "our Big Four."

It was noted by hundreds of critical and admiring eyes that "our" Mrs. Clare Gilbertson and Mr. Philmore Calhoun were seen "together more often than apart." Most were "too thrilled" for "lovely" Clare and agreed that there was bound to be an exchange of solemn vows between the happy couple.

Hundreds of critical and admiring eyes judged "our" Mrs. Philippa MacAdam's portrait of Dude as nothing less than masterful, which she neared completion sitting on the veranda to everyone's utter appreciation. Many swagger gentlemen had offered to buy the painting of Dude from Philippa for great sums, but she turned them down.

Philippa informed them that Colonel Marshe Williamson had expressed interest in the portrait before he had left (and promised to come back). She did not inform them that the colonel had told her, on the hay wagon, that it was "due to Dude" that they had discovered each other. Nevertheless, Philippa received so many commissions to paint portraits of resorters' favorite horses, she would not be able to complete half of them in five years.

Hundreds of critical and admiring eyes, by season's near end, still had not come unglued from "our enchanting" Countess Elizabeth Anne Gianotti. If anything, the countess was sought after by every group more than ever, and she joined most of them for their invitations morning, noon, and night. No matter how much she would have rather said no.

When the countess was seen with Clare and Philmore and Philippa and Beatrice and Sydney and Rutherford and Aki, and sometimes Professor Bellamy, on the veranda for the nightly concert, the guests noticed that Richard Anders and his father were constantly on either side of her.

The lancet-tongued old maids had been sure there was some sort of rivalry between father and son over the countess' attentions—until the countess herself had brought up the subject to them of her sickly Count Gianotti in Italy. The old maids, with their natural curly fake bangs and necks as long as salt cellars, loved speaking of illness rather than love affairs. From then on, the lancet-tongued old maids were not suspicious about what they heard was an "old island friendship" among father and son and Anna.

They even ignored Old Stinkweed when he had said to them, "Father and son are hankering after the same married woman. Humph." Little passed the armchair voyeur's attention. Never was so much seen by an old man who slept on the veranda most of the day . . . with one eye open and his tight shoes off.

In fact, not only had Anna kept herself busy with invitations, she even agreed to be honorary chairwoman of "Reminiscences of the Midway Plaisance"—an early evening lawn fete conceived by Jimmy Hayes, fashioned after the Midway Plaisance at the world's fair, to be held on the last night of the season followed by a fancy dress ball. Countess Gianotti had agreed to organize the lawn fete, which included designing tableaus depicting various nations, overseeing the painting of scenery, and signing up resorters to participate. Tickets were isssued for the costume ball, and the money collected was to be donated as "appreciation from the guests to the Grand Hotel help" (maids and waiters and cooks etc.) for their fine summer services.

Anna was so busy organizing the "Reminiscences . . ." that she made sure she had little time for either Richard or Arthur. Anna reasoned that less time spent with the two men, in spite of her own longings to feel "something of family" with them, would cool down the passions of father and son—and herself. It didn't.

Anna's reasoning was as off as cow's cream left on the cupboard for a week. If anything, to Richard and Arthur, the momentary nearnesses to Anna at night on the veranda, her wit and charm and freshness, so close, had built up their longings for her even more. After Anna insisted, father and son were even less spiteful to each other. In other words, there were no further slugfests between them, since neither of them had as yet lost Anna. But Richard had not moved back into his father's cottage. And his father would not have wanted him back. Not yet. For that night, among two weeks of nights, once again, Richard was to appear at Anna's hotel room door. And Arthur was to invite Anna to his cottage.

Yes, Anna skillfully avoided a confrontation with Richard and Arthur—until the fancy dress ball.

In the two weeks that passed, "our" Mrs. Beatrice Venn's portrait, repainted ten times, had finally been completed by Sydney Froilan and appraised by hundreds of critical eyes. They all wondered why Mr. Froilan needed so many sittings with Mrs. Venn.

Sydney had answered them, "I must capture Mrs. Venn in a free study that requires many sittings . . . she does not look the same each time. You see it is not only the characteristics of her face I must capture, but her spirit as well."

But the truth was that he repainted Beatrice over and over again because of her accusations, her challenge, after she had seen her finished portrait one night. Before lovemaking. She had declared, "Sydney, you have a fetish for the female figure. You paint a woman as you would paint an ikon. You paint a symbol of the ideal female form rather than a real woman. You create nothing but superfluous creatures. You do not know what a woman is . . . ."

Not surprising, there was no lovemaking that night between Sydney and Beatrice. Sydney could not have—done it—if he had wanted to.

Among the veranda crowd, the collective opinion formed that Mr. Froilan had not captured "our" Mrs. Venn's beauty. That the portrait did not do her justice. That her face was out of proportion. That her eyes looked too sad. But then few had noticed, other than her Big Four sisters and Professor Bellamy and Rutherford Haverhill and Sydney Froilan, that after the "never to be forgotten" Field Day, (after Professor Bellamy's shocking discovery on *Calla*), Beatrice Venn's eyes had, indeed, a slightly vacant look.

Yes, the veranda guests saw the "exquisite" Beatrice they had come to adore, as she was the first five weeks of the season . . . full of appetite and expression and experimentation.

World famous Sydney Chase Froilan took all the criticism that day about Beatrice's portrait in stride. As a man of the world should. Because he realized the veranda crowd wanted an ikon, an idealized portrait of their Mrs. Venn. And Sydney forgot the origin of the idea and made it his own.

"Froilan . . . I see you have finally finished Beatrice's portrait." Rutherford's expert eye caught every detail of the painting and he sniffed.

"Isn't it quite obvious, Haverhill."

"It is most unlike your usual style, Froilan. I imagine that is because it was not painted under the usual circumstances."

"Shut up, Haverhill."

"I only meant . . ."

"I do not care what you meant."

Rutherford gazed at Aki Shima on his arm.

Sydney Froilan looked, almost enviously, at what he thought was their, almost smug, happiness together.

"Look Froilan, let me say this, and I will leave. I have seen many of your portraits, frankly ad nauseum, in most of the society sitting rooms I have entered in America and abroad. Whenever I have seen your work I say . . . there is Sydney Froilan . . . not there is so and so, the sitter for the portrait. But with this painting, Froilan . . . for what it is worth . . . I say . . , there is Mrs. Beatrice Venn . . . and . . . Beatrice's soul." Rutherford looked directly into Sydney's eyes and concluded in his most anglophiliac voice, (a voice which did not in the least bother Aki Shima, able to accept other's weaknesses), "Excuse us . . . Sydney."

If Rutherford Haverhill had not forgiven Sydney Froilan—for publishing the insulting cartoon depicting him as an American anglophile in Paris wearing cowboy boots, which resulted in an unforgivable insult when his dearest aristocratic English friend winked at his French enemy—Rutherford had thanked him. Through the highest compliment he had ever bestowed upon a contemporary portrait painter. He had, without saying it, called Sydney Chase Froilan a first-rate artist.

The reason Rutherford thanked Sydney was because if it had not been for Sydney's cynical cartoon, the incident in Paris never would have happened—that caused Rutherford to leave Paris early for the Chicago World's Fair—and subsequently travel to Mackinac Island. No, without Sydney Chase Froilan, Rutherford never would have met his first real love, Aki Shima. In fact, what Sydney, the Vermont farmboy turned world famous, sketched four years ago—was to be the catalyst for what was to happen to the rest of Rutherford Earle Haverhill V's life. The entire remaining life of the richest man in America from the oldest family.

For the past two weeks, every member of the veranda had gossiped daily about the love affair between the "easterner" and the "far easterner." Why, some days the Japanese woman received as much attention as the Big Four themselves. The matriarchal group concurred that if "anything came of it," meaning marriage, the children would undoubtedly have slanted eyes. The crafty crackpots argued, with total agreement, that the oriental was a shrewd business woman after Rutherford's money. The "You'll be damned if you play cards on Sunday" group found out that Aki was a Buddhist, and disapproved of a Christian man falling in love with a "pagan."

The New Woman and intellectual flirt college girls were thrilled with the western-eastern romantic alliance between Rutherford Haverhill and Aki Shima. They saw the relationship as "true love" because it was "so unlikely." They figured that since Aki Shima was from a culture that was "as yet founded on human relations, rather than relations to the stock market," it was possible for such "true love" to blossom overnight with such a person from such a culture.

The college men did not analyze the love affair like their female counterparts. They only wondered what exotic love-making the oriental may have introduced to Rutherford.

Belinda Gaines, who wished to be seen frequently strolling

the veranda on the arm of Rutherford—in spite of her love affair with the millionaire from Hot Springs, Arkansas—was prevented from doing so because of Aki. So Miss Gaines spread rumors that the Japanese was really a woman of the night, a geisha; in Belinda's uninformed malicious mind, a prostitute.

But they all came to the same conclusion that Rutherford had changed perceptibly since the beginning of the season because of Aki Shima. In what way they were not quite sure. Until the Mesdames Muldoon pointed out that he smiled more. Then everyone agreed that Rutherford's looks had changed as well. They even noticed that he possessed beautiful teeth. As a matter of fact, seeing his teeth for the first time was quite startling to the guests. For it changed Rutherford's looks considerably.

But no matter what their opinion, most every member of the veranda treated Aki Shima with warm respect. After all, when she was not with Rutherford, she was with the Big Four. Even Aki's embroidery in the parlor had sold out the past two weeks. A matriarchal group member had seen the countess and Mrs. Venn and Mrs. Gilbertson and Mrs. MacAdam purchase one piece each. After that, Aki had received so many orders for her embroidery, she could not have personally filled them in three years.

Truly, Aki Shima, with no attachments left in her world, had never been so happy in her life. She floated through those glorious Mackinac summer days, like a lighted candle in a buoyant vessel upon the waters during the O-Bon festival; a magical Japanese festival when departed ancestors who have returned to earth are sent back to the netherworld in symbolic, lighted little vessels on the water.

Aki floated until Rutherford . . . having relieved himself of his happiness . . . having written to his beloved mother in

Newport about falling in love with Aki . . . and his intention to marry her . . . received a second fateful letter regarding his intentions . . . .

August 1893

Dearest Ruthey,

Will you not accept our firm reply to your revelation of love and intention to marry? Think long and hard before you make a final decision that will adversely affect the lives of those you hold most dear. Your father simply will not hear of a marriage that will produce slant-eyed grandchildren. I cannot believe that your children would be brought up as true Christians, since you have clearly and honestly stated she is a devoted Buddhist. My dear, it seems to us that your love has blinded you to the considerations of your future and ours.

You have caused your father sleepless nights. He has even implied to me, in the privacy of our moments, a complete disinheritance. My dear, please, reconsider these rash impetuous threats of marriage. We have always known you to be a clear-headed and logical son who would someday take over leadership of the family money from your father. We cannot rely on your spendthrift brother to settle into a responsible position. And now we read that you appear to have lost, in a mattter of weeks, all that we trusted in you.

My dear, would it not be wise to enjoy your time with this undoubtedly lovely creature, perhaps for the remainder of the summer season, and then return to New York. Alone. Your father would like you to begin to attend his office on a regular basis.

You must agree that we have allowed you much freedom of expression and financial freedom from the daily cares and challenges of Wall Street. Now it is time for you to settle down with a woman of our type and background. We look forward to grandchildren before we are too old and feeble to enjoy them. It is time that you pass on your personal freedom and enjoyment to your sons.

Believe me, my dear son, no female from a far eastern culture, from the other side of the world, can fulfill the needs and expectations of a male in our special society right here at home. After the blossoms of love have faded, you will find yourself locked in a relationship of cultural conflicts. You are not such a young man who cannot easily get over a summer infatuation. You have had so many infatuations before, that you should certainly realize the symptoms and know the cure.

I beg you to reconsider. If this marriage should occur, your fortune to inherit and our special relationship shall have no recourse but to wither and die. And that, dear son, shall for certain be the death of me.

Your grieving,
Mother

After reading his dear mother's devastating letter, Rutherford, stunned and torn with anguish, forgot his observation that the pale fawn envelope, thick in texture with a smooth, soft finish, was not stamped with a postmark on the front. It was the only letter from his mother that entire summer season—he did not read to the Muldoons.

The veranda crowd observed that the Big Four and, of all people, Mrs. Vivian Larron, were assisted into old Owen Corrigan's carriage by a young coachman.

"Go lang, Charley."

The guests had not seen Mrs. Larron for two weeks, ever since her accident in the hurdle jumping competition. They figured she had hurt herself and left the Grand Hotel quietly. Now they surmised, she had been quietly recuperating at the Grand Hotel. But the big question, that particular minute, on every guest's mind was why the distinguished group of four ladies was associating with that "parvenue." If they had known the truth—and other "truths" about the Big Four—they would not have believed any of them.

In fact, Mrs. Larron had been "watched," out of sight, for two weeks. Until negotiations between the Big Four and the little muslim Ibrahim G. Kheiralla could be finalized.

"Whoa, Charley."

Owen helped each of the ladies, and Mrs. Larron, out of the carriage in front of the quaint Island House hotel. But not without his customary joke.

"Leddies, I must tell ye, one fine day me and ol' Charley met a portly ledy, broader than a sugar barrel brimmin' with bricks, on the Cadotte Avenue hill leadin' up to the Grand palace. Her bumbershoot had to be three times wider 'an the next ledy. She must 'ave weighed nigh 350 pounds. She between huffin' and puffin' asked me, 'Will ye take me up the short distance to the Grand for ten cents?' And I answered her, 'Ach ya, me dear ledy. Ten cents a hunderd.' "

The countess and Beatrice and Clare and Philippa laughed heartily. Although Mrs. Larron found it funny, she did not laugh. She was too nervous wondering what was in store for her.

Gracious Mrs. Rose van Allen Webster, proprietress of the Island House, who remembered Anna from the ten summers her family had stayed at the hotel, greeted the Big Four warmly upon arrival. Then she led the four ladies and Mrs. Larron to Ibrahim's suite.

Little Ibrahim, smiling his oiliest smile, opened the door to the sitting room. A waft of shisheh smoke slightly blurred the eyepopping scene, and each woman's heart beat bellydance rhythms. For perched crosslegged and perpendicular to a light filled window, his ample body flashing sunstruck jewels, sat the bedazzling Shah of Harremajarra; a breathing confection of splendor.

The regal shah sat boldly upright upon a large yellow silk

pillow, upon a raised platform, upon a silk oriental carpet. Sun rays played upon his magnificent purple silk turban some fifty yards long, adorned with sparkling sprigs of rubies and diamonds and a rare emerald. Sun rays heated his dark ears, bored and adorned with large gold rings, and touched the shiny pearls, as big as marbles, hanging from his neck in two long strands of white pearly drops, bearing a cluster of glistening diamonds.

Sun rays brightened his persimmon silk caftan, which covered puffed trousers of purple muslin, tied on the right with a purple sash. Sun rays warmed his dark feet decked in leather shoes, really persimmon slippers turned up in a sinuous arabesque to a long point at the toe. Sun rays bounced off gold armlets and gold bracelets studded with emeralds, and off gold rings bearing topaz and turquoise and tourmaline on his fingers . . . flexuous fingers there for what but to feel female flesh . . . his arms and wrists and hands seeming like dummy appendages serving only to show off such extravagant wealth.

The shah peered at the four beautiful ladies, and the one stunning Mrs. Larron, dressed in tailored outing costumes. But he did not get up. If he had thought to rise in the western fashion, which he did not, the fifty-yard turban, out of balance with the movement, would have fallen off his bald black-bearded head.

Ibrahim seated the Big Four separately from Mrs. Larron.

He spoke in Arabic to the shah, who smiled at all of them vaguely. Then it occurred to the countess that she had seen the shah's face somewhere before. And it came to her that he was at the Grand Hotel's Field Day hop, dressed in plain western clothes, and accompanied by Ibrahim.

At the hop, Anna thought the shah was just another Islamic, whom Ibrahim had probably picked up at the Chicago World's

Fair. The Midway Plaisance was crawling with them. Truly, the Shah of Harremajarra was traveling—incognito. And never in her wildest daydreams would Anna have imagined such a sight as the resplendent shah, in Rose van Allen Webster's modest Island House hotel, on homey Mackinac Island. It was downright disconcerting.

Ibrahim would have taken all day in the negotiations if the countess had not handled him with firmness. And within two hours' time, after much haggling between the two of them, Mrs. Vivian Larron had been bought by the shah for $40,000 in gemstones.

In addition, Anna asked one "favor" of the shah, which was sure to be a surprise joke on Jimmy Hayes. The shah, blessed by Allah not only with wealth and fifty women, was also blessed with a sense of humor. He promised to cooperate with the countess when the time came to enact the "favor."

Beatrice and Clare and Philippa, awestruck with the shah and the countess' creative and diplomatic abilities, tried to refrain from smiling when Ibrahim concluded the negotiations in dead seriousness with, "Countess Gianotti, the shah wishes me to ask you, how much would it take to buy you . . . he would rather have you."

Anna smiled regally and quipped, "His kingdom."

Ibrahim relayed the countess' answer to the shah.

The shah, with piercing gleaming eyes, the kind that strip a woman bare with her clothes on, smiled and stated in a deep tone, in English, "Done."

Suddenly, the cavalier smiles of Anna and Clare and Beatrice and Philippa faded, and they quickly rose and politely took their leave. The whole unseemly situation had gone too far even for the sophisticated Big Four. But before they left, they saw Mrs. Vivian Larron being led into the shah's bedroom.

The four ladies caught a strong whiff and stole a long look beyond the bedroom door. Perfumed and jeweled harem wo-men with artificial moles and juice tinted feet, reclining in layer upon layer of rustling light silks, and caftans glinted with gold thread and glistening with bright silk embroidery, with veils draped over their black hair, smoked shisheh with the windows open to a picturesque view of the crescent shaped harbor.

Beautiful prisoners of a polygamous animal, Anna thought. A humane place for pitiable Mrs. Vivian Larron, prostitute since the age of ten, who by all standards should have been put behind bars in prison. But who was now a beautiful prisoner for life in the Shah of Harremajarra's harem.

Anna and Philippa and Beatrice felt utter relief knowing that Clare would never be blackmailed again by the dangerous Mrs. Larron. They felt somewhat avenged for Clare's sake, knowing that she had received $40,000, almost one quarter of the money Mrs. Larron had blackmailed from her. They felt comforted for Clare, knowing that no one else would ever hear about the Gilbertson scandal. And most importantly, they felt lighthearted, knowing that Clare could put her head to her pillow at night . . . for the first time in some five years . . . in peace.

Clare, exhausted, simply did not feel anything.

But the Big Four's lightheartedness was to last exactly two minutes. For when they passed a suite at the end of the hallway, as fate would have it, a door once again opened to a scene of surprise.

"Mrs. Venn?"
"Mrs. Haverhill?"
It did not take long before the Big Four and Mrs. Haverhill IV, yes, Rutherford's rich and old money mother who could have been a sister to the Muldoons, were having tea together in

her sitting room; the service overseen by Mrs. Rose van Allen Webster herself.

No wonder Rutherford had received his mother's letter without a postmark. The aristocratic white-haired lady, in her late sixties, had secretly traveled to Mackinac Island with a maid and a footman. And up to that moment, only the proprietress of the Island House hotel knew Mrs. Haverhill IV's real name.

A few hours before, when Mrs. Haverhill had observed five exceedingly fine ladies exiting Owen Corrigan's carriage, she she had said to herself that no true lady would be seen in such a dilapidated vehicle . . . and then recognized Mrs. Beatrice Venn climbing out of it. After immediate inquiries, Mrs. Haverhill found out that Mrs. Venn was one of four society queens up at the Grand Hotel—the hotel where Rutherford had fallen in love with the "foreigner."

And then Mrs. Haverhill had asked to be told when the four ladies would be leaving the hotel room of "whoever it was" they had come to visit. But Mrs. Rose van Allen Webster, a discreet lady always, would not tell Rutherford's mother whom the Big Four were visiting. But she did knock on Mrs. Haverhill's door . . . after the four ladies left the shah's suite at the other end of the hallway.

No, Mrs. Haverhill, of New York and Newport, did not let on to the four ladies sharing tea, that she was in a desperate state regarding her Rutherford and the Japanese woman. Mrs. Haverhill was sure that the foreigner was after her son's extravagant wealth. And in her desperate state she would use even Mrs. Beatrice Venn—a "divorcee" and really "quite fallen out" of the highest echelon of New York society these days—to help her.

"What a delightful view you have of the harbor, Mrs. Haverhill."

"Yes, Mrs. Venn. It is quite something."

Mrs. Haverhill IV hated the delightful view. She hated the hustle and bustle and noise of steamship whistles. What invigorated most people drove her nerves to rattle. Although the hotel was most accommodating with excellent service and food, she would rather have been in her own cottage in Newport. All twenty-five rooms of it. And on her own grounds—private—which stretched to the sea. Mrs. Haverhill IV admitted, only to herself, that it was dull in Newport. But it was a dullness of her own making. She could not take excitement unless it was of her own making.

The five ladies discussed mutual friends and acquaintances in America and abroad. Then it did not take long for exquisitely polite Mrs. Haverhill to get to the point, after learning that the four women had associated often with her son and the "Japanese woman in question." Nor did it take long for Mrs. Haverhill to judge Mrs. Beatrice Venn's lovely friends as high society ladies who could probably be trusted to keep her presence at the Island House hotel a secret from her son, for the time being.

"Mrs. Venn, may I ask, do you know Miss Shima very well?"

Beatrice answered for everyone, "We have known Aki Shima on a first name basis for some time, Mrs. Haverhill. And in that time, we have passed many pleasant and meaningful hours together."

The Big Four exchanged loaded glances thinking of the night of the Field Day . . . at Crack-in-the-Island.

Clare added, "She is graceful and kind hearted and lovely to look upon."

"I must confess that I am so interested in the far east. Along with Rutherford, I have quite a collection of Japonaise objets d'art. I have also heard that Miss Shima is skilled with the needle."

Philippa, catching the slightly demeaning tone in an otherwise amicable Mrs. Haverhill, added politely, "Aki is considered masterful by all who see her embroidery."

"I see. Is it possible that one of you could arrange an introduction for me to Miss Shima? I would be so delighted to meet her. Ah . . . would it be possible . . . that you would keep my name a secret from her, for the time being. You see, Rutherford intends to be engaged to Miss Shima. And I cannot judge the foreigner objectively if I do not have a chance to observe her in public."

Beatrice and Anna and Philippa and Clare exchanged loaded glances once more. They realized that Rutherford and Aki were smitten by love at first sight, but never would they have guessed that Rutherford intended to marry her. Yet, they thought Mrs. Haverhill IV's request a reasonable one and decided to comply with it.

Beatrice answered, "A group of us are gathering for a picnic tomorrow at one o'clock in a meadow near Early Farm. Aki will demonstrate how to put on a kimono. She has many with her and the four of us and some college girls and their MaMas have volunteered to model them. She will also teach us to dance. There will be some seventy-five ladies, girls and children there. You would not stand out, Mrs. Haverhill. I shall write down the directions for you. If you would care to join us."

"What a lovely idea," answered Mrs. Haverhill hesitantly. She hated picnics and thought, all those flies and ants and bees to contend with . . . all that is lovely about alfresco eating is the idea. Whenever Mrs. Haverhill ate outside, out of sheer kindness to her dearest friends with "predilections for pastoral fantasies," she would suffer dyspepsia and could not sleep the entire night after the affair. She asked, "Will gentlemen be invited?"

"It is an affair Jimmy Hayes has arranged just for the female resorters."

"I imagine there is much interest among the gentlemen regarding this Japanese woman . . . ."

The Big Four thought this a strange statement.

Philippa said cautiously, "I find that most everyone is interested in someone from a culture unlike their own."

"It is unfair to these exotic creatures to be used as objects of curiosity. I hear that the Midway Plaisance at the fair is like a zoo," said Rutherford's mother with emphasis.

The countess, beginning to regard the little accidental tea with Mrs. Haverhill suspiciously, purposefully countered Mrs. Haverhill's disguised insult; that the foreigners were nothing more than circus animals. Anna spoke up, "I visited the Midway Plaisance every day for a week . . . I found it fascinating. The people of foreign lands seemed to find us as interesting as we found them. Of course, I went through the Plaisance disguised as a man. With the Princess Eulalia. But I did not go so far as to smoke cigars. Though the princess must have smoked a hundred of them."

Mrs. Haverhill stared at the countess, totally unable to relate to such actions. In her day a woman would have been shunned by society as the result of such unladylike actions. But somehow, that Anna was a countess and roamed around dressed like a man with the Princess Eulalia, the Infanta of Spain no less, the toast of the world's fair, Mrs. Haverhill found it in herself to dismiss the startling revelation. She even wondered if the countess said this intentionally to shock her. Mrs. Haverhill decided not to think upon it again. Besides, she thought, this Countess Gianotti might come in handy.

After a short discussion about the natural curiosities on Mackinac Island, which Mrs. Haverhill pretended to be interested in, she asked the ladies to greet her as Mrs. Seward at the picnic.

Then the Big Four took leave of . . . Mrs. Seward. They were to regret this tea for the rest of their lives.

A day later, Mrs. Haverhill, disguised with the name Mrs. Seward, arrived at the Island House after the picnic near Early Farm with a heavy heart, and wrote immediately to her husband. While she wrote she could not get out of her mind the sight of pretty Aki Shima, with a disposition of sunshine and a smile of goodwill, playing the shamisen, while the countess and Mrs. Venn and Mrs. Gilbertson and Mrs. MacAdam danced with fans in the beautiful kimonos among the wild-flowers, in the way Aki had taught them to dance.

August 1893

Dearest,

My prayer is that you are feeling well again and sleeping at last. I am not sleeping and suffer much dyspepsia.

By sheer coincidence, too lengthly to explain in this letter, I accidently met that divorcée, Mrs. Beatrice Venn. Remember her? With your eye for beautiful ladies, I doubt if you could have forgotten her if you had wanted to. It was through Mrs. Venn I met the foreigner, Miss Shima, at a picnic. Yes! I had to endure eating out of doors. One lady's hat was dirtied by a black bird. She laughed and made the least little thing of it. These westerners. What to make of them. Oh, how I detest picnics.

But as a result of this affair, I have spent an afternoon with the Jap. Mrs. Venn introduced me as a Mrs. Seward. Once or twice I forgot myself, and did not answer when she addressed me by that strange name. Most distressing, as you can imagine. I think the other ladies thought me deaf. Except for some lovely ladies by the name of Muldoon, who confided to me that my accent was most pleasing to them and reminded them of a gentleman from out east, from New York and Newport, who spoke just like me. Can you imagine dearest, they were referring to our Rutherford! Such a small world. Such a nice compliment.

With much sorrow I must report to you, my dear, that the oriental is sweet in nature, beautiful in a foreign sort of way, altogether pleasing to speak with, and wise for her thirty years of age. Too wise. I believe she is a shrewd oriental business woman. And in that time, I learned how she will needed to be handled.

Really, it is all too dreadful what I must do. I am becoming too old for these rescue missions for the sake of the family. And my Rutherford was the last person I would ever have dreamed to place me in such a distasteful predicament. Where did I fail with him.

Anyway, I will do what I have to do tonight. I have invited the Japanese woman here on pretext of an order for embroidery. She appeared very happy to comply with my request. I admit finding this strange. For if she is only after Rutherford's money, why would she continue to take orders like a common shopgirl for embroidery? I simply do not understand the women today.

A Countess Gianotti, whom I have met, took me aside this afternoon and told me that Rutherford "appears to have found an exquisite happiness with Miss Shima." She added, "Like Rutherford, Miss Shima's life is discipline and art. And if marriage should be founded on sympathy of cultivated perceptions and consequent enjoyments, then Rutherford and Miss Shima should be married." I was moved by the countess' words and by the rapt way she had spoken them. In fact, I wondered if she would keep her promise and not tell Rutherford that I am here. I fear she suspects my motives. She appears a highly instinctive sort of sophisticated woman. And extremely well-liked, I must add. Why, the ladies at the picnic seemed to worship the very ground she walked on.

Nevertheless, I thought to instruct her, that to people of our position there is far more to consider in life than personal, selfish happiness. Then she informed me, in quite a grand way, mind you, that she has lived beyond this consideration of personal happiness her entire adult life. And now she believes that "position is a curse."

I was astonished to hear such a comment coming from a countess. But then she had also disguised herself as a man and walked through that Midway Plaisance at the Columbian Exposition. Imagine! When I think on it, I must question if an opinion from such a woman can be taken seriously. I can only think she is one of those ladies who fancies herself a New Woman.

I will take dinner now, my dear, so as I will not be eating when the foreigner arrives. My heart aches but, as you had so aptly put it at the train station, we must preserve our son's future. And yet, dearest, lately I must confide to you that I ponder if we are preserving a future, or a past.

With all my love,

Margaret

P.S. I must mention that the train takes only twenty-four hours from New York to Chicago. Such speed is quite incomprehensible to me. I am also reminded of the last words Cornelius Vanderbilt said to us a month before he died. Do you recall dearest that he was president of the Grand Hotel here on the island? He said, "You must go to Mackinac Island and see where the Astor fortune was built." This ensuant irony is galling. To think I should come here, not to see where the new Astors' fortune was built by Frenchmen and Indians—but to see where the old Haverhill's future might have been torn down by a Japanese foreigner.

Aki Shima entered Mrs. Haverhill's room and bowed.

"Good evening, Miss Shima. Thank you so much for coming."

"I am honored that you have asked me, Mrs. Seward."

Rutherford's mother flinched ever so slightly. "Please, Miss Shima, come and sit down beside me."

Aki took out the last piece of embroidery—an elaborate piece she wouldnot sell, but which she showed as an example of her abilities—from a satchel. The same satchel she had carried Mrs. Larron's letters and the . . . glass jar . . . to Crack-in-the-Island.

"Why this piece is truly masterful. I had no idea you were this gifted. I would like to buy this from you."

"Thank you for your most generous compliment. I am so sorry, Mrs. Seward, but I cannot offer this piece to you."

Mrs. Haverhill fliched again.

Aki noticed that the lady, who reminded her ever so much of the Muldoons except for her accent, was extremely nervous and figured she suffered from an extreme case of Americanitis.

"But Miss Shima, I am willing to offer you a great deal of money for it. I have quite a collection of Japonaise objets d'art, but nothing to match the design and skill you display here. Certainly you must be in need of money. Are you not?"

Aki thought, in Japanese, what lack of civility this Mrs. Seward displays. Aki had been told that this lady fared as an oligarch of New York society. Yet she lacked cultural sophistication. The woman's questioning was so direct. Even the tone was offensive to her ears. She figured that Mrs. Seward was nouveau riche.

"Mrs. Seward, I would be most happy to fashion a similar

piece for you. But I completed this piece at the time of my mother's death. She honored me so in her praise that I . . ."

"I offer you ten thousand dollars for it."

Aki gasped and covered her smiling mouth with her hand. She thought, only a rich American would be so cavalier about money. "Mrs. Seward, I humbly thank you for such a compliment. But if I would sell one similar to this, I would kindly ask five hundred dollars and no more."

Mrs. Haverhill realized that she was not going to be able to buy Aki Shima. She said to herself, what then is ten thousand dollars to a woman who stands to gain millions through marriage to my Rutherford. But she gave it one more try. "Miss Shima, I am willing to go as high as twenty thousand, but no more."

Aki began to wonder if Mrs. Seward was in her right mind, until the lady got up and came back with a photograph. Aki gasped yet again. Her prince, her Rutherford stood next to Mrs. Seward . . . .

"Yes, Miss Shima . . . I am Rutherford's mother."

Aki immediately fell noiselessly and gracefully to the floor. At one fell swoop. Beaten, cut, knocked down. And bowed till her face met the rug.

Mrs. Haverhill turned red with embarrassment. In a quiet, demanding tone of voice she told Aki to get up from "that lowly position."

Stunned at such coarse behavior, Aki could not move.

Lowering her voice in a sort of inverted yell, Mrs. Haverhill demanded, "My goodness girl . . . get up! We do not grovel before each other like this in America. It is unseemly. Undemocratic."

Aki forced her body into an upright position, but instinctively stayed on the floor.

Mrs. Haverhill, feeling "armored" because of a quick read through of Ottiwell's *History of Japan*, thought there was no

point in delaying any longer what she had to do. She understood that there were no absolute morals in Japan, and she
would hit upon the young woman with this ammunition.

"My son has informed me that you have chosen to climb
our genealogical tree."

"I am sorry I do not understand."

"Ah, but you do. Perhaps not the words. But the concept you
understand perfectly. You have indulged my son and flattered
his considerable pride. In my opinion, your relationship with
my son hints of a salacious nature."

"I am so sorry, I do not understand."

"Salacious . . . it means lascivious."

Aki desperately tried to follow Mrs. Haverhill's words and
their meaning.

"Licentious . . . .Lecherous . . . .Lustful!"

"Ah . . . I understand. Mrs. Seward . . . ah . . . many
pardons . . . Mrs. Haverhill . . . I have been most kind in my
affections to your son. You need not think that I have been
selfish. The water has been raised."

"Water? You misunderstand me, Miss Shima."

"Forgive me. But it is you who misunderstands me, Mrs.
Haverhill."

Aki Shima said this with such extreme politeness that
Rutherford's mother sensed the Japanese had insulted her. She
spoke gravely, "You have no God and no morals. You come
from a people who act from obedience to authority, not from a
religious viewpoint. How do you expect to enter a society
founded on the belief in God and built with the structure of
religion. I wonder that you have not thought of these practical
obstacles to your future with a man of Rutherford's stature.
No, how could you. You have known Rutherford less than a
month."

"Future . . . with your son . . ."

"Do not play the innocent oriental with me. Do not deny he

has not stated or inferred very strongly his intentions to marry you."

Mrs. Haverhill observed Aki Shima slump, ever so slightly. She peered at the Japanese woman, who stared at the floor as if in a trance.

Stunned at the news that Rutherford actually intended to marry her, Aki heard her heart beating like five kodo drums pounded in unison. Never would she have dared to dream such a dream. Out of the open window, Aki's spirit flew with the speed of wind, over the village, and up to the hotel where she knew Rutherford was playing croquet with Frederick and Monica and the Muldoons. Her spirit fell to Rutherford's feet and thanked him for this honor. His spirit lifted her. Embraced her. And they melted into one.

And as Rutherford's mother peered at the Japanese, she had to admit that Aki's personality and atmosphere and hands and face and hairdo and kimono were a synthesis of aesthetic cultivation. She suspected that the young woman was a geisha, looking for a patron—to marry her. Mrs. Haverhill said to herself, this Jap is an artiste. Her sensualness is learned and therefore artificial. Why is it my son does not see through her? And Mrs. Haverhill became deeply jealous, that her Ruthey had not chosen a more suitable woman to marry—one like herself.

Yes, Mrs. Haverhill's suspicions were true. But Aki Shima had no idea that Rutherford Earle Haverhill V was going to bond with her legally. Obviously, he had not asked her. Rutherford was going to wait until the last night of the season. After the fancy dress ball when he and Aki would, yet again, share a sunrise tea, when the nighttime moon still graced the sky. After lovemaking.

"Rutherford is a beautiful man. I have come to love him. I had no idea that he intended to tie together our destinies . . . legally."

Mrs. Haverhill decided to pull the truth of the Jap's background out of her. She became slyly gentle and asked, "Miss Shima, is my guess correct that you have at some point lived in a teahouse."

"Hai."

Mrs. Haverhill smiled at her own cleverness, and thought, at least the girl is honest. "Then tell me about your family."

"My mother was the daughter of an upper class family fallen on hard times. At the age she was to marry, her family was too poor to expect a suitable match to her upbringing. And because of her upbringing, she could not become the wife of a farmer. She was accepted into a teahouse. I was brought up in a teahouse in the flower district of Gion, in Kyoto. A teahouse my mother eventually came to own."

Mrs. Haverhill thought, it is no wonder Rutherford has found her tempting. She has been taught from a child how to please a man. Of course an uncommon passion has been ignited. No American girl, unless she is the daughter of a whore, knows how to please a man in uncommon ways. That is why my Rutherford has never loved an American girl of his own class in the same way. She has obviously bewitched Ruthey with ancient and exotic practices.

"Did you learn to embroider at the teahouse?" Mrs. Haverhill tried to mask her sarcasm.

"No. I was required to attend a handicraft workshop."

"I see."

"I will come to the point, Miss Shima. You should understand coming from a culture such as yours, what a marriage partner means to a family of class and rank."

"Hai. I understand. And in my country, a union between the classes, such as your son and myself, should he allow me to share the respectable role as his wife, would be accepted."

"In my society it may happen. But it is not accepted. And

whether geisha are prostitutes or not, they are women of the night in the minds of our social set."

"Rules between geisha and patrons are bound by a strict sense of etiquette."

"I am not referring to etiquette. I am referring to morals. And you are missing my point. Mr. Haverhill and myself do not agree to a marriage between two races."

"Please . . . in two ways you remind me of my mother . . . Mrs. Haverhill. Who is now dead," Aki said softly.

This was not the thing to say to Mrs. Haverhill IV. Not only did she think it a sentimental trick, she abhored being compared to a little Jap.

Aki continued, "You are as discerning, and obviously schooled in artistic pursuits as she was. My mother had a rich patron, as you have legitimately in your husband, only hers died. My father was sixty years old when he died. My mother told me that when my father died she would have killed herself if she did not have life in her. I was born three days after his death. She said that she hated me inside her those three days and still wanted to kill herself. Then I was born and she realized that my helplessness seemed greater than her unbearable sorrow. And she began to love me as much as she loved my father, her patron.

"My brother was illegitimate as well. But my father had a wife who consented to adopt my brother. I know which family my brother belongs to, but I have never met him. He does not know he is the son of a geisha. I have no other close relatives.

"When my mother died, five years ago, I sold her teahouse and could afford to move to Paris for the Exposition and sell my embroidery. Although I know the arts of a geisha, I never had a patron in Japan.

"I have lived with nuns in Paris for the past five years. They have taught me English and much of western ways. And I have shared my embroidery designs with them. Mrs. Haverhill, I would not be an embarrassment to your family. I would respect you as my new mother. You are as intelligent and businesslike as my own mother now gone forever from me."

Mrs. Haverhill would have been touched, if she had not almost burst at the seams having been compared with the "madame of a pleasure house." Rutherford's mother was deeply and irreconciably insulted.

Aki Shima erred in thinking that her compliment would be accepted. No rich, pampered American woman wanted to admit, even to herself, that she is a good businesswoman in keeping a husband to provide for her by whatever means necessary. Including overlooking her husband's secret hobby—women of the night.

Aki concluded, "Is it not true that in America marriages between cultures and social groups take place . . . because here one has the freedom and liberty to do so?"

"It happens in some families. Not ours. Look my dear, I like you very much. Your speech shows you to be intelligent and informed. But there is one piece of information which might change your mind. You see, we desire grandchildren of our own culture.

"If you and my son continue in this folly, my husband will disinherit Rutherford. You would be left with nothing. Mr. Haverhill is not in the habit of making empty threats. How would you support yourselves? My son has never done a day's work in his life. You will soon grow tired and cold to each other. You who have learned all the arts between men and women must also be aware of the realities."

Aki Shima fought her nature to be a passive victim of fate. She tried to argue respectfully with the western woman; she tried to show Rutherford's mother she could be western too in showing strong individuality. But in the end, Aki realized that she would ruin Rutherford's life. For his family would not accept Rutherford, accepting Aki Shima, and producing slant-eyed grandchildren. And obviously, Rutherford had found it in himself to love children.

Although Aki had tried to assert her personal will upon Mrs. Haverhill, it had been to no avail. And although Mrs. Haverhill was not quite as convinced that Aki was using her son, or as convinced that Aki Shima did not love her son, and was a shrewd Japanese business woman after his money, she shuddered with increased passion at the thought of slant-eyed grandchildren.

Aki Shima was powerless. Her cause was hopeless. She was alone.

In seconds Aki summed up her future. She had no one to go back to in Japan. Although the world of the geisha was never more popular, she had tasted the relative freedom of the western woman of small means, and the illusory freedom of the American woman. She could not go back to a restricted life in Japan. Her spirit would feel a prisoner. She could not go back to the nuns in Paris. Her body now yearned for a man.

But before Aki Shima succumbed to her fate, she railed at the paradox that as a woman she was free—but as a rich man Rutherford was not. And she inwardly railed against Mrs. Haverhill. Aki's body filled with hate for the smug eastern woman until she realized—it was too easy to hate.

There was only one way to prove her pure love of Rutherford to his mother. Aki went back to the Grand Hotel where she wrote a letter to Rutherford. Then she planned a surprise visit to Mrs. Haverhill once more on the last morning of the season. After "Reminiscences of the Midway Plaisance." After the fancy dress ball. After pillowing with Rutherford. After sunrise tea.

18

As Kindred One and All Unite

"Oh! A fairyland . . ."

"A late summer's night dream . . ."

At twilight, five hundred veranda guests gazed upon the great lawn below the Grand Hotel. A thousand and one colored lights nestled in tree branches and bushes, like delicate magical lacework, and defined outlines of ten canvas tents. Chinese lanterns, row upon row of yellow and pink and red and blue thin paper cases around incandescent lamps, bobbing in the gentle and cool Mackinac breezes, formed an arcade.

Under the colorful arcade would pass costumed guests through the "Reminiscences of the Midway Plaisance"—wonders from the four corners of the world—an international sideshow—a symposium of exotica—the gala Grand Hotel lawn fete, organized by the Countess Gianotti, as a prelude to the "goodwill" fancy dress ball. The very last ball, the very last night of the summer season of '93.

Sparkling rainbow fireworks exploded noisily, signaling the festivity and gaiety to come. Jimmy Hayes, dressed as "beer" in a fawn colored costume, with hops growing out of his pocket and barley plants growing from his shoulders, led his elite costumed resorters down the veranda stairway, through the porte-cochere, and down another stairway to the tents in the illuminated garden.

Between kettles full of leaping orange flames lining the pathway to the festive scene, passed "beer" followed by kings and queens, and pirates and knights, and angels and devils, and vestal virgins and Greek gods, and jesters and jugglers, and wizards and witches, and peasants of many nations, and hundreds of other historical characters, and creative choices (like beer and lemon and money and wastebasket and playing cards).

On the great lawn, from the tents of ten nations containing tableaux and pageantry, seeped weird melodies from "barbarous" instruments, strange and monotonous with odd rhythmic sweetness, or familiar folk tunes or national anthems played on instruments "of refinement" by the Salisbury Orchestra. Inconsonant sounds and clashing rhythms—the beat of deep toned congo drums, the three-quarter time of a waltz, the loud rattle of tambours, the sweet notes of a piccolo, the twanging and strange strumming of strings, notes ear piercing and discordant, notes melodic and soothing—intermingled in the air around the two rows of tents and under the arcade of Chinese lanterns connecting them.

From inside her "American Indian" tent, even above the pounding of tom-toms by local Indians dressed in full regalia, Anna heard the excited chatter of the resorters dividing up and heading for the various tents, hurrying first to the countries where a friend or relative was part of the "living picture" and pageantry. Or to tents where they knew the Big Four could be seen. Anna wondered if this gala "Reminiscences . . ." was to come off as she planned. And she wished she could see Jimmy Hayes' face when he entered the "Persian Palace."

Before the countess had time to think any more about it, her tent had filled to capacity. Richard and Arthur dressed in fringed untanned leather, moccasins, necklaces and collars of beads and feathers, struck an Indian pose.

Anna, dressed as a North American Indian queen, wearing sandals, a fringed leather dress with copious colored glass and bead embroidery, a diadem of colored eagles' and vultures' feathers and bead jewelry, sat upon a platform behind scenery representing Lover's Leap on Mackinac Island. Yellow feathery plumes of Canada goldenrod and purplish common burdock decorated the base of the papier-mâché rock.

The audience clapped appreciatively. Not because the costumes were authentic and the scenery so well done, but because the countess, in a black wig, looked strangely beautiful and earthy as an Indian with blue eyes. Truly, a much younger woman should have played the part. Twenty years younger to be exact. But Anna could find no one who wanted to play an Indian. Not even a New Woman college girl wanted to play the part of a broken people.

Richard, feeling his horn headdress slowly tipping to one side, pointed to Anna and began, "Upon a high rock sits Lo-tah, beautiful daughter of the Ojibway. Many many moons ago, her young brave Ge-niw-e-gwon had left her to attain more eagle plumes by destroying the Iroquois enemy in the east. Every day from this rock, Lo-tah watched the empty waters for her lover's return. And every day she waited, she sang this love song." Richard straightened his tipping headdress, with one hollow and one solid horn.

Anna, looking lovestruck, sang in a voice laced with heartache:

" 'A loon, I thought, was looming,
Mong-e-do-gwain, in-de-nain-dum,
Why! it is he, my lover,
Wain-shung-ish-ween, neen-e-mo-shane,
His paddle in the waters gleaming.
A-nee-wan-wan-san-bo-a-zode.' "

Arthur continued the narration and boomed, "Ah see! Something has moved in the horizon."

From behind the rock scenery, hidden Negro waiters held up little canoes on sticks from Fenton's Indian Bazaar.

Arthur continued, "Lo-tah soon identified the small spots far away as a flotilla of canoes. And as they neared Mackinac Island, Lo-tah heard the Ojibway warriors singing. She leaped up with joy. But soon she identified the song as a death song. Her eyes searched the canoes for her beloved. But he was no where to be seen. He had been killed."

Richard resumed narration, gazing at the countess with lovestruck eyes that everyone in the audience, especially the matriarchal group members and old maids, could not help but notice, "Beautiful . . . beautiful Lo-tah remained upon the high rock for seven sleeps. Each night a handsome bird appeared to her . . . and she realized that her lover bid her to join him." And Richard smiled to himself and thought, I have appeared at Anna's bedroom door for—fourteen sleeps. But Anna has not leaped for me.

Suddenly—Anna leaped off the papier-mâché rock. The audience gasped as she landed in a graceful heap on the grass. Her shapely legs protruded from underneath her leather skirt. The gentlemen stared appreciatively. One of the youngish old maids, from the "You'll be damned if you play cards on Sunday" group who was dressed as an (odd) Queen of Hearts, quickly, respectfully, stooped down to cover the countess' too lovely legs. But she was too late. The scene had had its stimulating effect. Especially on the men.

Arthur concluded, gazing at Anna with an intensity equal to Richard's rapture, "Lo-tah's father found her broken body on the morning of the eighth day at the base of the high rock. And Lo-tah's spirit was joined forever with her lover. Since that day, this high rock on Mackinac Island has been called . . . Lover's Leap."

The saddened audience did not applaud until Anna stood up. Then they cheered and clapped until the tent shook. A few old maids quickly wiped a stray tear from their cheeks, and that particular group of fifty resorters moved on to the tent next to the American Indian—the "Irish Village"—while a new group gathered inside Anna's tent.

The "Irish Village" tent, complete with a professional piper playing reels and jigs, enclosed painted scenery of Blarney's Castle, a papier-mâché Celtic cross, and an inside outside view of an Irish cottage on a slanting stage to give the effect of perspective. The cottage had a thatched roof and a small peat turf fire smoldering on the hearth, a potato pot hanging above it, and three pretty, red-cheeked Irish peasants, (really young millionairesses), crocheting or working needle-point lace or spinning wool on an old-fashioned wheel.

But the "Irish Village" would not have been complete without a dairy—or old Owen Corrigan in gray clothes and ruffles and green stockings, swelled up with pride that the Countess Anna had asked him to stand next to Glendora and Dora (the cow's calf), and tickled to stand near a half a dozen pretty young Munster milkmaids (really intellectual flirts)—who sat nearby not only for Old Owen to wink at, but to carve posies of lilies and roses from cakes of butter.

Owen played his part to perfection, but he wondered what was happening in the other tents, and half-wished he was free to attend them. After all, Owen had not been off the island in forty years, and he was a wee bit curious what life was like elsewhere. Especially what life was like in the "Street in Cairo" in the next door tent.

Music came forth from that Cairo tent on Mackinac Island that Owen thought, was more oddish than a Israelite singin' "Rose of Killarney" in Hebrew. Although Owney's foot kept tapping to the rhythm of the Irish jig played by the piper in his tent, his mind was imagining all sorts of things in the next tent and he thought . . . ach ya, ach ya, ach ya . . . such queer twangy pangs my ears 'ave never been destroyed with.

Bismallah. The music coming from the "Street in Cairo"

was strange. Anna had managed to get seven Algerine "children of Mahomet" to come up to the island from the Chicago World's Fair, to entertain the summer "infidels" with their music. No they were not Egyptians, but their flageolet, shrill and discordant, sounded the same to Anna. The musicians, dressed in turbans and jackets and trousers or red robes and a fez, sat on oriental rugs crosslegged and lined the walls of the tent, which were adorned with oriental tapestries and rugs and flags and lamps. With studied indifference, they played the mandolin, a fiddle on the knee, a tiny cello-like instrument, little tambours, a flageolet, and deep toned congo drums.

Portraying snake charmers and jugglers and other characters, a raft of college men and Sydney Chase Froilan had volunteered to man the "Street in Cairo." No wonder. The scandalous and voluptuous *danse du ventre* was to be performed. Just like that "carnal" dance performed by sexy "Little Egypt" at the Midway Plaisance in Chicago. The prudes of the Grand Hotel, never anticipating that the Countess Gianotti would include such a sinful show, were to have silent conniptions—but they stayed cooly curious until the end.

Dancing girl figures—with veiled faces and morphino-maniac eyes lined with black kohl, fully clothed in baggy trousers of blue or gold or lavender or green, and gold embroidered jackets, their necks and chests weighted with brass chains, and wearing layers of shimmering gauzy veils extending from under their caps—stamped and shuffled and undulated the *dance du ventre* to the ear-piercing, monotonous music. With voluptuous hot passion, their bodies, rattling brass ornaments, swayed and twisted and jerked and wiggled downward as they waved silken handerkerchiefs from their gloved hands, until they almost touched the grass. One fell over.

And only the gentlemen, who had oggled such creatures at the Midway Plaisance in Chicago, realized they were fakes.

Until the end. And then the entire crowd knew instantly and broke into a howl. Even the prudes half smiled when Sydney Froilan and the college men—snatched off their veils and bowed. It was middle-aged Sydney who had not managed to get down to the grass and had . . . fallen over.

If Beatrice had seen Sydney perform, in spite of a recent row between them, she would have laughed . . . till she cried. For Sydney was heading back to Paris . . . tomorrow.

The wild music from the "Street in Cairo" tent swallowed the simple and haunting shamisen music seeping from the tent next to it.

When the audience entered the "Fashions of Japan" tent, they were struck by the classic beauty and the implicit sanity in the simple forms and magnificent details of Aki Shima's costumes. All but one observer breathed a sigh of relief from mad Cairo, where the hypocondriacs had imagined gross smells. The observer, a masked woman in a black Puritan cap, portrayed Rose Standish. And instead of relaxing, she caught her breath and clutched her teeth at the beautiful sight of Aki Shima . . . and the glowing face of Rutherford gazing at the Japanese woman. The masked woman had never seen such a look on Rutherford's face. She could not even define it. She would always remember it. Mrs. Haverhill IV may have portrayed Rose Standish . . . but she played the Muse of Tragedy.

On one platform faced with tatami mats—enclosed on three sides with authentic Japonaise screens depicting mountains and waterfalls and pine trees, a shapely ikebana flower arrangement set to the side—sat resplendent Aki. With whitened face and wearing a uchikake robe fully embroidered in gold and red and green and white threads, once worn by a feudal lord's daughter, Aki plucked "Sakura, Sakura" on her stringed cat belly instrument.

Standing perfectly still nearby, Beatrice, looking as tall and attenuated as a courtesan in a Utamaro print, showed off her exquisite robe printed with the curving blue lines of a running stream and embroidered with bold flowers. Beatrice knew that her robe had been worn by a Japanese woman of the night, and the thought excited her. Next to Beatrice sat Monica, beaming, her embroidered robe of large flowered parasols spread out like a fan around her small body.

On a platform nearby stood Rutherford holding little Frederick's hand, who in turn held the hand of Professor Bellamy. All three stood perfectly still in cotton yukata robes printed with abstract designs. No easy feat for four-year-old Frederick dressed in an orange and white striped tsutsusode kimono. For not only was it hard for the little boy to stand perfectly still— because before the festivities, Belinda Gaines (costumed as a "bonbon") had sneaked him a handful of black licorice from her basket of candy—it was also hard for the four-year-old to hold back the loud grumbling in his stomach from the licorice. He was sure everyone smiled at him, because his stomach made girgling noises.

Professor Bellamy, dressed in a heavily starched indigo blue and white yukata robe with huge orange symbols, satisfied that Sydney Froilan was not in this tableau, relaxed at the gorgeous sight of glorious Beatrice and pretty little Monica. (He did not realize that Beatrice wore a robe . . . from the gay quarters. Nor that Aki had comforted Beatrice, regarding the old gentleman's stern censure of Beatrice's love affair with married Sydney, by telling her an old Japanese saying: "In his starched yukata, the old man looks as starchy as ever.")

Standing perfectly still, Professor Bellamy thought, perhaps dear Beatrice will come to her senses away from this gay fairy isle, when she gets back to gray New York. And then the old gentleman decided to release his singing mice on Mackinac

Island. He had no idea why he should feel so deeply about leaving the little creatures behind before he left tomorrow. How odd, he thought, in the forty summers I have stayed on the island, I never felt to do something this strange before. I must release them early in the morning, with the children. They must watch me teach the mice how to survive. They must watch me teach them fear. For without the instinct of fear we cannot survive. Then his chest grew tight thinking that he might not see dear Frederick and Monica, so trusting, and Beatrice, so vulnerable, again.

Rutherford, in the plainest robe, stood dreaming of how he would ask Aki to tie their destinies, legally, after lovemaking in the early hours of morning. He was not aware that the utterly simple indigo blue and white yukata robe Aki had asked him to wear, bearing a striped design—was considered elegant to the point of foppishness in Japan. Although he did notice that Aki, with unusually sad eyes, had giggled softly when she graciously helped him on with the yukata; and she told him she had played a joke on him.

To Aki, the narrow striped robe made Rutherford look even taller than his six feet and larger than life. To Aki's eyes, her western lover looked more handsome, more elegant, more narcissistic than ever.

And Rutherford, with eyes only for Aki, did not notice Rose Standish in the audience. It was good he did not. For he would have recognized the costume . . . it was authentic and had been in his mother's side of the family since the seventeenth century. The recognition of his dear mother, and his consequent attentions bestowed upon her, would have taken him away from Aki. And the next six hours were to be the happiest hours in his life.

The beautiful Aki Shima appeared so sad and her music sounded so unearthly that many resorters, especially those who had not found love that summer of '93, left this tent with a wet eye . . . without knowing why. Only Rose Standish knew why Aki Shima sounded so sad.

If the "Fashions of Japan" experience sweetly sobered the resorters, the next tent revved them up again. For it was the "Scottish Village" complete with scenery of Edinburgh Castle, and bagpipers droning music for highland sword dancers. (The dancers were really ruddy cheeked multimillionaire Grand Hotel guests, having the time of their lives showing off.)

Next to the Scots they visited the "South Sea Islanders" tent. The crowd chuckled at a sign next to the entrance stating: "Please do not ask about former custom of cannibalism." Inside, professional "savage" drummers, up from the world's fair, sat next to painted scenery depicting the tropical luxuriance of a south seas island. And college men, in short kilts of bark and grass armlets and necklaces, shouted savage chants and performed their hammed up version of a cannibal feast dance, much to the spectators' lively amusement.

From the "Ferris Wheel" tent next door, where two of the Big Four could be seen, a Salisbury band cheerfully blasted Sousa like sounds while high-spirited singing shook the tent. Upon entering the "Ferris Wheel" tent the audiences broke into peals of laughter. For Eugene "Sully" Sullivan, dressed as a champagne bottle with a cork on his head, a wine glass on one shoulder, and a sign on his chest with the words "Jules Mumm, Rheims, Very Dry," stood next to the Ferris Wheel— a carriage wheel he turned with a crank.

Sully gleefully sang the verses to "There's a Tavern in the Town," and Philippa, dressed as a "Lady Jockey" in orange and red satin wearing a jocky cap, and Philmore Calhoun, dressed as a "Pirate King," and Clare, dressed as a "Sea Queen"—in a robe of opalescent moire trimmed at the hem with seashells, a waist belt of coral, a train of silver cloth cut like a fish-tail and trimmed with clam shells and, to every-one's amusement, a miniature aquarium with two swimming goldfish as a headdress above her radiant face—all sang along with Sully during the choruses and bid the audience to join in the jolly songs. The resorters sang—"We Won't Go Home Till Morning," and "Say 'Au Revoir' but not Good-bye," and "They Kissed I Saw Them Do It"—as if there were no tomorrow.

Putting on a smiling face, Philippa sang as if tomorrow would come too soon. For Marshe Williamson had not made it back to the hotel from Lexington after all. And each word she sang felt as if it was coming up from her stomach rather than carried on her breath.

Yes, the countess would have been utterly surprised to see that the sophisticated resorters got the biggest kick out of the "Ferris Wheel" tent with little more than a carriage wheel as a prop. But when Jimmy Hayes popped inside to view it, he was not surprised at his guests' jolly reactions. With two of the Big Four in the tent, he could have predicted the "Ferris Wheel" would be a success no matter what.

But the countess would not have been surprised to see Jimmy Hayes turn ruby red in utter astonishment and disbelief when he entered the opulent "Persian Palace" tent. For Ibrahim stood at the entrance to the tent, and announced to Jimmy with piercing eyes and a smug sounding voice, "Jimmy Hayes . . . please bow before his royal highness, the Shah of Harremajarra!"

Even the Big Four took a back seat—to the Shah of Harremajarra, sitting erect on a golden throne and dressed in a sparkling robe of precious gems—for the rest of the glorious unforgettable evening.

And at the fancy dress ball, which followed the illuminated "Reminiscences of the Midway Plaisance," claimed a "howling success" by all, the Shah of Harremajarra was given a seat of honor. Ibrahim sat on one side of the resplendent shah and a "mysterious lady" with a veiled face sat on the other side. Not one excited guest would have dreamed that the veiled "lady" was a harem woman by the name of Vivian Larron.

"It is a fanciful merry-go-round!" exlaimed one of the Muldoons, dressed as a "rose garden" in a green gown covered with garlands of pink roses.

"I am deliciously dizzy from watching!" proclaimed the other Muldoon, dressed as a "bunch of sweet peas."

Among all the old couples, and old maids, and widows and widowers, and crafty crackpot members in the gallery, the Muldoons looked the most cheerful. Although the old members of the "You'll be damned if you play cards on Sunday" group, who played cards every other day of the week, looked spiffy dressed as red or black diamonds, hearts, spades or clubs, the rest of the gallery crowd were less than merry looking.

One hypocondriac from the crafty crackpots dressed as "influenza," with a water bottle on one shoulder, a packet of mustard leaves on the other, and the letters quinine attached to a bandeau in her gray hair. Other lancet-tongued old maids and spies came as "lemon" or "saltarella" or "superstition" or "fruitcake." Old Stinkweed came as "sour grapes." (Everyone joked that the old man should have come as "stinkweed.")

From the gallery, the smiling old Muldoon ladies gazed down at the whirling costumed figures, dancing in large circles on the glossy casino floor. After much discussion they finally agreed as to who was who among the matriarchal group members and chaperones lining the walls, and their girls seated in front of them. The old ladies smiled knowingly when they recognized that the intellectual flirts who did not wear colorful peasant costumes, came as (social) "butterflies" with diaphanous gauze wings, or "bridal cakes" hinting to their beaus to pop the question before morning, or "forget-me-not" hopefuls. The jilted ones, (kissed often), came as "souvenir spoons."

The Muldoons noticed that the New Woman college girls were no less satirical. Most of them came as a "new woman" wearing severe tailor-made gowns with a bicycle and rowing oar and *Sporting Times* newspaper pictured on the front of their skirts. They wore bicycle lamps on their Tam o'Shanter caps, latch-keys at their sides, and carried guns slung over their shoulders and resting on their backs. Needless to say, these "new woman" New Woman college girls were seldom asked to dance.

The New Woman college girls who came either as "queen of the Amazons" or "doctress of music" or "oarswoman" or "vestal virgin" or "lawn tennis"—faired better and were asked to dance more frequently than their "new woman" New Woman sisters.

The pretty Muldoons sighed at the extravaganza below them and glanced at their ballcards. Their hearts fluttered a bit when they noticed that the next promenade had a gentleman's name next to it. In fact, it was the only name on their cards. It had been years since either of them had been invited to the dance floor. And sure enough they turned around and there stood elegant Rutherford, in his simple yukata, smiling. Of all people, the Muldoons realized that Rutherford Earle Haverhill V wore the plainest costume at the fancy dress ball. He offered one of his arms to each Muldoon and escorted them down to the dance floor.

The old female population in the gallery turned green that such a young man should ask, not one, but two old ladies. And the Muldoons, so happy to be on Rutherford's arms, just about burst inside trying to hold back their emotions. For tomorrow they would not be hearing the affected accent of the gentleman from out east, as they had every morning for eight weeks. And without saying it to each other, it was not the accent of the man that they were going to miss.

The bewitching hours of music and dancing and flirting and last minute falling in love and out of love passed all too swiftly. And soon the clock struck half past one.

"Beatrice . . . how beautiful you are again this evening." Sydney Froilan guided her into a box step during the "Charming Waltz."

"Thank you, Sydney . . . may I return the compliment and say . . . how voluptuous you must have looked as a dancing girl in the Street in Cairo."

"I was the prettiest, no doubt."

Beatrice laughed softly.

Sydney smiled charmingly. "I shall always remember your laugh."

"I shall never remember all your jokes."

"Then I will have to visit you when I travel to New York. To tell you new jokes . . . for you to forget."

"To make me laugh."

"Yes, yes to make you laugh. But now I shall make you giddy twirling in my arms."

"I have been . . . giddy . . . since the Sault."

"Ah . . . the Sault . . . .I . . . I shall miss making you . . . giddy . . . my dear Beatrice."

"As the sun outshines the moon . . . so shall I, dear Sydney . . . oh so shall I!"

"Once more tonight . . . very discreet . . . like at the Sault?"

"Dui-du . . . ."

Sitting in the box with Clare the "sea queen," Philmore the "pirate king" stopped talking for a moment to relight his pipe.

The well-blackened meerschaum from Fenton's. To Philmore, this magical meershaum led him to Clare Gilbertson, as surely the magical axe he named Calla had led him to his fortune on Iron Mountain and allowed him to buy his "boat." Big Philmore Calhoun believed in tall tales. In fact, he made them happen.

"How beautiful you look as a 'sea queen,' dear Clare. If I were Neptune I would ravish you deep within my coral castle at the bottom of a turquoise sea," Philmore whispered in Clare's ear.

"Dear Philmore . . . I see that the 'pirate king' in you is coming out."

"Yes and something more is coming out." Philmore reached into his pocket and took out a scarf. He wrapped it around Clare as a sash and tied it at her shapely waist. The scarf had the letters *Calla* embroidered on it. But placed over *Calla*, in origami paper letters graciously sewed by Aki, were the letters *Clare*.

"Tomorrow, if you agree, the boat will be renamed."

Clare's enchanting smile would have melted Scrooge. "Oh Philmore . . . I agree."

"Then as my sea queen will you travel the world with me? I want to see the world, Clare, before the world changes, before cannibals are civilized, before we are all alike, before I am too old . . . I do."

"I will travel with you, Philmore . . . anywhere . . . I want to see the world . . . before the world changes . . . before cannibals are civilized . . . before we are all alike . . . before I am too old . . . I do."

"You will never be too old, dear Clare. May I have this dance, my sea queen? If I promise not to break any more clam shells on your gown's trailing fin?"

"Where we are going, Philmore, there will be plenty more clam shells to replace them . . . if by accident they should break. But I foresee no such clamity."

Philmore chuckled at Clare's pun but replied seriously, "Never again, if I can help it, will there be such calamity in your life, dear Clare . . . ."

For the fifth time that evening, Clare (without the aquarium on her head) danced with big Philmore Calhoun. Not one guest gossiped that one of "our Big Four" danced two times beyond respectability with a gentleman. Seeing the sash on radiant Clare, they silently congratulated the happy couple on the unannounced engagement. For the Grand elite knew that no sportsman changes the name of his yacht . . . unless he has caught a rare fish.

Philippa MacAdam, in kindly old Professor Bellamy's arms, whirled about the dance floor with resignation and a heavy heart. Colonel Marshe Williamson never came back. He had not even bothered to send her a telegram in three weeks. She decided to never look at a man again. Never again! Especially a gentleman. They were no good. Not to be trusted even with their mothers.

Yes, Philippa MacAdam absolutely, positively, without exception gave up on men—until a masked "Austrian hussar," wearing a light blue jacket and pantaloons heavily trimmed with silver and high boots with spurs, appeared at her side. And as planned between himself and Professor Bellamy, the old man regretfully stepped aside and let the younger man take over the dance.

"May I introduce myself, Madame?" he asked in an exceptionally pleasing voice and moderate southern accent.

"Please do . . ."

"My name is Captain Cupid and I have a message for you."

"I am sorry, I do not understand."

"There is a certain gentleman, who bid me to appear to you at half past two and beg you to forgive him for my late entrance and his obvious absence. He said the time would be meaningful to you. And he asked me to hand you a note I have in my pocket. Then he asked that I remain for your reply. Will you allow me to present the letter to you?"

Stunned, lovely Philippa took some time to reply.

The young "Austrian hussar" continued, "Please . . . perhaps behind that large palm over there, you could read your letter in privacy."

"Yes . . . of course."

As if in a dream, her heart pounding a three-beat gait, Philippa danced to the big palm in a dark corner of the ballroom while the Salisbury Orchestra played "Explosions Polka." The "Austrian hussar" handed her an envelope sealed with a coat of arms impressed in wax. Philippa did not recognize the seal or the handwriting. But she did recognize the message.

Smiling without control, she said, "Please, Captain Cupid, tell your colonel that I will forgive him for not writing or coming back to the island. And that I will . . . consider . . . his proposal . . . for accepting his horse Armande as a gift."

"In that case, with your permission, the colonel has instructed me to seal your consideration." The young masked man grabbed Anna, bent her over and kissed her hard on the lips and immediately repositioned her. "That is what he would have done if he were here. Now, with your permission, I will escort you back to your box."

Surprised, Philippa giggled and said, "Captain Cupid, are you sure he asked you to—seal—the proposal, if I answered only that I would give it my—consideration? Or to seal it if I said yes?"

"Suddenly . . . I must admit . . . I am not sure. But if the colonel had been here . . . if he had any instinct in him . . . he would have done likewise at the sight of your tempting southern beauty. Therefore, Mrs. MacAdam . . . would you accept that I have performed well for the colonel?"

"Please . . . tell the colonel for me . . . you performed . . . almost to distraction. And if this ever happens again . . . to send a less handsome messenger."

The young "Austrian hussar" fell in love with Philippa MacAdam then and there. It made no difference to him this new woman of his dreams was ten years older . . . and almost belonged to another man.

"I am honored, Madame. May I escort you to your box or will you consent to dance one waltz with me?"

"Captain Cupid, I may consent to dance two."

Philippa smiled charmingly at the young hussar. Then she watched the countess in her "Indian queen" costume whirling around the ballroom on the strong arms of her young Indian brave, Richard Anders. Philippa remembered Richard, bare-chested at the Sault. She wondered how her Captain Cupid would look in the same au naturel condition. Hmm.

But then she thought again of Colonel Marshe Williamson's proposal. And she sobered just a bit. For everyone knows that when a gentleman gives a woman his favorite horse . . . he is not engaging in horseplay . . . and certainly would not expect such from the female recipient of such a generous pre-marriage proposal gift.

"Anna, may I tell you . . . how beautiful you are . . . as always tonight?"

"Richard, I have given you leave to say that three times this evening." Anna tried to cover up any reaction to the utter warmth and contentment she felt with the younger man.

"But you have not given me leave to escort you back to your room after the ball."

"Nor have I given it to your father."

"Thank you, Anna."

"There is no need to thank me, Richard."

"Yes, there is. You kept us from going at each other these

past weeks. You have made such fun for us . . . you have done everything you could to ease our anger. Father mentioned this to me tonight . . . before the ball . . . almost in a conciliatory tone. I know that you still have feelings for my father. But dear Anna, I know that you . . . love me . . . with the same intensity I love you. You do not need to say it. And Anna . . . I will not let you deny it."

Anna could not deny that Richard both soothed and aroused her. Nor could she deny, that if her invalid husband in Italy died, she would run off with the younger man, never to be heard of or seen again.

The big bushy palm, placed in the dark corner of the ballroom for quick spoonological purposes, caught Richard's eye. Decisively, skillfully, he maneuvered Anna behind the same large palm where Philippa had been a few minutes before.

"Richard! People will notice!" Anna pulled away but Richard gently pulled her back.

"Only a number of old lemons and fruitcakes and an odd Queen of hearts and old jokers and Old Stinkweed in the gallery might notice. The rest of them cannot see this far. And those with disfiguring eyeglasses will only think a couple of lowly Indians, in sympathy with their uncivilized natures, are hiding in the bush and making love."

Anna's eyes twinkled but she only half smiled and insisted, "Richard, I simply cannot dally behind this palm with you like a schoolgirl."

"Then come outside with me for a stroll. I must talk with you. I must." Richard parted the palm froths. "Look Anna, my father is dancing. Come on. We can sneak past him."

"It is three o'clock in the morning. I certainly cannot sneak outside for a stroll with you."

"Why not dear Anna? Why not?"

Anna could not think of a good answer. And suddenly she wanted nothing more than to run outside of the stuffy ballroom into the clear and cool air of her Mackinac Island. Away from hundreds of admiring and critical eyes. Especially the Shah of Harremajarra's piercing eyes all over her body.

Richard and Anna slowly left the casino. Slowly and quietly, in their sandals and moccasins, they walked past the stables to Cadotte Avenue nearby.

"Race you to the pond in the common pasture . . ."

"The common pasture? At night?"

"Why not?"

"But the cow plats!"

"The moon will guide us."

A deep voice behind them boomed, "What moon?"

"Arthur—" Anna turned but could not see him, "where are you?"

"In your heart, dear Anna."

Struck by the intensity of his father's words, Richard could not respond. He could not say, get the hell out of here, old man. This is my affair. Do not interfere. For passionate words of twenty years back suddenly replayed themselves in his mind. Words of love between his father and Anna he had not remembered until now.

Anna knew she should never have allowed Richard to talk her into such a compromising dilemma. Her heart beat wildly. She wondered if father and son were going to have yet another argument, or worse another fight as they had had on the Field Day. But they remained silent. There were no sounds in the still Mackinac morning, except for the sudden rush of—ten bats around their heads.

"Ugh!" Anna was not fond of bats.

"Anna . . . I did not know you spoke Ojibway," Arthur joked.

Richard laughed in a tone free from malice. That one simple laugh of Richard's sounded like a chorus of—father, you are forgiven. It was as if an evil spell between father and son, born through death thirty years ago, had been broken in the release of Richard's laugh.

Anna wanted to run to Richard and hug him and tell him . . . what he told her in the ballroom . . . that she loved him . . . was true. His generosity . . . his spirited youthful energy lodged itself in Anna and made her feel so young. But with Arthur standing there, so much older and broken from some twenty years more of life, she could not answer her need to run to Richard.

Instead she ran from both of them gleefully. Free to run without corsets, one of the few times in her life as as adult in the outdoors, and wearing sandals, she ran as if invisible wings held her up. Ecstatically free, she ran down the Cadotte Avenue hill from the bats that had swarmed around them.

"Whoopee!" Anna called softly. Something deep and powerful and dangerous stirred up her spirit. The men sensed it. They sprinted after her.

She called gleefully, "Don't you see the clouds are breaking?"

Sure enough. The clouds broke and a three quarter moon bleached a white hole in the sky. Richard caught up to Anna and grabbed her hand as he had twenty years back. Anna stopped.

"Ah, dear Richard, let me catch my breath." But she really waited for Arthur.

Arthur appeared at Anna's side breathing heavily and grabbed Anna's other hand without thinking. He said, in the voice of a man who had wedded suffering and finally divorced his old worn out sorrows, "I remember watching both of you leaping about this pasture like gazelles and laughing until your sides hurt. I remember feeling . . . so left out . . . I remember . . . if I had stepped into the muck . . . I would have been too proud to let you see or smell me, Anna . . . I . . . I intend to jump with both of you, if I may. Son . . . I mean Richard . . . may I join you?"

Richard and Anna heard the bare apology in Arthur's tone. No further words of explanation were necessary. All three understood. And it struck Anna that to make families whole, all her life she had seen the children give in and always forgive—before the proud parent could even imply apology. Are the children, full of instinct, wiser after all? Yes, she thought, age does not beget wisdom; of that she was sure. In the cool night air, wet with perspiration from running, the wet leather skins against her own soft skin, Anna shivered.

"There is a technique to jumping cow plats correctly, Father. And may I add . . . from years of experience . . . you do not step into the plats . . . you either smoosh into them . . . or slide into them. Am I right, Anna?"

Anna and Richard and Arthur laughed with abandon.

Arthur said, "Will this help? A little Indian whiskey?"

"Is it from Owney's still?" Anna asked gaily.

"None other."

"Well, then it may give us the—kick—over the plats we need!" Anna smiled at Arthur lovingly.

"Here. Ladies first."

Anna joked, "I do not see ladies with corsets here. I only see wild Indians."

"Well then I will take the first slug." Arthur gulped down a shot.

Anna shivered again in the cool and damp Mackinac morning.

"Here, dear Anna, this will keep you warm."

Richard watched his father place his hand on Anna's hand

and feed the spirits to her almost as if it were a caress. His father's gentle tone and manner surprised Richard. But he instantly related to it. Richard put his arm around Anna's shoulders and said, "Does this help warm you as well?"

"Oh very much, Richard." How good it felt to Anna, Richard's arm around her shoulder. And again Anna's present realities away from corsets and Europe and the court of Queen Marguerite and her invalid husband faded and something from long ago, before she was born, stirred her. Deep feelings . . . instinctive . . . primeval sensations excited dim memory. And it was not only Anna who felt she was losing civilized control.

Arthur, having dropped layers of provincial righteousness in a few short weeks, looked knowingly and said, "Here . . . Richard. Have a drink. It will warm up your Injun bones." And after that drink—as if it were some sort of pact without words—Richard never heard his father refer to him as "son" again. There was a reason for this. It was yet to come. In triple time.

"We must begin with a running start," Anna said lightheartedly.

"And remember," Richard reminded them, "you must never let go of the hand you are holding. And you might have to sacrifice yourself in some way so that the other two do not muck up as well."

Anna thought to herself, the story of my life.

"Go!"

In the faint moonlight over Mackinac Island, the three Indian clad figures leaped across the common pasture hand in hand. Their six feet jumped to avoid one by two by three by four by five cow plats they could barely see . . . unless they were fresh and caught a faint reflection of the moonlight . . . and seven by eight by nine by ten they could not see, but knew they were there. Ah . . . what excitement for a continental countess and worldly gambler and small town judge, dressed as Indians. And Anna realized that it was even more fun jumping cow plats hand in hand in hand in trio—rather than in duo.

"Whoa, Charley!" Owen Corrigan demanded in low tones. He said to his old horse, "May the blessed Holy Mother preserve me, me peepers are gettin' old. I dreamt I'd seen three Injuns leapin' in the cow pasture. Forty winks would do well by me."

"Whoopee!"

"Whoopee!"

Owen swore on the blessed book itself that he was not only seeing things, but hearing things.

"Whoopee!"

Owen strained his tired eyes to see the Indian ghosts in the pasture. But without warning the clouds covered the moon.

"Oops!"

"Oops!"

"Oops!"

Anna and Richard and Arthur could not stop laughing till their sides hurt. But in the dark they could not see who had taken the worst spill when the clouds covered the moon. In other words who had fallen into the swill. So they sniffed instead.

Old Owen overheard the following conversation, of sorts.

"Oh no!"

"It is you, Richard."

"Not me, it is Father."

"Call me Arthur."

"After all these years?"

"Why not?"

"I feel awkward. What the hell. Then it is you, Arthur."

"It is not me. It is Anna."

"Oh no. It cannot be me!"

"It is!"

"Oh no. How awful!"

"Not the delicate scent I usually associate with you, dear Anna."

"Oh no! What am I to do? I cannot go back to the hotel reeking of cow manure!"

"Come to the cottage. You can bathe there."

"We'll leave a note with your maid to send your garments to the cottage."

"Here, dear Anna, have some of Owen's whiskey. It will ease the . . . perfume."

Owen's ears perked up at the mention of his name and he yelled out towards the pasture, "If it's a drink ye'll be havin' 'ave the courtesy to invite the fella who made it fer ye!"

"Owen?" Anna called.

"Tis me. And is it ye, Countess Anna?"

"Not the way you remember me, Owney. I fell into the muck."

Owen took off his Tam o' Shanter and scratched his head. What next will the fancy women be a doin' in this world, he asked himself.

Anna and Richard and Arthur appeared at his carriage. Giggling and guffawing they handed Owen a flask of whiskey.

He guzzled a shot, or two, and said, "Ah . . . good stuff. Oh me stars. I need a clothespin on me wee nose, I do. I hope me Charley can take the stink. Let me throw a oilcloth on me hack's seats afore ye crazy Injuns sit down."

On the way to Arthur's cottage in the Annex, Owen explained to the threesome, "Me and Charley took off most of the day, an' after standin' in the Irish Village, 'ave worked all night, bein' it is the last night of the Grand's season. I was slowly headin' up to the grand palace to pick up Miss Shima, when I heard the ruckus nearby. I strained me eyes, an' as sure as a leprechaun wears green, when the clouds fell upon the moon, I saw a Injun ghost with blue heron feathers and long beak on his head. One side of the wild creature's face and body were black. The other side were red. Me own peepers bear witness to white circles makin' rings 'round its beady eyes. An' a shiny deer bone stuck in through its nostrils. It leaped right in front of me Charley. I saw me Charley leap three feet into the air and almost toppled me carriage."

Owen swore he saw an Indian sha-man ghost of olden times, probably leaving the lodge-shaking ceremony; a ritual when Indians asked and found out their future. He shuddered to think that ghosts of the red man still came back to Mackinac Island, after all these years since the white man took it away from them.

Anna and Richard and Arthur grinned quietly. But Anna wondered why Aki Shima had ordered a carriage before sunrise.

"Whoa, Charley."

"Here ye all are finally at yer fine cottage, Arthur Andryer. And forgive me, Countess Anna, but ye smell like a barn, and I don't mind if ye step out of me hack."

"I am sorry, Owney. And I thank you with all of my heart. This is the second time you have come to my rescue this summer."

Richard and Arthur wondered what the first time rescue was about. They were never to find out (until many years later).

"I canna say twas a pleasure. But fer ye . . . Anna . . . anything. I'm after yer very heart."

"Ye have it then, Owney. Here." Anna, reeking, planted a kiss on Owney's cheek.

In all his living days, Owen Corrigan had never received a sweeter kiss from such a fine Indian lady under such stinking circumstances.

"Afore we head back to the grand palace, may I say, cow plat jumpin' is no sport fer a cloudy moonlit night. Ach ya."

"Good night, Owen. And many thanks."

"Go lang, Charley."

"Anna, could you use some more hot water? We have four kettles here. They're damned heavy."

Anna thought long and hard about the proposal for more hot water coming from the other side of the door. Her bath water was merely tepid, and she was freezing in the cold bathroom of the cottage. But Anna was not yet sure.

"Cover yourself up and we will close our eyes and pour it in."

Anna smiled to herself. She was not born yesterday. And wondered how the men thought she was supposed to cover herself unless she got out of the water. And then, once again that evening, in spite of the humor or because of it, she felt the very pulsebeat of life rushing through her veins. She thought of her dear count in Italy who once said to her, "If I am no longer here for you, do not lie beneath the trees, climb them," and Anna pondered what her count would do in a similar circumstance. If she were an invalid. If he were loved not by one, but by two. Something clicked inside her and she called, "Dui-du . . . ."

The two men walked into the candlelit bathroom. They stopped in their tracks. Anna had not covered herself and her white Venus de Milo breasts seemed to beckon them. Her eyes sparkled with joy and her mouth expressed experience of past and present bliss. Both men took long breaths and sighed deeply. And like God in Genesis, they liked what they saw. But unlike God they did not rest on the seventh day. For it was

Sunday. And it was more tempting to do something creatively naughty on Sunday, when such threesomes seem more sinful, than on any other day of the week.

Anna noticed the veins in Richard's and Arthur's hands as they poured the hot water from the heavy kettles into her bath. Veins protruding, veins leading to their hearts. She imagined red blood pumped through blue veins from their hearts to their groins. Blood bursting forth and shooting up the formerly downward slopes. She smiled lovingly. And the time between her bath and their baths and bed did not exist.

It was not as if, simply, a lusty bacchanalia inspired by instinctual feeling was in full swing at the modest Andryer cottage. In spite of years of pent-up passion inside all of them, the threesome did not tear down the walls in fits of passion. Because the walls were needed to conceal the sighs and little animal noises of true lovers loving. The two men did not look at each other. Only at Anna. Filled with pure love for her. Those moments the men did not exist to each other.

As if floating in a cloud of elevated sensation, Anna kept her eyes shut, while four hands carressed her soft naked body, and mouths kissed her throat and lips and eyes and brow and breasts . . . and they all laughed softly for wild love. And when the time came, she did not open her eyes to see if it was the father or the son inside her. For she loved. Simply loved. And it did not matter.

"I wish . . . to press ten hundred nights of love . . . into these moments," whispered Aki to Rutherford after they made love.

Rutherford gently kissed the cherrylike lips that spoke so softly. Caught up in passion, he did not realize that he instinctively tried to kiss away Aki Shima's mysterious sadness.

"Dear Aki . . . I love you . . . ."

Aki shivered. Rutherford's words charged through her like a jolt of joy. "I should like to stay on this island forever and watch myself leave tomorrow."

"Darling Aki . . . we shall go to Newport tomorrow to meet my mother. She will be so surprised and delighted to meet you."

Rutherford noticed Aki's eyes looked frightened.

"Please have no fears regarding my family, my darling. They will be fond of you. Especially when they hear the news. Dear Aki . . . will you do me the honor . . . will you consent to be my wife?"

Aki fell into Rutherford's arms, fighting tears, fighting resignation. Thinking of her promise to his mother. She could not look into his eyes. She tried to cover up her pain and asked, "Oh my love . . . you honor me more than you know . . . but your family . . . your New York and Newport society friends . . . will they approve?"

"There will be some stuffy ones who will not approve . . . initially . . . but the very sight of you will convince them . . . after five minutes with you . . . you will win them over."

"But will I win over your father . . ."

"Yes, Aki. You will win him over too."

"Then you do love me . . . to take this chance with all you hold dear."

"I say I love you, Aki, and know for the first time its meaning. I say I sense something within me, I do not remember since a very small child."

"You do not ask me if I love you?"

"I do ask it, Aki. I wait for you to say it . . . if it is in your heart. I asked it in my heart at the same time I asked you to be my wife. If I could have said both sentences at the same time . . . I would have."

"I love you . . ."

Rutherford embraced her again and kissed her. And it struck him that no woman, except his mother, had ever told him that she loved him.

"Oh Aki . . . I have such plans for us. We will come back to the island next summer. I will have a yacht built twice as large as *Calla* . . . I mean *Clare* . . . and we will sail it down the Atlantic coast from Newport, through the New York harbor, up the mightly Hudson River, into the St. Lawrence Seaway, down to Lake Ontario, through Lake Erie to Lake Huron and finally here to the magnificent Straits of Mackinac. We will anchor in the harbor and marry at Trinity Church. Or we will marry at Trinity Church before we leave tomorrow. It does not matter to me. Whatever you agree to, my Aki."

"I have no one to tell of this marriage, Rutherford. It matters not if we marry tomorrow or next year or next life . . . whatever . . . ."

Ecstatic, Rutherford did not pursue what Aki might have meant by "next life." He continued, "We will invite everyone we know on the island to a wedding feast here at the Grand. Then we will board the yacht and sail back to New York where we will board a ship. A ship to Japan. And then we will marry again there. According to your tradition. I want to learn your ways and know your people as we begin our lives together. It would not be fair to you to have to be the only one to adapt. Perhaps we will stay in Japan and never come back."

Rutherford added that last statement with his mother's recent letter in mind. Just in case he could not convince his father to accept his marriage to Aki Shima. In case he was disinherited. He had decided to escape the "office jail" and escape to Japan if necessary. He convinced himself that his father had a dozen better men than himself to run his Wall Street office. He was not really needed. Already his family had more money than they could spend in ten generations, if they were careful.

He had told himself, why should I imprison myself in the confines of an office when there is so much world to discover and taste. The thought of being indoors when the sun is out is too depressing for words. I would rather be a peasant than sit in an office.

For a man who would not sit his privileged behind in a private (if public) hotel bathtub without an India rubber mat, this was quite a statement. And since Rutherford Earle Haverhill V chose his words carefully, he meant exactly what he thought.

"I must leave your room now, my love."

"Hai. The night sky fades into a new day." Aki clung to Rutherford.

"I dread to leave you. But I must before departing guests begin to stir. I should not want to be seen compromising my future wife. Dear Aki . . . but you did not answer me."

"Rutherford I have already married you . . . in my heart. I want you to know that I believe . . . many centuries ago . . . you and I were once great lovers and married. We have come together again and we must be thankful for the time we have together. Please. We will talk of the practicalities of marriage later. But before you go . . . my love . . . please hold me just once more—"

Rutherford embraced Aki as if they were one.

To Aki . . . their spirits were one.

And before Rutherford left, Aki fell to the floor, her head bowed. Tears spotted the rug. Aki remained motionless.

If Rutherford had not been so overjoyed, if he had not been a man, he would have cried as witness to such expression of overwhelming feeling. Though Aki's body was bent over, he sensed her static position charged with love. He figured Aki felt as overjoyed as himself and could not control her utter happiness.

Rutherford picked Aki up and carried her to her bed. He

covered Aki and said softly, "Sleep now, Aki dearest. I will meet you on the veranda as planned." And he kissed her slanted eyelids.

At half past five in the morning, Aki Shima quietly paid her bill to the desk clerk, and left the Grand Hotel. The clerk noticed she had no bags with her and wondered if she had sent them on ahead or was coming back. Owen Corrigan helped her into his carriage and drove her to the Island House hotel, where he waited for her. Saying something to Owen about not wanting to miss the sunrise at Arch Rock, Aki practically ran in and out of the hotel. It looked to Owen that she had delivered a piece of her embroidery. He thought it a strange time of the day for social calls. But then he figured that Aki was leaving on the early ferry and there had been no other time.

Yet old Owen thought all this mighty odd. This early excursion to Arch Rock. But then he remembered that the oriental was particularly fond of the natural bridge. Whenever the Big Four could not decide which natural curiosity to revisit, the oriental always suggested Arch Rock. He remembered it reminded her of a bridge somewhere on the other side of the world.

"Whoa, Charley."

Owen helped the sad looking Aki Shima out of his carriage.

"Miss Shima . . . how long would ye like me and Charley to wait? Till the sun exposes its firey face upon the waters?"

"No. Thank you Owen. You may leave now." Aki handed him some money wrapped in red paper.

Owen did not take the money and said, "But how are ye goin' to get back to the grand palace?"

"Someone is meeting me here, Owen. Thank you for your gracious concern." Aki bowed forty-five degrees and remained there for some time.

Owen bowed back, all forty-five degrees, but could not

bend back up. Aki graciously helped him. Owen noticed Aki smile for the first time that morning and she slipped the paper-wrapped money into his torn pocket.

"It's too old I'm a gettin', Miss Shima. Enjoy yer youth while ye got it." Owen sneaked a long look at pretty Aki out of his covered eye. Something stirred in his bones and he felt all was not right with the young woman. He wondered if that Haverhill dandy from out east hurt her in some way. He knew that Haverhill and Miss Shima were in love's embrace. Gallant lovers, of that he had no doubt. But Owen had also seen hundreds of such summer love affairs develop on the island and die off of the island. He remembered Countess Anna and Arthur Andryer, so much in love they only had eyes for each other. Ah, such passion is wasted on the young, he said to himself.

Then Owen wondered if the same thing had happened to the "easterner" and the "far easterner." For to Owen Corrigan who had seen so much sorrow in his long life—Aki Shima's slanted eyes looked like open wounds.

"Go lang, Charley."

19

Poker Faces and Four-flush

"Are you four ladies leaving on the afternoon ferry?" asked Jimmy Hayes after he walked up to their breakfast table in the mammoth Grand Hotel dining room.

The Big Four smiled warmly. Sadly. Beatrice and Clare and Philippa were leaving but the Countess Gianotti was staying on a few more days. Although the official summer season at the Grand closed that afternoon, the hotel would remain open for a couple of weeks. But the countess would not be staying at the hotel . . . .

"Well, ladies, be sure to stop by at my office before you leave. I should like to say good-bye to all of you." Jimmy Hayes' eyes twinkled and he looked at each lady one by one. And each lady's lovely orbs twinkled back at him. Never had he seen such beauty of form and beauty of soul gathered together in one little group, in any hotel he had ever managed or visited in the world. He had the feeling he would never see such a group of society queens again.

Every guest at the Grand had the same feeling. They could not imagine waking up the next day and not sharing chatter with "our Big Four" or about "our Big Four." It was as if they were losing their queen mother and her sisters. And hundreds of seasonal guests stopped at the Big Four's breakfast table . . . and wished them all safe journey and invitations to visit them in Chicago or Detroit or New York or St. Louis or Charleston or Galveston or New Orleans or Denver or Richmond or Grand Rapids or Wilmington or Philadelphia . . . and wished them good-bye. The four ladies barely had a chance to eat. But this one morning they did not mind. For the wishes they received seemed heartfelt.

And the spirit of good will among all the guests in the dining room that morning reflected upon the spectacular season now finished. It would be talked about and remembered and passed onto children and grandchildren alike. For the summer of 1893, the year of the Chicago World's Fair, the season at the Grand Hotel on Mackinac Island . . . became the highlight of most of their lives.

"It is beautiful, Belinda . . ."

"So large . . ."

"Look at it, you all . . . if you all can . . . when I point it into the glorious sunlight on this simply magnificent veranda. Mercy. How my fiancé and I will miss strollin' upon this portico. And how I shall miss all of you! I simply must have all of your addresses before I leave."

Some twenty college girls exchanged loaded glances.

"When did he ask you, Belinda?"

"At the fancy dress ball, of course."

New Woman and intellectual flirt college girls had gathered around Belinda, on the longest porch in the world, as they waited for carriages to take them and their mothers and trunks down to the dock in the village. Good sportswomen to the end, they congratulated the southern belle they could not stomach, on her last minute engagement to the middle-aged millionaire from Hot Springs, Arkansas.

Yes, Belinda Gaines had been out to catch a millionaire that summer. She did just that. And not without a little gloating. But Belinda really wished she could have flashed the diamond in front of Mrs. Price's and Cynthia's faces. That would have added an extra dash of meaning to her triumph. She reminded herself, first thing when I get back to New Orleans, I must write a letter announcing my engagement to the dear Prices.

"Well then, Belinda, since you are to be married, it looks like you will not be going to college," said a college girl from Grand Rapids, Michigan, goading Belinda on, just a bit.

"College! I wouldn't think upon it. I declare, you develop coarse manly ways of thinkin' in college. Men notice it and are scared off. They don't like women who act like men." Belinda looked around, lowered her voice, and as an engaged woman of experience lectured instructively, "Men may like to converse with thinkin' women, but they don't like them in their beds. Men don't like to have to think in bed too! So you all better think carefully if you all want to be a . . . brainworker . . . or a gentleman's wife. It just doesn't work out bein' both."

"Do you really think so?" asked a sister from New Bedford with a satirical smile.

Staring down at her first ten carat diamond Belinda answered, "I know so. I declare, many college women don't even get married. They end up old maid school teachers. If you're a brainworker, you're doomed to a joyless life. Besides, college is just a fad for girls right now. I just don't understand why women don't leave all the thinkin' to men. It's so much easier that way. Why, my wise old grandma says that when women, especially club women, start actin' like men the world will come to an end. 'Cause its women who keep families together and keep children moral. And 'cause if the women act like men, all that is soft and sweet will die out and there won't be anythin' beautiful left in the world worth livin' for . . . ."

By the time Belinda had finished her speech, only two college girls were standing next to her. They had remained, only because their trunks were nearby. And they were not listening.

"Professor Bellamy . . ."

"Froilan . . ."

"I am leaving for the dock in a couple of minutes, Professor. I am taking the lake route back to New York . . . I . . ."

"Yes?"

"I . . . I am . . . the Grand is not wearying in its splendor is it? That is what sets it apart from so many Grand Hotels in the world . . ."

"I imagine that as a world famous artist . . . you have visited every Grand Hotel in the world."

"Yes . . . we Vermont farm boys dream big."

"And what have you got with your big dreams, Froilan . . . what have you really got?"

Sydney had given the professor his chance to get back at, if not get even, with him. And now that the old man had released some steam, Sydney could leave. The artist could leave in good faith, knowing that he had fulfilled this—one last favor to Beatrice.

" 'Fessor . . . please hurry."

"Professor Bellamy . . . Nanna says we must go now or we cannot go with you. She says we have to be back here soon. Because we have to catch the ferry." With sweet if earnest expressions, Monica and little Frederick stared up at the kindly old grandpa-like man. They ignored Sydney Chase Froilan— the man who took their mother away from them for most of the summer.

"Good-bye then, Professor . . . children."

"Froilan . . ."

"We must be off then," said Professor Bellamy to the children with urgency in his voice. He turned and saw Beatrice a distance down the porch. She clutched her left hand to her heart and stared at Sydney as he climbed into the carriage. Then the old professor saw Sydney, still playing cock of the walk and ham of the world, stand up in the carriage, take off his hat in a broad gesture and bend over in Beatrice's direction. And while he held his bow, the carriage jolted forward and he landed back on his behind, grinning from ear to ear and waving his hat. The professor saw Beatrice throw her head back and laugh with all her spirit. And once again clutch her hand over her heart.

"Come, children."

The professor and Frederick and Monica hurriedly walked over to the common pasture near the hotel. Enroute they picked up some tree branches on the ground.

"Lots of splooshed cow poop in this pasture 'Fessor!"

Monica scolded importantly, "Freddy, you know Nanna says you are never to say that word!"

"Cow poop cow poop cow poop cow poop . . ."

"Now now, Frederick," Professor Bellamy tried to hold back a grin, let's just make our way to the pond without unnecessary fighting . . . and without stepping into one."

"O.K. 'Fessor." Little Frederick considered Professor Bellamy his best buddy and would do anything in the world for him.

"Well, here we are. Now, children. Before we let the singing mice go we must teach them fear."

"Why 'Fessor?"

"So that they can survive, Frederick. All creatures . . . even human beings must have fear in order to protect themselves . . . in order to survive."

"I do not have fear, Professor Bellamy," spoke up Monica in her most adult voice.

The old professor said to himself, neither does your mother.

And without fear she will be used and abused by men less caring than Sydney Froilan. That damned Froilan opened a Pandora's box.

She was lucky . . . this time.

"Here we are, little Caruso . . . little Nelly Melba . . . we must say good-bye."

The mice sat on the ground and stared up at the professsor. Then they scampered up his leg, sat in his hand, and looked at his face expectantly.

"They don't want to go. They don't want to go."

"Well then, Monica, we must teach them to fear us."

"How?"

"Pinch them and hoot like an owl."

"But it will hurt them."

"Pinch them."

Monica pinched the little animal gently and hooted like an owl. The little mice raced down the Professor's leg. But ten seconds later they came back.

"Wave a branch over them, Frederick, like it might be a hawk's wings. Turn them over carefully and shake them up."

"They ran away!"

"They are coming back!"

"Wiggle your stick like a creeping fox."

And the professor wielded the final careful blows. With deep sadness he switched the little mice sharply with the stick.

The mice squealed with pain and no longer trusted Professor Bellamy.

"They are running away!"

"Oh, have we saved them from the robbers out to eat them?"

The old professor replied, "If we have taught them fear, they have great chances for survival." And the professor started strolling away as if in a daze, holding Monica's hand,

and wondering if the lesson would somehow sink into Monica and Frederick Venn—who were brought up without fear by a mother—who had abandoned them without even realizing it.

Frederick dallied behind, as four-year-olds do. He was curious to see where Caruso and Nelly Melba had gone. So he quietly crept up to the place where he had last seen the singing mice. Frederick grew wide-eyed. For he saw the mice drag something to the edge of the pond, get on it, and drift out into the water. Upon closer inspection, he noticed it was dried cow dung, and the mice used their tails for an oar and a rudder. And as little Frederick watched the singing mice sail away from the shore . . . journeying across what must have seemed an ocean to them . . . he heard them singing a sad duet.

And he decided not to tell anyone about the wonder he had seen or heard. For he knew the adults, why even Monica, would think he had imagined it. He knew they would just smile knowingly.

Yes, sometimes one has to keep things to oneself. Like secrets. And few were better at it than the Big Four. For not one guest ever found out why the countess really stayed at the hotel so long, away from her dying count in Italy. And no one even suspected that Clare and Philippa and Beatrice might also have a veiled motive for staying at the hotel.

"Countess Gianotti . . . Mrs. Gilbertson . . . Mrs. Mac-Adam . . . Mrs. Venn . . . thank you for coming." Jimmy Hayes smiled. "And thank you for everything!" He poured the four ladies his driest champagne and handed each of them a glass as he talked.

The Big Four smiled charmingly.

"I met Old Stinkweed before he left. You might get a kick out of this. I said, I hope you're pleased with us, sir. He responded impatiently, 'Perfectly, perfectly.' I said, thank you sir, thank you. I trust you will come again next summer? He replied, 'No, Jimmy Hayes, I will not come back.' I asked him why? And Old Stinkweed responded, 'What's the use of spending your summer at a resort if you can't complain all winter of the discomforts you've endured, and gab about how much better off you'd have been—had you stayed at home.' "

Anna and Clare and Philippa and Beatrice laughed in high spirits. Jimmy Hayes tried to fix in his mind the mirthful blended sound of the merry laughter.

"Ladies . . . now that it is over I will refer to our big secret. I cannot tell you how often you saved the season for me . . . for one reason or another . . . in spite of the Mrs. Larron incident. I must admit to having grave doubts about putting four women together, every day for eight weeks. But you are true sportsmen . . . or should I say true sportswomen . . . and you must agree we pulled it off splendidly. The veranda conversations . . . the introductions . . . the dances . . . the balls . . . the picnics . . . the Field Day . . . the Reminiscences of the Midway . . . ." A toast to you four ladies for a brilliant season!"

The four high society ladies looked at each other triumphantly—with delighted conspiratorial smiles—and stood up and toasted each other.

"You quenched all nasty rumors . . . you entertained the fun-loving . . . you visited with the lonely . . . you brought lovers together . . . you worked overtime every day . . . you even played matchmaker for yourselves. You have banded together to make people happy . . . and keep them in order, I might add. And we can sleep in peace knowing that you are exactly what you united to be. To all of you fine ladies . . . cheers!"

And they gleefully toasted each other again.

Ah yes, sometimes life's realities are beautiful illusions.

The Big Four was the brilliant idea of the Napoleon of hotel proprietors, Jimmy Hayes. Each lady in the Big Four group played her part—her real self—to perfection. And since not one guest was suspicious about the ladies' secret roles as socialite hostesses at the hotel, they never had to lie. If there was any deception in the merry band of four it was in—what was not said—in not admitting the roles they played.

Jimmy smiled at Anna and remembered how the clever idea came to him, when he had met the Countess Gianotti quite by chance in Paris, and he learned she was a lady-in-waiting at the court of Queen Marguerite. He discovered that the beautiful noble lady had summered on Mackinac Island for eighteen years and that she was returning to the area to take care of family business, after accompanying the queen's laces to the Chicago World's Fair.

Jimmy had offered to help her find someone to buy her family estate in Michigan. One thing led to the next . . . and the countess revealed she was in desperate need of money to keep the Gianotti palazzo for at least one more year. She revealed that her beloved husband was dying and she wanted for him, and for his family, that he pass away in the palace that had been in his family for five hundred years. All the family heirlooms, including her jewels, had been pledged for money to pay debts. There was little left to support his family and small staff.

And then Jimmy had been hit with his brilliant idea. He told the countess that at his Grand Hotel and all hotels like it in the world, the summer season was always marred by seasonal guests fighting vicious social climbing battles. He asked her if that sort of animosity was controlled among the court ladies of her Queen Marguerite. The discussion took quite a turn. Soon the countess and Jimmy put their heads together and came up with the idea of—planted summer society leaders—or court ladies incognito.

Jimmy Hayes knew that beyond controlling the atmosphere

at the hotel, once the news was published that a real countess was staying the season at the Grand—it would do wonders for his business. (And he was right.) So he had offered the countess room and board and one percent of the gross.

Anna, knowing she had nothing else to do after accompanying the queen's laces to Chicago, except wait for her family's estate to be sold in Michigan, and then accompany the laces back to Italy when the world's fair closed, decided to accept Jimmy's handsome offer, and play a disguised court lady on her beloved Mackinac Island. In fact, the countess was not playing a role. She was a court lady. But she never dreamed she would see her first love Arthur Andryer again on the island—and fall in deep love with his son.

It was Anna who had given Jimmy the idea of finding other "court ladies" to assist her. She had told Jimmy, we need ladies whose gestures and words and manners and airs are refined. Whose feminine sweetness shines in their carriage. Whose virtues of mind are as strong as a man's. Who are free from affectation, not proud or curious, discreet and prudent, not conceited or railing, knowing how to obtain and maintain favor to all.

Yes, Anna had told Jimmy all she knew about being a court lady. She had mastered the job in twenty years. She told him to find ladies who were capable of great regard . . . who took care not to be spotted with any fault . . . who would never be suspected or give occasion to be spoken ill of. To be a court lady she insisted he find women . . . who were pleasant, and affable, and able to entertain all sorts of company.

At the time, Jimmy Hayes was not sure women like that existed in America. So he started by looking for women free from husbands and well-disciplined. And soon, he found Philippa MacAdam and Beatrice Venn and Clare Gilbertson, who were generally thrilled to be in on the glamorous intrigue . . . and assist an American born countess as disguised court ladies. Jimmy figured that the Big Four were the first planted high society leaders to exist incognito, for the purpose of keeping order and making guests feel happy. Especially female guests. Yes, Jimmy Hayes was an innovator.

Jimmy smiled at Philippa MacAdam and remembered with some sadness her story before she had joined the "court ladies." Philippa had told Jimmy that she returned to the south from studying art in Rome, and found that her in-laws would not return her three children to her. She had found her holdings in her dead husband's horse farm had been sold in her absence, and her money from the estate was held up in the courts for reasons even she could not understand. Emotionally broken and without substantial funds to reestablish herself, Philippa had traveled to New York to a friend who would introduce her to possible commissions for horse portraits.

He remembered meeting Philippa by pure chance, in New York (after he came back from Paris), at the Metropolitan Museum of Art in front of Rosa Bonheur's *The Horse Fair*. Immediately he invited her to tea under the guise of commissioning a portrait of his favorite horse.

After an hour with lovely Philippa, Jimmy knew she would make an excellent "court lady." He convinced Philippa to accept his intriguing proposal, when he said that she would find the perfect opportunity to obtain commissions for her horse paintings at the hotel. Under much easier conditions than in heartless New York. And that she could escape the torrid heat of New York in the summer, and be rewarded for her help with room and board. Philippa had accepted, hesitantly.

Jimmy smiled at Beatrice Venn and remembered that he did not have to convince her to be a court lady. Beatrice had practically begged to be a part of the "fun." And her acceptance had nothing to do with money. Beatrice had so many millions she did not even know what she was worth.

By a remarkable coincidence, call it fate, Beatrice had

been stood up by a former best friend for tea—on the same day that Jimmy Hayes had explained his scheme to Philippa at a table nearby. She had overheard him say he needed two more "court ladies," and Beatrice instantly decided this fantastic idea would allow her to escape all her boring and judgmental relatives and friends on the east coast. For now that Beatrice was a divorced lady, society and in-laws had cooled to the point of ice in their relationship with her.

Of course, when Beatrice boldly introduced herself to Jimmy and Philippa, she did not tell him that she was divorced. She told him that her husband had "departed" from her two years ago. Naturally, Jimmy had figured her husband was dead.

Beatrice even had told Jimmy that she would join the "court ladies" for the sheer amusement of it all. But he had insisted upon rewarding her with room and board, to keep her serious about her—summer job.

Jimmy smiled at Clare Gilbertson and remembered that she had joined the "court ladies," after an introduction to him at the Palmer House hotel in Chicago one evening. She told Jimmy she would join because she was lonely and bored and wanted to escape the heat of Chicago in summer. Clare did not tell Jimmy that she joined to put herself into a state of mind away from Mrs. Vivian Larron and her husband's murder, which plagued every moment of her life. And although Clare's resources were drained by Mrs. Larron, she still had enough money to retain the facade of a high society lady.

Clare was so delighted to be on the receiving end for a change, that she accepted her room and board in exchange for her social services, as if she were a child receiving a present every day for eight weeks.

Jimmy poured some more champagne and exclaimed with gusto, "One last toast to our Big Four! How great is the generalship of women!"

Once again Anna and Clare and Beatrice and Philippa laughed together for the sheer joy of their many accomplishments that summer. And the room was filled with the atmosphere of their almost child-like gaiety.

The radiant ladies looked at each other warmly. Without saying it, they realized their united feeling was due to recognizing—their own inner upheavals and driven desires for joy and happiness—in each other as well. And they supported each other in attaining what the four of them so desired. No wonder they glowed.

Gazing at the four women smiling warmly, Jimmy remembered having panicked now and then. When he had overheard resorters at the hotel saying, "how strange that 'our' Big Four do not seem to mind so many intrusions on their time . . . so many admirers seizing possession of their privacy." But standing in his office with the beautiful four women at that moment, Jimmy figured that the resorters had witnessed the Big Four's generosity of spirit (no matter that it was planned), and they too had found it in themselves to share more of their time with others.

Yes, Jimmy figured the Big Four's generosity of spirit accounted for the many strong new friendships made that summer of '93. For strong friendship requires more than a few hours now and then. Jimmy Hayes, who elevated friendship to a creed, knew this better than most. And he was one of those left, in the world of 1893, who still put aside the making of money as secondary . . . to the making and keeping of friends.

Jimmy's voice broke as he said, "Ladies . . . if I keep you much longer you will miss your ferry. Please, Countess . . . would you stay a few minutes more."

Anna turned to Clare and Beatrice and Philippa, who were taking the ferry together to Mackinaw City. She did not know which new friend to look upon first. And her friends knew it and rushed to her side. Although they had said all their good-byes earlier in the day. Although they had made arrangements to gather together again, somewhere, this final parting was too difficult for words.

So no words were uttered. Only the deepest looks of kindred spirits were exchanged. It was enough. Clare and Beatrice and Philippa hugged Anna and fled from the room. And the Big Four felt they had abandoned something more precious . . . than they had ever known before in their lives.

Coda

"Countess," Jimmy began.

"Please, you may call me Anna."

"Thank you, Anna . . . please accept this. You will see that we did very well this season. Please open it."

Anna was so embarrassed to receive money as payment for her services, she hesitated.

"I do not mean to embarrass you, Anna. But I should like to see the look of surprise on your face. You will be able to keep the palazzo for two years if you are careful."

Anna opened the envelope and saw a note for $47,500. She gasped. "But surely . . . this is more than one percent of your gross earnings."

Jimmy laughed heartily and said, "If only it were. No, the $40,000 was contributed by one of your friends. In thanks for dealing with you know who."

Anna thought of Clare and Mrs. Larron and Ibrahim and the shah and Aki Shima. Aki Shima!

Clare had mentioned to Anna in the morning that she had looked everywhere for Aki. That she wanted to remind Aki to come and stay with her in Chicago once more. And say one more final good-bye and thank her yet again for her help with Mrs. Larron. For without Aki's idea of finding some sort of "evidence" in Mrs. Larron's room, on that fateful Field Day, Clare felt she would still be in bondage to the blackmailer.

Anna remembered that Clare had said she could not find

Aki. Nor had Beatrice and Philippa found her to say their final good-byes. Then Anna recalled that when Owen drove Richard and Arthur and herself up to the cottage, he had mentioned that he must pick up Miss Shima before sunrise.

Suddenly, the door to Jimmy Hayes' office crashed open. Rutherford stood like a man out of his mind, clenching his hands at his sides. Anna rushed across the room to Rutherford and Jimmy dashed to the door and shut it.

"What is it, Rutherford?" Anna's heart fell to her stomach.

"What is it good man, I say, speak up."

But Rutherford could not talk. He was in shock.

Anna and Jimmy led him to a leather chair and helped him sit down. Jimmy quickly poured his finest brandy and offered it to him. Rutherford simply stared and showed no signs of awareness that he was being addressed. His skin was a white as a geisha's in the moonlight.

"Send for Dr. Bailey," Anna demanded softly.

Jimmy ran from the room.

"Rutherford . . . dear Rutherford . . . please . . . you must tell me . . . what has happened?" Anna caressed his clenched fist and his hand finally released a piece of red paper, smelling faintly of sandalwood. It dropped to the floor as lightly as an autumn leaf falls from a tree. Hesitantly, Anna picked the paper up. To read or not to read was the question. It did not take Anna long to make up her mind. Or to know who the unsigned note was from. As Anna read, it was as if Aki Shima's soft voice spoke out loud.

"My dearest,

As I write this to you, the sun sinks lovesick into the twilight of nighttime. And I feel to bite you on the neck."

Anna smiled at Aki's humor, in spite of her suspicions, and continued reading, "I must leave you, my love. For you are a man of fine ancestry. Your father is a lord. And you must obey him.

"Cherish our pure love together, for in the hereafter it has no value.

"As I listen to the mourning of the wind blowing across the Straits of Mackinac, I feel my fate blows me away from the fleeting world and you. I must follow my feelings. And now I feel my soul departing from my body and lodging itself within you, my love."

Anna lost her breath and clasped her hand to her heart. Aki's final words blurred before her eyes.

"Oh! Life you are the cryptic light
From darkness in the womb,
A comic tragic interlude,
To darkness in the tomb;
I bow to my foredoom."

Rutherford suddenly cried out, "Damn all feeling!"

Anna knew well the joy and pain of the fine instinct that had awakened in Rutherford. She held tightly the hand of one who had finally . . . unearthed feeling . . . for the first time in his life.